HAGAR'S DAUGHTER

broadview editions
series editor: Martin R. Boyne

Yours for humanity,
Pauline E. Hopkins

Pauline Elizabeth Hopkins from the *Colored American Magazine* (January 1901). Reproduced from *The Digital Colored American Magazine*, coloredamerican.org. Original held at the Beinecke Rare Book and Manuscript Library, Yale University.

HAGAR'S DAUGHTER.

A Story of Southern Caste Prejudice

Pauline Elizabeth Hopkins

edited by John Cullen Gruesser
and Alisha R. Knight

broadview editions

BROADVIEW PRESS – www.broadviewpress.com
Peterborough, Ontario, Canada

Founded in 1985, Broadview Press remains a wholly independent publishing house. Broadview's focus is on academic publishing; our titles are accessible to university and college students as well as scholars and general readers. With 800 titles in print, Broadview has become a leading international publisher in the humanities, with world-wide distribution. Broadview is committed to environmentally responsible publishing and fair business practices.

Library and Archives Canada Cataloguing in Publication

Title: Hagar's daughter : a story of Southern caste prejudice / Pauline Elizabeth Hopkins ; edited by John Cullen Gruesser and Alisha R. Knight.
Names: Hopkins, Pauline E. (Pauline Elizabeth), author. | Gruesser, John Cullen, 1959- editor. | Knight, Alisha R., editor.
Description: Originally serialized in Colored American Magazine from 1901-1902.
Identifiers: Canadiana (print) 20200364901 | Canadiana (ebook) 20200365053 | ISBN 9781554815630 (softcover) | ISBN 9781770487918 (PDF) | ISBN 9781460407424 (EPUB)
Classification: LCC PS1999.H4226 H34 2020 | DDC 813/.4—dc23

Broadview Editions
The Broadview Editions series is an effort to represent the ever-evolving canon of texts in the disciplines of literary studies, history, philosophy, and political theory. A distinguishing feature of the series is the inclusion of primary source documents contemporaneous with the work.

Advisory editor for this volume: Norah Franklin

Broadview Press handles its own distribution in North America:
PO Box 1243, Peterborough, Ontario K9J 7H5, Canada
555 Riverwalk Parkway, Tonawanda, NY 14150, USA
Tel: (705) 743-8990; Fax: (705) 743-8353
email: customerservice@broadviewpress.com

For all territories outside of North America, distribution is handled by Eurospan Group.

Broadview Press acknowledges the financial support of the Government of Canada for our publishing activities.

Typesetting: George Kirkpatrick
Cover design: Aldo Fierro

PRINTED IN CANADA

for Eileen Cullen Gruesser (1931-2020)

Contents

Illustrations

Acknowledgements

We wish to thank Sam Houston State University's Department of English, the Beinecke Rare Book and Manuscript Library at Yale University, the Charles L. Blockson Afro-American Collection at Temple University, the Schomburg Center for Research in Black Culture, and the Smithsonian Institution for their support and access to rare materials. Garrett Lawrence, our graduate assistant at Sam Houston State, provided research and editorial support for which we are sincerely appreciative. We would also like to express our gratitude for the insightful conversations we've had and the valuable feedback we've received from the following colleagues and fellow scholars: Hanna Wallinger, JoAnn Pavletich, Lauren Dembowitz, Ira Dworkin, Michael Winship, John Barton, Eurie Dahn, and Brian Sweeney. We would also like to thank Don LePan and Marjorie Mather at Broadview Press for their enthusiastic support for this project.

Introduction

Prior to 1980, few scholars and teachers were familiar with and, consequently, even fewer students were introduced to the writings of Zora Neale Hurston (1891–1960), Charles Chesnutt (1858–1932), and Harriet Jacobs (1813–97). Today it is impossible to imagine African American and American literature without them. Over the last forty years, Pauline Hopkins (1859–1930) has undergone a similar transformation. In the 1970s, one of the few published articles about her was subtitled "A Biographical Excursion into Obscurity" (Shockley). Even in the early 1990s, when over a thousand pages of her fiction had been brought back into print thanks to Oxford University Press's Schomburg Library of Nineteenth-Century Black Women Writers series (*Contending Forces*, *The Magazine Novels of Pauline Hopkins*, and *Short Fiction by Black Women*), little was known about Hopkins since only a handful of people had published essays, reference-book entries, or book-chapter sections devoted to her or her texts. Since then, as a result of the efforts of researchers and the digitization of white and black newspapers, a wealth of information about her life has come to light and a treasure trove of Hopkins criticism has been published.[1] Moreover, she has achieved canonical status, consistently appearing in anthologies of African American and, increasingly, American literature. Despite these remarkable gains, her writings have fallen short of being fully accessible to undergraduate students and general readers because the Schomburg volumes— now three decades old—and online versions of Hopkins's novels and short stories, which have become available in recent years, provide neither contextualizing materials nor annotations. The present volume aims to initiate the process of remedying this situation.

---

1 In 2007, Rutgers University Press published *Daughter of the Revolution: The Major Nonfiction Works of Pauline E. Hopkins*, edited by Ira Dworkin, making another significant portion of Hopkins's corpus readily available.

Pauline E. Hopkins

A generation ago, those seeking information about Hopkins encountered seemingly unbridgeable gaps in her life's story. Her career as a performer and pioneering playwright in the second half of the 1870s and the first half of the 1880s was documented. Yet she appeared to have fallen out of the official record from that time until 1899, when she copyrighted her first novel, *Contending Forces*, and then worked as an editor for and published a remarkable number of writings in the Boston-based *Colored American Magazine* between 1900 and 1904. There seemed to have been another extended period of silence between 1905, when articles by Hopkins appeared in the *Voice of the Negro* and she self-published the pamphlet *A Primer of Facts about the Early Greatness of the African Race*, and early 1916, when she served as the editor-in-chief for and contributed fiction and nonfiction to the short-lived *New Era Magazine*. Biographies of Hopkins published in 2005 and 2008 by Hanna Wallinger and Lois Brown,[1] respectively, as well as materials now available in newspaper databases, however, attest that for forty years she was more or less continuously in the public eye, primarily in the Boston area, as a singer, actress, playwright, lecturer, fiction writer, journalist, editor, activist, and public intellectual.

Pauline Elizabeth Hopkins was born in Portland, Maine, in 1859 to Sarah A. Allen and Benjamin Northup. The couple divorced, and in 1864 her mother married Civil War veteran William A. Hopkins, whose last name Pauline would adopt as a teenager. When she was very young, Hopkins moved with her mother to Boston, where she graduated from Girls High School in 1875. The previous year, she won an essay contest sponsored by the Congregational Publishing Society of Boston. The prize of $10 in gold was provided by William Wells Brown (c. 1814–84), whose intertextual approach to authorship and publications in multiple genres would have a profound influence on Hopkins's own writings. In the late 1870s and early 1880s, she gained a reputation as "Boston's favorite colored Soprano"[2] for

---

1 Some of the biographical information in this Introduction has been derived from these books.

2 See, for example, the page-three advertisement for a "Grand Sacred Concert" featuring the Virginia Jubilee Singers in the 15 January

her performances both as a soloist and as part of Hopkins Colored Troubadours, a group that included her mother and stepfather, as well as, at various times, such well-known actor-singers as the Hyers Sisters and Sam Lucas (c. 1848–1916). In 1877, she began writing for the theater, and her musical *Peculiar Sam; Or, the Underground Railroad* (see Appendix E1) toured Illinois, Wisconsin, Michigan, Iowa, Kansas, and Missouri in the spring of 1879 and was performed that December in Boston, where it was reprised in the summer of 1880 and the fall of 1881 (Southern xxiv; Metzler 118). According to Lois Brown, Hopkins's play "provided American audiences with the first staged reenactments of slavery that were not offered through the lens of the white imagination" (117). Although William Wells Brown had written and recited *Experience* and *The Escape* in the 1850s, Lucas and other commentators considered *Peculiar Sam* to be the "first colored drama" ("Sam Lucas' Theatrical Career").[1]

Even though Hopkins had apparently stopped singing professionally by 1886, her appearances on stage did not come to an end. In 1889, she began a career as a public speaker, giving lectures to black and white audiences on Haiti and other topics, at times accompanied by copious illustrations ("The Rise of the Black Republic"). A January 1901 profile, very likely written by Hopkins herself, states that she abandoned playwriting in favor of fiction on the advice of a theater manager ("Pauline E. Hopkins" 218). Although it is not known when she completed her earliest stories, the footnote at the bottom of the first page of the initial installment of her serial novel *Hagar's Daughter* announces that she had copyrighted some portion of it in 1891 (Allen 337), which indicates that she had turned her talents to fiction by that time. During the 1880s and 1890s, Hopkins delivered

---

1882 issue of the *Boston Globe*. A similar item for a performance by the Hopkins Colored Troubadours refers to her as the "well known Gifted and Cultivated Solo Soprano" (*Boston Herald*, 21 June 1885, p. 11).

1 The "Gossip of the Stage" column in the 14 December 1912 issue of the Indianapolis *Freeman* states, "To those who can go back many years it may be remembered that Sam Lucas was the first colored man to appear in a big dramatic play. The play was written by Miss Pauline Hopkins and entitled 'The Underground Railroad'" (5).

"readings," likely of her own compositions, as part of church programs and concerts; she also directed the choir at Boston's Charles Street African Methodist Episcopal Church ("Charles-Street Church"; "Colored Folks Thanksgiving"; "In the West End"). In the final years of the nineteenth century, she made speeches addressing issues related to race and social justice, such as the convict lease system and lynching, and read selections from her soon-to-be-published novel *Contending Forces* to the Woman's Era Club and the Colored National League ("Colored Women Protest"; "Read a Paper on Lynching"). The previously mentioned sketch of her life asserts that she has "struggled to the position she now holds in the same fashion that *all* Northern colored women have to struggle—through hardships, disappointments, and with very little encouragement. What she has accomplished has been done by a grim determination to 'stick at it,' even though failure might await her at the end" ("Pauline E. Hopkins" 218). It also states that Hopkins strived to produce stories "in which the wrongs of her race will be so handled as to enlist the sympathy of all classes of citizens, in this way reaching those who never read history or biography" (219).

Beginning in May 1900, Hopkins published a torrent of writings in a wide variety of genres in the *Colored American Magazine*, under her own name and at least two pseudonyms. These included three serial novels (*Hagar's Daughter. A Story of Southern Caste Prejudice*, *Winona: A Tale of Negro Life in the South and Southwest*, and *Of One Blood; Or, the Hidden Self*), two extended biographical series (Famous Men of the Negro Race and Famous Women of the Negro Race), a large number of unsigned editorial pieces, several short stories, and many journalistic articles. Contemporary accounts by Hopkins (see Appendix F3) and others reveal that she played a major editorial role at the *Colored American Magazine* long before she received recognition on the masthead for doing so. She chose and shaped its literary content, solicited and published a large number of articles about places beyond the borders of the United States (particularly Africa, Cuba, and the Philippines), and often curated individual issues of the magazine in such a manner that the contents related to each other in compelling and fascinating ways.[1] In addition, she

---

1 See Sweeney for a discussion of the connections between the layout, fiction, nonfiction, illustrations, and photographs in the

advanced a neo-abolitionist argument in her *Colored American Magazine* fiction and nonfiction, asserting that the relationship between US blacks and whites had grown so dire that the times demanded an activist movement as committed and widespread as the one that had worked tirelessly and courageously to put an end to slavery prior to and during the Civil War.

Hopkins addresses the policies and position of prominence of educator and race leader Booker T. Washington (1856–1915) in her fiction and nonfiction, typically criticizing him implicitly but at times doing so overtly. *Contending Forces* features major characters who represent the rival positions of Washington and leading intellectual and race leader W.E.B. Du Bois (1868–1963); her 1901 short story "A Dash for Liberty," concerning the 1841 insurrection on the slave ship *Creole*, changes the rebel leader's surname from Washington to Monroe (see Appendix E3); her Famous Men of the Negro Race series begins with Toussaint L'Ouverture (1743–1803) and Frederick Douglass (1818–95; see Appendix C1), continues with abolitionists, Union soldiers, and Reconstruction-era politicians, and concludes with Washington, who does not fare well by comparison; and her 1902 essay "Munroe Rogers" proclaims that the race sorely needs a new Toussaint to guide it (see Appendix C4). In 1904, she would pay a steep price for her pro-agitation, anti-imperialist, and women-centered stances when Fred Moore (1857–1943), an agent of Washington, bought the *Colored American Magazine*, moved it to New York, and dismissed her.

Hopkins continued to appear in public for several years, giving addresses in Boston in honor of abolitionist editor William Lloyd Garrison (1805–79) in 1905 and Massachusetts US Senator Charles Sumner (1811–74) in 1911; speaking on "behalf of the colored women of Atlanta" at a Faneuil Hall event protesting the white-on-black violence in Georgia's largest city in 1906; lecturing to a crowd of 100 people in nearby Roxbury in 1907 as part of a program sponsored by the Boston Literary and Historical Association; participating in an "anti-Roosevelt, anti-Taft mass meeting" at Faneuil Hall in 1908; and, three years later, denouncing a Pennsylvania lynching ("Protest at Faneuil Hall"; "Miss Lee Entertained"; "Anti-Roosevelt-Taft"; "To Protest Lynching"). In 1916, the 57-year-old Hopkins returned to the

---

January–February 1902 issue.

helm of a Boston-based race publication entitled the *New Era Magazine*. Like its predecessor, the *New Era Magazine* emphasized literature, black biography, and international issues of particular interest to African Americans. When the magazine folded after only two issues, Hopkins seems to have retired from public life.[1]

Beginning in the early 1890s, Hopkins supported herself (and, following her stepfather's death, her mother) by working as a stenographer, except when she was employed full time as an editor and/or writer. In 1892, the Indianapolis *Freeman* announced that she had taken such a job with Republican Party politicians in Boston. Two years later, a *Boston Post* item reported that Washington had invited Hopkins to Alabama to do stenographic work for the Tuskegee Institute's treasurer. She declined the offer, passed a civil-service exam, and secured a position with the Massachusetts Census Bureau, which she held from 1895 to 1899 ("Woman's World"; "West End News"; "Pauline E. Hopkins" 219). In 1898 and from 1906 onward, the Cambridge City Directory identified her as a stenographer. The 1910 US Census also listed her as pursuing this line of work at the "State House," and during the final decade of her life she was engaged in this profession at a "college," presumably the Massachusetts Institute of Technology, located close to the room she rented for the last dozen years of her life at 19 Jay Street in Cambridge. It was there, in August 1930, that an oil stove explosion resulted in burns that ended her life at the age of 71 ("Central Square").[2]

Contexts for *Hagar's Daughter*

A critical edition of *Hagar's Daughter* is particularly appropriate in light of the fact that Hopkins integrates the serial novel into

---

1 One event in which she did participate during her later years was a 1927 exhibition of her "100 Pictures of Haiti," no doubt connected to her lectures about the black republic almost four decades earlier, at Boston's Columbus Avenue A.M.E. Zion Church (*Cambridge Chronicle*, 15 April 1927, p. 8).

2 Prior to renting the room on Jay Street, Hopkins lived for many years with her parents in a mortgaged home at 53 Clifton Street in North Cambridge.

the multifaceted quilt that is the *Colored American Magazine*. In this way, she makes it inseparable from the other writings—and the social and ideological contexts they engage—that she weaves into the fabric of the periodical. Because *Hagar's Daughter* demonstrates Hopkins's keen sense of history, use of multiple literary genres, emphasis on gender roles, and political engagement, it provides the perfect introduction to the author and her era. The novel features concealed and mistaken identities, dramatic revelations, and extraordinary plot twists. In Part 1, Maryland plantation heirs Hagar Sargeant and Ellis Enson fall in love, marry, and have a daughter. However, Ellis's covetous younger brother, St. Clair, claims that Hagar is of mixed-race ancestry, putting her and her infant in a precarious position. When Ellis is presumed to be dead, St. Clair sells Hagar and her child into slavery, and they apparently die when Hagar, in despair, leaps into the Potomac River with her daughter. These events provide the backdrop for Part 2 (set 20 years later), which includes a high-profile murder trial, an abduction plot, and a steady succession of surprises as the young black maid Venus Johnson assumes male clothing to solve a series of mysteries that are both current and decades-old.

The novel may be fruitfully approached from a variety of contexts: antebellum, bellum, and postbellum history; US race relations; the Bible; genre; and gender. In addition to depicting slave auctions and Southern secession, it refers to the Compromise of 1850 and the fugitives from slavery Shadrach Minkins (c. 1814–75), Thomas Sims (1834–1902), and Anthony Burns (1834–62); Civil War battles, such as Fort Wagner, Fort Pillow, and Honey Hill, in which black soldiers participated, as well as the heroics of the men, led by Robert Smalls (1839–1915), who commandeered the C.S.S. *Planter*; the conspiracy to assassinate Abraham Lincoln (1809–65) and the ensuing manhunt and trial; the founding of the Secret Service; the so-called Lost Cause, which was increasingly used to justify the Confederate rebellion; the Reconstruction era; the Gilded Age; and the actions taken to deprive African Americans of their citizenship rights during the period known as the nadir (see Appendix C). For those interested in exploring the role of race in American fiction (and American society), *Hagar's Daughter* draws attention in its subtitle to "Southern caste prejudice," but the novel also suggests that "the sin is the nation's"—not just a peculiarity of the South. The serial also explicitly evokes Hagar, the Egyptian woman who bears the child of and then is cast off by the Jewish patriarch Abraham in the book of Genesis, a figure frequently evoked by American women writers and visual artists during the 1800s (see Appendix D). For those interested in exploring the conventions of popular literature, *Hagar's Daughter* serves as a fascinating example of nineteenth- and early-twentieth-century melodramatic fiction. It employs and updates minstrel stereotypes and makes copious use of dialect, similar to Hopkins's pioneering 1879 drama *Peculiar Sam*. The narrative also draws on the trope of the tragic mulatta, incorporates Gothic conventions, and, together with Hopkins's story "Talma Gordon" (see Appendix E2), stands among the earliest examples of African American detective fiction. On the one hand, the novel underscores the vulnerability of women, especially those of African descent, subjected to or threatened with slavery, imprisonment, concubinage, sexual exploitation, workplace discrimination, accusations of insanity and immorality, and a lifetime of domestic service. On the other hand, it demonstrates their strength, bravery, and brilliance, and at times it challenges traditional gender roles (see Appendix F). For the increasing number of instructors and students who are interested in exploring the ethical, aesthetic, and political issues related to plagiarism, literary borrowing, and Signifying,[1] *Hagar's Daughter* offers an extraordinarily rich case study. Hopkins reproduces and/or reworks episodes and passages from not only such well-known texts as William Shakespeare's plays, John Milton's *Paradise Lost* (1667), Charlotte Brontë's *Jane Eyre* (1847), and the first African American novel, William Wells Brown's *Clotel* (1853), but also 1880s and 1890s popular fiction by white women appearing in *Frank Leslie's Monthly*, *Frank Leslie's Weekly*, and other periodicals (see Appendix G).

The Publication History and Structure of *Hagar's Daughter*

In *Hagar's Daughter*, Hopkins notably incorporates a variety of socially relevant issues into a dramatic plot while working within the framework of the serial novel. Serials emerged in Britain at

---

1 An African American form of repetition, word play, and revision.

the turn of the eighteenth century and rose to immense popularity during the Victorian era. Although Charles Dickens (1812–70) is generally recognized as the most successful author to utilize this publishing practice, several African American writers—namely Martin Delany (1812–85), William Wells Brown, and Frances E.W. Harper (1825–1911)—also published their fiction a few chapters at a time in weekly or monthly periodicals. Hopkins published her first novel, *Contending Forces*, as a bound book; however, her decision to publish her next three novels as serials is indicative of her professional and financial investment in the *Colored American Magazine*. Cliffhangers were standard elements in serials that were used to create a sense of anticipation among readers and a demand for subsequent issues of the magazine. Although Hopkins would have received any profits generated from the sale of *Contending Forces* directly, she would have seen the proceeds from the sale of her serialized novels reinvested in the *Colored American Magazine* for its continued publication. Since she served as the magazine's editor and as a member of the parent company's board of directors, she would have understood that the success of each of her serial novels was dependent upon the success of the *Colored American Magazine* enterprise, and vice versa. Furthermore, as Rachel Ihara observes, Hopkins "makes strategic use of [the] serial structure" not only to "maximize suspense and stimulate desire for subsequent installments" (133) but also to "please a specifically black audience" (134) by carefully constructing key scenes to show racial justice and black empowerment.

Authors who serialized their work often felt pressure to satisfy both readers' expectations and publishers' deadlines. Hopkins, however, appears not to have had these stressors. The novel was announced as forthcoming with "original drawings" in the October 1900 issue, suggesting that Hopkins wrote most if not all of the novel before the first installment appeared five months later in the *Colored American Magazine*. The twelve installments, beginning in March 1901 and ending in March 1902, comprise thirty-seven chapters that unfold over two time periods separated by roughly two decades. The events in the first three installments (Chapters I–VIII) transpire at the beginning of the 1860s, while those in the remaining nine installments (Chapters IX–XXXVII) take place during and after 1882, and each installment ends with an explicit or implicit cliffhanger:

Part One: Chapters I–VIII, set approximately 1858–1862
Installment 1, March 1901, Chapters I–III
Installment 2, April 1901, Chapters IV and V
Installment 3, May 1901, Chapter V concluded–VIII

Part Two: Chapters IX–XXXVII, set 1882 and afterward
Installment 4, June 1901, Chapters IX–XII
Installment 5, July 1901, Chapters XIII–XVI
Installment 6, August 1901, Chapters XVII–XIX
Installment 7, September 1901, Chapters XX–XXII
Installment 8, October 1901, Chapters XXIII–XXV
Installment 9, November 1901, Chapters XXVI–XXVIII
Installment 10, December 1901, Chapter XXVIII
    concluded–XXX
Installment 11, January/February 1902, Chapters
    XXXI–XXXIII
Installment 12, March 1902, Chapters XXXIV–XXXVII

The Illustrations for *Hagar's Daughter*

Born in what is now Guyana in January 1874, J. Alexandre Skeete came to Boston in August 1888 and, beginning around 1895, had a career as a model for (and was apparently also a lover of) the photographer F. Holland Day (1864–1933). Likely with Day's help, he attended Cowles Art School in Boston, after which he spent some time in London. On his return to the United States, he supplied the *Boston Herald* and other papers with illustrations (Elliott; Fanning 82). From May 1900 until the fall of 1901, he held the position of the *Colored American Magazine*'s leading staff artist, and his design for its cover, featuring early African American poet Phillis Wheatley (1753–84) and Frederick Douglass, debuted in May 1901. Although he apparently tried to continue his artistic career following his departure from the journal, by 1914 he was working as a janitor in Boston, a job he held until his death, which occurred in or sometime before 1937 (Shand-Tucci).

Each of Skeete's illustrations for *Hagar's Daughter*, which appeared in the March, April, May, July, August, and September 1901 issues (all as frontispieces except for the one in the April issue), have been reproduced in this Broadview edition. These illustrations function as counter-caricature, according to Adam

J. ALEXANDRE SKEETE.

On Our Art Staff.

J. Alexandre Skeete, from the *Colored American Magazine* (May 1901). Reproduced from *The Digital Colored American Magazine*, coloredamerican.org. Original held at the Beinecke Rare Book and Manuscript Library, Yale University.

Sonstegard, who argues that Hopkins played a major role in their conception (190–98). Skeete's images evoke not only 1850s illustrations for Harriet Beecher Stowe's *Uncle Tom's Cabin* and William Wells Brown's *Clotel* but also, as Lauren Dembowitz has asserted ("Sources"), for the 1882 story "Two Women" in *Frank Leslie's Weekly* (see Appendix G).

Reception and Criticism

Whatever emphasis an instructor, student, or general reader wishes to place on *Hagar's Daughter*, ample critical commentaries exist on which to draw. The only known review, written in response to the novel's first installment, was published in the 15 March 1901 issue of the white Elizabeth City, North Carolina, *Weekly Economist* (see Appendix H1). In addition, the *Colored American Magazine*'s serial fiction elicited a white reader's letter to the editor, to which Hopkins responded at length, defending her choices in narratives such as *Hagar's Daughter* (see Appendix H2). Beginning with Claudia Tate and Hazel Carby in the mid- to late-1980s, scholars have commented on Hopkins's blending and subversion of popular genres and types in her three *Colored American Magazine* novels—especially *Hagar's Daughter*. Kristina Brooks and Jessica Metzler both discuss the serial in relation to minstrelsy, while Stephen F. Soitos, Catherine Ross Nickerson, M. Michelle Robinson, and John Gruesser all address its use of the tropes of detective fiction. Janet Gabler-Hover compares Hopkins's novel to other American Hagar narratives. Eugenia DeLamotte shows how Hopkins reworks the female Gothic tradition established by Ann Radcliffe (1764–1823); Hanna Wallinger focuses on the figure of the tragic mulatta; Lois Brown argues that the serial pays homage to John Milton's *Paradise Lost* as well as to William Wells Brown's *Clotel*; Mikko Tuhkanen addresses various forms of passing (racial, temporal, spatial, and economic) in the text; Alisha Knight asserts that it critiques the American Gospel of Success; and Jill Bergman discusses the narrative in connection with the trope of the motherless child. Lauren Dembowitz has charted Hopkins's extensive borrowings in *Hagar's Daughter* from late-nineteenth-century fiction, most of it published in *Frank Leslie's Popular Monthly*; in doing so, she has added to the work of JoAnn Pavletich, Geoffrey Sanborn, and Richard Yarborough on what some have called

Hopkins's plagiarism and others her "inspired borrowings" in connection with her serial novels. In *Untimely Democracy: The Politics of Progress after Slavery*, Greg Laski posits that for writers living in a white supremacist nation obsessed with "progress" and a "better future," including Hopkins, Douglass, Chesnutt, Du Bois, Stephen Crane (1871–1900), and Sutton Griggs (1872–1933), "the best (if not the last) chance to realize democracy is to embrace the past [of slavery and race prejudice] that refuses to pass away" (4). Laski uses *Contending Forces* to make his case for viewing Hopkins as a political thinker who portrays and grapples with "untimely democracy" more profoundly and powerfully than any of her post-Reconstruction–era peers; however, this argument applies equally well—and perhaps even more clearly and convincingly—to *Hagar's Daughter*, as several critics, in particular Holly Jackson, have shown. In "Throwing Stones across the Potomac: *The Colored American Magazine*, the *Atlantic Monthly*, and the Cultural Politics of National Reunion," Brian Sweeney reads the novel in light of and as a pointed response to the Northern renunciation of Reconstruction and retreat on black civil rights at the turn of the twentieth century, especially on the part of New England's most influential periodical. He contends that *Hagar's Daughter* strives to answer the otherwise unasked question "What happens when the reconciliation of the North and South is imagined in a way that *includes* rather than excludes African Americans, and that rests not on concealment but on an honest reckoning with the nation's racial histories?" (156).

Pauline Elizabeth Hopkins: A Brief Chronology

1859	Born in Portland, Maine, to Sarah Allen and Benjamin Northup. Following a divorce, Allen marries Civil War veteran William A. Hopkins in 1864.
1874	Receives a $10 Gold Prize, donated by William Wells Brown, for "The Evils of In-temperance and Their Remedy" in a Congregational Publishing Society of Boston essay contest.
1875	Graduates from Girls High School in Boston, her place of residence since infancy.
1877	Performs in the two-act operetta *Pauline; Or, the Belle of Saratoga*. Registers the copyright for *Aristocracy: A Musical Drama in 3 Acts*.
1878	Registers the copyright for *Winona; A Drama in 5 Acts*.
1879	Registers the copyright for the "first colored drama," *Peculiar Sam; or, The Underground Railroad, A Musical Drama in 4 Acts* (aka *Slaves' Escape and A Flight for Freedom*), which toured the Midwest that spring and was performed multiple times in Boston.
1870s–80s	Performs with family members and well-known stars, including the Hyers Sisters and Sam Lucas, as part of the Hopkins Colored Troubadours. Gains a reputation as "Boston's Favorite Colored Soprano."
1880s–90s	Lectures on such topics as "The Rise of the Black Republic" and Toussaint L'Ouverture at sites including Boston's Tremont Temple and Providence, Rhode Island's (white) Friends' Academy.
1890s	Works as a stenographer for Republican politicians and the Massachusetts census bureau. Declines Booker T. Washington's offer of a stenography job at the Tuskegee Institute in 1894.
Late 1890s	Denounces the convict lease system at a public meeting of Boston's Woman's Era Club in 1897. Represents the Woman's Era at the annual meeting

of the New England Federation of Women's Clubs in 1898. Speaks about lynching, reads from *Contending Forces* at women's clubs and other venues, and registers the copyright for the novel in 1899.

1900   The US Census lists her as a stenographer and writer, living with her stepfather (a tailor) and mother in a mortgaged home at 53 Clifton St. in Cambridge, Massachusetts. The Colored Cooperative Publishing Company issues *Contending Forces* and, beginning in May, publishes the *Colored American Magazine* (CAM), in which a remarkably large number of writings by Hopkins in multiple genres appear. CAM announces that she will edit its Women's Department and publishes her pioneering anti-imperialist detective/mystery story, "Talma Gordon." She lectures at Boston's St. Paul's Baptist Church on the "Problems of the South."

1900–01   CAM publishes her 12-part Famous Men of the Negro Race biographical series.

1901–02   CAM publishes her novel *Hagar's Daughter* in 12 installments and her 11-part Famous Women of the Negro Race biographical series.

1902   CAM publishes her novel *Winona* in six installments.

1902–03   CAM publishes her novel *Of One Blood* in 13 installments.

1903   CAM's masthead identifies her as its Literary Editor. A "direct descendant of the colored revolutionary soldier, Tobias Cutler," she leads the effort to establish the Sons and Daughters of the American Revolution, a "Patriotic Society."

1904   CAM's masthead identifies her as chief editor for the first and only time in its March issue. Fred R. Moore, an ally of Booker T. Washington, purchases CAM and moves it to New York City, to which she briefly relocates after being demoted. Moore later fires her. The Atlanta-based *Voice of the Negro* publishes her journalistic piece "The New York Subway."

1905   Offers her "Thoughts on the Negro Problem" to the Literary Circle of Brooklyn's Concord Baptist Church of Christ in March. The *Voice of the Negro* publishes her six-part ethnographic series, The Dark Races of the Twentieth-Century. Self-publishes the pamphlet *A Primer of Facts Pertaining to the Early Greatness of the African Race*. Delivers an address at the Citizens' William Lloyd Garrison Centenary Celebration in Boston in December.

1906   Speaks on "behalf of the colored women of Atlanta" at a mass meeting at Faneuil Hall protesting the killing of blacks in Atlanta. Stepfather William Hopkins dies.

1907   Lectures on the "Crown of Manhood" at the Twelfth Baptist Church in Roxbury, Massachusetts.

1908   Speaks at an "anti-Roosevelt, anti-Taft" meeting at Faneuil Hall organized by the National Negro American Political League.

1910   The US Census lists her as a stenographer, working at the "State House" and living with her mother at 53 Clifton St., Cambridge.

1911   Speaks at the Boston event honoring the 100th anniversary of the birth of Charles Sumner and at a Boston mass meeting protesting the lynching of Zachariah Walker in Coatesville, Pennsylvania.

1913   Mother Sarah Allen dies.

1916   Founds and edits the short-lived *New Era Magazine*, which publishes two installments of her Men of Vision biographical series and two installments of her serial novel *Topsy Templeton*.

1918–30   Boards with the Carter family, a widow and her son, at 19 Jay St. in Cambridge, Massachusetts.

1920   The US Census lists her as a lodger working as a proofreader in a mechanical laboratory.

1930   The US Census lists her as a lodger employed as a stenographer at a college. Dies at the Cambridge Relief Hospital from injuries resulting from a fire at her Jay St. residence.

A Note on the Text

Hagar's Daughter was originally published as a serial novel in 12 monthly installments in the *Colored American Magazine* between March 1901 and March 1902. This Broadview edition is based on original issues of the *Colored American Magazine* held at the Beinecke Rare Book and Manuscript Library at Yale University and accessible online at *The Digital Colored American Magazine* (coloredamerican.org), with the exception of the September 1901 and December 1901 installments, which are based on the Negro Universities Press reprint of the *Colored American Magazine*.

Typographical errors have been silently corrected, but in order to retain as much of the original format and serial structure of the novel as possible, we have retained Hopkins's variant spelling and punctuation along with the "To be continued" notations marking the end of each installment.

Chapter titles were provided only for Chapters IX–XVI, and we have retained this feature of the original text. Each of the fourth through twelfth installments was originally preceded by a synopsis, which we have abbreviated (to eliminate repetition) and moved to footnotes. The full synopsis is reprinted in Appendix A.

HAGAR'S DAUGHTER.

A Story of Southern Caste Prejudice

"I'D DO ANYTHING THAT WOULD BREAK THIS CURSED LUCK I'M HAVING." *Colored American Magazine* frontispiece (March 1901). Reproduced from *The Digital Colored American Magazine*, coloredamerican.org. Original held at the Beinecke Rare Book and Manuscript Library, Yale University.

HAGAR'S DAUGHTER.

A Story of Southern Caste Prejudice.
SARAH A. ALLEN.

CHAPTER I.

IN the fall of 1860 a stranger visiting the United States would have thought that nothing short of a miracle could preserve the union of states so proudly proclaimed by the signers of the Declaration of Independence, and so gloriously maintained by the gallant Washington.

The nomination of Abraham Lincoln for the presidency by the Republican party was inevitable. The proslavery Democracy was drunk with rage at the prospect of losing control of the situation, which, up to that time, had needed scarcely an effort to bind in riveted chains impenetrable alike to the power of man or the frowns of the Godhead; they had inaugurated a system of mob-law and terrorism against all sympathizers with the despised party. The columns of partisan newspapers teemed each day in the year with descriptions of disgraceful scenes enacted North and South by proslavery men, due more to the long-accustomed subserviency of Northern people to the slaveholders than to a real, personal hatred of the Negro.

The free negroes North and South, and those slaves with the hearts of freemen who had boldly taken the liberty denied by man, felt the general spirit of unrest and uncertainty which was spreading over the country to such an alarming extent. The subdued tone of the liberal portion of the press, the humiliating offers of compromise from Northern political leaders, and the numerous cases of surrendering fugitive slaves to their former masters,[1] sent a thrill of mortal fear into the very heart of many a

---

1 In accordance with the national Fugitive Slave Law, part of the Compromise of 1850, Thomas Sims (1834–1902) in 1851 and Anthony Burns (1834–62) in 1854 were tried in Boston and (*continued*)

household where peace and comfort had reigned for many years. The fugitive slave had perhaps won the heart of some Northern free woman; they had married, prospered, and were happy. Now came the haunting dread of a stealthy tread, an ominous knock, a muffled cry at midnight, and the sunlight of the new day would smile upon a broken-hearted woman with baby hands clinging to her skirts, and children's voices asking in vain for their father lost to them forever. The Negro felt that there was no safety for him beneath the Stars and Stripes, and, so feeling, sacrificed his home and personal effects and fled to Canada.[1]

The Southerners were in earnest, and would listen to no proposals in favor of their continuance in the Union under existing conditions; namely, Lincoln and the Republican party. The vast wealth of the South made them feel that they were independent of the world. Cotton was not merely king; it was God. Moral considerations were nothing. Drunk with power and dazzled with prosperity, monopolizing cotton and raising it to the influence of a veritable fetich the authors of the Rebellion did not admit a doubt of the success of their attack on the Federal government. They dreamed of perpetuating slavery, though all history shows the decline of the system as industry, commerce, and knowledge advance. The slaveholders proposed nothing less than to reverse the currents of humanity, and to make barbarism flourish in the bosom of civilization.

The South argued that the principle of right would have no influence over starving operatives; and England and France, as well as the Eastern States of the Union, would stand aghast, and yield to the master stroke which should deprive them of the material of their labor. Millions of the laboring class were dependent upon it in all the great centers of civilization; it was only necessary to wave this sceptre over the nations and all of them would

---

returned to their masters; however, Shadrach Minkins (c. 1814–75), another self-emancipated person, was tried in Boston, freed by the Boston Vigilance Committee in 1851, and escaped to Canada. Hopkins writes about Shadrach in the Famous Men of the Negro Race sketch about Lewis Hayden (1811–89) in the April 1901 issue of the *Colored American Magazine*. She also uses J. Shirley Shadrach as one of her *Colored American Magazine* pseudonyms.

1   As a result of the Compromise of 1850, self-emancipated people had to escape to Canada to ensure their freedom.

acknowledge the power which wielded it. But, alas! the supreme error of this anticipation was in omitting from the calculation the power of principle. Right still had authority in the councils of nations. Factories might be closed, men and women out of employment, but truth and justice still commanded respect among men. The proslavery men in the North encouraged the rebels before the breaking out of the war. They promised the South that civil war should reign in every free state in case of an uprising of the Southern oligarchy, and that men should not be permitted to go South to put down their brothers in rebellion.

Weak as were the Southern people in point of numbers and political power, compared with those of the North, yet they easily persuaded themselves that they could successfully cope in arms with a Northern foe, whom they affected to despise for his cowardly and mercenary disposition. They indulged the belief, in proud confidence, that their great political prestige would continue to serve them among party associates at the North, and that the counsels of the adversary would be distracted and his power weakened by the effects of dissension.

When the Republican banner bearing the names of Abraham Lincoln for President and Hannibal Hamlin for Vice-President flung its folds to the breeze in 1860, there was a panic of apprehension at such bold maneuvering; mob-law reigned in Boston, Utica and New York City, which witnessed the greatest destruction of property in the endeavor to put down the growing public desire to abolish slavery. Elijah Lovejoy's[1] innocent blood spoke in trumpet tones to the reformer from his quiet grave by the rolling river. William Lloyd Garrison's[2] outraged manhood brought the blush of shame to the cheek of the honest American who loved his country's honor better than any individual institution. The memory of Charles Sumner's brutal beating by Preston Brooks stamped the mad passions of the hour indelibly upon

---

1 Elijah Lovejoy (1802–37), minister, journalist, and abolitionist murdered by a pro-slavery mob in Alton, Illinois. The January 1901 issue of the *Colored American Magazine* has an article entitled "Elijah Parrish Lovejoy: The First American Martyr" by John Livingstone Wright.

2 William Lloyd Garrison (1805–79), the co-founder and editor of the abolitionist newspaper *The Liberator*.

history's page.[1] Debate in the Senate became fiery and dangerous as the crisis approached in the absorbing question of the perpetuation of slavery.

At the South laws were enacted abridging the freedom of speech and press; it was difficult for Northerners to travel in slave states. Rev. Charles T. Torrey[2] was sentenced to the Maryland penitentiary for aiding slaves to escape; Jonathan Walker had been branded with a red-hot iron for the same offense. In the midst of the tumult came the "Dred Scott Decision,"[3] and the smouldering fire broke forth with renewed vigor. Each side waited impatiently for the result of the balloting.

In November the Rubicon was passed, and Abraham Lincoln was duly elected President contrary to the wishes and in defiance of the will of the haughty South. There was much talk of a conspiracy to prevent by fraud or violence a declaration of the result of the election by the Vice-President before the two Houses, as provided by law. As the eventful day drew near patriotic hearts were sick with fear or filled with forebodings. Would the certificates fail to appear; would they be wrested by violence from the hands ordered to bear them across the rotunda from the Senate Chamber to the hall of the House, or would they be suppressed by the only official who could open them, John C. Breckenridge of Kentucky, himself a candidate and in full sympathy with the rebellion.

A breathless silence, painfully intense, reigned in the crowded chamber as the Vice-President arose to declare the result of the

---

1 On 22 May 1856, two days after Massachusetts US Senator Charles Sumner (1811–74) made a speech decrying pro-slavery outrages in Kansas territory, South Carolina US Congressman Preston Brooks (1819–57) beat him nearly to death with a walking stick on the floor of the Senate. Hopkins recounts Brooks's caning of Sumner in her February 1901 Famous Men of the Negro Race sketch of Robert Browne Elliott (296–97).

2 Charles T. Torrey (1813–46), abolitionist and Underground Railroad organizer who died of tuberculosis in prison after being convicted of stealing slaves.

3 An 1857 US Supreme Court case ruling that enslaved men and women and their descendants could not be US citizens. Hopkins comments on this ruling in "Hon. Frederick Douglass" (see Appendix C1).

election. Six feet in height, lofty in carriage, youthful, dashing, he stood before them pale and nervous. The galleries were packed with hostile conspirators. It was the supreme moment in the life of the Republic. With unfaltering utterance his voice broke the oppressive stillness:

"I therefore declare Abraham Lincoln duly elected President of the United States for the term of four years from the fourth of March next."

It was the signal for secession, and the South let loose the dogs of war.[1]

CHAPTER II.

DURING the week preceding the memorable 20th of December, 1860,[2] the streets of Charleston, S.C., were filled with excited citizens who had come from all parts of the South to participate in the preparations for seceding from the Union. The hotels were full; every available space was occupied in the homes of private citizens. Bands paraded the streets heading processions of excited politicians who came as delegates from every section south of Mason and Dixon's line;[3] there was shouting and singing by the populace, liberally mingled with barrelhead orations from excited orators with more zeal than worth; there were cheers for the South and oaths for the government at Washington.

Scattered through the crowd traders could be seen journeying to the far South with gangs of slaves chained together like helpless animals destined for the slaughter-house. These slaves were hurriedly sent off by their master in obedience to orders from headquarters, which called for the removal of all human property from the immediate scene of the invasion so soon to come. The traders paused in their hurried journey to participate in the festivities which ushered in the birth of the glorious Confederate States of America. Words cannot describe the scene.

---

1 William Shakespeare, *Julius Caesar* 3.1.273.
2 The day South Carolina became the first Southern state to secede from the Union.
3 Eighteenth-century demarcation of the border between Pennsylvania and Maryland that was used figuratively to denote the division between slave states and free states.

"The wingèd heralds by command
Of sovereign power, with awful ceremony
And trumpet sound, proclaimed
A solemn council forthwith to be held
At Pandæmonium, the high capital
Of Satan and his peers."[1]

Among the traders the most conspicuous was a noted man from St. Louis, by the name of Walker.[2] He was the terror of the whole Southwest among the Negro population, bond and free; for it often happened that free persons were kidnapped and sold to the far South. Uncouth, ill-bred, hard-hearted, illiterate, Walker had started in St. Louis as a dray-driver,[3] and now found himself a rich man. He was a repulsive-looking person, tall, lean and lank, with high cheek-bones and face pitted with the small-pox, gray eyes, with red eye-brows and sandy whiskers.

Walker, upon his arrival in Charleston, took up his quarters with his gang of human cattle in a two-story flat building, surrounded by a stone wall some twelve feet high, the top of which was covered with bits of glass, so that there could be no passage over it without great personal injury. The rooms in this building resembled prison cells, and in the office were to be seen iron collars, hobbles,[4] handcuffs, thumbscrews, cowhides, chains, gags and yokes.

Walker's servant Pompey had charge of fitting the stock for the market-place. Pompey[5] had been so long under the instructions of the heartless speculator that he appeared perfectly indifferent to the heartrending scenes which daily confronted him.

On this particular morning Walker brought in a number of customers to view his stock; among them a noted divine, who was considered deeply religious. The slaves were congregated in

---

1 John Milton, *Paradise Lost* I.752–57.
2 Lois Brown has shown that Hopkins based this character on an "uncouth" St. Louis slave trader and former "dray driver" of the same name for whom William Wells Brown (c. 1814–84) worked (345–46).
3 Sturdy cart for hauling heavy loads.
4 Ropes or straps used to impede movement.
5 As Lois Brown notes, "Pompey," "Jeems," and "Tobias" are the names of enslaved characters in William Wells Brown's 1853 novel *Clotel* (348).

a back yard enclosed by the high wall before referred to. There were swings and benches, which made the place very much like a New England schoolyard.

Among themselves the Negroes talked. There was one woman who had been separated from her husband, and another woman whose looks expressed the anguish of her heart. There was old "Uncle Jeems," with his whiskers off, his face clean shaven, and all his gray hairs plucked out, ready to be sold for ten years younger than he was. There was Tobias, a gentleman's body servant educated at Paris, in medicine, along with his late master, sold to the speculator because of his intelligence and the temptation which the confusion of the times offered for him to attempt an escape from bondage.

"O, my God!" cried one woman, "send dy angel down once mo' ter tell me dat you's gwine ter keep yer word, Massa Lord."

"O Lord, we's been a-watchin' an' a-prayin', but de 'liverer done fergit us!" cried another, as she rocked her body violently back and forth.

It was now ten o'clock, and the daily examination of the stock began with the entrance of Walker and several customers.

"What are you wiping your eyes for?" inquired a fat, red-faced man, with a white hat set on one side of his head and a cigar in his mouth, of the woman seated on a bench.

"'Cause I left my mon behin'."

"Oh, if I buy you, I'll furnish you with a better man than you left. I've got lots of young bucks on my farm," replied the man.

"I don't want anudder mon, an' I tell you, massa, I nebber will hab anudder mon."

"What's your name?" asked a man in a straw hat, of a Negro standing with arms folded across his breast and leaning against the wall.

"Aaron, sar."

"How old are you?"

"Twenty-five."

"Where were you raised?"

"In Virginny, sar."

"How many men have owned you?"

"Fo."

"Do you enjoy good health?"

"Yas, sar."

"Whipped much?"

"No, sar. I s'pose I didn't desarve it, sar."

"I must see your back, so as to know how much you've been whipped, before I conclude a bargain."

"Cum, unharness yoseff, ole boy. Don't you hear the gemman say he wants to zammin[1] yer?" said Pompey.

The speculator, meanwhile, was showing particular attention to the most noted and influential physician of Charleston. The doctor picked out a man and a woman as articles that he desired for his plantation, and Walker proceeded to examine them.

"Well, my boy, speak up and tell the doctor what's your name."

"Sam, sar, is my name."

"How old are you?"

"Ef I live ter see next corn plantin' I'll be twenty-seven, or thirty, or thirty-five, I dunno which."

"Ha, ha, ha! Well, doctor, this is a green boy. Are you sound?"

"Yas, sar; I spec' I is."

"Open your mouth, and let me see your teeth. I allers judge a nigger's[2] age by his teeth, same as I do a hoss. Good appetite?"

"Yas, sar."

"Get out on that plank and dance. I want to see how supple you are."

"I don't like to dance, massa; I'se got religion."

"Got religion, have you? So much the better. I like to deal in the gospel, doctor. He'll suit you. Now, my gal, what's your name?"

"I is Big Jane, sar."

"How old are you?"

"Don' know, sar; but I was born at sweet pertater time."

"Well, do you know who made you?"

"I hev heard who it was in de Bible, but I done fergit de gemman's name."

"Well, doctor, this is the greenest lot of niggers I've had for some time, but you may have Sam for a thousand dollars and Jane for nine hundred. They are worth all I ask for them."

"Well, Walker, I reckon I'll take them," replied the doctor.

"I'll put the handcuffs on 'em, and then you can pay me."

---

1 Examine.

2 While considered derogatory and highly offensive, this word was commonly used in the era.

"Why," remarked the doctor, "there comes Reverend Pinchen."

"It is Mr. Pinchen as I live; jest the very man I want to see." As the reverend gentleman entered the enclosure, the trader grasped his hand, saying: "Why, how do you do, Mr. Pinchen? Come down to Charleston to the Convention, I s'pose? Glorious time, sir, glorious; but it will be gloriouser when the new government has spread our institootions all over the conquered North. Gloriouser and gloriouser. Any camp-meetin's, revivals, death-bed scenes, or other things in your line going on down here? How's religion prospering now, Mr. Pinchen? I always like to hear about religion."

"Well, Mr. Walker, the Lord's work is in good condition everywhere now. Mr. Walker, I've been in the gospel ministry these thirteen years, and I know that the heart of man is full of sin and desperately wicked. Religion is a good thing to live by, and we'll want it when we die. And a man in your business of buying and selling slaves needs religion more than anybody else, for it makes you treat your people well. Now there's Mr. Haskins—he's a slave-trader like yourself. Well, I converted him. Before he got religion he was one of the worst men to his niggers I ever saw; his heart was as hard as a stone. But religion has made his heart as soft as a piece of cotton. Before I converted him he would sell husbands from their wives and delight in doing it; but now he won't sell a man from his wife if he can get anyone to buy them together. I tell you, sir, religion has done a wonderful work for him."

"I know, Mr. Pinchen, that I ought to have religion, and that I am a great sinner; and whenever I get with good, pious people, like you and the doctor, I feel desperate wicked. I know that I would be happier with religion, and the first spare time I have I'm going to get it. I'll go to a protracted meeting, and I won't stop till I get religion."

Walker then invited the gentlemen to his office, and Pompey was dispatched to purchase wine and other refreshments for the guests.

Within the magnificent hall of the St. Charles Hotel[1] a far dif-

---

1 Founded as the Pavilion Hotel in 1838 and located on the corner of Charleston's Meeting and Hasell streets; the King Charles Hotel now stands at this location.

ferent scene was enacted in the afternoon. The leading Southern politicians were gathered there to discuss the election of Lincoln, the "sectional" candidate, and to give due weight and emphasis to the future acts of the new government. There was exaltation in every movement of the delegates, and they were surrounded by the glitter of a rich and powerful assemblage in a high state of suppressed excitement, albeit this meeting was but preliminary to the decisive acts of the following week.

The vast hall, always used for dancing, was filled with tables which spread their snow-white wings to receive the glittering mass of glass, plate and flowers. The spacious galleries were crowded to suffocation by beautiful Southern belles in festive attire. Palms and fragrant shrubs were everywhere; garlands of flowers decorated the walls and fell, mingled with the new flag—the stars and bars—gracefully above the seat of the chairman. In the gallery opposite the speaker's desk a band was stationed; Negro servants in liveries of white linen hurried noiselessly to and fro. The delegates filed in to their places at table to the crashing strains of "Dixie";[1] someone raised the new flag aloft and waved it furiously; the whole assembly rose *en masse* and cheered vociferously, and the ladies waved their handkerchiefs. Mirth and hilarity reigned. The first attention of the diners was given to the good things before them. After cigars were served the music stopped, and the business of the day began in earnest.

There was the chairman, Hon. Robert Toombs of Georgia; there was John C. Breckenridge of Kentucky, Stephen A. Douglas, Alexander H. Stevens, and Jefferson Davis.[2]

---

1 Song of disputed origin that first appeared on the minstrel stage and became the unofficial anthem of the Confederacy during the Civil War.

2 Robert Toombs (1810–85) was the first secretary of state of the Confederate States of America. John C. Breckinridge (1821–75) was the 14th vice president of the United States and later a Confederate officer. Stephen A. Douglas (1813–61) was the Democratic US Senator from Illinois and was defeated by Abraham Lincoln (1809–65) in the 1860 presidential election. Alexander H. Stephens (1812–83) was a Georgia politician who served as vice president of the Confederate States of America. Jefferson Davis (1808–89) was a US Senator from Mississippi, a US secretary of war, and the president of the

"Silence!" was the cry, as Hon. Robert Toombs, the chairman, arose.

"Fellow Delegates and Fellow Citizens: I find myself in a most remarkable situation, and I feel that every Southern gentleman sympathizes with me. Here am I, chairman of a meeting of the most loyal, high-spirited and patriotic body of men and their guests and friends, that ever assembled to discuss the rights of humanity and Christian progress, and yet unable to propose a single toast with which we have been wont to sanction such a meeting as this. With grief that consumes my soul, I am compelled to bury in the silence of mortification, contempt and detestation the name of the government at Washington.

"I can only counsel you, friends, to listen to no vain babbling, to no treacherous jargon about overt acts; they have already been committed. Defend yourselves; the enemy is at your door; wait not to meet him at the hearthstone,—meet him at the door-sill, and drive him from the temple of liberty, or pull down its pillars and involve him in a common ruin. Never permit this federal government to pass into the traitorous hands of the black Republican party.[1]

"My language may appear strong; but it is mild when we consider the attempt being made to wrest from us the exclusive power of making laws for our own community. The repose of our homes, the honor of our color, and the prosperity of the South demand that we resist innovation.

"I rejoice to see around me fellow-laborers worthy to lead in the glorious cause of resisting oppression, and defending our ancient privileges which have been set by an Almighty hand. We denounce once and for all the practices proposed by crazy enthusiasts, seconded by designing knaves, and destined to be executed by demons in human form. We shall conquer in this pending struggle; we will subdue the North, and call the roll of

---

Confederate States of America. As Lois Brown points out, Hopkins "places in Charleston five leading antebellum Southern politicians who were not present at the historic meeting" (339).

1 Hopkins here rearranges lines from a speech that Toombs made in the US Senate on 24 January 1860; the topic was self-emancipated persons. See *A Political Textbook for 1860*, edited by Horace Greeley and John F. Cleveland (Tribune Association, 1860), pp. 171–72.

our slaves beneath the very shadow of Bunker Hill.[1] 'It is a consummation devoutly to be wished.'[2]

"And now, I call upon all true patriots in token of their faith, to drink deep to one deserving their fealty,—the guardian and savior of the South, Jefferson Davis."

Vociferous cheers broke forth and shook the building. The crowd surrounding the hotel took it up, and the name "Davis!" "Davis!" was repeated again and again. He arose in his seat and bowed profoundly; the band played "See the Conquering Hero Comes"; a lady in the gallery back of him skillfully dropped a crown of laurel upon his head. The crowd went mad; they tore the decorations from the walls and pelted their laurel-crowned hero until he would gladly have had them cease; but such is fame. When the cheers had somewhat subsided, Mr. Davis said:

"I must acknowledge, my fellow-citizens, the truth of the remarks just made by our illustrious friend, Senator Toombs. I was never more satisfied with regard to the future history of our country than I am at present. I believe in state rights, slavery, and the Confederacy that we are about to inaugurate.

"The principle of slavery is in itself right, and does not depend upon difference of complexion. Make the laboring man the slave of *one* man, instead of the slave of society, and he would be far better off. Slavery, black or white, is necessary. Nature has made the weak in mind or body for slaves.[3]

"In five days your delegates from all the loyal Southern States will meet here in convention. I feel the necessity that every eye be fixed upon the course which will be adopted by this assembly of patriots. You know our plans. South Carolina will lead the march of the gallant band who will give us the liberty we crave. We are all united in will and views, and therefore powerful. I see before me in my colleagues men to whom the tranquility of our government may be safely confided—men devoted and zealous in their interest—senators and representatives who

---

1 Toombs repeatedly denied making this claim, which was often attributed to him from 1856 onward. See "Roll-Call of Slaves in the North," *New York Times*, 24 March 1863, p. 4.

2 Shakespeare, *Hamlet* 3.1.62–63.

3 Hopkins took this language, attributed to George Fitzhugh and the editors of the *Richmond Inquirer*, from William Wells Brown's *My Southern Home* (A.G. Brown, 1880), p. 152.

have managed everything for our aid and comfort. Few of the vessels of the navy are available at home; the army is scattered on the Western frontier, while all the trained officers of the army are with us. Within our limits we have control of the entire government property—mints, custom-houses, post-offices, dockyards, revenue-cutters, arsenals and forts. The national finances have been levied upon to fill our treasury by our faithful Southern members of the late cabinet. Yes, friends, all is ready; every preparation is made for a brief and successful fight for that supremacy in the government of this nation which is our birthright. (Tremendous applause.)

"By the election just thrust upon us by the Republican party the Constitution is violated; and were we not strong to sustain our rights, we should soon find ourselves driven to prison at the point of the bayonet (cries of 'Never, never!'), ousted from the council of state, oblivion everywhere, and nothing remaining but ourselves to represent Truth and Justice. We believe that our ideas are the desires of the majority of the people, and the people represent the supreme and sovereign power of Right! (Hear! hear! cheers.) For Abraham Lincoln (hisses) nothing is inviolate, nothing sacred; he menaces, in his election, our ancient ideas and privileges. The danger grows greater. Let us arise in our strength and meet it more than half way. Are you ready, men?"

"We are ready!" came in a roar like unto the waters of the mighty Niagara. "What shall we do?"

"No half measures; let it be a deed of grandeur!"

"It shall be done!" came in another mighty chorus.

"In such a crisis there must be no vacuum. There must be a well-established government before the people. You, citizens, shall take up arms; we will solicit foreign re-enforcements; we will rise up before this rail-splitting[1] ignoramus a terrible power; we will overwhelm this miserable apology for a gentleman and a statesman as a terrible revolutionary power. Do you accept my proposition?"

"Yes, yes!" came as a unanimous shout from the soul of the vast assembly.

"Our Northern friends make a great talk about free society.

---

1 Literature for Lincoln's 1860 presidential campaign used the nickname Rail Splitter (i.e., someone who chops logs into rails for fences) to emphasize his lowly origins.

We sicken of the name. What is it but a conglomeration of greasy mechanics, filthy operatives, small-fisted farmers, and moon-struck Abolitionists? All the Northern States, and particularly the New England States, are devoid of society fitted for well-bred gentlemen. The prevailing class one meets with is that of mechanics struggling to be genteel, and farmers who do their own drudgery, and yet who are hardly fit for association with a gentleman's slave.[1]

"We have settled this matter in the minds of the people of the South by long years of practice and observation; and I believe that when our principles shall have been triumphantly established over the entire country—North, South, West—a long age of peace and prosperity will ensue for the entire country. Under our jurisdiction wise laws shall be passed for the benefit of the supreme and subordinate interests of our communities. And when we have settled all these vexed questions I see a season of calm and fruitful prosperity, in which our children's children may enjoy their lives without a thought of fear or apprehension of change."

Then the band played; there was more cheering and waving of handkerchiefs, in the midst of which John C. Breckenridge arose and gracefully proposed the health of the first President of the Confederate States of America. It was drunk by every man standing. Other speakers followed, and the most intemperate sentiments were voiced by the zealots in the great cause. The vast crowd went wild with enthusiasm.

St. Clair Enson, one of the most trusted delegates, and the slave-trader Walker sat side by side at the table, and in the excitement of the moment all the prejudices of the Maryland aristocrat toward the vile dealer in human flesh were forgotten.

The convention had now passed the bounds of all calmness. Many of the men stood on chairs, gesticulating wildly, each trying to be heard above his neighbor. In vain the Chair rapped for order. Pandemonium[2] reigned. At one end of the long table two

---

1 Statements attributed to the Muscogee (Alabama) *Herald* and raised as an issue by Lincoln in his debates with Stephen Douglas in 1856. Hopkins may have encountered these statements in the Preface to William Lloyd Garrison's *Southern Hatred of the American Government* (R.F. Wallcut, 1862).

2 The place where Satan gathers his minions in Milton's *Paradise Lost*, here used as a term suggesting complete chaos.

men were locked in deadly embrace, each struggling to enforce his views upon the other by brute strength.

One man had swept the dishes aside, and was standing upon the table, demanding clamorously to be heard, and above all the band still crashed its brazen notes of triumph in the familiar strains of "Dixie."

A Negro boy handed a letter to Mr. Enson. He turned it over in his hand, curiously examining the postmark.

"When did this come, Cato?"

"More'n a munf, massa," was the reply.

Mr. Enson tore open the envelope and glanced over its contents with a frowning face.

"Bad news?" ventured Walker, with unusual familiarity.

"The worst possible for me. My brother is married, and announces the birth of a daughter."

"Well, daughters are born every day. I don't see how that can hurt you."

"It happens in this case, however, that this particular daughter will inherit the Enson fortune," returned Enson, with a short laugh.

Walker gave a long, low whistle. "Who was your brother's wife? Any money?"

"Clark Sargeant's daughter. Money enough on both sides; but the trouble is, it will never be mine." Another sharp, bitter laugh.

"Sargeant, Sargeant," said Walker, musingly. "'Pears to me I've had business with a gentleman of the same name years ago, in St. Louis. However, it can't be the same one, 'cause this man hadn't any children. Leastways, I never heard on eny."

"Perhaps it is the same man. Clark Sargeant was from St. Louis; moved to Baltimore when the little girl was five years old. Mr. and Mrs. Sargeant are dead."

"Same man, same man. Um, um," said Walker, scratching the flesh beneath his sandy whiskers meditatively, as he gazed at the ceiling. "Both dead, eh? Come to think of it, I moight be mistaken about the little gal. Has she got black hair and eyes and a cream-colored skin, and has she growed up to be a all-fired pesky fine woman?"

"Can't say," replied Enson, with a yawn as he rose to his feet. "I've never had the pleasure of meeting my sister-in-law."

"When you going up to Baltimore?" asked Walker.

"Next week, on 'The Planter.'"

"Think I'll take a trip up with you. You don't mind my calling with you on your brother's family, do you, Mr. Enson? I would admire to introduce myself to Clark Sargeant's little gal. She moight not remember me at first, but I reckon I could bring back recollections of me to her mind, ef it's jes' the same to you, Mr. Enson."

"O, be hanged to you. Go where you please. Go to the devil," replied Enson, as he swung down the hall and elbowed his way out.

"No need of goin' to the devil when he's right side of you, Mr. Enson," muttered Walker, as he watched the young man out of sight. "You d—d aristocrats carry things with a high hand; I'll be glad to take a reef in your sails, and I'll do it, too, or my name's not Walker."

CHAPTER III.

St. Clair Enson was the second son of an aristocratic Maryland family. He had a fiery temper that knew no bounds when once aroused. Motherless from infancy, and born at a period in the life of his parents when no more children were expected, he grew up wild and self-willed. As his character developed it became evident that an unsavory future was before him. There was no malicious mischief in which he was not found, and older heads predicted that he would end on the gallows. Sensual, cruel to ferocity, he was a terror to the God-fearing community where he lived. With women he was successful from earliest youth, being possessed of the diabolical beauty of Satan himself. There was great rejoicing in the quiet village near which Enson Hall was situated when it was known that the young scapegrace had gone to college.

The atmosphere of college life suited him well, and he was soon the leader of the fastest set there. He was the instigator of innumerable broils, insulted his teachers, and finally fought a duel, killing his man instantly. According to the code of honor of the time, this was not murder; but expulsion from the halls of learning followed for St. Clair, and much to his surprise and chagrin, his father, who had always indulged and excused his acts as the thoughtlessness of youth's high spirits, was thoroughly enraged.

There was a curious scene between them, and no one ever knew just what passed, but it was ended by his father's saying:

"You have disgraced the name of Enson, and now you dare make a joke to me of your wickedness. Let me not see your face in this house again. Henceforth, until you have redeemed yourself by an honest man's career, I have but one son, your brother Ellis."

"As you please, sir," replied St. Clair nonchalantly, as he placed the check his father handed him in his pocket, bowed, and passed from the room.

That was the last heard of him for five years, when at his father's death he went home to attend the funeral.

By the terms of the will St. Clair received a small annuity, to be enlarged at the discretion of his brother, and in event of the latter's death without issue, the estate was to revert to St. Clair's heirs "if any there be who are an honor to the name of Enson," was the wording of the will.

In the event of St. Clair's continuing in disgrace and "having no honorable and lawful issue," the property was to revert to a distant branch of cousins, "for I have no mind that debauchery and crime shall find a home at Enson Hall."

After this St. Clair seemingly dropped his wildest habits, but was still noted on all the river routes of the South as a reckless and daring gambler.

His man Isaac was as much of a character as himself, and many a game they worked together on the inexperienced, and many a time but for Isaac, St. Clair would have fared ill at the hands of his victims. Isaac was given to his young master at the age of ten years. The only saving grace about the scion of aristocracy appeared in his treatment of Isaac. Master and slave were devoted to each other.

As a last resource young Enson had gone in for politics, and the luck that had recently deserted him at cards and dice, favored him here. The unsettled state of the country and the threatening war-clouds were a boon to the tired child of chance, which he hailed as harbingers of better times for recreant[1] Southern sons. He would gain fame and fortune in the service of the new government.

All through the dramatic action of the next week when history was made so fast in the United States, when the South

---

1 Disloyal, but also cowardly.

Carolina convention declared that "the union then subsisting between herself and other states of America, was dissolved" and her example followed by Mississippi, Florida, Alabama, Georgia, Louisiana, Texas, Virginia, Arkansas, North Carolina and Tennessee, all through that time when politics reached the boiling point, St. Clair, although in the thickest of the controversy, busy making himself indispensable to the officials of the new government, was thinking of the heiress of Enson Hall. He was bitter over his loss, and ready to blame anyone but himself.

In his opinion, Ellis was humdrum; he was mild and peaceful in his disposition, because his blood was too sluggish and his natural characteristics too womanish for the life of a gentleman. Then, too, Ellis was old, fifteen years his senior, and he was twenty-five.

St. Clair shared the universal opinion of his world (and to him the world did not exist north of Mason and Dixon's line), that a reckless career of gambling, wine and women was the only true course of development for a typical Southern gentleman. As he thought of the infant heiress his face grew black with a frown of rage that for the time completely spoiled the beauty women raved over. His man Isaac, furtively watching him from the corner of his eye, said to himself:

"I know dat dar's gwine to be a rippit;[1] Marse St. Clair never look dat a way widout de debbil himself am broked loose." In which view of the case Isaac was about right.

St. Clair made up his mind to go home and see this fair woman who had come to blast his hopes and steal his patrimony for her children. Perhaps as she was young, and presumably susceptible, something might be done. He was handsome—Ah, well! and he laughed a wicked laugh at his reflection in the mirror; he would trust to luck to help him out. He ordered Isaac to pack up.

"Good Lawd, Marse St. Clair! I thought you'd done settled here fer good. How comes we go right off?"

"We're going home, Isaac, to see the new mistress Enson and my niece. Haven't I told you that your master, Ellis was married, and had a daughter?"

"Bress my soul! no sar!" replied Isaac, dropping the clothes he held upon the floor. His master left the room.

"Now de Lawd help de mistress an' de little baby. I love my

---

1 Uproar.

master, but he's a borned debbil. He's jes' gwine home to tare up brass, dat's de whole collusion[1] ob de mystery."

St. Clair Enson took passage on board "The Planter," which was ready to start upon its last trip up Chesapeake Bay before going into the service of the Confederate government. At that time this historic vessel was a side-wheel steamer storing about fourteen hundred bales of cotton as freight, but having accommodations for a moderate number of passengers. No one of the proud supporters of the new government dreamed of her ultimate fate.[2] The position of the South was defined, and given to the world with a loud flourish of trumpets. By their reasoning, a few short months would make them masters of the entire country. Wedded to their idols, they knew not the force of the "dire arms"[3] which Omnipotence would wield upon the side of Right. One of the most daring and heroic adventures of the Civil War was successfully accomplished by a party of Negroes, Robert Smalls[4] commanding, when the rebel gunboat "The Planter" ran by the forts and batteries of Charleston Harbor, and reaching the flagship "Wabash" was duly received into the service of the United States government.

St. Clair Enson went on board the steamer with mixed feelings of triumph and chagrin—triumph because of the place he had made for himself in the councils of the new government and the adulation meted out to him by the public; chagrin because of his brother's new family ties and his own consequent poverty.

For a while he wandered aimlessly about, resisting all the tempting invitations extended by his numerous admirers in the sporting and political world to "have something" at the glittering bar. But his pockets were empty—they always were—and he finally allowed himself to be cajolled to join in a quiet game in

---

1 An example of the double meaning Hopkins achieves through dialect. Isaac means "conclusion" here, but "collusion" foreshadows St. Clair and Walker's scheme.

2 After being stolen, the *Planter* became a Union vessel.

3 Milton, *Paradise Lost* 1.93–94.

4 Robert Smalls (1839–1915), born enslaved in Beaufort, South Carolina. Smalls served in the US military from 1862–68 and as a US Congressman from 1882–83 and 1884–87. Hopkins discusses Smalls at length in "Heroes and Heroines in Black Part I," *Colored American Magazine*, January 1903, pp. 208–11. See also Appendix C3.

the hope of replenishing his purse, where he saw the chances were all in his favor.

The saloon was alight with music and gaiety; the jolly company of travelers and the gaudy furniture were reflected many times over in the gilded mirrors that caught the rays of a large chandelier depending from the center of the ceiling. To the eye and ear merriment held high carnival; some strolled about, many sought the refreshment bar, but a greater number—men and even women—took part in the play or bet lightly on the players, sotto voce,[1] for pastime. The clink and gleam of gold was there as it passed from hand to hand. Six men at a table played baccarat; farther on, a party of very young people—both sexes—played loo for small stakes. There were quartets of whist[2] players, too; but the most popular game was poker, for high stakes made by reckless and inveterate gamblers.

St. Clair and his party found an empty table, and Isaac, obedient to a sign from his master, brought him the box containing implements for a game of poker. All the men were inveterate gamblers, but Enson was an expert. Gradually the on-lookers gathered about that one particular table. Not a word was said; the men gripped their cards and held their breaths, with now and then an oath to punctuate a loss more severe than usual.

The slave-trader Walker sauntered up to the place where St. Clair sat, and stood behind him.

"What's the stakes?" he asked of his next neighbor. The man addressed smiled significantly: "Not a bagatelle[3] to begin with; they've raised them three times."

"Whew!" with a whistle. "And who is winning?"

"Oh, Enson, of course."

"Why 'of course?'" asked Walker with a wicked smile on his ugly face.

"He always wins."

"I reckon not now," returned Walker, as he pointed to the play just made.

"He's dealing above board and square, and luck's agin him."

---

1 Quietly.

2 Baccarat is a card game in which one player competes directly with the banker; loo and whist are also card games, the latter a forerunner of bridge.

3 Trifle.

It was true. From this time on Enson played again and again, and lost. The other players left their seats and stood near watching the famous gambler make his play. Finally, with a muttered curse, he staggered up from his chair and started to leave the table with desperate eyes and reeling gate.[1] But he stopped as if struck by a sudden inspiration, and resumed his seat.

"What will he do now?" was the unspoken thought of the crowd.

"Isaac, come here," called out Enson. "I will see you and five hundred better," he continued, addressing his opponent, as the boy approached, and at a signal from him climbed upon the table. The crowd watched the strange scene in breathless silence.

"What price do you set on the boy?" asked the winner, whose name was Johnson, taking a large roll of bills from his pocket.

"He will bring eighteen hundred dollars any day in the New Orleans market."

"I reckon he ain't noways vicious?" said Johnson, looking in the Negro's smiling face.

"I've never seen him angry."

"I'll give you fifteen hundred for him."

"Eighteen," returned Enson, with an ominous tightening about the mouth.

"Well, I'll tell you what I'll do, the very best; I'll make it sixteen hundred, no more, no less. That's fair. Is it a bargain?"

Enson nodded assent. The crowd heaved a sigh of relief.

"Then you bet the whole of this boy, do you?" continued Johnson.

"Yes."

"I call you, then," said Johnson.

"I've got three queens," replied Enson.

"Not enough," said the other.

"Then if you beat three queens, you beat me."

"I have four jacks, and the boy is mine." The crowd heaved another sigh as one man.

"Hold on! Not so fast!" shouted Enson. "You don't take him till you *show* me that you beat three queens." Johnson threw his five cards upon the table, and four of them were jacks! "Sure," said Johnson, as he looked at Enson and then at the crowd.

"Sure!" came in a hoarse murmur from many throats. For a moment all things whirled and danced before Enson's eyes as he

---

1 I.e., gait.

realized what he had lost. The lights from the chandelier shot out sparkles from piles of golden coin, the table heaved, faces were indistinct. He seemed to hear his father's voice again in stern condemnation, as he had heard it for the last time on earth. His face was white and set. He was a man ready for desperate deeds. It seemed an hour to him, that short second. Then he turned to the winner:

"Mr. Johnson, I quit you."

Isaac was standing upon the table with the money at his feet. As he stepped down, Johnson said:

"You will not forget that you belong to me."

"No, sir."

"Be up in time to brush my clothes and clean my boots; do you hear?"

"Yas, sir," responded Isaac, with a good-natured smile and a long side-glance at Enson, in which one might have seen the lurking deviltry of a spirit kindred to his master's. Enson turned to leave the saloon, saying:

"I claim the right of redeeming that boy, Mr. Johnson. My father gave him to me when I was a lad. I promised never to part with him."

"Most certainly, sir; the boy shall be yours whenever you hand me over a cool sixteen hundred," returned Johnson. As Enson moved away, chewing the bitter cud of disappointment, Walker strolled up to him.

"That's a bad bargain Johnson's got in your man, Mr. Enson."

"How? Explain yourself."

"If he finds him after tomorrow morning, it's my belief it won't be the fault of Isaac's legs."

"Do you mean to say, sir, that I would connive at robbing a gentleman in fair play?"

"Oh, no; it won't be your fault," replied Walker with a familiar slap on Enson's back, that made the latter wince; "but he's a cute darkey that you can sell in good faith to a man, but he won't stay with him. Bet you the nigger'll be in Baltimore time you are."[1]

"I'll take you. Make your bet."

Walker shook his head. "No, don't you do it. Luck's agin you, an' I won't rob you. That nigger'll lose you, sure."

---

1 This episode closely resembles a scene in Chapter 2 of William Wells Brown's *Clotel* (350). See Appendix G2.

Enson made no reply, but stood gazing moodily out upon the dark waters of the Atlantic, through which the steamer swiftly ploughed her way. Finally Walker continued:

"Why don't you try another game? Keep it up; luck may change. I'll lend you."

Enson waved his hand impatiently and said: "No; no more tonight. I have not a cent in the world until I eat humble pie and beg money from my brother."

"Tough!"

"Thank you. I do not want your sympathy."

"My help, then. Perhaps I can help you." Enson smiled derisively at the endless black waves and the moonless sky.

"No man can do that. I have made my bed hard and must abide the issue."

"Oh, rot! Be a man, and keep on fighting 'em. You'll be all right presently. Never say die."

"Perhaps you have a plan to compass the impossible," returned Enson with a sneer.

"I should say so. I've been thinking a good deal about your brother's marriage, and my old friends, the Sargeants. What would it be worth to you now to find a way to break off this marriage?"

"Break it off! Why, man, that can't be done. What are you driving at?"

"Easy there, now. I said 'break it off,' and I meant 'break it off.' They used to tell me when I was a boy that two heads was better'n one ef one was a sheep's head. Same case here. Job's worth ten thou. I can see three thou right in sight, that would make your bill about seven thou." Walker settled his hat at the back of his head, thrust his hands deep in his hip pockets, and gazed out over the dark waters with a glance from his ferret-like gray eyes that seemed to pierce the blackness.

"I don't understand you, Walker; explain yourself."

"I understand myself, and that's enough. All you've got to do is to put your I O U to a paper calling for seven thousand dollars conditional on my rendering you valuable service in a financial matter. Savey?"[1]

"I'd do anything that would break this cursed luck I'm having. Can you do anything? What do you mean, anyhow, Walker?"

---

1 I.e., savvy.

"Never mind what I mean. You meet me at Enson Hall. Wait for me if you get there first. Be ready to sign the paper, and I'll show you as neat a job as was ever put up by any man on earth. That's all." Walker turned as he finished speaking and walked away. St. Clair looked after him, uncertain what to think of his strange words and actions.

(To be continued.)

"MY DEAR, ARE YOU ACQUAINTED WITH THIS GENTLEMAN?"
Hagar's Daughter illustration, *Colored American Magazine* (April 1901). Reproduced from *The Digital Colored American Magazine*, coloredamerican.org. Original held at the Beinecke Rare Book and Manuscript Library, Yale University.

CHAPTER IV.

THE morning sun poured its golden light upon the picturesque old house standing in its own grounds in one of the suburban towns adjacent to Baltimore—the Baltimore of 1858 or 1860.

The old house seemed to command one to render homage to its beauty and stateliness. It was a sturdy brick building flanked with offices and having outbuildings touching the very edge of the deep, mysterious woods where the trees waved their beckoning arms in every soft breeze that came to revel in their rich foliage. This was Enson Hall. The Hall was reached through a long dim stretch of these woods—locusts and beeches—from ten to twelve acres in extent; its mellow, red-brick walls framed by a background of beech-trees reminded one of English residences with their immense extent of private grounds. In the rear of the mansion was the garden, with its huge conservatories gay with shrubs and flowers. Piazzas and porticoes promised delightful retreats for sultry weather. The interior of the house was in the style that came in after the Revolution. An immense hall with outer door standing invitingly open gave greeting to the guest. The stairs wound from the lower floor to the rooms above. The grand stairway was richly embellished with carving, and overhead a graceful arch added much to the impressive beauty which met the stranger's first view. The rooms, spacious and designed for entertaining largely, had panelled wainscotting and carved chimney-pieces.

Ellis Enson, the master of the Hall, was a well-made man, verging on forty. "Born with a silver spoon in his mouth," for the vast estate and all invested money was absolutely at his disposal, he was the envy of the men of his class and the despair of the ladies. He was extremely good-looking, slight, elegant, with wavy dark hair, and an air of distinction. Since his father's death he had lived at the Hall, surrounded by his slaves in lonely meditation, fancy free. This handsome recluse had earned the reputation of being morose, so little had he mixed with society, so cold had been his politeness to the fair sex. His farms, his lonely rides, his favorite books, had sufficed for him. He was a good manager, and what was more wonderful, considering his Southern temperament, a thorough man of business. His crops, his poultry, his dairy products, were of the very first quality. Sure it was that his plantation was a paying investment. Meanwhile the great house, with all its beautiful rooms and fine furniture, remained closed to the public, and was the despair of managing mammas with many daughters to provide with eligible husbands. Enson was second to none as a "catch," but he was utterly indifferent to women.

Just about this time when to quarry the master of Enson Hall seemed a hopeless task, Hagar[1] Sargeant came home from a four years' sojourn at the North in a young ladies' seminary.

The Sargeant estate was the one next adjoining Enson Hall; not so large and imposing, but a valuable patrimony that had descended in a long line of Sargeants and was well preserved. For many years before Hagar's birth the estate had been rented because of financial misfortunes, and they had lived in St. Louis, where Mr. Sargeant had engaged in trade so successfully that when Hagar was six years old they were enabled to return to their ancestral home and resume a life of luxurious leisure. Since that time Mr. Sargeant had died. On a trip to St. Louis, where he had gone to settle his business affairs, he contracted cholera, then ravaging many large cities of the Southwest, and had finally succumbed to the scourge. Hagar, their only child, then became her mother's sole joy and inspiration. Determined to cultivate her daughter's rare intellectual gifts, she had sent her North to school when every throb of her heart demanded her presence at home. She had developed into a beautiful girl, the admiration and delight of the neighborhood to which she returned, almost a stranger after her long absence.

A golden May morning poured its light through the open window of the Sargeant breakfast-room. A pleasanter room could scarcely be found, though the furniture was not of latest fashion, and the carpet slightly faded. There was a bay window that opened on the terrace, below which was a garden; there was a table in the recess spread with dainty china and silver, and the remains of breakfast; honeysuckles played hide-and-seek at the open window. Aunt Henny, a coal-black Negress of kindly face, brought in the little brass-bound oaken tub filled with hot water and soap, and the linen towels. Hagar stood at the window contemplating the scene before her. It was her duty to wash the

---

1 Genesis 16 and 21 recount the story of Hagar, an Egyptian hand-maiden whose relations with Abraham result in the birth of the out-cast Ishmael. See Appendix D1.

heirlooms of colonial china and silver. From their bath they were dried only by her dainty fingers, and carefully replaced in the corner cupboard. Not for the world would she have dropped one of these treasures. Her care for them, and the placing of everyone in its proper niche, was wonderful to behold. Not the royal jewels of Victoria were ever more carefully guarded than these family heirlooms.

This morning Hagar was filled with a delicious excitement, caused by she knew not what. The china and silver were an anxiety unusual to her. She felt a physical exhilaration, inspired, no doubt, by the delicious weather. She always lamented at this season of the year the lost privileges of the house of Sargeant, when their right of way led directly from the house to the shining waters of the bay. There was a path that led to the water still, but it was across the land of their neighbor Enson. Sometimes Hagar would trespass; would cross the parklike stretch of pasture, bordered by the woodland through which it ran, and sit on the edge of the remnant of a wharf, by which ran a small, rapid river, an arm of Chesapeake Bay, chafing among wet stones and leaping gaily over rocky barriers. There she would dream of life before the Revolution, and in these dreams participate in the joys of the colonial dames. She longed to mix and mingle with the gay world; she had a feeling that her own talents, if developed, would end in something far different from the calm routine, the housekeeping and churchgoing which stretched before her. Sometimes softer thoughts possessed her, and she speculated about love and lovers. This peaceful life was too tranquil and uneventful. Oh, for a break in the humdrum recurral of the same events day after day.

She had never met Ellis Enson. He was away a great part of the time before she left home for school, and since she had returned. If she remembered him at all, it was with the thought of a girl just past her eighteenth birthday for a man forty.

This morning Hagar washed the silver with the sleeves of her morning robe turned up to the shoulder, giving a view of rosy, dimpled arms. "A fairer vision was never seen," thought the man who paused a moment at the open window to gaze again upon the pretty, homelike scene. As Hagar turned from replacing the last of the china, she was startled out of her usual gay indifference at the sight of a handsome pair of dark eyes regarding her intently from the open window. A quick wonder flashed in the eyes that met hers; the color deepened in his face as he saw he was observed. The girl's beauty startled him so, that for a moment he lost the self-control that convention dictates. Then he bared his head in courteous acknowledgment of youth and beauty, with an apology for his seeming intrusion.

"I beg pardon," Enson said in his soft, musical tones; "is Mrs. Sargeant at home? I did not know she had company."

"I am not company; I am Hagar. Yes, mamma is at home; if you will come in, I will take you to her."

He turned and entered the hall door and followed her through the dark, cool hall to the small morning-room, where Mrs. Sargeant spent her mornings in semi-invalid fashion. Then a proper introduction followed, and Ellis Enson and Hagar Sargeant were duly acquainted.

At forty Enson still retained his faith in womanhood, although he had been so persistently pursued by all the women of the vicinity. He believed there were women in the world capable of loving a man for himself alone without a thought of worldly advantage, only he had not been fortunate enough to meet them.

He had a very poor opinion of himself. Adulation had not made him vain. His face indicated strong passions and much pride; but it was pride of caste, not self. There was great tenderness of the eye and lip, and signs of a sensitive nature that could not bear disgrace or downfall that might touch his ancient name. After he left the Sargeant home Hagar's face haunted him; the pure, creamy skin, the curved crimson lips ready to smile,—lips sweet and firm,—the broad, low brow, and great, lustrous, long-lashed eyes of brilliant black—soft as velvet, and full of light with the earnest, cloudless gaze of childhood; and there was heart and soul and mind in this countenance of a mere girl. Such beauty as this was a perpetual delight to feast the eyes and charm the senses—aye, to witch a man's heart from him; for here there was not only the glory of form and tints, but more besides,—heart that could throb, soul that could aspire, mind that could think. She was not shy and self-conscious as young girls so often are; she seemed quite at her ease, as one who has no thought of self. He was conscious of his own enthralment. He knew that he had set his feet in the perilous path of love at a late day, but knowing this, he none the less went forward to his fate.

After that the young girl and the man met frequently. She did not realize when the time came that she had grown to look for his coming. There were walks and drives and accidental meetings in the woods. The sun was brighter and the songs of the birds sweeter that summer than ever before.

Ellis fell to day-dreaming, and the dreams were tinged with gold, bringing a flush to his face and a thrill to his heart. Still he would have denied, if accused, that this was love at first sight— bah! That was a well-exploded theory. And yet if it was not love that had suddenly come into his being for this slender, dark-eyed girl, what was it? A change had come into Ellis Enson's life. The greatest changes, too, are always unexpected.

It was a sultry day; there was absolutely no chance to catch a refreshing breeze within four walls. It was one of the rare occasions when Mrs. Sargeant felt obliged to make a business call alone. From the fields came the sound of voices singing: the voices of slaves. Aunt Henny's good-natured laugh occasionally broke the stillness.

"Now I shall have a nice quiet afternoon," thought Hagar, as she left the house for the shadow of the trees. Under the strong, straight branches of a beech she tied three old shawls, hammock-like, one under another, for strength and safety. It was not very far from the ground. If it should come down, she might be bruised slightly, but not killed. She crawled cautiously into her nest; she had let down the long braids of her hair, and as she lolled back in her retreat, they fell over the sides of the hammock and swept the top of the long, soft grass. Lying there, with nothing in sight but the leafy branches of the trees high above her head, through which gleams of the deep blue sky came softly, she felt as if she had left the world, and was floating, Ariel-like,[1] in midair.

After an hour of tranquility, footsteps were audible on the soft grass. There was a momentary pause, then someone came to a standstill beside her fairy couch.

"Back so soon, mamma? I wish you could come up here with me; it is just heavenly."

"Then I suppose you must be one of the heavenly inhabitants, an angel, but I never can pay compliments as I ought," said a voice.

"Mr. Enson!" Hagar was conscious of a distinct quickening of heart-action and a rush of crimson to her cheeks; with a pretty, hurried movement she rose to a sitting posture in her hammock; "I really am ashamed of myself. I thought you were mamma."

---

1 A reference to the spirit in Shakespeare's *The Tempest*.

"Yes," he answered, smiling at her dainty confusion.

"Mr. Enson," she said again, this time gravely, "politeness demands that I receive you properly, but decency forbids I should do it unless you will kindly turn your back to me while I step to earth once more."

The man was inwardly shaking with laughter at the grave importance with which she viewed the business in hand, but not for worlds would he have had her conscious of his mirth.

"I can help you out all right," he said.

"No, I am too heavy. I think I will stay here until you go."

"Oh—but—say now, Miss Hagar, that is hard to drive me away when I have just come; and such an afternoon, too, hot enough to kill a darkey. Do let me help you down."

"No; I can get out myself if I must. Please turn your back."

Thus entreated, he turned his back and commenced an exhaustive study of the landscape. Hagar arose; the hammock turned up, and Ellis was just in time to receive her in his arms as she fell.

"Hagar—my darling—you are not hurt?" he asks anxiously, still holding her in a close embrace.

"No; of course not. It is so good of you to be by to care for me so nicely," she said in some confusion.

"Hagar—my darling," he said again, with a desperate resolve to let her know the state of his feelings, "will you marry me?" She trembled as his lips pressed passionate kisses on hers. The veil was drawn away. She understood—this was the realization of the dreams that had come to her dimly all the tender spring-time. Never in all her young life had she felt so happy, so strangely happy. A soft flush mounted to cheek and brow under his caresses.

"I don't understand," murmured the girl, trembling with excitement.

"My darling, I think I have said it more plainly than most men do. Hagar, I think you must know it; I have made no secret of my love for you. Have you not understood me all the days of the spring and summer?"

"Are you quite sure that you love me? You are so old and wise, and I so ignorant to be the wife of so grand a man as you."

She glanced up fleetingly, and flushed more deeply under the look she met. He folded her closer still in his arms. His next words were whispered:

"My love! lift your eyes to mine, and say you love me."

Hagar had not dreamed that such passion as this existed in the world. It seemed to take the breath of her inner life and leave her powerless, with no separate existence, no distinct mental utterance.

Gently Ellis drew back the bright head against him, and bent over the sweet lips that half sought his kiss; and so for one long moment he knew a lifetime of happiness. Then he released her.

"Heaven helping me, you shall be so loved and shielded that sorrow shall never touch you. You shall never repent trusting your young life to me. May I speak to your mother tonight?"

"Yes," she whispered.

And so they were betrothed. Ellis felt and meant all that he said under the stress of the emotion of the moment; but who calculates the effect of time and cruel circumstance? Mrs. Sargeant was more than pleased at the turn of events. Soon Ellis was taking the bulk of the business of managing her estates upon his own strong shoulders. These two seemed favored children of the gods all that long, happy summer. She was his, and he was hers.

The days glided by like a dream, and soon brought the early fall which was fixed for the wedding festivities. All was sunshine. The wedding day was set for October. On the morning of the day before, Hagar entered her mother's room as was her usual custom, to give her a loving morning greeting, and found nothing but the cold, unresponsive body, from which the spirit had fled. Then followed days that were a nightmare to Hagar, but under Ellis' protecting care the storm of grief spent itself and settled into quiet sadness. There was no one at the Sargeant home but the bereaved girl and her servants. At the end of a month Ellis put the case plainly before her, and she yielded to his persuasions to have the marriage solemnized at once, so that he might assume his place as her rightful protector. A month later than the time originally set there was a quiet wedding, very different from the gay celebration originally planned by a loving mother, and the young mistress took her place in the stately rooms of Enson Hall. When a twelve-month had passed there was a little queen born—the heiress of the hall. Ellis' happiness was complete.

CHAPTER V.

IT was past the breakfast hour in the Hall kitchen, but Marthy still lingered. It was cold outside; snow had fallen the night before; the clouds were dull and threatening. The raw northern blasts cut like bits of ice; the change was very sudden from the pleasant coolness of autumn. The kitchen was an inviting place; the blaze shot up gleefully from between the logs, played hide-and-seek in dark corners and sported merrily across the faces of the pickaninnies[1] sprawling on the floor and constantly under Aunt Henny's feet.

Aunt Henny now reigned supreme in the culinary department of the Hall. Her head was held a little higher, if possible, in honor of the new dignity that had come to the family from the union of the houses of Enson and Sargeant.

"'Twarn't my 'sires fer a weddin' so close to a fun'ral, but Lor', chile, dars a diffurunce in doin' things, an' it 'pears dis weddin's comin' out all right. Dem two is a sight fer sore eyes, an' as fer de baby"—Aunt Henny rolled up her eyes in silent ecstasy.

"Look hyar, mammy," said Marthy, Mrs. Enson's maid and Aunt Henny's daughter, "why don' you see Unc' Demus? He'd guv you a charm fer Miss Hagar to wear; she needn't know nuthin' 'bout it."

"Sho, honey, wha' you take me fo'? I done went down to Demus soon as dat weddin' wus brung up."

"Wha' he say, mammy?"

"Let me 'lone now tell I tells you." Aunt Henny was singeing pin-feathers from a pile of birds on the floor in front of the fire. She dropped her task to give emphasis to her words. "I carried him Miss Hagar's pocket-hankercher and he guv me a bag made outen de skin ob a rattlesnake, an' he put in it a rabbit's foot an' er sarpint's toof, an' er squorerpin's[2] tail wid a leetle dust outen de graveyard an' he sewed up de bag. Den he tied all dat up in de hankercher an' tell me solemn: 'Long as yer mistis keep dis 'bout her, trouble'll neber stay so long dat joy won't conquer him in de end.' So, honey, I done put dat charm in Missee Hagar draw 'long wid her tickler fixins an' I wants yer, Marthy, to take keer ob it," she concluded, with a grave

---

1 Now offensive term for black children.
2 Scorpion's.

shake of her turbanned head. Marthy was duly impressed, and stood looking at her mother with awe in every feature of her little brown face.

"'Deed an' I will, mammy."

"My young Miss will be all right ef dat St. Clair Enson keeps 'way from hyar," continued the woman reflectively.

"Who's St. Clar[1] Enson?" asked Marthy.

"Nemmin' 'bout him. Sometime I'll tell you when you gits older. All you got ter do now is ter take mighty good keer o' your mistis and de baby," replied her mother, with a knowing wag of her head. "Fling anudder chunk on dat fire!" she called to one of the boys playing on the floor. "Gittin' mighty cole fer dis time ob year, de a'r smell pow'rful lack mo' snow."

A shadow fell across the doorsill shutting out the light for a moment, that came through the half-open doorway. Marthy gave a shriek that ended in a giggle as a young Negro, tall, black, smiling, sauntered into the kitchen; it was Isaac. Aunt Henny threw her arms high above her head in unbounded astonishment.

"En de name ob de Lawd! Isaac! What's gwine ter happen ter dis fambly now, Ike, dat you's come sneakin' home?"

Isaac grinned. "Isn't you pow'rful glad ter see me, Aunt Henny? I is ter see you an' Marthy. Marfy's a mighty likely lookin' gal, I 'low." He gave a sly roll of his eye in the direction where the girl stood regarding the athletic young Negro with undisguised admiration.

"None o' dat," sputtered Aunt Henny. "Don' you go tryin' ter fool wid dat gal, you lim' ob de debbil.[2] Take yo'sef right off! What yer doin' hyar, enyhow? Dis ain't no place fer you."

"My marse tell'd me ter come," replied Isaac, not at all ruffled by his reception. "I ain't gwine ter go right off; ain't tell'd none o' de folks howdy yit."

"*Your marse tell'd you ter come!* What fer he tell'd yer to come?" stormed Aunt Henny, with a derisive snort. "Dat's what I want ter know. *My* marse'll have somethin' ter say I reckon, ef *yer* marse *did* tell'd yer ter come. An' I b'lieve you's a liar, 'deed r do. I don' b'lieve yer marser knows whar you is at, dis blessid minnit."

---

1   Hopkins occasionally uses St. Clar instead of St. Clair.

2   An evil or impish child.

Isaac chuckled. "I'se come home ter see de new mistis an' de leetle baby; I cert'n'y hopes dey is well. Marse St. Clar'll be hyar hisself bimeby."[1]

Aunt Henny stood a moment silently regarding the boy. Fear, amazement and curiosity were blended in her honest face. Plainly, she was puzzled. "De debbil turn' sain'," she muttered to herself, with a long look at the unconscious Isaac, who sat toasting his cold bare toes before the roaring fire. "Dis house got mo' peace in it, an' Marse Ellis happier den he been sence his mar, ol' Missee Enson, died; but," and she shook her turbanned head ominously, "'tain't fer long. I ain't fergit nuffin'; I isn't lived nex' dis Enson Hall so many years fer nuffin."

"I'se walk'd a long way slippin' officers"—began Isaac.

"Um!" grunted Aunt Henny, with the look of alarm still in her eyes, "officers! dat's what's de matter."

"Dey'll hab ter see Marse St. Clar, tain't me. He sol' me. I runned 'way. I come home, dat's all. Kain't I hab suthin' to eat?"

"Ef tain't one it's t'odder. Befo' God, I 'lieve you an' yo' marse bof onhuman. Been sol'! runned 'way! hump!" again grunted Aunt Henny.

Meanwhile Marthy had made coffee and baked a corncake in the hot ashes. Isaac sniffed the aroma of the fragrant coffee hungrily. There was chicken and rice, too, he noticed as she placed food on the end of a table and motioned him to help himself. Isaac needed no pressing, and in a moment was eating ravenously.

"Tell you de troof, Aunt Henny," he said at last, as he waited for a fourth help, "Marse St. Clar git hard up de oder night in a little play comin' up de bay, an' he sell me to a gempleman fer sixteen hundred, dollars. But, Lor', dat don' hol' Isaac, chile, while he's got legs."

"Dat's jes' what I thought. No use yer lyin' ter me, Isaac, yer Aunt Henny *was born wif a veil.*[2] I knows a heap o' things by seein' 'em fo' dey happens. I don' tell all I sees, but I keeps up a steddyin' 'bout it."

"Dar's no mon can keep me, I don' keer how much Marse St. Clar sells me; he's my onlies' marser," continued Isaac, as he kept on devouring food a little more slowly than at first.

---

1 By and by, in time.

2 Gifted with second sight, clairvoyant.

"Lawd sakes, honey; you's de mos' pow'rfulles' eater[1] I'se seed fer many a day. Don' reckon you's had a good meal sence yer was home five years ago. Dog my cats ef I don' hope Marse Ellis will jes' make yer trot."

"He kin sen' me back, but I isn't gwine stay wid 'em," replied Isaac, with his mouth full of food.

"You cain't he'p yo'se'f."

"I kin walk," persisted Isaac doggedly.

"Put you in de caboose[2] an' give yer hundred lashes," Aunt Henny called back, as she waddled out of the kitchen to find her master.

"Don' keer fer dat, nudder."

Isaac improved the time between the going and coming of Aunt Henny by making fierce love[3] to Marthy, who was willing to meet him more than half way.

The breakfast-room was redolent with the scent of flowers, freshly cut from the greenhouses; the waxed floor gleamed like polished glass beneath the fur rugs scattered over it, and the table, with its service for two, was drawn in front of the cheerful fire that crackled and sparkled in the open fireplace. All the luxuries that wealth could give were gathered about the young matron. It was a happy household; the hurry and rush of warlike preparations had not reached its members, and the sting of slavery, with its demoralizing brutality, was unknown on these plantations so recently joined. Happiness was everywhere, from the master in his carriage to the slave singing in the fields at his humble task. Breakfast was over, and as Ellis glanced over the top of his morning paper at his wife and baby, he felt a thrill of intense pride and love.

As compared with her girlhood, Hagar's married life had been one round of excitement. Washington and many other large cities had been visited on their brief honeymoon. They were royally entertained by all the friends and relatives of both families, and the beautiful bride had been the belle of every assembly. Ellis was wrapped up in her; intimate acquaintance but deepened his love. Her nature was pure, spiritual, and open as the day. Gowned in spotless white, her slender form lost in a large

---

1 Consuming large quantities of food was a common minstrel-show convention.

2 Calaboose, prison.

3 To engage in courtship, to woo.

armchair, she sat opposite him, dandling the baby in her arms. She looked across at him and smiled.

"Well, pet," he smiled back at her, "going to ride?"

She shook her head and set every little curl in motion.

"I won't go out today, it is so cold; we are so comfortable here before the fire, baby and I."

"What a lazy little woman it is," he laughed, rising from his seat and going over to stand behind her chair, stroke the bright hair, and clasp mother and child in his arms. Hagar rested her head against him, and held the infant at arm's length for his admiration.

"Isn't she a darling? See, Ellis, she knows you," as the child cooed and laughed and gurgled at them both, in a vain effort to clinch something in her little red fists.

"This little beggar has spoiled our honeymoon with a vengeance," he replied with a laugh. "I cannot realize that it is indeed over, and we have settled down to the humdrum life of old married folk."

"Can anything ever spoil that and its memories?" she asked, with a sweet upward look into his face. "Indeed, I often wonder if I am too happy; is it right for any human being to be so favored in life as I have been."

"Gather your roses while you may, there will be dark clouds enough in life, heaven knows. No gloomy thoughts, Mignon;[1] let us be happy in the present." He kissed the lips raised so temptingly for his caress, and then one for the child. He thought humbly of his own career beside the spotless creature he had won for life. While not given to excesses, yet there were things in the past that he regretted. Since the birth of their child, the days had been full of emotion for these two people, who were, perhaps, endowed with over-sensitive natures given to making too much of the commonplace happenings of life. Now, as he watched the head of the child resting against the mother's breast, he ran the gamut of human feelings in his sensations. Love and thanksgiving for these unspeakable gifts of God—his wife and child—swept the inmost recesses of his heart.

"Please, Marse Ellis!" cried Aunt Henny's voice from the doorway, "please, sah, Marse St. Clar's Isaac done jes' dis minnit come home. What's I gwine ter do wid him?"

---

1 Lover, darling.

"What, Henny!" Ellis cried in astonishment; "St. Clair's Isaac? Where's his master?"

"Dunno, Marse Ellis, but dar's allers truble, sho, when dat lim' o' Satan turns up; 'deed dar is."

Ellis left the room hurriedly, followed by Aunt Henny. Hagar sat there, fondling the child, a perfect picture of sweet womanhood. She had matured wonderfully in the few months of married life; her girlish manner had dropped from her like a garment. Eve's perfect daughter, she accomplished her destiny in sweet content. Presently the door opened, and her husband stood beside her chair again; his face wore a troubled look.

"What is it?" she asked, with a sweeping upward glance that noted every change of his countenance.

"St. Clair's Isaac."

"Well, and is he so serious a matter that you must look so grave?"

"My dear, the slaves all look upon him as a bird of evil omen; for myself, I look upon it as mere ignorant superstition, but still I have a feeling of uneasiness. They have neither of them been at the Hall for five years. Isaac says his master is coming—that he expected to find him here. What brings them is the puzzler."

"News of your marriage, Ellis; a natural desire to see his new relative. I see nothing strange in that, dear."

"He can't feel very happy about it, according to the terms of the will; probably he has been counting on my not marrying, and now, being disappointed, comes for me to pay his debts, or perform some impossible favor."

"Why impossible?"

"St. Clair is an unsavory fellow, and his desires are not likely to appeal to a man of honor," replied Ellis, with a short, bitter laugh.

"So bad as that?" said his wife regretfully; it was the first shadow since the beginning of their honeymoon. She continued: "Promise me, Ellis, to bear with him kindly and grant him anything in reason, in memory of our happiness."

In the kitchen Aunt Henny, with little braids of hair sticking out from under her turban, talked to Marthy.

"Ef Marse Ellis listen to me, he gwine ter make dat Isaac quit dese diggin's."

"Law, mammy," laughed Marthy, showing her tiny white teeth and tossing her head, "you don' want ter drive de po' boy 'way from whar he was born, does yer?" Marthy was a born coquette,[1] and Isaac was very gallant to her.

"Dat all I gwine ter say. Nobody knows dat Marse St. Clar an' his Isaac better'n I does. I done part raise 'em bof. I reckon my ha'r'd[2] all turn plum' white ef dem two hadn't done lef' dese parts."

"How you come to raise 'em, mammy, an' what made 'em try ter turn yo' ha'r plum' white?"

"Dev'ment,[3] honey, pur' dev'ment! It 'pears lack 'twas only yisterday dat I was a gal wurkin' right yere in dis same ol' kitchen. Marse Sargeant he lose heap money, an' all ob dem move ter St. Louis ter 'trench[4] an' git rich ergin; Marse Enson he want me fer ol' Miss, an' so Marse Sargeant done leave me hyar at Enson Hall. While I was hyar bof ob dem imps was born, but Marse St. Clar he good bit older dan Isaac. Many's de time he run me all ober dis plantation when he no bigger'n dat Thomus Jefferson, 'cause I wouldn't give dat Isaac fus' help from de chickuns jes' roasted fer dinner befo' de fambly done seed nary leg ob 'em. Chase me, chile, wid a pissle[5] pinted plum' at me."

"Lordy! wha' you reckon he do ef he come back hyar now?"

"I don' reckon on nuffin but dev'ment, jes' same as he done time an' time agin when he were a boy—jes' dev'ment."

"Mammy, you say oder day when Missee Hagar git married to Marse Ellis: 'Now dat St. Clar'll stan' no chance ob gittin' de property'; what you mean by dat?"

"Didn't mean nuffin," snapped her mother, with a suspicious look at her. "G' 'long 'bout yo' bisness; you's gittin' mighty pert sence you git to be Miss Hagar's maid; you's axin' too many questions."

In a day or so the family settled down to Isaac's presence as a matter of course. Aunt Henny's predictions about the weather were verified, and the week was unpleasant. The wind blew the

---

1 Flirt, wench; as Kristina Brooks points out, the mammy (Aunt Henny), the buck (Isaac), and the wench (Marthy) were all minstrel stereotypes.
2 Hair would.
3 Mischief.
4 Re-intrench.
5 Pistol.

bare branches of the trees against the veranda posts and roared down the wide fireplaces; snowflakes were in the air. Hagar and Ellis had just come in from a canter over the country roads; she went immediately to her room to dress for dinner, but Ellis tarried a moment in the inviting room which seemed to command his admiration. The luxuries addressed themselves to his physical sense, and he was conscious of complete satisfaction in the knowledge that his wealth could procure a fitting setting for the gem he had won. Other thoughts, too, crept in, aroused by the talk of a friend where they had called on the way home. He had not thought of war, and was not interested in politics; still, if it were true that complications were arising that demanded a settlement by a trial of arms, he was ready. "Perhaps we are too happy for it to last," he muttered; "but, come what will, I have been blessed." His gaze followed Marthy's movements mechanically, as she lighted the wax candles and let fall the heavy curtains, shutting the gloom outside in the gathering darkness. He was aroused from the deep revery into which he had fallen by the sound of wheels on the carriage drive. In a moment, before he could cross the room, the door opened and St. Clair Enson entered, followed by the slave-trader, Walker.

"St. Clair! Is it possible!" he cried, striding forward to grasp his brother's hand. "Is it really you? Welcome home!" They shook hands warmly, and then Ellis threw his arm about St. Clair's shoulders, and for a moment the two men gazed in the depths of each other's eyes with emotion too deep for words. The younger man *did* feel for an instant a wave of fraternal love for this elder brother against whom he meditated a [fell][1] deed.

"Why, Ellis, I do believe you're glad to see me. You're ready to kill the fatted calf to feast the prodigal,"[2] St. Clair said, as they fell apart. "My friend, Mr. Walker—Walker, my brother."

"Glad to see you and welcome you to Enson Hall," said Ellis in cordial greeting, his hospitable nature overcoming his repugnance for this man of unsavory reputation.

"Thanky, thanky," said Walker, as he awkwardly accepted the armchair Ellis offered him, and drew near the blazing fire.

"Just in time for dinner; you will dine with us, Mr. Walker." Walker nodded assent.

---

1 I.e., evil. The original text reads "a fe l deed."
2 Reference to Christ's Parable of the Prodigal Son in Luke 15.11–32.

"Well, Ellis, how's the world using you? You're married, lucky dog. Got your letter while I was at the nominating convention; it must have followed me about for more than a month. Thought I'd come up and make the acquaintance of my new sister and niece," remarked St. Clair, with careless ease.

"Yes," replied Ellis. Somehow his brother's nonchalant air and careless words jarred upon his ear. "You are always welcome to come when you like and stay as long as you please. This is your home."

"Home with a difference," replied St. Clair, as an evil smile for an instant marred his perfect features.

"He won't stand much show of gittin' eny of this prop'ty now you's got a missus, Mr. Enson," ventured Walker, with a grin. "He's been mighty anxious to meet your missus. Most fellers isn't so oneasy about a sister-in-law, but I reckon this one is different, being report says she's a high-stepper,"[1] said Walker, as he grinned at Ellis and cleared his mouth by spitting foul tobacco juice on the polished hearth. Ellis bowed coldly in acknowledgment of his words.

"Mrs. Enson will be down presently. This certainly is a joyful surprise," he said, turning to St. Clair. "Why didn't you send word, and the carriage would have met you at the station?"

"Oh, we came out all right in Walker's trap."

"I'll have it put up." Ellis rose as he spoke.

"No, no; my man will drive me back to the city shortly," Walker broke in.

"I hope you are doing well, St. Clair; where are you from now?"

"Just from Charleston, where I have made a place for myself at last. Politics," he added significantly.

"Ah!"

"Great doin's down to Charleston; great doin's," Walker broke in again.

"No doubt of it; how do you think this matter will end?"

"It's goin' to be the greatest time the world ever saw, Mr. Enson. When we git a-goin' thar'll be no holdin' us. The whole South, sah, is full of sodjers, er-gittin' ready to whup the Yanks t'uther side of nex' week. That's how it's goin' to end."

---

1 Fashionable or attractive person but also a social climber or a pleasure seeker.

"Then it will really be war?"

"The greatest one the worl' ever seen, sah, unless the Yanks git on their knees and asks our pardon, and gives up this govinment to their natral rulers. Why, man, ain't yer heard? You's a patriot, ain't you? Yer a son of the sunny South, ain't yer?"

Ellis smiled at his enthusiasm, although filled with disgust for the man.

"When one has his family to think of, there are times when he forgets the world and thinks of nothing but his home. Be that as it may, I am no recreant son of the South. I stand by her with all I possess. I can imagine nothing that would turn me a traitor to my section."

"Spoken like a man. That's the talk, eh, Enson?" he said, appealing to St. Clair, who nodded in approval. "Do all you can, I say, for the Confederate States of America, from givin' 'em yer money down to helpin' 'em cuss."

"When the time comes I shall not be found wanting. By the way, St. Clair, your boy Isaac is here. Came on us suddenly the other day."

"Ha, ha, ha! the little black rascal. Didn't I tell you he'd do Johnson out of that money? He's the very devil, that boy."

"Like master, like man," replied St. Clair, with a shrug of his handsome shoulders.

"What is it?" asked Ellis sternly; "no cheating or swindling, is there?"

"He's a runaway. I sold him to a gentleman about a week ago," was St. Clair's careless answer.

"What is the man's name, and where is he to be found? he must be reimbursed or Isaac returned to him," said Ellis, looking sternly at his brother. "Enson Hall is no party to fraudulent dealings."

"I'm glad to hear you say that, Mr. Enson; I'm up here lookin' for a piece of property belonging to me, and said to be stopping on this very plantation."

"Impossible, sir; all our slaves have been here from childhood, or have grown old with us. You have been misinformed."

"I reckon not. As I was tellin' your brother here, it's a mighty onpleasant job I've got before me, but I must do my dooty." Walker put on a sardonic smile, and continued:

"I see, sah, that you don' understan' me. Let me explain further: Fourteen years ago I bought a slave child from a man in St.

Louis, and not being able to find a ready sale for her on account of her white complexion, I lent her to a Mr. Sargeant. I understand that you have her in your employ. I've come to get her." Here the slave-trader took out his large sheepskin pocketbook, and took from it a paper which he handed to Ellis.

Ellis gazed at Walker in bewilderment; he took the paper in his hand and mechanically glanced at it. "Still your meaning is not clear to me, Mr. Walker. I tell you we have no slave of yours on this plantation," but his face had grown white, and large drops of perspiration stood on his forehead.

"Well, sah, I'll explain a leetle more. Mr. and Mrs. Sargeant lived a number of years in St. Louis; they took a female child from me to bring up—*a nigger*—and they passed her off on the commoonity here as their own, and you have *married* her. Is my meaning clear now, sah?"

"Good God!" exclaimed Ellis, as he fell back against the wainscotting, "then this paper, if it means anything, must mean my wife."

"I can't help who it means or what it means," replied Walker, "this yer's the bill of sale, an' there's an officer outside there in the cart to git me my nigger."

"This paper proves nothing. You'll take no property from this house without proper authority," replied Ellis with ominous calm. Walker lost his temper, apparently.

"I hold you in my hand, sah!" he stormed; "you are a brave man to try to face me down with stolen property."

Ellis rose slowly to his feet. Pale, teeth set, lips half parted, eyes flashing lightning—furious, terrible, superb in his wrath. His eyes were fixed on Walker, who, frightened at his desperate look, rose to his feet also, with his hand on his pistol. "You would murder me," he gasped.

Ellis laughed a strange, discordant laugh.

"There is, there must be some mistake here. My wife was the daughter of Mr. Sargeant. There is not a drop of Negro blood in her veins; I doubt, sir, if you have ever seen her. And, Mr. Walker, if you do not prove the charges you have this day insulted me by making, your life shall pay the penalty."

"Well, sah, fetch her in the room here; I reckon she'll know me. She warn't so leetle as to fergit me altogether."

Just at this moment Hagar opened the door, pausing on the threshold, a fair vision in purest white; seeing her husband's visitors, she hesitated. Ellis stepped quickly to her side and took her hand.

"My dear, are you acquainted with this gentleman? Do you remember ever seeing him before?"

She looked a moment, hesitated, and then said: "I think not."

Walker stepped to the mantel where the wax-light would fall full upon his face, and said:

"Why, Hagar, have you forgotten me? It's only about fourteen years ago that I bought you, a leetle shaver,[1] from Rose Valley, and lent you to Mrs. Sargeant, ha, ha, ha!"

Hagar put her hand to her head in a dazed way as she heard the coarse laugh of the rough, brutal slave-trader. She looked at Ellis, put out her hand to him in a blind way, and with a heart-rending shriek fell fainting to the floor.

(To be continued.)

---

1 Child.

"With one bound she sprang over the railing of the
bridge." *Colored American Magazine* frontispiece (May 1901).
Reproduced from *The Digital Colored American Magazine*, col-
oredamerican.org. Original held at the Beinecke Rare Book and
Manuscript Library, Yale University.

CHAPTER V.—(CONCLUDED.)

"I thought she'd remember," exclaimed Walker.

Ellis raised his wife in his arms and placed her upon a sofa. St. Clair stood watching the scene with a countenance in which curiosity and satisfaction struggled for the mastery.

"Throw a leetle water in her face, and that'll bring her to. I've seen 'em faint befo', but they allers come to."

Ellis was deathly white; he turned his flaming eyes upon the trader:

"The less you say, the better. By God! I have a mind to put a ball in you now, you infernal hound!"

"Yes, but she's mine; I want to see that she's all right," and Walker shrank away from the infuriated man.

Ellis took his wife in his arms and bore her from the room. Shortly, Aunt Henny brought them word to dine without him, their rooms were ready, and he would see Mr. Walker in the morning after he had communicated with his lawyer. The officer was dismissed, and drove back to the town. As they sat at the table enjoying the sumptuous fare and perfect appointments, St. Clair said to Walker:

"Is this thing true?"

"True as gospel. The only man who could prove the girl's birth is the one I took her from, and he's dead."

"Well, you've done me a mighty good turn, blame me if you haven't. I shan't forget it. Here's to our future prosperity," and he touched his wineglass to his friend's.

"I don't mean you shall forget," was Walker's reply as he sat his glass down empty. "Now, siree, you hang about here for a spell and watch the movements. He'll pay me all right, but you mustn't let him snake her off or anything. Ef things look queer, jes' touch the wires and I'll be with you instanter."

On the following morning Ellis Enson's lawyer, one of the ablest men of the Maryland Bar, pronounced the bill of sale genuine, for it had been drawn up by a justice, and witnessed by men who sent their affidavits under oath.

"There is but one thing to be done, Mr. Walker," Ellis said, after listening to his lawyer's words. "What do you want? How much money will it take to satisfy you to say no more about the matter?"

"I don't bear you any malice for nothing you've said ter me;

perhaps I'd do about the same as you have ef it was my case. Five thou, cash, will git her, though ef I toted her to New Orleans market, a handsome polished wench like her would bring me any gentleman's seven or eight thou, without a remark. As for the pickaninny—"

"What!" thundered Ellis, "the child, too?"

"In course," replied Walker, drawing his fingers in and out his scraggy whiskers, "the child follows the condition of the mother,[1] so I scoop the pile."[2]

Ellis groaned aloud.

"As I was sayin'," continued Walker, "the pickaninny will cost you another thou, and cheap at that."

"I would willingly give the money twice over, even my whole fortune, if it did not prove my wife to be of Negro blood," replied Ellis, with such despair in his tones that even these men, inured to such scenes from infancy, were touched with awe.

The money was paid, and within the hour the house had resumed its wonted quiet and all was apparently as before; but the happiness of Enson Hall had fled forever.

CHAPTER VI.

Marthy was horrified to see how her mistress arose from the couch where her husband placed her, fall on her knees beside it, and burst into wild tempestuous sobbing.

"Lor', Missee Hagar! Lor', honey! Don' cry so, don', honey!"

Hagar suddenly arose, caught her by the shoulders and turned her toward the light, minutely examining the black skin, crinkled hair, flat nose and protruding lips. So might her grandmother have looked.

"Fo' mercy sake, is you sick, Miss Hagar?" cried the girl, frightened at the strange glare in the large dark eyes. But Hagar turned away without replying. Marthy hurried down stairs.

"My soul, Mammy," she cried as she burst into the kitchen, "Miss Hagar done gone clean destructed."[3]

---

1 According to the slave system, if the mother was enslaved, her children were as well.

2 Take it all.

3 Distracted.

Once more Hagar crouched upon the floor. She felt like writhing and screaming, only her tongue seemed paralyzed. She thought and thought with agonizing intensity. Vaguely, as in a dream, she recalled her stay in Rose Valley and the terror of her childish heart caused by the rough slave-trader. Could it be true, or was it but a hideous nightmare from which she would soon awake? Her mother a slave! She wondered that the very thought did not strike her dead. With shrinking horror she contemplated the black abyss into which the day's events had hurled her, leaving her there to grovel and suffer the tortures of the damned. Her name gone, her pride of birth shattered at one blow! Was she, indeed, a descendant of naked black savages of the horrible African jungles?[1] Could it be that the blood of generations of these unfortunate ones flowed through her veins? Her education, beauty, refinement, what did they profit her now if—horrible thought—Ellis, her husband, repudiated her? Her heart almost ceased beating with the thought, and she crouched still lower in the dust of utter humiliation.

Then she rose and walked about the room; it was crowded with her wedding finery. She touched an article here and there with the solemnity that we give to the dead—they were relics of a time that would never return to her. She examined her features in the mirror, but even to her prejudiced eyes there was not a trace of the despised chattel. One blow with her open hand shattered its shining surface and the pieces flew about in a thousand tiny particles; she did not notice in her frenzy that the hand was torn and bleeding. Then she laughed a dreadful laugh: first, silently; then in a whisper; then a peal that clashed through the quiet house[2] and reached the sorrow-stricken man in the silent library. He shuddered, but did not move; he could not face her yet. Aunt Henny and Marthy stood outside the locked door and whispered to each other: "Missee Hagar done gone mad!"

She paused an instant, in her ceaseless promenade about the room, beside the dressing table where her husband's picture reposed in its nest of silk and lace; she paled and shuddered.

---

1 A typical white perception of Africans and Africa at the turn of the twentieth century.

2 John Gruesser asserts that these lines rework a passage regarding the laughter of Bertha Mason, the prototype of the "madwoman in the attic," in Chapter 11 of Charlotte Brontë's *Jane Eyre* (*Edgar* 121).

Could she expect him to forget all his prejudices, which were also her own? Slavery—its degradation, the pining and fretting of the Negro race in bondage—had always seemed right to her. Although innocent of cruelty to them, yet their wrongs were coming home to her in a two-fold harvest. Yes, Ellis would give her up; he must; it was his duty. Only this morning she was his wife, the honored mistress of his home; tonight what? His slave, his concubine! Horrible fatality that had named her Hagar. Somewhere she had read lines that came back to her vividly now:

"Farewell! I go, but Egypt's mighty gods
Will go with me, and my avengers be.
And in whatever distant land your god,
Your cruel god of Israel, is known,
There, too, the wrongs that you have done this day
To Hagar and your first-born,
Shall waken and uncoil themselves, and hiss
Like adders at the name of Abraham."[1]

Then she gazed once more upon the pictured face with the strained look we place upon the face of the dead before they are hidden from us forever. They brought the child to the door and begged her to open to it. She heeded it not. Let it die; it, too, was now a slave.

The night passed; it was dawn again. There were sounds of life from the house below. Some one came slowly up the stairs and paused at her door. Then Ellis's voice, sounding harsh and discordant said:

"It is I, Hagar."

She opened the door. She nerved herself to hear what he might say. The sense of her bitter shame overpowered her, and she shrank before him, cowering as he closed the door, and stood within the room.

Twice he essayed to speak, and twice a groan issued from his white lips. How could he bear it! She stood before him with clasped hands and hanging head as became a slave before her master. How changed, too, he thought, a blight had even fallen

---

1 Final stanza of Eliza Poitevent Nicholson's "Hagar," published in the November 1893 issue of *Cosmopolitan*. Hopkins has dropped the name Ishmael from the end of the third-last line. See Appendix D3.

upon her glorious beauty. He who had always upheld the institution as a God-given principle of humanity and Christianity, suddenly beheld his idol, stripped of its gilded trappings, in all its filthiness. Then in his heart he cursed slavery.

"Hagar, I have bought you of that man—Walker—he will not annoy you again."

She did not speak or raise her eyes. Ellis bit his lips until the blood ran in the effort to restrain himself for her sake.

"I have thought the matter over and much as I wish it might be otherwise, much as I would sacrifice for you, I feel it my duty as a Southern gentleman, the representative of a proud old family, to think of others beside myself and not allow my own inclinations to darken the escutcheon[1] of a good old name. I cannot, I dare not, and the law forbids me to acknowledge as my wife a woman in whose veins courses a drop of the accursed blood[2] of the Negro slave."

Still she stood there motionless.

Ellis was in torture. Why did she stand there like a forlorn outcast, in stony despair?

"Speak!" he cried at last, "for God sake say something or I shall die!"

Then she raised her eyes to his for one fleeting moment, "I do not blame you. You can do nothing else."

He moved a step toward her with a smothered groan, "Dearest, dearest," he whispered, and the tone of his voice carried in it his unshaken love.

"Do not,—do not—," broke from her white lips and with a smothered cry of agony her reserve broke down and she flung herself upon the couch face down.

Ellis went to her and knelt beside her with his arms about her. Five minutes must have passed while they communed in spirit. There was no sound but the girl's hysterical sobbing.

"I am going away," he said at length: "I cannot stay here and live. I may never return, but I shall leave you amply provided for." Then he rose to his feet and rushed from the room. She

---

1 A heraldic shield bearing a family's coat of arms. (To put a blot on—here "darken"—an escutcheon is to damage the reputation of a family.)

2 The one-drop rule specified that even the smallest amount of African blood disqualified a person from being deemed legally or socially white.

heard his footsteps echoing down the empty corridor and pause before the door of the nursery.

Ellis loved his wife devotedly, but the shame of public ostracism and condemnation seemed too much for inherited principles. An hour passed. Once more Ellis resumed his measured pacing in the library. The clock ticked slowly on the mantel, but the beating of his heart outstripped it. He could not follow the plans he had laid out as the path of duty. His visit to the nursery had upset them; parental love, love for his innocent wife, was too strong to be easily cast aside. The ticking of the clock maddened him. It seemed the voice of doom pursuing him—condemning him as a coward—coward—coward. He could stand it no longer. Once more he mounted the stairs to his wife's room.

"Hagar, I cannot do it. We cannot alter the fact that we are bound by all the laws of God and man for better or worse. I have thought it all out, and I have planned a way."

"It is impossible," she said in quiet despair. "You cannot overcome this fearful thing that has fallen upon us. I myself think and feel as you do. It is enough; I accept my fate."

"Oh, no, no; do not say that!"

"Yes, Ellis," she repeated, her face like snow in its pallor.

"Hagar, you do not know what you are saying. You love me, and I love you as my very soul. How were we to know? How could we tell? Therefore, having committed a sin in innocence— if sin it be, and I do not so believe it, for things appear in a different light to me now—we will together live it down. Surely heaven cannot fix the seal of this crime on us forever." The supplication of his voice, his speaking eyes, shook Hagar's heart, so tired and worn with emotion. Her eyes were full of compassion as they rested on him, her lips firm and cold. "I love you, Ellis; you know that, and by that love, although I am your slave and chattel, I know that your love demands naught for your wife but honor. The force of circumstances cannot degrade you—cannot change your chivalrous nature."

"Great heavens! You misunderstand me. I have no hope, no life, apart from you, and I hold you as I cling to salvation, my love, my soul! Listen, Hagar, I have a plan." Bending over her he rapidly outlined a plan of life abroad. They would be remarried, and sail from a Northern port for Europe; there, where the shadow of this crime could not come, they would begin a life anew. He had mapped it all out carefully and as she listened she was convinced—it was feasible; it could be done.

Neither of them noticed that the door was ajar; neither did they hear the light footfall that paused beside it. It was St. Clair.

"Walker was right. We must stop that game," he muttered to himself.

CHAPTER VII.

Two weeks had passed since Ellis left his home on the pretext of urgent business, but in reality to make necessary arrangements for an indefinite stay abroad. Ill news travels fast and it was well known all over the plantations and in the neighborhood that the terrible discovery of Hagar's origin had broken up the home life at Enson Hall. Save for St. Clair's presence, the Hall had settled back into its old bachelor state with one difference—in the mistress's suite a beautiful despairing woman sat day after day, with her infant across her knees, eating her heart out in an agony of hope and fear waiting the reprieve from a living death that Ellis's return would bring her.

Here was a woman raised as one of a superior race, refined, cultured, possessed of all the Christian virtues, who would have remained in this social sphere all her life, beloved and respected by her descendants, her blood mingling with the best blood of the country if untoward circumstances had not exposed her ancestry. But the one drop of black blood neutralized all her virtues, and she became, from the moment of exposure, an unclean thing. Can anything more unjust be imagined in a republican form of government whose excuse for existence is the upbuilding of mankind!

These were sorrowful days for the Negroes who could not bring themselves to look upon their beloved mistress as one of their race, a share in their sad destiny.

Aunt Henny spent most of her spare time praying and coaxing Hagar out of the apathy into which she had fallen.

"Bless de Lawd! I know'd dev'ment was on han' when Marse St. Clar done comed home," she said one morning to Marthy. "Las' time he was here ol' Marse he bus' a blud vessel in his head an' never know'd a blessed thing fer a munf, den he die. 'Fore dat he shoot a mon to de college an' beat de prefesser 'mos' to def. Dais[1] a cuss on dat boy, sho."

"How you tink it come so, Mammy?"

"I hern tell from Aunt Di, who nussed Missee Enson. See hyar, chile, I don' no 'bout tellin' a disrespons'ble gal like you fambly secrets,—an' ef you goes to 'peatin' my words all 'roun' de plantation, I hope Marse Ellis whop yer back." Marthy rolled her eyes in terror and promised to keep her mammy's revelations as sacred as Scripture.

"You know's dat no one neber goes nigh de ole summer house down dar close to de wharf at de foot ob de garden don' you?"

Marthy nodded, and her eyes grew larger as she listened with bated breath for the ghostly story she was sure would follow.

"Jes' 'fore Marse St. Clar was born, ole Missee Enson was settin' in there an' a turrible thunder storm came up an' jes' raised Jeemes Henry[2] with houses an' trees, an' tored up eberythin'. Ol' Miss so dar 'feared to move even one teeny bit her li'l' finger. While she sot dar all white an' trimbly de debbil jes' showed he face to her an' grinned."

"Sure nuff debbil, mammy?" whispered Marthy in awed accents. Her mammy nodded solemnly in reply.

"Ol' Miss jes' went into conwulshuns an' when dey fin' her she in dead faint. Dat night Marse St. Clair was born, an' ef de debbil ain't de daddy den dat ol' rapscalion neber had a borned servant in dis sinful wurl'."

"Mammy what you tink de reason de debbil show hisse'f to ole Missee Enson?"

"De trubble wid you is, Marthy, dat you is de mos' 'quis'tive gal on dis plantation; you want to know too much, but de ol' fo'ks been hyar long time say dat ol' Marse git mad one day wid Unc' Ned, an' tell oberseer 'whop him.' Unc' Ned conjure man; neber been whopped in all he life. He jes' rub hisse'f all ober wid goopher,[3] put a snake skin 'roun' he neck, a frog in one pocket an' a dry lizard in de oder, an' den he pray to de debbil: 'Dear debbil, I ax you to stan' by me in dis' my trial hour, an' I'll neber

---

1 There's.

2 Havoc.

3 A conjure man (or woman) practices African American folk medicine, folk magic, or rootwork; goopher is a powder used in this practice.

'sert you as long as I live. I's had de power, continer de power; make me strong in your cause, make me faithful to you, an' help me to conquer my enemies, an' I will try to deserve a seat at your right han'!'"

As Marthy listened an ashy hue overspread her face and she asked breathlessly:

"Did dey whop him?"

"Bless yer soul, gal, dat was de afternoon 'fore dey was 'gwine ter whop him in de mornin', an' dat bery night de debbil 'pear to ole Miss, an' Unc' Ned neber was whopped tell de day he died, neber."

"He must a been a power, mammy, he cert'nly must."

"But de strangest part was dis: At de bery time ole Miss seen de debbil in de summer house, de oberseer was in de barn an' he 'clar' dat ober in de east corner he saw de lightnin' play, an' while he looked he see hell wid all its torments an' de debbil dar, too, wid his cloven foot, an' a struttin' 'bout like he know'd he was boss; de oberseer was so skeered dat he run, an' he run, an' he run an' he neber stop runnin' tell he git plum inter Baltymo'."

"'Spec' he know'd he 'long'd to be debbil."

"Course! An' den he sen' ol' Marse word to sen' him his clo's: 'neber lib on dat plantation agin fer twice yer money; money no 'ducemen'.'"

"Mammy, mammy," this in a whisper, "do you b'lieve Miss Hagar got nigger blud in her?"

"Course not, honey. Somebody roun' hyar done conjured her. Dat debbil, St. Clar, I spec. Now, Marthy, take dat big silver tray of things up dar to dat po' chile, an' you keep a poundin' 'tell she ope de do', po' li'le chile."

Marthy obediently disappeared to execute orders and Aunt Henny with a dubious shake of her head lifted up her voice in song:

I'm a gwine to keep a climbin' high,
See de hebbenly lan';
Till I meet dem er angels in a de sky,
See de hebbenly lan'.

Dem pooty angels I shall see,
See de hebbenly lan';

Why don' de debbil let-a-me be,
See de hebbenly lan'.[1]

* * * * * *

Day succeeded day. There was little communication between the town and Enson Hall. Inclement weather prevailed for it was now the latter part of January. The fire of curiosity still burned fiercely among the rich planters over the "Enson horror," as it was called, but up at the Hall all seemed quiet. One bitter morning St. Clair sat at breakfast the picture of luxurious ease. He felt himself master of the situation already, and had assumed all the airs of ownership. Aunt Henny felt drawn, sometimes, to "shy[2] a plate at him," as she expressed it to herself.

The odor of roses and lilies mingled pleasantly with that of muffins and chocolate. A man came striding up the avenue. It was Dr. Gaines, the family physician, who owned a neighboring plantation.

"Where is Mr. Enson?" he asked of Isaac, who answered his clamourous call on the resounding brass knocker.

"At breakfas', massa."

"I must see him at once. I have news for him."

As the doctor entered the room, St. Clair Enson was leaning back in his chair snapping his fingers at a hound stretched on a rug at his side. The doctor was unceremonious:—

"I regret to say, that I come as the bearer of evil tidings."

"Shall I bid Isaac set another plate, doctor? No? You have taken breakfast? At this hour? You are a primitive people in this rural district, truly. You should mingle with the world as I have and become capable of enjoying the delights and privileges of civilized life. May I ask the nature of the news you bring?" The doctor was a kind old man though somewhat brusque. He averted his eyes, and answered in a low voice.

"It relates to your brother. Mr. Enson, when did Ellis leave home, and when was he expected back?"

"My brother Ellis? He left home about two weeks ago, for what reason he did not state. I do not know when to look for his return; he may drop in, unexpectedly, at any moment."

---

1 Plantation song that appears in Chapter 5 of William Wells Brown's *My Southern Home.*

2 Throw.

The doctor was preternaturally grave.

"And you have heard nothing from him since?"

"No, I have not."

The doctor grew graver yet.

"My dear sir, early this morning my boy Sam had occasion to cross the foot of your land, where the remains of the old wharf enter the stream, and there he stumbled upon a frightful thing— the dead body of a man!"

"Not a pleasant sight," said St. Clair as he helped himself to another hot cake.

"Evidently, the body has been there two or three days. There is an ugly wound in the head that completely disfigures the face, and an empty pistol by the side of the body tells its own pitiful tale. St. Clair Enson that dead man was—"

St. Clair shifted uneasily in his chair as he looked the speaker in the eye, then started to his feet.

"My brother?"

"Your brother!"

To Dr. Gaines's eyes the cold, pale face into which he gazed did not change, only the gaze sought the floor.

"That is strange. Was he robbed also?"

"No. A large sum of money is on the body; papers and his watch. Sam ran home to me, and I summoned help, and was among the first to reach the spot."

The hound leaped suddenly to his feet and began to howl.

"Was it murder or suicide?" asked St. Clair in a calm voice.

"That cannot be decided yet. Finding his valuables untouched, and his hand frozen to his pistol, seems to point to suicide; that will be determined at the inquest." Dr. Gaines turned from the window by which he was standing, and said: "The remains of your brother are being brought home."

A little procession of Negroes, with heads uncovered, advanced up the avenue, slowly, between the grand old beeches, their tread echoing in a solemn thud upon the frozen ground. A cloth was spread decently over the mangled face. In the silence and majesty of death the master returned to his home. His unlucky life had come to a sudden close. In midnight solitude and shadowed by mystery the curtain fell on the tragedy.

St. Clair advanced with a firm step to meet the bearers; there was no sign of grief in his face. The servants crowded the hall, standing in terrified silence broken only by Aunt Henny's sobs and lamentations. St. Clair lifted the cloth that covered the dead face with a hand that did not tremble, under the curious gaze of Dr. Gaines.

"Mr. Enson," said the doctor at length, "your brother had a wife or one whom we believed his wife," he corrected at St. Clair's negative gesture. "Will you not notify her of his death? She must be suffering anxiety concerning him."

"True; I had forgotten her," muttered St. Clair with a shrug of his handsome shoulders. "Yes, doctor, you break the news to her." The doctor left the room. Presently there was a scream in a woman's voice as of one in mortal agony, an opening and closing of doors and a hurrying of feet; then silence broken only by the pitiful wail of a young child.

There was an inquest at which Walker, the speculator, corroborated the evidence of St. Clair Enson—that the deceased was laboring under great depression at the time of his leaving home, and of his avowed purpose to shoot himself as the shortest way out of his family difficulties. This testimony so clearly given produced a profound impression upon the listeners. It was hoped by many that Hagar would testify, but they were doomed to disappointment. The pistol was well-known to many friends as well as to his servants, as the one Ellis Enson always carried. The watch was the old-fashioned timepiece that his father had carried before him. The papers were legal documents made by the family lawyer and having no bearing on the case.

The jury rendered a verdict of suicide. Plainly, Ellis Enson had died by his own hand.

There was a stately funeral: St. Clair Enson buried his brother with every outward mark of wealth and pomp. The servants moved about the house with red eyes and stealthy steps while from the quarters the wind bore the sound of mournful wailing.

It was a bleak night. The new master of the Hall and the slave-trader, now his inseparable companion, sat before the fire consulting about the disposal of the slaves.

"I'm going to let them all go, Walker, and only keep a small working gang to till the ground and look after the Hall."

"Jes' so," replied Walker, as he folded a fat bundle of bills into his pocket-book and carefully replaced the same in his hip pocket.

"That's a sensible thing to do. It won't be six months from now before we'll all be fighting Yankees like mad, and then where'd your niggers be so nigh as this plantation is to Washington. Best be on the safe side is my idee. And there's the missis—" At this moment the door opened unceremoniously and Hagar came straight up to the two men, seated before the blazing fire. Her dark eyes shone like stars, her face was white as the snow that covered the fields outside, her long hair hung in a straggling mass, rough and unkept, about her shoulders and over her sombre dress. A more startling apparition could not well be imagined.[1] An exclamation broke from the lips of both men.

"I have come without your bidding, sir, for I have something to say to you," she said, addressing St. Clair without bestowing a glance on the man Walker. She cast a wild look around the sumptuous room.

"So you take your ease while he sleeps in his coffin. You need not frown. I do not fear you. Life has no terrors to offer me now." She towered above him as he sat crouched in his chair, and she looked down upon him with a wicked glare in her eyes.

"The question I came to ask is this—St. Clair Enson, do you believe that your brother died by his own hand?"

"Most certainly," Enson constrained his white lips to answer.

"Ellis was killed, murdered—shot down like a dog! What did the pistol prove? Nothing. His pockets had not been rifled. That proves nothing. Neither his great trouble brought to him by his marriage with me—a Negro—would have driven him to self-destruction. He was murdered!"

A chill crept over her listeners. No one had ever seen the gentle Hagar Sargeant in her present character.

"Murdered?" gasped St. Clair.

"Yes," she shouted. "You are his murderer!"

He recoiled as if she had struck him a blow.

"Mad woman! You are mad I say, trouble has turned your brain!"

"It was you who drove him forth from a happy home. You who found your twin demon and brought home the story that broke his heart, ruined his life and gained for you the wealth you have always coveted. I repeat, you are his murderer!"

---

1 John Gruesser suggests that this passage echoes Charlotte Brontë's description of Bertha Mason during her nocturnal visit to Jane's room in Chapter 25 of *Jane Eyre* (*Edgar* 121).

St. Clair cringed; then he sprang to his feet and seized her by the arm.

"This is too much for any man to stand from a nigger-wench. You have sealed your own fate. Off you go, my fine madam, to the Washington market in short meter.[1] I would have kept you near me, and made your life as easy as it has been in the past, but this settles it. Walker," he said as he turned to the speculator, "you have my permission to take this nigger and her brat whenever it pleases you." Then he released her.

Hagar eyed the man critically from head to foot.

"Selfish, devilish, cruel," she said slowly, "think not that your taunts or cruelties can harm me; I care not for them. No heart in your bosom; no blood in your veins! You are his slayer, and his blood is crying from the ground against you this very hour."

It was more than he could bear. Again he sprang from his seat and seized her arm. Walker took her by the other one and between them they dragged her toward the entrance.

"Easy, easy!" exclaimed Walker in a warning voice to St. Clair. "Don't injure the sale of your property, Enson." St. Clair dropped his hold and again returned to his seat by the fire.

"There, there, my dear, you're a leetle bit excited an' no wonder. Go to your room and rest yourself, my dear, I recommend gin. Gin with a leetle hot water, sugar and spice is very nice, very nice for hysterics, and soothing, very soothing to a gal's nerves." Walker punctuated his remarks with many a little thump and pat in her back.

With a defiant smile, Hagar paused on the threshold and said:

"It's the truth! you're his murderer, and in spite of the wealth and position you have played for and won, you have seen the last on this earth of peace or happiness." Then striking her breast, she added:

"As I have parted with the same friends! Pleasant dreams to you, St. Clair Enson, master of Enson Hall!"

---

1 Quickly.

CHAPTER VIII.

It will be remembered that on February 4, 1861, a provisional government was formed for the "Confederate States of America." This provisional government was soon superseded by a "permanent" one, under whose constitution Jefferson Davis, Alexander H. Stevens and other officials were to serve six years, from February 22, 1862. A Peace Congress composed of delegates from twenty states, held a session for three weeks at Washington, in February, 1862. In March, same year, a Commission also went to the Capital City to negotiate for a settlement of difficulties; but all these overtures failed. Being called to Washington as a leading delegate, with power to help settle all these great questions that were then agitating the country, St. Clair Enson and Walker decided that it would be best to close the Hall, leaving Isaac, Aunt Henny and Marthy in charge of the house, and take the rest of the hands to Washington, where so many rich and influential men would congregate from the most southern parts of the country, that they would be assured of quick sales and large profits.

On the morning of departure, the small colony of black men and women sat and stood about the familiar grounds stunned and hopeless. Here most of them were born, and here they had hoped to die and be buried. The unknown future was a gulf of despair. Ellis was a good master, kind and considerate; their sincere mourning for him was mingled with grief at their own fate.

In the midst of a motley group Hagar stood with her child clasped in her arms,—hopeless, despairing. She had felt her degradation before, but not until now had she drained the bitter cup of misery.[1]

Ellis Enson's lawyer had questioned her about her husband's business.

"Did he give you free papers?" with a pitying glance at the fair, crushed woman.

"When he returned, he intended to take me and the child abroad after making ample settlements."

The legal gentleman sighed.

"It was a great oversight—a great mistake."

So no papers, bearing upon the case, being found, all the

---

1 An echo of Lamentations 3.15.

Sargeant fortune reverted by law to the master. Nothing could be done.

Then began the humiliating journey to Washington, herding with slaves, confined in pens like cattle, the delicately nurtured lady tasted of the torments of those accursed. Her brain grew wild; she folded her infant closer to her breast—sang, whispered, laughed and wept.

Upon reaching the private slave-pen, a number of which then disgraced the national capital, she fell into a state of melancholy from which nothing aroused her but the needs of the child.

A purchaser was soon found for the handsome slave, in a New Orleans merchant who agreed to take the child, too, for the sake of getting the mother out of the city without trouble.

At the dusk of the evening, previous to the day she was to be sent off, as the prison was being closed for the night, Hagar, with her child closely clasped in her arms, darted past the keeper and ran for her life. It was not far from the prison to the long bridge which passes from the lower part of the city, across the Potomac, to the forests of Arlington Heights.[1] Thither the fugitive directed her flight. The keeper by this time had recovered from the confusion incident to such a daring and unexpected attempt, he rallied his assistants and started in pursuit. On and on she flew, seeming tireless in her desperate resolve. It was an hour when horses could not be easily obtained; no bloodhounds were at hand to run her down. It was a trial of speed and endurance.

The pursuers raised the hue-and-cry as they followed, gaining steadily upon the fugitive. Astonished citizens poured forth from their dwellings to learn the cause of the alarm, and learning the nature of the case fell in with the motley throng in pursuit. With the speed of a bird, having passed the avenue, she began to gain, and presently she was upon the Long Bridge. Panting, gasping, she hushed her babe, appealed to God in broken sentences, and gathered all her courage to dash across the bridge and lose herself in the friendly shelter of the woods. Oh, will she,—can she, make it! Already her heart began to beat high with hope. Courage! She had only to pass three-quarters of a mile more and all would be well, the woods would shelter her, night would cover her and save her.

---

1 Section of Virginia close to Washington, DC, that is now a national historic district.

Just as the pursuers passed the draw they beheld three men slowly approaching from the Virginia shore. They called to them to help arrest the runaway slave. As she drew near they formed a line across the bridge to intercept her. Now the panting woman, hard-pressed on every side, suddenly stopped.

She looked wildly and anxiously around to see if all hope were indeed gone; far below the bridge rolled the dark waters, sullen, angry, threatening. Before and behind were the voices of the profane, inhuman monsters into whose hands she must inevitably fall. Her resolution was taken. She kissed her babe, clasped it convulsively in her arms, saying:

"Alas, poor innocent, there is one gift for thee yet left for your unfortunate mother to bestow,—it is death. Better so than the fate reserved for us both."[1]

Then she raised her tearful, imploring eyes to heaven as if seeking for mercy and compassion, and with one bound sprang over the railing of the bridge, and sank beneath the waters of the Potomac river.[2]

(To be continued.)

---

1 This mirrors not only the title of Chapter 25 of William Wells Brown's *Clotel* (1853), "Death Is Freedom" (see Appendix G2), but also Harriet Jacobs's assertion in Chapter 11 of *Incidents in the Life of a Slave Girl* (1861) that "[d]eath is better than slavery."

2 A similar scene occurs in *Clotel*, Chapter 25, in which the title character "vaulted over the railings of the bridge, and sunk for ever beneath the waves of the river!" See Appendix G2.

CHAPTER IX.[1]
Twenty Years Later.

It was a fine afternoon in early winter in the year 1882, in the city of Washington, the beautiful capital of our great Republic. Pennsylvania Avenue was literally crammed with foot-passengers and many merry sleighing parties, intent on getting as much enjoyment as possible out of the day.

---

1 Synopsis of Chapters I to VIII. During December, 1860, the rebellious political spirit of the country leaped all barriers and culminated in treason.

    Closely associated with the Confederate leaders was St. Clair Enson, son of an aristocratic Maryland family, who hoped, by rendering valuable aid to the founders of the government, to re-establish himself socially and financially. While in Charleston, SC, attending the convention preliminary to the formation of the new government, he received a letter announcing the birth of his brother's heiress. This enraged Enson who saw in it the loss of his patrimony. He fell in with a notorious slave-trader named Walker, who accompanied him on his homeward trip on the steamer "Planter." Walker offers to show him a way out of his difficulties for ten thousand dollars.

    St. Clair Enson's brother Ellis had married Miss Hagar Sargeant a beauty and an heiress. A daughter was born. Soon after this St. Clair arrives at Enson Hall accompanied by Walker. He claims that Enson has a slave of his on the plantation. Enson denies the charge.

    Walker explains that, being childless. Mr. and Mrs. Sargeant, while living at St. Louis, took an octoroon [one-eighth black] slave from him to bring up. He declares that Hagar is that child, and produces papers to prove his claim. Hagar recognizes the man, and faints at the sight of him.

    Ellis buys Hagar and the child of Walker. Unable to bear the disgrace of having married a Negress, he decided to leave home, but loving his wife very dearly, concludes to go abroad, and live where they are unknown. St. Clair overhears the plan and informs Walker. Enson leaves home to make arrangements for the journey. At end of three weeks his dead body is found in some woods on the estate.

    Hagar accuses St. Clair and Walker of murdering Ellis. Then St. Clair gives Walker permission to sell Hagar and the child in the Washington slave market. Hagar, with the child, leaps into the Potomac River.

Freezing weather had been followed by a generous fall of frozen, down-like flakes. Quick to take advantage of a short-lived pleasure, vehicles of every description were flying along the avenue filled with the elite of the gay city. The stream of well-dressed pedestrians moved swiftly over the snowy pavements, for the air was too cold for prolonged lingering, watching with interest, in which envy mingled to some extent, the occupants of the handsome carriages gliding along so rapidly on polished runners. Every notable of the capital was there from the President in his double-runner[1] to the humble clerk in a single-seated modest rig.

A sumptuous Russian sleigh drawn by two splendid black horses, with a statuesque driver in ebony handling the ribbons, attracted the attention of the crowd as it dashed down the avenue and paused near the capitol steps. Two ladies were its occupants. The elder was handsome enough to demand more than a passing glance from the most indifferent, but her young companion was a picture as she nestled in luxurious ease among the costly robes, wrapped in rich furs, from which her delicate face shone out like a star upon the curious throng. That she was a stranger to the crowd could be easily told from the questioning glances which followed the turn-out.

As they passed the Treasury Department two men, both past their first youth, though one was at least twenty years older than the other, came down the steps, and paused a moment, to follow with their eyes the Russian sleigh with the beautiful girl, before mingling with the living stream that flowed from between the great stone columns and spread itself through the magnificent streets of the national capital.

"Really, Benson," remarked the elder man as they resumed their walk, "the most beautiful girl I have seen for many a day. You know everyone worth knowing; who is she?"

At this moment an elderly man of dark complexion, in stylish street costume, but with a decidedly Western air, came down the capitol steps followed by a young man. Both were warmly greeted by the occupants of the sleigh. The dark man spoke a few words to the driver, then both men entered the carriage and it dashed off rapidly.

---

1 Type of sleigh.

"That is Senator Bowen,[1] his wife and daughter. He is the new millionaire senator from California. I am not acquainted with the ladies, but after their ball I intend to become assiduous in my attentions."

"Oh! then they are the Bowens! How I wish I knew them. I predict a sensation over the young beauty. Who's the young man?"

"Cuthbert Sumner, my private secretary. Deuced fine fellow, too."

The conversation drifted away from the Bowens, and they were apparently forgotten.

"How was it at the Clarks' last night, Benson, as bad as you expected?"

"Worse if possible. It was dev'lish slow! Nothing stronger than bouillon, not a chance to buck the tiger[2] even for one moment, not a decent looking woman in the rooms. All the women fit for pleasant company give that woman's house a wide berth. Dashed if I blame 'em. The only thing that gives the Clarks a standing is his position. I can't see how he puts up with her. If I had a sanctimonious woman like her for a wife I'd cut and run for it, dashed if I wouldn't."

His companion laughed long and loud.

"No fun for you there, eh, Benson? My boy, you'll never fit into the dignified position of a father of his country, I fear. Oh, well; it's hard to teach an old dog new tricks."

"Yes, but think of not being able to give your friends a decent time, because your wife has a fad on temperance and thinks it a sin to smell a claret cup or a brandy-and-soda. A man with a wife of that sort ought to leave her at home, where she could rule the roost to her heart's content. The seat of government is no place for a missionary."

"Well, there's always a way to remedy such things when you know your hostess."

"Of course, of course," General Benson hastened to reply. "Our bouillon was washed down with Russian tea a la Russe.[3] We doctored it in the coatroom."

The two men indulged in a hearty laugh.

---

1 Brook Thomas points out that California US Senator Aaron Sargent (1827–87) was the likely inspiration for Zenas Bowen (294).

2 Gamble.

3 In the Russian manner. Presumably alcohol is added to the tea.

"Well, Benson, you'll do," remarked the elder when their mirth had somewhat subsided. "For a dignified chief of a division you're a rare bird."

After a moment's silence, General Benson asked:

"Is Amelia[1] come?"

"Yes, got here last night?"

"Good. It's a relief to be with a woman who can join a man in a social glass, have a cigar with him, or hold her own in winning or losing a game with no Sunday-school nonsense about her. It's hard work keeping up to it, Major; one needs a friend to help one out."

"When's the session end?"

"Next week, thank heaven."

"Sick of politics, too, old man?"

"No; but it's been nothing but wind. Words—words—words—"

"And mutual abuse," broke in the Major, laughing.

"Exactly; with nothing accomplished. Can't seem to throw much dust in the eyes of these old fossils."

"The truth is, Benson, the South has a hard, rough road before her to even things up with the North; we've got to go slow until some of the old fire-eaters[2] die out and a new generation comes in."

"It'll be slow enough, never you fear. At present we are in a Slough of Despond;[3] heaven knows when we'll get out of it. My position in the Treasury brings the secret workings under my eye. I know."

"Slough!" retorted the Major; "call it a bog at once. And to think of the money we have lost for the Cause."[4]

"And my exile abroad that my mix-up in the Lincoln assassination caused me.[5] Do you know, Major, if it were known

---

1 Hopkins introduces this character as Amelia but changes her name to Aurelia in Chapter XI.

2 Pro-slavery Southerners who supported secession from the United States.

3 A state of degradation or depression. The phrase comes from John Bunyan's *Pilgrim's Progress* (1678).

4 I.e., the Lost Cause, a romanticized view of the South's doomed struggle against superior Union forces in the Civil War.

5 Following the death of Lincoln on 14 April 1865, and the ensuing manhunt, the surviving conspirators were put on trial and nine

that I am my father's son, they'd hang me even now with little ceremony."

"Thank God they don't know it, my boy, and take courage."

"I'll get mine out of it by hook or by crook," replied Benson with a savage look. "The country owes me a fortune, and I'm bound to have it."

The two had reached the corner made historical by the time-honored political headquarters, Willard's Hotel.[1] They paused before separating.

"By the by, Major, I'll get you cards for the Bowens' ball if you like. It would be a great chance for Amelia."

"If I like! Why, man, I'll be your everlasting debtor."

"Very well; consider it done."

"A thousand thanks." The friends parted.

General Benson entered the hotel, where he had apartments, and the Major wended his way to his home, a handsome house in a quiet side street.

CHAPTER X.
THE FAMILY OF A MILLIONAIRE.

Senator Zenas Bowen, newly elected senator from California, and many times a millionaire, occupied a mansion on 16th Street, N.W., in close proximity to the homes of many politicians who have made the city of Washington famous at home and abroad.

There were three persons in the Bowen family—the Honorable Zenas Bowen, his wife Estelle and his daughter Jewel. This was his second season in Washington. The first year he was in the House and his work there was so satisfactory to his constituents that the next season he was elected with a great flourish of trumpets to fill the seat in the Senate, made vacant by a retiring senator.

The Honorable Zenas was an example of the possibilities of individual expansion under the rule of popular government.

---

people were sentenced to execution or prison on 30 June 1865. One suspected conspirator, John Surratt (1844–1916), fled the country and was later captured in Europe.

1   Founded in 1847 by Henry and Edwin Willard, the hotel still stands on the corner of 14th Street and Pennsylvania Avenue.

Every characteristic of his was of the self-made pattern. In familiar conversation with intimate friends, it was his habit to fall into the use of ungrammatical phrases, and, in this, one might easily trace the rugged windings of a life of hardship among the great unwashed[1] before success had crowned his labors and steered his bark[2] into its present smooth harbor. He possessed a rare nature: one of those genial men whom the West is constantly sending out to enrich society. He had begun life as a mate on a Mississippi steamboat. When the Civil War broke out, he joined the Federal forces, and at its close was mustered out as "Major Bowen." His wife dying about this time, he took his child, Jewel, and journeyed to California, invested his small savings in mining property in the Black Hills.[3] His profits were fabulous; he counted his pile way up in the millions.

His appearance was peculiar. Middle height, lank and graceless. He had the hair and skin of an Indian, but his eyes were a shrewd and steely gray, wherein one saw the spirit of the man of the world, experienced in business and having that courage, when aroused, which is common to genial men of deadly disposition. Firm lips that suggested sternness gave greater character to his face, but his temper was known to be most mild. He dressed with scrupulous neatness, generally in black broadcloth. There was no denying his awkwardness; no amount of polish could make him otherwise. His relation to his family was most tender, his wife and daughter literally worshipping the noble soul that dwelt within its ungainly casket.

After Fortune had smiled on him, one day while stopping at the Bohemian, a favorite resort in 'Frisco, he was waited on by a young woman of great beauty. The Senator fell in love with her immediately and at the end of a week proposed marriage. Fortunate it was for him that Estelle Marks, as she was called, was an honorable woman who would not betray his confidence. She accepted his offer, vowing he should never have cause to regret his act. One might have thought from her eager acceptance that in it she found escape, liberty, hope.

"Yes," she said, "I will marry you."

---

1 Ordinary people, especially of the lower class.
2 Ship.
3 Mountain range in South Dakota where a gold rush occurred in the mid-1870s.

He was dazed. He could not speak for one moment so choked was he with ecstasy at his own good fortune. He covered his eyes with his hand, and then he said in a hoarse voice: "I swear to make you happy. My own happiness seems more than I can believe."

Then she stooped suddenly and kissed his hand. He asked her where she would like to live.

"Anywhere you think best," was her reply.

He assured her that the North Pole, Egypt, Africa,—all were one to him, with her and his little daughter. And so they were married.

He had never regretted the step. Estelle was a mother to the motherless child, and being a well-educated woman, versed in the usages of polite society, despite her recent position as a waitress in a hotel, soon had Jewel at a first-class school, where she could be fitted for the position that her father's wealth would give her. Nor did Estelle's good work end there. She recognized her husband's sterling worth in business and morals, and insisted upon his entering the arena of politics. Thanks to her cleverness, he made no mistakes and many hits which no one thought of tracing to his wife's rare talents. Not that Bowen was a fool; far from it. Mrs. Bowen simply fulfilled woman's mission in making her husband's career successful by the exercise of her own intuitive powers. His public speeches were marked by rugged good sense. His advice was sagacious. He soon had enthusiastic partisans and became at last a powerful leader in the politics of the Pacific Slope. All in all, Mrs. Bowen was a grand woman and Senator Bowen took great delight in trying to further her plans for a high social position for himself and the child.

Jewel Bowen's beauty was of the Saxon type, dazzling fair, with creamy roseate skin. Her hair was fair, with streaks of copper in it; her eyes, gray with thick short lashes, at times iridescent. Her nose superbly Grecian. Her lips beautifully firm, but rather serious than smiling.

Jewel was not unconscious of her attractions. She had been loved, flattered, worshipped for twenty years. She was proud with the pride of conscious worth that demanded homage as a tribute to her beauty—to herself.

Her tastes were luxuriously simple; she reveled in the dainty accessories of the toilet. To the outside world her dress was severely plain, but her dressmaker's bill attested to the cost of her elegant simplicity.

It was but a short time since Jewel had been transported from her quiet Canadian convent into the whirl of Washington life, a splendid house, more pretty dresses than she could number, a beautiful mother, albeit a step-mother, more indulgent than most mothers, fairly adoring the sweet and graceful girl so full of youth's alluring charm, and a father who was the noblest, tenderest and wisest of men. But she was a happy-hearted girl, full of the joy of youth and perfect health. She presented a bright image to the eye all through the fall, as she galloped over the surrounding country on her thoroughbred mare, followed by her groom and two or three dogs yapping at her heels.

There was perfect accord between her and her step-mother. Mrs. Bowen shared the Senator's worship of Jewel. From the moment the two had met and the child had held her little arms toward her, blinking her great gray eyes in the light that had awakened her from her slumbers, and had nestled her downy head in the new mother's neck with a sigh of content, almost instantly falling asleep, again, with the words: "Oh, pitty, pitty lady!"

Estelle Bowen had kissed her passionately again and again, and from that time Jewel had been like her very own. The young step-mother trained the child carefully for five years, then very reluctantly sent her to the convent of the Sacred Heart[1] at Montreal, where she had remained until she was eighteen. Then followed a year abroad, and her meeting with Cuthbert Sumner.

About this time events crowded upon each other in her young life. Her father's rise was rapid in the money world and, together with his political record, gave his family access to the wealthiest and most influential society of the country.

Cuthbert Sumner, her acknowledged lover, was an only child of New England ancestry favored by fortune like herself. His father, a wealthy manufacturer, was the owner of a business that had been in the Sumner family for many generations. His mother had died while he was yet a lad. It was a dull home. The son just leaving Harvard, had been expected to assume the responsibilities of his father's establishment, but having no taste for a commercial life, and being fitted by nature as well as education for a career in politics, his father reluctantly gave his consent that

---

1　The Sacred Heart School, a Catholic institution for girls, was founded in Montreal in 1861.

Cuthbert should have his wish after a few years spent in travel had acquainted him with the great world.

Mr. Sumner, senior, finding his son's desires still unchanged upon his return from abroad, used his influence and obtained for him a position in the Treasury as private secretary in General Benson's department. So young Sumner was duly launched upon the sea of politics. The world of fashion surged about him and he soon found himself a welcome guest in certain homes. He had little leisure for society, but sought it more after he attended Jewel Bowen's "coming-out" reception, a year previous to this chronicle. There he had seen a maiden in white, her arms laden with fragrant flowers, with beautiful fearless eyes which looked directly into the secret depths of his heart.

Sumner was twenty-six and this was not his first experience with women. He had been in love with the sex, more or less, since the day he left off knee-breeches. As he looked into Jewel's eyes he remembered some of his experiences with a pang of regret. He was no better, no worse than most young fellows. He had played some, flirted some, had even been gloriously hilarious once, for all of which his conscience now whipped him soundly. Jewel looked upon him with mingled feelings, in which curiosity was uppermost. In her world money was the potent factor; but in this man she saw the result of generations of culture and wealth combined.

One afternoon when they were calling, about the time of her "coming-out" party, a friend of Mrs. Bowen had mentioned him: "Such a fascinating man! and so handsome! Will you let me bring him? He's a man you must know, of course, and the sooner the better."

"We shall be very pleased," Mrs. Bowen replied; "any friend of yours is welcome."

"Thanks. That's settled then."

"He looks very different from the most of the men one meets in Washington," remarked Jewel, who was examining the pictured face that smiled at her from its ornate frame on the mantel.

"How?"

"Oh, I don't know. More manly, I suppose would explain it."

"Wait till you know him," returned the matron with a meaning smile.

"Cuthbert Sumner," Jewel repeated to herself. "Yes, they talk so much of him, all the women seem to have lost their hearts to him. I wonder if he will, after all, be worth the knowing."

That was the beginning. The end was in sight from the time they first met. It was a desperate case on both sides. None was surprised at the announcement of the engagement the previous winter. It was understood that the wedding would take place at Easter.

★ ★ ★ ★ ★ ★

"The Bowens are in town." That meant a vast deal to the important section of Washington's world which constitutes "society," for the splendid mansion, closed since the daughter's brief introduction to society, it was rumored, would be added to the list of places where one could dance, dine and flirt. Festivities were to open with a ball—a marvel of splendor, for which five hundred invitations had been issued.

Senator Bowen was walking down the avenue the next afternoon, on his way home, when he was joined by General Benson, who had developed lately a passion for his society. The two men frequented the same clubs and transacted much official business together, but there had been nothing approaching intimacy between them. If the shrewd Westerner had given expression to his secret thoughts they would have run somewhat in the following vein:

"Got a hang-dog look about that off eye[1] which tells me he's a tarnation mean cuss on occasion. He's all good looks and soft sawder.[2] However, that don't worry me any; it's none o' my funeral."

After the two men had exchanged the usual civilities, the latest political question looming up on the horizon was discussed; finally, the conversation turned upon the coming ball.

"By the by, Senator, I wish I dared ask for cards for a friend of mine and his daughter. They have just arrived in town for the season, and know no one. He, the father, is the newly-appointed president of the Arrow-Head mines; the daughter is lovely; a fine foil for Miss Jewel. Unexceptional people, and all that."

"Certainly, General," the Senator hastened to reply. "What address?"

---

1   As opposed to the dominant eye used in shooting.
2   Flattery.

With profuse thanks, General Benson handed him a card, on which appeared the name:

HENRY C. MADISON.
Corcoran Building. Washington, D.C.

"I will speak to Mrs. Bowen right away."

★ ★ ★ ★ ★ ★

Mrs. Bowen and Jewel were enjoying a leisure hour before dinner, in lounging chairs before the blazing grate-fire in the former's sitting-room. There was a little purr of gratification from both women as they heard a well-known step in the hall.

"Well here you both are," was Senator Bowen's greeting as he kissed his wife and daughter and flung himself wearily into a chair.

"Tired?" asked his wife.

"Yes, some of these dumb-headed aristocrats are worse to steer into a good paying bit of business for the benefit of the government treasury, than a bucking broncho."

"How late you are, papa," here broke in Jewel from her perch on her father's knee, where she was diligently searching his pockets. It had been her custom from babyhood, and never yet had her search been unrewarded.

"I'd have been here earlier only I met General Benson and he always has so many questions to ask, especially about my little lass, that he kept me no end of time."

"Don't be wicked, papa," smiled Jewel, "because you spoil me; you think everyone must see with your eyes."

"Ah! pet; it's just wonderful how well all the old and young single fellows know me since you have grown up. But we won't listen to 'em just yet, Blossom; not even Sumner shall part us for a good bit; your pa just can't lose you for a good spell, I reckon."

"No man shall part us, dad; if he takes me, he must take the whole family," replied Jewel with a loving pat on the sallow cheek.

"We'll see, we'll see. There's another bid for an invite to your shin-dig," he continued, with a laugh, as he tossed the card given him by General Benson into his wife's lap. "It's mighty pleasant to be made much of; it's worth while getting rich just to see how money can change the complexion of things, and how cordial the whole world can be to one man if he's got the spondulix."[1]

"My dear Zenas," said Mrs. Bowen, with a shake of her head and a comical smile on her face, "don't talk the vernacular of the gold mines here in Washington. You'll be eternally disgraced."

"Well, Mrs. Senator, I've fit the enemy, tackled grizzlies, starved, been locked up in the pens of Libby Prison,[2] and I've come out first best every time, but this thing you call society beats me. The women make me dizzy, the men make me sick, and a mighty little of it makes me ready to quit, fairly squashed. Them's my sentiments."

A cry of delight broke from Jewel,—"O dad!" as she brought to view a package in a white paper. Mrs. Bowen left her seat to join in the frolic that ensued to gain possession of it. At last the mysterious bundle was unwrapped, the box opened and a pearl necklace brought to view of wonderful beauty and value. The senator's eyes were full of the glint and glister of love and pride as he watched the faces of his wife and daughter. After a moment he brought out another package, which he gave to his wife.

"There, Mrs. Senator, there's your diamond star you've been pining after for a month. I ordered them quite a while ago; happened to be passing Smith's and stopped in, found 'em ready and here they be. What women see in such gewgaws[3] is a puzzler to me. I can tolerate such hankering in a young 'un, but being you're not a chicken, Mrs. Senator, and not in the market, and still good looking enough to make any man restless with no ornaments but a clean calico frock, your fancies are a conundrum to yours truly. But these women folks must be humored, I suppose."

With this the Senator plunged into his dressing-room, which adjoined his wife's sitting-room, and began the work of dressing for dinner and the theatre.

"Cuthbert coming?" he called to his daughter, who still lingered.

"Yes, papa."

"Jewel, dear, have Venus be particular with your toilet tonight; I will overlook you when she has finished."

---

1 Money, cash.
2 A notoriously cramped, pestilential Confederate prison in Richmond, Virginia.
3 Trinkets, baubles.

"That the name of your new maid, Blossom?" the Senator's voice demanded. There were many grunts, groans and growls issuing from the privacy where his evening toilet was progressing because of refractory collar buttons and other unruly accessories.

"Yes, papa."

"Hump! Name enough to hang her: Venus, the goddess of love and beauty! Can she earn her salt?"

He appeared at the door now struggling into an evening vest. He employed no man, declaring no valley de chamber[1] should boss him around. He'd always been free and didn't propose to end his days in slavery to any slick-pated fashion-plate who didn't know the color of gold from the inside of a brass kettle.

"I don't know what I would do without her. I have been intending to speak to you for some time concerning her brother. He is a genius, and Venus has given up her hopes of becoming a school teacher among her people to earn money to help develop his talents. Can't we do something for them, papa? I have said nothing to her yet."

"Hump! You're always picking up lame animals, Blossom; from a little shaver it's been the same. If you keep it up in Washington, you'll have all the black beggars in the city ringing the area bell.[2] However, I'll look the matter up. If the girl ain't too proud to go out as a servant to help herself along, there may be something in her."

CHAPTER XI.
WHO IS SHE?

At eight that evening—Theatre was filled to overflowing, for Modjeska[3] was to interpret the heart-breaking story of "Camille."

---

1 I.e., valet de chambre.

2 Doorbell.

3 Helena Modjeska (1840–1909), a Polish actress known for her portrayal of Marguerite Gautier in *Camille* (1852), based on the 1848 novel *La Dame aux Camélias* by Alexandre Dumas *fils* (1824–95), which tells the story of a French prostitute who dies of consumption. Through the reference to Dumas's character, Hopkins hints that Aurelia Madison is a fallen woman. Lauren Dembowitz has shown in "Sources for *Hagar's Daughter*" that Hopkins derived (*continued*)

Senator Bowen and his handsome wife; Jewel and Cuthbert Sumner occupied a box, and were watching intently the mimic portrayal of life. Jewel was listening earnestly to Modjeska's words; the grand rendering of the life story of a passionate, loving, erring, noble woman's heart touched her deeply. The high-bred grace, the dainty foreign accent, the naturalness of the actress, held her in thrall and she did not take her eyes from the stage. As the curtain went down on the second act she lifted her glass and slowly scanned the house. Suddenly she paused with a heart that throbbed strangely. Directly across from her sat a woman—young in years, but with the mature air of a woman of the world. "Surely," thought Jewel, "I know that face." The girl had a woman's voluptuous beauty with great dusky eyes and wonderful red-gold hair. Her dress of moss-green satin and gold fell away from snowy neck and arms on which diamonds gleamed. Just then Sumner uttered an exclamation of surprise. He had turned, almost at the same moment with Jewel, and swept a careless glance over the house, bowing to several, mostly well-known people either by profession or social standing, but had declined to see more than one fair one's invitation. Passing, as it were, a box on the left, his glance had rested on a face that instantly arrested it and caused him to exclaim. An elderly man sat with the vision of loveliness. In repose the girl's face lost some of its beauty and seemed care-worn; one felt impressed that girlhood's innocence had not remained untouched.

The lady was watching their box intently, and seeing herself discovered smiled a brilliant smile of recognition as she inclined her head in Sumner's direction holding his glance for one instant in a way that seemed to call him to her side. He bowed, then turned his head away with a feeling of confusion that annoyed him. He did not offer to go to her, however.

"Do you know her? Who is she, Cuthbert?" asked Jewel, intercepting both smile and bow.

"It is Miss Madison," he replied, lifting his glass nonchalantly. "I did not know she was in Washington. I have not seen her for three years. Looking remarkably well, is she not?"

"She is glorious! Her face somehow seems familiar to me. I must have met her. Have you seen much of her?"

---

much of this scene and several others in the novel from Fanny Driscoll's "Two Women" (1884). See Appendix G3.

"Can't say that I have. Met her at a ball at Cape May.[1] But I found the place so dull I packed up and went home. After that I went abroad. Then I met a sweet little woman who has led me captive at her chariot wheels ever since."

Then followed some talk dear to the souls of lovers and the beauty opposite was forgotten. But throughout the next act Jewel felt her heart contract as the dusky eyes followed her movements with a restless, smouldering fire in their depths that pained her to see.

Amelia Madison watched the box opposite with hungry intensity. She was studying Jewel's face mentally saying: "There is not another woman in the house like her. She is like a strain of Mozart, a spray of lilies. My God! how he looks at her—he never looked at me like that! He respects her; he worships her—"

She sank back in breathless misery.

Aurelia Madison and Cuthbert Sumner had met one summer at Cape May. They had loved and been betrothed; had quarreled fiercely over a flirtation on her part and had separated in bitterness and pain; and yet the man was relieved way down in a corner of his heart for he had felt dimly, after the first rapture was over, that he was making a mistake, that she was not the woman to command the respect of his friends nor to bring him complete happiness. Yet after a fashion she fascinated him. Her grace, her beauty, thrilled his blood with rapture that he thought then was Love. Love came to him a later guest, and the purity and tenderness of Jewel's sweet face blotted out forever the summer splendor of Aurelia Madison's presence. Now it was all over; he knew he had never loved her, and that he was fortunate to have found it out in time.

No one knew of this episode in Aurelia Madison's life. Her father had been away on one of his periodical tours, and the girl was accountable to none but an old governess who acted as chaperone.

Since that time she had led a reckless life. Had lived at Monte Carlo[2] two seasons, aiding her father in his games of chance, luring the gilded youth to lose their money without murmuring. Hers had been a precarious life and a dangerous one. Sometimes they were reduced to expedients. But through it all the girl held

---

1 Resort town in southern New Jersey, situated on the Atlantic Ocean.
2 The principality of Monaco, known for its casinos.

her peace, set her teeth hard, and waited for the day when she should again meet Cuthbert Sumner, trusting to the effect of her great beauty, and the fact that he had once loved her passionately, to re-establish her power over the man she worshipped. Once his wife, she told herself, she would shake off all her hideous past and become an honest matron. Honesty she viewed as a luxury for the wealthy to enjoy. Thank heaven, Cuthbert Sumner's wife could afford to be honest. They had met again, but how? All her hopes were dust.

Now she saw Jewel lift her eyes to his with devotion, love and faith in them; she saw him look down eagerly, with truest, tenderest love. The last act was on. She could bear it no longer, but rose impatiently, with rage and hatred in heart, and attended by her father, left the house. When next Jewel stole a glance in the direction of the stranger her place was empty.

CHAPTER XII.
A PLOT FOR TEN MILLIONS.

It was near nine o'clock the next morning and General Benson was still invisible. His colored valet was moving about noiselessly, making ready for his master. Breakfast was on the table in its silver covers. A bell rang; Isaac disappeared.

General Benson's renown as a great social leader rested, not only on his lavish expenditure and luxurious style of living at Willard's Hotel, where he monopolized one of the most expensive suites, but upon his mental and physical attributes as well. The ladies all voted him a charming fellow. He had a remarkably sweet and caressing voice, which added to his attractions. The many women to whom he had vowed eternal fidelity at one moment, only to abandon heartlessly the next at the rise of a new star in the firmament of beauty, sighed and wept at his defection and voted him the most perfect lover imaginable. It was hinted that one girl had committed suicide solely on his account. But still the ladies believed in his professions.

The members of the various clubs that he affected acknowledged him to be an admirable card-player, a good horseman, an expert with sword or revolver, as well as an unusually agreeable companion in a search after pleasure; generous, too, with his money. But with all his popularity and increase of fame, his fortune declined, and he found himself at the present time embarrassed for money, his capital growing smaller each month in spite of a large salary. Debts of honor must be met, and to keep a good name one's opponent must sometimes win. Then, too, he was growing old; he carried his years well, but fifty was looming perilously near.

He and his friend Major Henry Clay Madison, President of the Arrow-Head Mining Company of Colorado, newly established in the city, had a mutual interest in the great scheme that was to make the fortunes of the different share-holders, but even the generous payments he received as his share of the profits made out of verdant[1] men of means who became easy prey because of General Benson's sweet persuasive voice and exalted position in the political world, failed to assist him out of his financial dilemma. Within a month a new scheme had entered his mind,—one that dazzled him the possibilities were so great, a scheme which if successfully handled would put millions in the pockets of a trio of unscrupulous adventurers,—Major Madison and his daughter and himself.

As the clock chimed nine, General Benson entered the room and seated himself at the breakfast table. A moment later his valet informed him that Major and Miss Madison wished to see him.

"Very well; show them in, at once."

Presently the valet ushered them in. The major we have mentioned before; he was short, stout, more than fifty, with gray hair and ferret-like eyes, close-set, and a greenish-gray of peculiar ugliness; a close observer would take exception to them immediately. He was scrupulously attired in the height of fashion. He was accompanied by the strange beauty who had attended the theatre the night before.

"Well, General, you sent for us and here we are. How are you?" was the major's greeting as he shook hands with General Benson and then flung himself into an arm-chair.

"Very well, indeed, thanks, Madison. What is it indeed you, Aurelia?" he exclaimed on beholding the girl. "How delightful to have you with us once again!"

The lady inclined her head slightly in answer to her host's warm greeting, ignored his offered hand, and subsided onto

---

1 Green, inexperienced.

a chair with a preoccupied air, a slight frown puckering her forehead.

"Don't mind Aurelia, General; she's mooning as usual," laughed her father.

"You are looking very fit, Major," remarked Benson, recovering from the confusion caused by Aurelia's coolness. "Have a B. and S.?"

"Don't care if I do."

Benson poured a brandy-and-soda for his guest and another for himself; passed the cigars to him and the cigarettes to Miss Madison. She took one, lit it, and drew away in a manner that showed her keen enjoyment. A smile passed over Benson's face as he covertly watched her.

"Well, Madison," the General said, after a few moments' enjoyment of the weed, "I sent for you to come here this morning on a matter of business, because I shall not be able to call on you at any time today, for I may have to go out of town at any moment on some confounded office business. It's a nuisance, I say. The office interferes too much with a man's pleasure. If my plans succeed I'll cut the whole thing."

"Indeed! I imagine we are mutually interested when you speak of business. You're not ruined I take it. Do you want to borrow money of me?" said the Major with a laugh as he drew his chair a trifle closer to his friend. The lady evinced no interest in the conversation.

"On the contrary, I wish to offer you a chance to make some."

"You are extremely kind, Benson; you could not have chosen a more opportune time for your offer. Will you believe it—I was compelled to part with a diamond pin this morning," replied Madison, touching his polished shirt-front. "But what can I do for you?"

"Since we joined forces, Madison, on the strictly respectable basis, we have gained fame and influence, and but little money. It takes money to maintain our position, and plenty of it. This you know. I have studied the situation and I am convinced that our only surety for providing for the future lies in a coup that shall net us millions, on which we may retire."

"Yes, but how to get it," replied Madison with a mournful shake of the head. "Work is not in our line, unsafe expedients are dangerous and not to be thought of. I do not fancy running my head into a noose. One can't do much but go straight here, and money's a scarce article."

"Be patient. You need have no apprehension that I shall suggest anything dangerous, Madison; though the time was when you were the risky one and I the one to hesitate," with a significant uplifting of the eyebrows.

"True; but time has changed my ideas. I have a hankering for respectability that amounts to a passion."

"Remain as respectable as you wish, my friend; I have a legitimate scheme that will make us masters of ten millions! No risk; nothing necessary but judicious diplomacy."

Miss Madison had evinced no interest until now, but at the words "ten millions" uttered by this man whom she knew to be practical, astute in business and no dreamer, she seemed to awaken from her lethargy. She retained her self-possession, however, and maintained her unruffled calm, remarking carelessly, even sarcastically: "May I ask the nature of the plan, General, and where my usefulness comes in?"

"I was about to explain that point, my dear; but first permit me to ask a question,—has the idea of acquiring a fortune by a wealthy marriage ever occurred to you?"

"Yes, I admit it has. But you know too well my reasons for hesitating in such a course."

Benson moved uneasily in his seat, and for a moment his eyes dropped under the steady gaze that the girl bent upon him—eyes large, dreamy, melting, dazzling the senses, but at this moment baleful. A dull flush mounted to his brow.

"See here, Aurelia, have you tried to find an opportunity?"

"Possibly," she answered coldly.

"And you met with no success?"

"Evidently not, as I am single."

"Then your efforts were misdirected."

"Do you think so?" mockingly.

"Most assuredly I do. Your attention was bestowed upon men for whom you had conceived a real liking. That is not the way to bring success in such a venture."

"It is the wrong lead for a woman like me,—an adventuress,[1] to forget her position for one instant and allow her heart to guide her head. What fool wrote 'Poverty is no crime'?[2] I know of none

---

1 Woman who uses any means necessary to advance socially or financially.
2 Perhaps a reference to an 1854 three-act comedy of that name about a poor apprentice by the Russian realist Alexander Ostrovsky (1823–86).

greater. It is responsible for every crime committed under the sun. It is a foul curse!"

"Why, Aurelia, girl, what has come to you this morning? You talk like a man with the blue devils[1] after losing all night at poker," said her father.

Her answer was a shrug of her handsome shoulders as she resumed her listless attitude.

"Listen to me; I will unfold a scheme that shall remove the curse of poverty, and give you for a husband a man who will fill the bill, heart and all."

He rose, approached the mantel, and turning his back upon it, rested both elbows on the marble—a position which brought him face to face with his guests, and asked: "Are you acquainted with Cuthbert Sumner?"

"Know him by sight and reputation. Clerk in your department," replied Madison. Aurelia did not speak, but a flush came into her face, a light to her eyes. One might have felt the thrill that passed over her form.

"What do you think of him?"

"He's all right; a genial fellow, but careful not to go too far; handsome, too, by Jove. No money, though?"

"O yes," nodded Benson. "Only in the department for experience in political life. His father's very wealthy. New England manufacturer."

"Indeed!"

"He's the one I've picked out for our lady here."

"But he's engaged," broke in Aurelia.

"Exactly. And that brings me to the rest of the scheme. Sumner is about to marry Bowen's daughter. By the way, Aurelia, you got the cards, for the ball, did you not?" Aurelia bowed in assent.

"Jewel Bowen is the Senator's only child, and his heiress. She will receive ten millions upon her wedding day. What I propose is that Aurelia fascinate the gentleman, thus leaving the field clear for me. I have taken a decided fancy to Miss Bowen and her fortune. If I succeed there is a million for you, Madison, and another for Aurelia. Sumner, too, has pots of money, and we shall all be able to settle down into quiet respectability. What do you think of my plan?"

---

1 Low spirits, depression.

"By Jove, Benson," blurted out Major Madison, fairly thunder-struck at the magnificence of the vista opened before him, "what a splendid idea! how admirably you have planned things!" Benson nodded and smiled:

"All remains with Aurelia, and certainly with her magnificent beauty to help us, we need fear no failure."

"Spare me your compliments. This is probably your last chance, General. So you think I can win this Mr. Sumner from his betrothed?" she said.

"Precisely."

"That is a droll idea. Do you think—"

"I think, I repeat, that you can easily make the person referred to sufficiently in love with you to do anything you ask."

"Suppose he proves, obdurate? What then? You cannot judge all men alike."

"Break the engagement, if you can do nothing more. During a fit of insanity, if it lasts but a week, an hour even, you will have ample time to accomplish my desires."

"And then?"

"I will look after mademoiselle. It will make no difference to you. Your compensation will be my affair. It is only his money that you would want."

"Oh, I see!" There was a world of sarcasm in the three words uttered by a smiling mouth. "My dear General, you are indeed a marvel! No one knows better than you how to make love to a young girl."

"You are the cleverest woman I know, Aurelia. I knew you would comprehend the situation perfectly." After a moment's reflection the girl replied: "Yes, I think I'll try it. It will probably be announced before long that the marriage is broken off. I will earn my million, never fear. I shall, doubtless, find it an agreeable task."

"And a husband, too, my girl," added her father.

"Perhaps."

"Are we to be intimate friends or simply business acquaintances?" asked the Major of General Benson.

"Business friends will be best. Let us have no appearance of collusion."

"When shall we see you again?" asked the Major as they rose to go.

"Just as soon as you have something to tell me. How fortunate that Aurelia has never been introduced to Washington society. She will take the place by storm."

Then the friends separated.

(To be continued.)

"A DEEP SIGH STARTLED HIM." *Colored American Magazine* frontis-piece (July 1901). Reproduced from *The Digital Colored American Magazine*, coloredamerican.org. Original held at the Beinecke Rare Book and Manuscript Library, Yale University.

CHAPTER XIII.[1]
PLAYING WITH FIRE.

About lunch time that same morning, as Sumner was leaving the office, a note was brought to him by a servant in plain livery:

"May we not be friends for the sake of the old days, when no other woman was dearer than I? Come to me just once."
AURELIA.
New York Avenue.

Sumner's brow was knit as he scanned the sheet of ivory paper in his hand, with its emblazoned monogram. He muttered an imprecation. Elise Bradford, the stenographer, glanced up from her work in surprise. Sumner was a gentleman in the office and a great favorite with all the employees; it was rare to hear an uncouth expression from the lips of this man, who honored all womanhood.

"I thought that was all over and done with," he muttered to himself. "What is the use of going through with it all again? Well, I suppose I must go once for decency's sake, but I'll take care to make short work of it. There shall be no misunderstanding."

Then softer thoughts came to him as he took from a pile of commonplace, business letters on his desk, a slim satiny envelope. It was from Jewel. He opened it and read the few lines it contained, reminding him of an appointment that he had with her for the evening.

---

1 SYNOPSIS OF CHAPTERS IX TO XII. [The synopsis of Chapters I to VIII has not been repeated here. See Appendix A for the full text.] The story next opens in the winter of 1882, in the city of Washington, DC.

The event of the season is a grand ball about to be given at the home of Senator Zenas Bowen who has a charming wife and a beautiful young daughter, Jewel, engaged to Cuthbert Sumner, a rich New Englander, private secretary for General Benson, chief of a department.

At the theatre one night, society is stirred by the advent of a new beauty, Miss Aurelia Madison, to whom Sumner was at one time engaged, a fact that he has concealed from Jewel.

General Benson has fallen in love with Jewel and determines to win her and her fortune of ten million. To this end, he plots with Major Madison and Aurelia to separate the lovers.

"My little Blossom!" he said gently.

But his little Blossom did not keep him from going to see Aurelia Madison. She was less than nothing to him. He had never met her from the day he left Cape May until the night before. He never even thought of her. Yet he went to call upon her. Reluctantly and distastefully—but he went.

He was ushered into the drawing-room, scented and flower-filled. A moment later Aurelia came into the room from the library. Ah, she stirred even his cold heart.

A white negligé clothed her from throat to foot, and her wonderful hair was caught in a mass low down on her neck. A deep light was in the dusky eyes that bewildered a man and weakened his energies. In an instant she came swiftly to him—the white arms were about his throat, the warm lips against his.

"My love! my love!" she murmured softly, and Cuthbert Sumner (blind and foolish) was not the kind of man to let the memory of little Blossom prevent him from holding a beautiful, yielding form closely clasped in his arms, and returning clinging kisses with interest when such a rare opportunity offered.

I question if there are many men that would.

She was playing a part in a desperate game that meant everything to her. This was her first move toward the end she had vowed to accomplish. She would be victorious; she swore it. Her rôle was not a hard one for she worshipped this man so cold and unyielding to her arts. She would have preferred the lilies of virtuous winning;[1] debarred from that she would take the torments of a love to which she had no right. By-and-by, she said:

"Bert, do you love her very much?"

He bowed with a long look in her face.

"And NOT as you loved ME!" she said passionately. "Tell me about her."

"My dear Aurelia, can a man sing the praises of one beautiful woman to another?"

"Tell me about her," she said again with the imperious gesture that Sumner remembered so well in that summer at the Cape. "I have not loved you for two long years, Bert Sumner, without learning every phase of your mind. When do you marry her?"

"At Easter," he replied proudly, disdaining further subterfuge.

---

1 From Algernon Charles Swinburne's 1866 poem "Dolores (Notre-Dame des Sept Douleurs)" (line 67).

"And you can sit there calmly and tell it to me—to me—," she bit her lip a moment; there was less time than she had thought.

"She is very wealthy?"

"Yes, as the world counts it, but I care not for that; if she had nothing it would be the same to me."

"I believe you. And I could see her beauty for myself; and she is good, not like me."

"She is an angel, my white angel of purity," he replied with a look of reverence on his face.

Aurelia was a gorgeous tropical flower; Jewel, a fair fragrant lily. Men have such an unfortunate weakness for tropical blooms, they cannot pass them by carelessly, even though a lily lies above their hearts. Cuthbert could not ignore this splendid tropical flower; it caused his blood to flow faster, it gave new zest to living—for an hour. Jewel was his saint, his good angel; and he loved her truly with all the high love a man of the world can ever know. He trusted her for her womanly goodness and truth. And Jewel returned his love with an intensity that was her very life.

Aurelia looked at him and sighed heavily.

"May I know her?"

"I am sure, I cannot say. You may possibly meet her at some party."

"Then you do not object absolutely. I am glad, for we have invitations to Mrs. Bowen's ball. I want to go."

She looked at him keenly. "I think I have met Miss Bowen before. If I mistake not, we were at the Montreal convent at the same time. I am older than she, and left just after she entered. I remember her as a sweet cherub who resembled a pictured saint."

"Quite a coincidence," he replied with all his usual courtliness for womankind; but for all that he mentally anathematized the idiot who had sent the cards and the convent where the girls had met. He was vexed, and she felt it.

"Yes, I shall go—"

She caught her breath sharply and then fell at his feet in all her exquisite beauty.

"Can you never, NEVER love me again, Bert? My life, my soul is yours! Can you not give me a little love in return?"

He lifted her up gently.

"It is too late to ask that now, Aurelia. Try and forget that you have ever loved me. Believe me, you will be happier. No one can more bitterly regret than I the misery of our past. Let us begin anew."

She thrust him from her wildly, and bade him go if he did not wish to see her fall dead at his feet.

Cuthbert went away sadly.

He knew the full power of Aurelia Madison's siren[1] charms. Nor was her emotion all feigned. She really felt all she had expressed. What was pride compared to the desolation that swept over her when she realized that his heart was hers no longer? Her great love obliterated even the thought of his wealth. She felt she should triumph, in spite of the coldness with which he had received her professions of love. Yes, she would be his wife, even though it were a barren honor, since his heart was not hers.

"If his love is not for me, it shall be for no one else," she told herself, as she thought over her afternoon's work and prepared for the next move in the drama.

And so Cuthbert Sumner went back to his little Blossom, whose calm, pure face was continually before him.

CHAPTER XIV.
RENEWING OLD ACQUAINTANCE.

The following afternoon Major Madison's carriage rolled up to the Bowen mansion on Sixteenth Street, and stopped. From it Aurelia stepped, clad richly and daintily in a becoming calling costume. She had determined to storm the citadel, as it were, and carry it by assault.

She rang the bell and asked the footman if Miss Bowen was at home.

"Yes, Miss—. What name please?"

She gave the man a card on which she had written, "Known to you as Aurelia Walker," and was shown into a morning-room to wait. Would Jewel recognize her, she wondered. Would she be pleased to meet her again?

Presently she heard the gentle froufrou of silken skirts down the broad stairway and the next instant Jewel Bowen stood

---

1 Tempting, seductive.

before her, holding out her hand in frankly-glad recognition—
Jewel in a tea-gown[1] that was a poem, a combination of palest
rose-satin and cream lace. Surprise and pleasure mingled in her
speaking face.

"The card said, 'Aurelia Walker.' Can it be possible that you
are the same Aurelia whom I knew in Montreal? How delightful
to meet you again."

Her greeting was most cordial, and put Aurelia instantly at
her ease. After a time spent in recalling reminiscences of school
life, and pleasant girlish chatter, Aurelia said:

"I must explain the change in name,—papa was embarrassed
financially, and he placed me at school, calling himself Walker
while he earned the money to satisfy his creditors; that saved him
much annoyance, and as soon as he could satisfy their demands,
we resumed our rightful name."

"Pray do not speak of it, Aurelia; such things are annoying,
but cannot always be helped," replied Jewel with a smile. "Won't
you come to the drawing-room and meet mamma?"

How beautiful everything was, thought the girl, as she passed
up the broad marble stairs with velvet carpet in the centre, on
which the foot fell noiselessly, and statues and flowers in niches
and on landings, while the walls were hung with lovely frescoes
that impelled one to pause and admire.

The drawing-room door was flung open, and they were in
a spacious apartment with painted ceiling, and all things rich
and harmonious in tone. In a moment, she was standing before
Mrs. Bowen, who greeted her warmly, as if truly glad to meet her
daughter's school friend. No lovelier vision was ever seen than
these two girls as they entered the Bowen drawing-room. Mrs.
Bowen was a cultured lady and their grace and beauty gratified
her taste.

She conversed freely and pleasantly with the unexpected
guest, although after the first feeling of wonder and satisfaction at so much loveliness, she was surprised and puzzled at the
vague feeling of distrust and dislike that personal contact with
her young guest brought to her. It was intangible. She shook it
off, however, the beautiful face and voice were so enchanting
that she could not resist them, and felt ashamed of her distrust.

"Come and sit down by the fire and let us have a long chat

---

1 Loose-fitting dress worn at afternoon teas.

before anyone else comes in. We never know how long we may be alone," said Jewel, indicating a seat near her own.

"This is very cosy and homelike," remarked Aurelia as she took the seat offered. "I have been so lonely since I came to the city."

"Poor child," remarked Mrs. Bowen in a sympathetic voice, "are you very much alone? How long since you lost your mother?"

"I cannot recall her at all, dear Mrs. Bowen," the girl answered, lifting a pair of dusky eyes, swimming in tears, for a moment to her face. "Papa is so intent on the fortunes of the mine, just at present, that he gives me very little attention. Indeed, I believe he forgets at times that he has a daughter," this last with a little sigh of martyrdom.

Mrs. Bowen melted more and more to her guest.

"Then stay and dine with us. Let me send away your carriage." She rang the bell and gave the order to the servant. "We have a few jolly people coming—not a dinner-party, you know, but just a few friends."

"I shall be delighted. How kind you are," replied Aurelia, feeling dizzy over her good luck.

"Thanks," said Jewel, pressing her hand. "Here comes tea, and with it papa."

Senator Bowen welcomed his guest with his usual Western heartiness.

"By Jove," he thought to himself, "she's a stunner! But my little girl doesn't lose a thing by contrast. What a sight for sore eyes the pair of them makes!"

Then he remarked aloud to the guest: "I know your father, my dear; I shall try and see more of him after this. My daughter's friends are my friends."

There were, beside Aurelia, four people to whom Mrs. Bowen introduced her. Two of them—the Secretary of the Treasury and his wife—she knew by sight, but Mr. Carroll West and a pretty widow, Mrs. Brewer, were total strangers. Lord Browning, the English Ambassador, and Lady Browning were shortly announced, and quickly following them came Cuthbert Sumner, completing the party.

"This is my dear friend, Aurelia Madison, Cuthbert; we were at school together. You remember that I told you at the theatre her face seemed very familiar to me."

"Delighted to meet you again, Miss Madison," he said as he

bowed over her hand, suppressing a start of amazement at the sight of her. To himself he added:

"Confound the woman; what does she mean? Is she following me up? That won't help her any."

Aurelia thoroughly ingratiated herself with Lady Browning, paying her the greatest deference. Finding her ladyship much interested in religious topics and charitable projects, she affected an enthusiastic interest in them, and was rewarded by overhearing Lady Browning express herself as delighted with Miss Madison.

"Such a beautiful girl, and so intelligent to talk with."

She went down to dinner with Mr. West, who seemed much impressed with his lovely partner.

Cuthbert's attention would wander to the couple opposite him at table. West was talking to her with animation, while Aurelia smiled and sparkled, and looked irresistibly bewitching. West had but a small income for a wealthy man, and had always been incorrigible until now, but he seemed to have surrendered at last. Cuthbert watched her covertly, not at all deceived by the gaiety of her manner.

"So, the moth is still fluttering about the flame. Let her beware; I would sacrifice her without a moment's hesitation if I thought she meant Jewel harm."

He showed nothing of this outwardly, being as calm, smiling and well-bred as ever. But he was seriously annoyed by the inscrutable conduct of the woman opposite him. It was a vague feeling that he could not grasp—a shadow no larger than a man's hand.

Dinner over, the gentlemen did not linger long behind the ladies. Back in the drawing-room once more, Mrs. Bowen whispered to her husband:

"Do ask Miss Madison to play, Zenas."

"I will when I get a chance. West seems to have such a lot to say to her that it would be cruel to spoil sport."

Mrs. Bowen looked and laughed:

"I'll ask her myself then. Miss Madison, I am sure you are musical," she said to the girl, with a smile. "Will you not favor us?"

Aurelia signified her willingness and Mr. West, a minute later, had installed her at the piano, and stood by listening with delight to her playing. And she was worth listening to for she was a cultured amateur of no mean ability, and gave genuine pleasure by her performance. Mr. West was more and more infatuated each moment he spent in her society. Mrs. Bowen thanked her warmly as she rose from the instrument, followed by the plaudits of the company.

"Miss Madison," said the pretty widow, "you play beautifully."

"Do I?" queried Aurelia, laughing, "but then I cannot sing, Jewel can, though—divinely, I hear."

"Flatterer!" said Jewel as she passed Aurelia's seat on her way to the piano, attended by Sumner.

"What is it to be?" he asked her as he turned over the contents of a folio.

"Will you choose, Cuthbert?"

A jealous pang shot through Aurelia's heart, as her ear caught the words, but she set her teeth hard.

Sumner took from the folio "Some Day," by Wellington.[1]

"Always a favorite of mine, you know," he said.

She gave him a quick, trustful look, and smiled as she began the accompaniment.

Conversation was hushed; everyone listened while the rich, pure voice filled the room, giving the old song with the dramatic fire of a professional. There was a buzz of admiration when Jewel had finished. Cuthbert bent over with pride and delight shining in his face, and his softly-spoken "Thanks, sweetheart," was heard distinctly by the woman sorely tried by jealous pain.

"Don't leave the piano; sing something else," came from all parts of the room.

"Very well," she said, and then gave with delicious pathos that sweet old song, "Dreaming Eyes."[2]

The listeners were charmed. The singer rose, crossed the room and seated herself beside Aurelia. Their renewed acquaintance seemed destined to ripen into a close intimacy.

"Aurelia," the girl said as they sat there somewhat apart from the others, "Will you come with us to the—Theatre tomorrow night—we have a box?"

Surnames were dropped from that night. How did it happen? CIRCE[3] alone knew. But after that these two were much together.

---

1   Likely a reference to Joseph Milton Wellings's "Some Day" (1881).
2   Possibly a reference to William Gooch's "Dreaming Eyes" (1873).
3   Temptress in Homer's *Odyssey* who turns men into animals.

"Such a lovely morning, Jewel! You must come for a turn with me," or, "I shall be alone all day; do come and make the hours bright for me."

Sumner's first undefined fears gradually subsided. Time, rolling on springs of pleasure, passed swiftly bringing the night of the ball.

CHAPTER XV.
THE BALL.

The Bowen mansion was ablaze with light. Servants in livery hurried about attending the arrival of guests. Outside the house a continuous stream of carriages deposited the fortunate ones bidden to the feast.

The ball-room was a vast apartment arched, with a gallery of carved oak, in which the orchestra was seated. The rooms were filling fast, yet at no time, even when the crowd was densest, was there a pressure for room. Flowers wreathed the gallery, the national colors hung in the angles, banks of roses were everywhere. Mrs. Bowen, in white velvet, old lace and diamonds, stood near the entrance, supported by her husband, her daughter and Cuthbert Sumner. The house party was enforced by several gentlemen of political importance and their wives.

"In glass of satin,
And shimmer of pearls."[1]

Jewel Bowen stood, a flush on her cheeks, her hair falling in waving masses, pearls clasping her white throat and arms, her large gray eyes like wells of light. An only child and heiress of many millions, she would have been the bright star of fortune to the gilded youth of Washington had not Cuthbert Sumner stood first in the field; albeit, a man might be pardoned for losing his head had she possessed only her youth and beauty.

---

1 The third line from Alfred, Lord Tennyson's 1855 poem *Maud* XXI, section 9, is "In gloss of satin and glimmer of pearls." Lauren Dembowitz has shown in "Sources" that Hopkins derived parts of this scene from Etta Pierce's serial *A Dark Deed* in *Frank Leslie's Popular Monthly* (1884).

A band hidden away in the great mansion discoursed Rossini's[1] dreamy music in a concert during the arrival of guests. Fashionable Washington greeted its world and congratulated itself on being there, discussed the host and hostess, admired the arrangements for dancing just as the dear five hundred[2] always have done and always will do. It was evident that the Bowen ball was to be the hit of the season. The Senator was voted charmingly original, and his wife attracted as much comment and attention as the debutantes who graced the occasion.

"I hear that we are to have a new beauty introduced tonight. A girl who is fairly startling," remarked one man to another. The rumor was started by Mrs. Bowen saying to a number of dancing men, with a roguish smile:

"Don't fill up all your dances, for there is another beauty coming. Nobody you know, either. A stranger in the city."

"We have heard something of her charms through West, I think, Madam Bowen. You mean Miss Madison. West is fairly a drivelling idiot over her at present. I'm worried over the poor chappie."

"Tiresome man, why couldn't he allow me the pleasure of trapping society. Have either of you met her?"

"Alas, for your intended surprise, dear Mrs. Bowen, I have seen her on the boulevard once or twice," replied the one who had not yet spoken. "What a perfect pair Miss Jewel and she will make, and puzzle anyone to award the palm."

"Mrs. Bowen is certainly a charming hostess," remarked one to the other as they walked away, displaced by fresh relays of guests.

"She is really a beautiful woman, but too cold to please me," was the reply.

"She has a throat and shoulders of alabaster, a superb head and a flowerlike face."

"Hear, hear! Wasting compliments on a passée elderly matron—it isn't like you, Rollins."

"A pretty woman is never passée; you fellows who are new in society have something to learn, let me tell you."

---

1 Gioachino Rossini (1792–1868), Italian composer best known for the opera *The Barber of Seville* (1775).

2 Likely a reference to William Cowper's lines in the 1785 poem *The Task*, Book II: "She that asks / Her dear five hundred, contemns them all, / And hates their coming" (lines 642–44).

"Granted. But we don't waste ammunition on elderly females who have had their day."

"Has a woman, once a beauty, ever had her day?"

"What a queer fellow you are tonight, making flowery speeches about old folks."

"There is no denying the truth of what I said, though. It is human nature. With a woman it is her good looks—with a man his strength, which at no age will he ever admit to be materially lessened any more than a woman will allow her good looks quite gone into the past, or if they do admit a decay of their charms or strength there is still a feeling of pride in what they were once."

"Here endeth the first lesson," laughed his companion as they separated to find partners for the opening number.

Other men, older than the two recorded, remarked the nobleness and charm of the hostess.

"There is a story written on her face, if I mistake not; I would give much for the power to read it," said a famous student of psychology to a celebrated physician, as they stood together surveying the brilliant scene.

"Granted she is beautiful, but she looks a creature of snow and ice. The daughter is more to my liking."

"Yes, but you must confess that they are alike."

"Alike, yet unlike; in the daughter there is fire and life, and a little diablerie,[1] if I mistake not."

"Ah! but the beautiful Mrs. Bowen is only step-mother to the lovely Jewel."

"Is it possible? I should have thought them of one blood.[2] Who was madam before her marriage?"

"No one knows," was the reply, accompanied by a suggestive shrug of the shoulders. "We do not inquire too closely into one's antecedents in Washington, you know; be beautiful and rich and you will be happy here."

Meantime the room was filling fast. Directly the butler announced "General Benson," Senator Bowen moved forward a pace and shook him warmly by the hand and then presented

---

1   Mischief, sorcery.
2   Indirect reference to Acts 17.26: "[God] hath made of one blood all nations of men for to dwell on the face of the earth." Hopkins's final *Colored American Magazine* serial novel would be entitled *Of One Blood* (1902–03).

him to his wife and daughter. A puzzled look swept over his face as he bent for an instant above Mrs. Bowen's hand. Then he stole a furtive glance at her white impassive countenance, started slightly—looked again with a quick indrawn breath. There was now a questioning look in her eyes of seeming surprise at his evident interest—a quick contraction of the straight brows, the next second the dark eyes drooped, but he felt conscious that under those long lashes they still watched him. It passed in a second of time, there was no change in the beautiful cold face of the elegant woman of the world save that one might have imagined that she grew whiter, if possible. Then he recovered himself and turned with easy self-complacency to Jewel:

"Am I too late for the first dance?" he asked in his most courtly style.

"The first is gone certainly," smiled Jewel.

"Well, never mind; the first waltz, then."

"So sorry, General, but it is promised," with an arch glance at Sumner, who was standing back of her.

"Oh! I see. You unprincipled fellow, to steal the march on the world of us who are in darkness. We must all give first place to your claim, Sumner, lucky boy," he said with a genial laugh. "The fourth then? I shan't get another chance, so I must secure my luck while I can."

"With pleasure."

"And the one right after supper, dare I ask?"

"Very well," she replied again, smiling at his persistency.

The General took her card, and inscribed his name against two members, and as the opening bars of the first dance sounded, and her partner came to claim her, bowed and moved away.

There was a movement near the door, and "Major Madison and Miss Madison" were announced. There was a moment's hush as they entered the ball-room, and every man present mentally uttered an exclamation of surprise and admiration. For once rumor had not lied. This woman was quite the loveliest thing they had ever seen, startling and somewhat bizarre, perhaps, but still marvellously, undeniably lovely. Her gown was a splendid creation of scarlet and gold. It was a magnificent and daring combination. Her hair was piled high and crowned with diamonds. A single row of the same precious stones encircled her slim white throat. She looked superbly, wondrously beautiful.

Truly this girl was an exquisite picture, but it bewildered one so that the eye rested on Jewel's slender, white-robed figure with pleasure, and intense relief.

Sumner was talking with Mrs. Vanderpool, the wife of a New York millionaire, as the Madisons entered, and turned at her exclamation:

"What a lovely girl! Who is she, Mr. Sumner?"

"She is the daughter of Major Madison, President of the Arrow-Head gold mines, so much talked about at present. You admire that vivid style?"

"Do introduce me, Mr. Sumner, I adore pretty girls." He was greeted by a flash from Aurelia's dark eyes, and a brilliant smile as he came up to give the desired introduction. Already she was surrounded and her ball card besieged.

"Miss Madison, Mrs. Vanderpool."

Both ladies bowed and immediately opened an animated conversation that ended in Aurelia's promising to grace Mrs. Vanderpool's german[1] with her presence. Then Sumner gave the elder lady his arm across the room to join Mrs. Bowen. He passed Aurelia again on his way to the card-tables, in an adjoining room.

"You are going to ask me to dance, Mr. Sumner, of course?" she said to him as he paused an instant beside her chair. Her manner gave the bystanders the idea that they were old and intimate acquaintances. Her words and way jarred on Cuthbert. He took her card, and after consulting her, scribbled his name down for the after-supper dance, bowed and passed on.

He drew a deep breath of relief as he saw Jewel talking to the Russian ambassador, an old man in gorgeous dress and orders blazing on his breast.

"You are lucky, Excellency, to have a moment of Miss Bowen's time bestowed on you."

His Excellency bowed his head.

"I was just telling this lovely little lady that I must not be selfish, that I must give way for others who have a better right to her company than an old man like me."

"I have enjoyed talking with you so much," Jewel said simply.

"Thank you, my child. I see a friend of mine over in the corner. I can leave you in safe hands, now Sumner has come.

---

1 Dancing party.

By-and-by, perhaps, you will let me return and have a few more pleasant moments."

Sumner felt his vague sense of repulsion, which his encounter with Aurelia had aroused, fade, as he came in contact with the pure fascination of his betrothed. He smiled down at her tenderly. How inexpressibly sweet and lovely she was!

The band was playing a delicious waltz. Aurelia, flashing in her jewels, was flying round in the arms of West, who was her shadow. Sumner's brows met in a frown.

"How lovely Aurelia is!" cried Jewel with eager enthusiasm. "She is the most beautiful woman in the rooms."

"Bar one," said Cuthbert, smiling.

"Oh, you; you don't count. You are prejudiced," replied Jewel, laughing. "She seems to get on very well with Mr. West. I wonder—"

"Little matchmaker! I imagine West stands no chance in that quarter. He has nothing but his salary."

"Would that make a difference with her?" in a surprised, regretful tone.

"I imagine that they are not wealthy. Miss Madison, if I read her correctly, will marry for money."

The next instant his arm encircled Jewel's waist, he held her form pressed closely to his throbbing heart, and they glided away from earth to a short period of heaven.

As an intimate friend of the family, and soon to be a son of the house, Cuthbert Sumner had shared the dispensing of hospitality with Senator Bowen.

"My boy," said the older man, "just fix the thing up when you see 'em lagging. I'm going into the card-room and have a game with Madison. He's an old duffer like myself. You understand all this sort of thing, but I'll be hanged if I ain't sick of it before I begin."

So Sumner had found himself pretty busy. After that waltz, however, which came just before supper, he and Jewel had a few precious moments together in the conservatory, sitting out the remainder of their dance. Then came supper, at which Sumner insisted upon being her escort. "I will not waive every enjoyment for the pleasure of others," he declared firmly.

CHAPTER XVI.
THE SPIDER'S WEB.

The first dance after supper Jewel had given to General Benson.

"A short Elysium[1] at last for me," whispered the gallant General as he passed his arm about her slight form. Jewel was a Western girl with all the independence that the term implies. She glanced up at her partner, as they whirled away, with a little amused smile slightly, sarcastic; "I expected something different from you. Something at least original."

"Well, it is Elysium to find one's step perfectly duplicated."

"Oh, that is easy where one's partner is master of the art as you are. I imagine that you are one of the best dancers here."

"You are fond of dancing?" asked the General, after a silence.

"Yes; that weakness was born with me."

"In the tremendous crowd, I could not judge. But I can speak from this waltz—you dance like a fairy. Are you pleased with Washington?"

"Oh, yes; but I miss the freedom of the ranch, the wild flight at dawn over the prairie in the saddle, and many other things."

He looked at her with glowing eyes: "There we have congenial tastes. I am never so happy as when in the saddle."

The ball-room was a whirl of fair faces and dazzling toilets— the light, the heat, the perfume almost oppressive.

Knowing himself to be a fascinating conversationalist, he took advantage of a pause in the music to speak of the heat and suggest a turn in the conservatory where he knew that he could exert this power of enchantment. Jewel was nothing loth.

They stood a moment, before taking seats, at an open glass door gazing out on the gardens sered and withered and covered in places with patches of snow, but bathed in moonlight. There was something solemn in the scene, merriment seemed out of place; even soft laughter jarred on the nerves. She looked up to the heavens, where the Southern cross shone in all its brilliancy surrounded by myriads of other stars. The glorious Southern moon rode high in the sky. The flutes and viols were pouring out their maddest music.

"How glorious," Jewel said softly.

"Ay glorious indeed!"

---

1 Paradise.

"I mean the moon," she said.

"I mean your eyes, fair lady."

"You will persist in saying pretty things, General," she replied, turning away indifferently.

The General bit his lip in vexation. It was not to be easy work, that was plain.

There was a subdued murmur of voices and sometimes a ripple of laughter, for many couples stood, or strolled about the extensive greenhouses. They were lighted softly, from the arched dome, by silvery lamps; fountains flashed scented waters into marble basins where aquatic plants of strange beauty had found a home. Leading from the main conservatory were many arbors and grottoes, transformed for the time being by draperies of asparagus vines and roses into a charming solitude for two. The cool stillness was refreshing after the heat of the ball-room.

"Really, this is well done," remarked the General, stopping to admire the effect. "None of the balls I have attended in Washington was so beautiful."

"Another compliment, General?"

"It is not flattery to speak the truth."

They seated themselves on a rustic chair for two, and the General entertained her with tales of his travels in Italy and India, of cyclone and typhoon, all very fascinating to the girl before whom life was just opening.

"Were you long out of the United States, General?"

"About ten years," he replied, looking down. "It was this way, Miss Jewel, I was a hot-blooded young fellow who could see no wrong in the decision of his section to secede from the union of states; and so, when it all ended disastrously, I gathered together what remained of my shattered fortunes, and went abroad until the pain of recollection should be somewhat dimmed. I returned almost a foreigner."

"Ah!" she said, with a gentle sigh of pity, "how dreadful that time must have been. Thank heaven, ours is a united country once more. And you are mistaken, too, in your judgment: we have no foreigners here. We have effaced the word by assimilation; so, too, we have no Southerners—we are Americans."

The General accented her remark by a courtly bow, and then he drifted into an animated description of a sail down the Mediterranean Sea. Jewel could imagine that she inhaled the odor from boatloads of violets, brought to her senses by his wonderful descriptive powers.

At this moment their enjoyable tête-à-tête was interrupted by the sound of a woman's voice in passionate pleading.

★ ★ ★ ★ ★ ★

Early in the evening Aurelia Madison had whispered to General Benson:

"If you can, take Jewel into the conservatory after supper. I shall have something interesting for her to hear."

"How are you getting on? Any progress?"

"Wait," was her answer.

After supper Sumner went to her to claim his dance. It was a duty-dance and a painful one he found it. As they floated down the long room, Aurelia gazed up at him with flushed cheeks and glittering eyes.

She had taken a great fancy to Jewel Bowen, not only because the latter was very kind to her—kinder than anyone had ever been to her in her lonely, reckless life, but because she really carried in her heart a spark of what passed for love and which would have developed but for Sumner. She could even admire Jewel's beauty without jealousy; she did not envy her her wealth although so pinched herself in money matters, and yet—strange nature of women, or of some women—for that reason she was the more determined to triumph over her as a woman, and, if she could, stab her. She had forced the friendship with that intention.

She felt instinctively that Cuthbert shrank from allowing a continuance of the intimacy between them, and she resented it. Yes, she would have her fling, her triumph; Jewel should know, beyond a doubt, that Cuthbert Sumner and his fortune was hers, belonged to her—Aurelia Madison.

Now she watched his face and resented his cold, preoccupied air.

"How quiet you are; aren't you well?"

"Never better," he replied, with an apology for his seeming indifference. After all she was a woman, and a beautiful one. Why should he try to mar her favorable reception among the élite.

"Only, I am not Jewel; is that it?"

"Pardon. Let us speak of something else. Shall I take you to have some refreshment?" he said coldly.

"Oh, let us go to the conservatory. I want air and rest," she said, slipping her hand through his arm. "I have seen nothing of you all the evening. Now you must devote a short time to me." Her air was bolder than Sumner had ever noticed before. He bowed low in acquiesce, though he would willingly have left her there.

She bit her lip and a dogged look came into her face that was not pleasant to see, and in her heart she felt that she could take the strong, handsome man and dash him senseless at her feet. She hid her feelings well, and glanced up at him with a pretty pleading look.

"Oh! Bert, I keep forgetting—of course—," then she broke out suddenly, "I wish you loved her less!"

"A useless wish," said Sumner coldly. "Happen what may, Jewel must always be my first thought."

"Aye, your best and truest love," she said through her teeth.

They were in the deserted conservatory where all was coolness and shadow; Sumner walked by her side until they reached one of the grottoes, where from between the folds of the rose-curtain drapery a rustic seat held its inviting arms toward them. Aurelia dropped upon it:

"I am afraid I can't give you many minutes," he said with a cool smile. "Senator Bowen naturally expects me to assist him in looking after the guests."

The band was playing divinely and the notes came to them in waves of undulating melody. Sumner never forgot that night, and the music of the band haunted him ever after.

She sat there in sad languor that would have touched any heart but his. They talked a moment on indifferent subjects, then he arose and offered his arm with a motion that indicated a return to the ball-room. But with a low and exceedingly bitter cry she stood up.

"Must we part like this? My God! I cannot bear it! Have you no mercy, no pity?"

The tears were streaming down her cheeks, she held out her hands imploringly.

With deepest sympathy and pity he took them in his.

"Aurelia, you will forget. Believe me, dear, you will forget all this in a very little while. What good would my love do you now? It could bring you nothing but sorrow. We must forget each other. I hope—I know you will be happy yet. God be with you, dear girl." He bent down and pressed his lips to her trembling hands, feeling himself a wretch for bringing sorrow to this beautiful woman who loved him so.

But she flung her arms about him, and clung to him in desperation and the abandonment of grief, sobbing hysterically, with low, quivering moans, that cut him to the heart.

"Aurelia, do not weep so. It is torture for me to hear you."

"I hope I may die! Oh, if I only could!" she sobbed, faltering and shivering, and clinging to him, and he put his arms about her and kissed her twice on the brow. Her lovely wet face was pressed close against his cheek.

A deep sigh startled him. He lifted his head. Standing in the doorway of the curtained recess, pallid as a ghost, all the graceful beauty gone from her wan face, with frightened woful eyes and despair in every feature, stood Jewel. With a loud exclamation, with rage and impatience and disgust, he shook the exquisite form from his bosom.

(To be continued.)

"WITH A CRY JEWEL STAGGERED TO HER FEET." *Colored American Magazine* frontispiece (August 1901). Reproduced from *The Digital Colored American Magazine*, coloredamerican.org. Original held at the Beinecke Rare Book and Manuscript Library, Yale University.

CHAPTER XVII.[1]

It was long after midnight and the guests were leaving, when Sumner, with white, set face, sought Mrs. Bowen and asked for Jewel. She was much concerned over her daughter.

"I do not understand it," was her reply to his eager questions; "Jewel sent word by General Benson that she was not well, and had gone to her rooms. She was all right, and as gay as possible all day. I thought you would know."

Finding that he could not explain matters that night, and would accomplish nothing by waiting, Sumner left the scene of revelry, desiring to be alone. How it had all happened he could not tell. But what a sentimental fool he felt himself to be, for allowing himself to be betrayed into acting such a scene in so public a place. Still, he felt that he could blame no one but himself. Aurelia was free from any intention of scheming for how could she know of Jewel's presence at just that moment? So he argued, lulling his suspicions to rest.

At eight o'clock, while breakfasting, there came a letter from Jewel with his ring enclosed. Then, indeed, it seemed to him that life was over. With mad and bitter wrath, he cursed Aurelia Madison; then he started for Jewel's home. The servant who answered the summons was one wont to have a welcoming smile for the familiar visitor. There was no expression in his well-trained face when he informed Sumner that the ladies were not at home. Night found him again at the Bowen mansion. Mrs. Bowen was coldness itself; Jewel begged to be excused.

Despair seized him. Everything, every one, was repulsive to him. Days of insane recklessness followed. A month went by in this manner—working furiously days, spending his nights in

---

1 Synopsis of Chapters XIII to XVI. [The synopsis of Chapters I to XII has not been repeated here. See Appendix A for the full text.] Aurelia Madison becomes fast friends with Jewel on the strength of an old school acquaintance at the Canadian convent. She secures an invitation to the ball and appears there, creating a sensation.

On the night of the ball, and near its close, by a series of preconcerted arrangements, Jewel, who had gone to the conservatory with General Benson, sees Aurelia in Sumner's arms; she believes him in love with her beautiful friend.

search of the excitement that is supposed to drown care. Then he grew calmer. He would seek Jewel again; he would force her trust; she should believe in him. Life was not worth living without her. For one touch of her cool hand, one glance from her calm eyes, one smile on the sweet, earnest lips, he would barter wealth and fame, and all the world had to offer—aye life itself!

They had met frequently in society during this memorable month, but Jewel passed her lover without a sign of recognition or with a slight bend of the head in acknowledgment of his reverential uncovering. General Benson was always in close attendance, and Aurelia Madison also, was often her companion.

After the usual nine days of wonderment[1] and surmises as to the cause of the estrangement between the lovers, public curiosity turned to speculating on the middle-aged general's chances with the fair heiress.

★ ★ ★ ★ ★ ★

At seven o'clock one evening, Cuthbert sat at his desk in his rooms lost in sombre thoughts. He had determined to devote himself to the hardest of tasks, heavy brain work, when his heart and soul were racked with agony. He was busy on a political treatise. He was considered a brilliant writer. If he could make a stir in the literary world, it would please his father, and he had no one else to think of now.

Work! Could he work? He flung out his arms over the papers on the desk before him, and bowed his head upon them.

"If I knew that the suffering was for myself alone, my Blossom, I could bear it better."

He lifted himself at last haggard and weary as with weeks of sleepless toil, resolved to devote himself to his chosen work.

"What I am I will live on to the end—Ambition my only bride." He was striving with all his young courageous heart to kill the memory of the girl he loved. It was a bitter task, and an impossible one.

Modern pessimists are fond of crying that love, as well as chivalry, has died out of our practical world. If this were true, then Sumner lived after his century, for his belief in higher and

---

1 Short-lived interest or curiosity.

better things was intense. He had a desire to worship purity in any shape, to champion the weak, and carve a pathway to honor that was characteristic of the chivalrous days of old.

The minutes passed, half-past seven ticked away, and then eight, and he never moved. He sat with his face on his two hands, his elbows planted on the table.

"I will not think more about her," he said to himself, doggedly. "I will not—I will not."

John, his servant, a New England colored man who had known him from his youth, had put his evening clothes out in the dressing-room, and now entered the room to remind his master of an engagement to dine.

"It's time you was dressed, Mr. Cuthbert," he said in his quiet way. John was eager for his master to leave Washington and return to Massachusetts and the family home.

"'Deed," he argued to himself, "this Washington's no city for me. Give me old New England every time; it's God's own country. They's nuthin' human about the South for chocolate complected gents like me, no matter how you fix it. The pint of the argument is in the scorpion's tail. Jes' so; and this here Southern idea of colored Americans aint good fer black nor white when you's done had a New England raisin'.

"Mr. Cuthbert's an altered man sense the night of that there Bowen ball," he told himself again and again, "if he ain't twenty years older in his looks then I'm blind in one eye and can't see out of the 'tother. He'll be best off if he gets back home to the old gentleman. Dog my cats but there's something strange in this whole kickup or my name ain't John Robinson."[1]

Sumner roused himself at last: "What's the time, John?" he was asking as the bell of the suite rang shrilly.

"If that's Mr. Badger, show him in," he said as John went out of the room.

Cuthbert stood gazing down into the fire. He heard voices outside, but he gave them no heed; there was always a good-natured controversy between his friend and his servant.

A slap on the back, and "Holloa, Sumner, old man!" made him start round and put his gloomy thoughts behind him, and greet his friends, Will Badger and Carroll West.

---

1 Perhaps a reference to the mythical Jack Robinson; elsewhere this character's name is John Williams.

"Ah! How are you, Will? How are you, West? How goes it?" he said, holding out his hand in greeting to his guests.

"Thought I'd bring West with me, and after we dine at the club, take a look in at the Madisons, this is their at home night. West's agreeable," with a laugh and a meaning look in the latter's direction.

Sumner hesitated. Aurelia had written him again and again, but he had not answered her impassioned letters. She had begged him to call and let her help set matters right, but as yet, he had not been able to bring himself to comply with her request.

"Well," he replied to Will Badger after a moment, "I don't mind. Have a glass of wine while I change."

"Thanks—we don't mind," said West.

West never did mind. He was fond of a social glass, and Sumner was noted for his fine wine and excellent brand of cigars.

"Yes, we'll have a little game with the Major," he remarked, as he helped himself from the side-board. "Great fun, the Major knows a thing or two about life does the old man."

"He knows enough to win your money, I suppose, you foolish boy," replied Sumner.

"It's very little I've lost there. He always insists on returning me my money."

"Have others been as fortunate?"

"That's their own fault; the Major wins fair every time," replied West hotly.

"Oh, West, you're prejudiced in his favor," broke in Badger.

"A pretty daughter is a trump card."

"She can't help being charming and attracting men to the house," stoutly maintained West.

"Charming, but dangerous, my dear fellow."

"She's my friend. I would be more to her if it were not for my poverty. Don't malign her, Badger, I won't stand it."

"My dear boy," broke in Sumner, soothingly, "Badger and I are your friends. Don't be angry with us; we mean it for your good. Aurelia Madison is one of those women with whom mere friendship is impossible. Men must always be half her lovers and therein lies the secret of her power—of any woman's power over our sex, if she is inclined to use that power to our detriment. Oh! she's circumspect," he continued as West attempted a vehement interruption. "I believe that it is not in her to care enough for anyone to kick over the advantages of respectability for his sake, but she'll sail close to the wind."

West laughed bitterly: "You speak from experience I suppose; the city is ringing with your broken engagement and its cause."

Sumner stood silent. The blow was a keen one because the wound was so recent.

"Oh, come, fellows; drop it," hastily exclaimed Badger. "What do we care for Miss Madison except as any man admires a handsome woman. She'll bowl you over, Carrie, my son; she's using you just now to suit her own purposes. You're young yet," he continued affectionately, "but when you've had two or three seasons of this sort of thing, you'll hold your own with the deepest of them."

"Yes, West," rejoined Sumner who had regained his self-possession, "there are scores of just such women in the world; I will own that once I thought Aurelia Madison divine, but," shrugging his shoulders, "I have changed my opinion, and I am not sorry to have escaped from her toils. If you enjoy her society, continue to do so, but be careful; don't let her snare you."

"You ought to do some of your preaching to old Bowen. Dogged if he ain't gone on her worse than I am; any way, it looks so; he's there every night."

"What!" exclaimed Sumner.

"Let up, West, why don't you?" said Will Badger giving him a meaning look. "It's my idea, Cuthbert, that Senator Bowen is putting money into the mine. That's what I think is the attraction. I intended to speak to you about it some days ago."

Sumner made no reply, and in a few moments the trio left the house.

Washington society, with all its proneness to overlook small trespasses, was beginning to talk about the Madisons. Some declared the beautiful daughter but a bait to snare the unwary, and openly voted the Major "shady." A good deal of money changed hands in the salon of the unpretentious house on New York Avenue; it was whispered also that the mine was a gigantic swindle. As yet these reports were but floating rumors; no one had made open complaint.

Meanwhile, the evenings were gay in the drawing-room where Aurelia smiled and flirted with the greatest intellects of the great Republic. There was an excellent buffet, obsequious servants, the soft shuffle of cards, and in the billiard room at the rear of the house, a chosen few rattled dice or gave themselves up to the fascinations of rouge-et-noir.[1]

It was past eleven when the servant opened the door of Major Madison's salon and the three friends entered. Sumner found himself in a fair-sized and well-furnished room, containing a semi-grand piano; it was the one he had entered on his former visit. Aurelia was the only woman present. The Major came forward from a group near the fire-place to receive them.

"So pleased to see you," he said, shaking hands in his cordial fashion. "Aurelia, my dear, here is Mr. Sumner." West was already standing by the beauty's chair, and Badger had passed on to a group of men in another part of the room.

Aurelia was exquisitely dressed in her favorite colors, cream and terra-cotta, combined in a wonderful gown.

"Well, Mr. Sumner, have you honored us at last?" she queried as she laid her hand lightly in his. Then as her father moved away she said with a bitter smile:

"The fault was not mine. I would have died rather than Jewel should have heard my foolish words."

Her manner, more than her words, broke down all Sumner's lingering suspicions, and he warmed perceptibly toward her. She was but a girl, impassioned, impressionable. What right had he to accuse her of perfidy. Some one came up to them and interrupted her.

Yes, she would give them music. She went to the piano and Sumner followed her. She played popular selections from the latest opera bouffe,[2] and then a morceau[3] in a style that satisfied the most critical taste.

Senator Bowen had just entered the house and paused for the music to cease before speaking to Miss Madison, then he went up to her passing Sumner with a cold nod. Presently Major Madison and he disappeared, and Sumner felt that they had gone to the card room. He wandered about for a while seeing enough to alarm him at the ascendency Major Madison had evidently gained over the Senator. As he stood at the door of the room watching the party where Senator Bowen sat staking large sums on rouge-et-noir and losing at every turn of the wheel, he

---

1 Roulette.
2 Light or comic opera.
3 Short piece (in this case musical).

felt dejected at his own helplessness. Gaming was Senator Bowen's only vice, a legacy from the old days when as mate he played every night for weeks as the cotton steamer made her trips up and down the river highways in the ante-bellum days. Sumner determined to rescue the honest old man from the toils of these sharpers.[1] Just then Aurelia came up to him and touched his arm.

"I wish to speak with you, Bert, come with me."

He gave her his arm and they went to the vacant library. As they passed from view one man standing back of Senator Bowen's chair watching the game said to another:

"Sumner rich?"

"Very."

"It would be a fine thing for Miss Madison to catch him in the rebound. He seems fascinated."

"Indeed it would. And why not? She is of good blood, and he does not need money."

"Ah, no! only beauty and love. She is worthy of a coronet."[2]

The soft light of tender sympathy was on Aurelia's face. Sumner clasped both her hands in his and begged her to tell him all she knew of Jewel.

"That is why I brought you here," was her serious reply. "I mean to undo this tangled web which I have unwittingly woven."

"Is she well? Does she hate me? Dare I go to her?" he asked with passionate earnestness.

Disengaging one of her hands, Aurelia laid it on his shoulder, while she answered in soothing tones:

"Jewel is quite well, Bert dear, but she is allowing General Benson to monopolize her attention; in fact, I sometimes fear that the mischief is beyond repair and that she is pledged to him. But I am sure she loves you still. Trust a woman's intuitive powers. She cannot deceive me. Whatever she has done has been in a spirit of pique which needs but your presence to overcome. We will save her if it is not too late."

"Bless you for those words," he said, "your sympathy is very sweet to me."

"Be patient, and leave it all to me; I will bring you together again."

---

1 Swindling gamblers.

2 Small crown.

"You have filled my mind with forbodings," he said deject-edly, "I fear it is too late."

"Not too late, Bert; leave me the hope, at least, of redeem-ing myself in the eyes of Jewel. I have arranged for a meeting between you on Tuesday. On that day the Senator and Mrs. Bowen go to the President's reception. Jewel has a cold and will not be able to accompany them. She expects me to spend the evening with her. I waive my engagement in your favor, Bert; see that you improve your opportunity."

Tears filled her eyes, her voice broke, she was pale with emo-tion. She was proud of the intense feeling she displayed, and felt that she was acting her part splendidly. For a moment Sumner was speechless, then he kissed her hand and said in a broken voice, as he turned to go:

"God bless you, Aurelia."

★ ★ ★ ★ ★ ★

At four A.M., General Benson, Major Madison and Aurelia stood alone in the deserted drawing-room.

The Major waved in triumph two checks for large amounts, bearing Senator Bowen's signature.

"That's all right, Madison, but it is slow work—too slow for me. How are you getting on, Aurelia?"

She looked at him with an evil smile on her face that destroyed all its marvellous beauty: "I have told Cuthbert Sumner to call on Jewel, Tuesday evening. The Senator and his wife will be out, the girl alone. I think, General, you can do the rest, and settle the matter once for all."

"By jove, Aurelia, I will convince him of my triumph against all odds. You've earned your husband and your million."

CHAPTER XVIII.

The burst of gaiety which the ball brought into Jewel's life, made the succeeding days of gloom more depressing. Her high spirits had received a severe shock in her supposed discovery of Cuth-bert's treachery, from which they rallied with difficulty.

"Don't stand there, my darling, those large windows are always draughty."

"I feel nothing of the sort, mama; don't libel this beautiful house, if you please."

"Beautiful house indeed; I shall be glad when June is come. I long for the breeze of the ranch."

"There will be more snow by tomorrow, mama."

"Of course! It seems to me that everything is out of joint. Think of snow in Washington in March!"

Jewel left the window where the light was darkening. She smiled at Mrs. Bowen and one could see how wan and delicate she looked.

"Mama, you are pessimistic to-day," she said kneeling beside the fire and stretching out her hands to the blaze.

Mrs. Bowen made no reply. In truth, her heart was bitter within her breast. She made an effort to appear cheerful before Jewel, not altogether successful.

The two ladies were in the favorite lounging room of the family—the small reception room. Jewel's great mass of bright hair rolled at the back of her small head, seemed too heavy a weight for it, while the hand that held the fleecy shawl about her was so shadowy as to fill one with apprehension. Yet she did not complain, only her parents noted the change in her since the night of the great ball, with feelings of uneasiness.

"My dear," said the Senator to his wife in one of their conversations about the best course in the matter, "My dear, if it were left to me, I'd shoot Sumner on sight. Out in 'Frisco his life wouldn't be worth a cuss. I've as much as I can do to keep decent and not put a ball into his miserable carcass. Think of a feller philandering after two women to once, either of them handsome enough to satisfy any reasonable man even if he is dead sot on looks in a female. Blast my eyes, Mrs. Senator, it's lucky we start for 'Frisco as soon as the session closes. I'd not answer for holding in much longer.

"Who'd have believed it possible! Sumner seems such a decent feller. Talk about deceit in women! Women ain't in it compared with these Eastern raised gents they call men!"

Then Senator Bowen retired to his club to vent his rage in pushing billiard balls about. It was during one of his fits of impotent wrath that he fell into Major Madison's toils and became an easy victim.

"Oh! my dove," murmured Mrs. Bowen to herself, as she had murmured many a time during the past few weeks; "my gentle, proud, suffering flower, how I wish I could take the pain out of your young heart and bear it for you; it is so hard to see that look on your child face, and feel that the sunshine is gone for you, and then realize that with all my love I can do nothing—nothing, nothing. A woman's life is hard, hard, from the cradle to the grave. O, God! why were we made to bear all the punishment for Adam's fall! Why are men so cruel? Why did he win her heart to throw it one side as a worthless bauble?"

Mrs. Bowen was crocheting an afghan and the needle dropped from her long white fingers and a settled look of pain crept like a veil over the beautiful proud face as she gazed into the fire.

Aurelia had been to see Jewel, had told her with many tears and sobs, of the broken engagement between herself and Cuthbert, that they still loved each other, that Sumner blamed himself for believing that he had forgotten her (Aurelia) and had engaged himself to Jewel without realizing the true state of his feelings, and now he would never marry—neither of them felt that they could know happiness without the thought of Jewel's wrongs before them. Could they not be friends still, she and Jewel? She was so lonely and miserable feeling that she had brought so much suffering on her dear friend. Mrs. Bowen heard it all but deep in her heart was a doubt of the specious pleader.

"I wish we had not been so hasty, and had given Cuthbert a chance to explain," she remarked to Jewel one day.

"There is nothing to explain," replied Jewel lifting her head proudly. "I saw and heard it all for myself. He told me he had only met Aurelia casually at the Cape, leaving almost immediately; now I find beyond a doubt, that they were actually engaged. Nothing can alter the fact that he had something to conceal and for that reason deceived me. Then, too, papa has met him at the Major's, and has heard the gossip of the clubs. It proves itself, mama; there is nothing more to be said. I—I have learnt my lesson—I shall never be so foolish again. I have to thank Mr. Sumner for teaching me worldly wisdom."

"I had thought better things of Cuthbert. I would never have believed him to be the cruel, selfish man he has proved. Well, may he have some peace before he marries Aurelia, for I suppose it will end that way. He will be punished if he marries her or I greatly mistake her nature."

Jewel knelt on, gazing into the fire. She was silent for a time, and then she said gently:

"You dislike Aurelia, mama, simply for my sake. It is not like you to be unjust."

Mrs. Bowen glanced at her sharply.

"It is not that alone, Jewel, but I believe her false. I have a presentiment that there is something wrong. O, my darling, do be careful. I think it would kill your father if anything happened to you," exclaimed Mrs. Bowen as she folded her daughter in her loving arms.

Jewel answered her tender embrace with warm kisses.

"Dear mama, the sting is taken out of all the pain when I remember that no matter what comes my own darling father and mother see no fault in their dear girl."[1]

Ah! children who have not needed it yet, believe that the wound must be mortal that cannot be soothed by parental balm and oil. Those dear ones have the power to restore self-respect though they may be powerless to restore happiness. Mrs. Bowen put the girl from her and left the room.

"Yes, I, too, shall be glad to return to the ranch. It will be quiet and peaceful there. I shall forget."

She shivered. "Forget," she repeated, pressing her hands to her breast, and moving to and fro in agitation, "no, no! I shall never forget—I shall remember as long as I live."

She rose to her feet and began walking the length of the room. The opening of the door aroused her, and turning with a slight frown, she saw General Benson.

The frown deepened as she saw him place a basket of lovely flowers on a table. She did not desire him to bring her gifts; but this did not cause her pain. It was the vision of a by-gone day, when some one else was wont to come softly into the room with beautiful flowers.

Her face flushed for a moment, then became paler than ever. She gave General Benson her hand silently, he bit his lip when he saw how quickly she withdrew it.

"Sam told me I should find Mrs. Bowen here," he said courteously.

"Mama is in her room. I will ring and let her know you are here."

---

1 Lauren Dembowitz has shown in "Sources" that Hopkins derived much of the preceding passage from Annie Thomas's "A Last Chance" in *Frank Leslie's Popular Monthly* (1884).

"Wait one moment," he pleaded. "I have brought you some flowers, Miss Jewel."

"They are very beautiful," she answered coldly; "and you are very kind, General Benson."

"Flowers suit you," he said in his soft caressing voice, that had never failed him with other women, but which was wasted on Jewel. "You should always be surrounded with them, Miss Jewel."

She did not smile. This man's admiration jarred on her. Her father liked his pleasant ways and found him a good companion to wile away the hours, but somehow she could not assume the easy familiarity of friendship with him.

She took herself to task for her growing dislike of him. Why should she be so ungenerous to one so kind? Why should she shrink from him with a loathing she could not repress? She had never voiced her feelings but she knew that her mother felt with her toward this suave, diplomatic gentleman. She had once seen him kick the dog that followed him, cowed and faithful only through fear, and she disliked him for the cowardly act. She spoke to him about it.

"Oh, one must be in the fashion!" he replied, never dreaming of the anger and disgust beneath the girl's cold exterior. "And dogs were made to kick. People talk a lot of rubbish about the faithfulness of dogs. It's all bosh! Their devotion means dread of the whip, or a strong boot, Miss Jewel."

Jewel's disgust was so great that for the moment she lost all other feeling, every remnant of respect and liking fled. He had forgotten the incident; and though resenting the girl's coldness, he did not associate his own cruelty with it. In fact, he put it down to coquetry, and it only inflamed his admiration and strengthened his determination to make this girl his wife. He wondered if Senator and Mrs. Bowen would oppose him?

Jewel's stepmother was a woman of the world, and between General Benson and herself there was no great liking. He felt uneasy in her presence, that under her rather haughty manner a keen sight was hidden that read his motives. Senator Bowen was more to his liking. In reply to Mrs. Bowen's cautious questioning concerning General Benson, the Senator's answer was:

"The government, my dear, gives him its confidence by placing him in a responsible position. That is enough for me. Uncle Sam never employs rascals to transact his business."

Opposition or not, General Benson meant to win in the end. Aurelia might fail with Cuthbert, but he would win with Jewel. He was irritated by the delay; apart from his vanity which was injured by Jewel's indifference, it was time the engagement was announced. His creditors were unpleasantly pressing. His property in Baltimore was mortgaged up to its full value. There was nothing for it but this marriage with the California millionaire's heiress.

Heiresses were not easily found. It was only a question of time and management, and Jewel must be his wife.

"Yes, you are one of those beings for whom it seems flowers were especially created. I always think of you as a delicate lily or a white rose."

The girl's face flushed, but not with pleasure.

"Mama must see them. She will admire them," she said as she rang the bell, and sent a message to Mrs. Bowen.

General Benson bit his lip. He had intended speaking to her today, but it was not an easy thing to do. She kept him at bay.

"Have you seen Miss Madison lately?" he asked sauntering up to the fire. Jewel shook her head.

"Not this week," and the troubled look returned to her eyes.

"She is a great girl," said Benson with a laugh—he leaned against the over-mantel and stroked his moustache. "She and Sumner are going the pace. I suppose we cannot expect lovebirds to remember anything outside their paradise." Jewel shivered.

"She loves him still," he said to himself between his teeth. "Well, it is no matter; she may love him now, but I shall alter that when she is my wife."

Then with the innate cruelty of his nature he continued:

"Sumner is to be congratulated, if what I hear is true; the Madisons are a fine old Southern family, and Miss Aurelia is worthy of her race." He hid a smile behind his hand.

"It is quite refreshing in these matter-of-fact days to come upon a real genuine romance. Love, they say, is out of fashion; if so, I am afraid Sumner is a long way behind the times, for I am told he is madly in love. That I guessed the first time I saw them together. One could read his infatuation in his eyes. Miss Madison's magnificent beauty easily accounts for it. Her face is her fortune, most assuredly." Jewel drew herself away a few steps. The pain he hoped to give her was not there. She had schooled herself to bear hearing the news of the engagement at any time. He could arouse her indignation—pride; this he did successfully.

"Then it is settled. Aurelia is very beautiful," she said quietly. "She is my friend, and I think her one of the most beautiful women I have ever seen."

He smiled.

"Ah, pardon, Miss Jewel; I had forgotten while speaking that you were more than ordinarily interested. Always sweet and generous, Miss Jewel, most rarely so, for one beautiful woman seldom acknowledges another."

"Here is mama." Jewel turned to the door with a faint sigh of relief. "Will you excuse me, General Benson, I want to catch the next mail?"

General Benson did not stay much longer. He was not at his ease with Mrs. Bowen. He was furious with Jewel for retiring and leaving him with her mother. He set it down against her in his book of reckoning to be settled in a future not far-distant.

Mrs. Bowen went to Jewel after he was gone. "You have not looked at your flowers, Blossom," she said gently. Her daughter colored.

"They are very beautiful, but—"

"They give you no pleasure?"

"I do not like presents from General Benson."

"You do not like him?" queried her mother, stroking the wonderful coils of shining hair.

The girl shivered.

"No—no. I do not like him at all; he is very kind, but I cannot bring myself to like him, mama, dear."

Mrs. Bowen kissed her brow.

"Nor do I; he is a bad man and I shall find a way to stop his calling here." She paused a moment lost in deep thought. "Perhaps it is well that we do not return to Washington next fall. I am glad your father has so decided."

The small hours of the morning found Jewel still sitting before her bedroom fire. She had returned from a reception, and had dismissed her maid, telling Venus that she would manage without her.

She was thinking of words she had heard that confirmed the report that Sumner and Aurelia were engaged. She had not seen the latter for a number of days, but she felt that she might expect her at any moment to confirm the report. What is first love? Some say first love is "calf love," a silly infatuation for an insipid hero or heroine.

Others will tell you first love is the only true passion; that it comes but once to every human being; that the intense yearning for the sound of a beloved voice, the sight of an adored face, the clasp of a hand, only fills the heart once in a lifetime. The question as to whether it is the deepest love must be answered by each individual.

"The heart knoweth its own bitterness,"[1] says Holy writ. So also it knoweth its own joy. Jewel was a firm believer in the strength of first love. And now she found herself suffering the pangs of love despised, the anguish of disappointment, the humiliation of neglect. Ever before her inner sight was the merry dancing, daring, the glancing fun in those dark eyes so recently her sun. How little she had been to him that he could so soon forget.

Oh, they were beautiful eyes, she thought, with a stirring of the old rapture at her heart. What a noble face he has! high-bred, refined, and manly, too! There was not another man to compare with him; and—he belonged to another. A bitter pang smote upon her, a keen memory of the events of the past weeks. She wept over her baseless dreams, and prayed for strength to solve the problem of her life.

"How shall I meet him?" she asked herself. "How shall I be calm, conventional to Mr. and Mrs. Cuthbert Sumner?" Long she sat there pondering many things.

CHAPTER XIX.

The last of March came, but winter still lingered in the lap of spring. Jewel's couch was drawn up before the blazing fire; the parlor was snug and comfortable, just cosey enough for a semi-invalid. The room was half-panelled with oak, and the furniture was of the same material covered with bright silk and embroidered cushions.

Jewel was not well and had excused herself from attendance at the President's reception. Her mother had ensconced her in the small reception parlor promising to return early, and bidding

---

1 Proverbs 14.10.

her doze away the time until then. She was not asleep. Her eyes were open, and fixed upon the fire; they were filled with intense pain, and her hands were clenched, while now and then a shiver ran through her frame, as she turned restlessly from side to side.

She sought solitude that evening, and yet the sound of Sam's voice in the hall admitting a visitor whose tones betrayed Gen. Benson, was not distasteful to her.

He was very much at home now, and drew a low chair round between her and the fire, after bidding her good evening, took his place there, and gazed steadfastly into her face a few moments without speaking.

"Of what are you thinking?" he asked gently.

"I am thinking what a horrible thing it is that we women are always loving the wrong men—worthless, heartless men, who cannot appreciate in even a small degree the love we waste upon them."

He took one of her hands in his.

"Look at me," he said. "You are very young—you will get over this happening—this episode in the life of every young girl. Don't start. How can anyone who cares for you, help knowing that you have suffered through loving the wrong man? But time is a great healer. Now don't try to free your hand. It must belong to me some day, so why not let it rest in mine now?"

She shivered as she turned from him.

"You don't understand," she said speaking very low. "My heart is dead, or only so much alive that I can feel it ache. I can never love—never marry. I must go on living—expiating my wilful blindness in being so reckless as to love a—a villain with all my heart and soul."

The tears rolled slowly down her face.

"Won't you let me try to comfort you?" he asked.

She shook her head. "You cannot give me back the man I believed in," she replied.

Benson rose, frowning heavily,

"Can't I horsewhip him or do something to punish the scoundrel?"

"No, no!"

"You don't love him still?"

"No," she answered. "But I can never hate him. Don't let's talk about it any more," she continued wearily. "Dead loves are like dead people—talking will not bring them back."

"I will make you forget him some day," he said, kissing her hand.

"I wish you could," she replied with a sigh.

Benson felt encouraged, and determined to follow up his advantage.

"What has put you in this state?" he asked tenderly.

"Why are you not at the reception?" she laughed evasively.

"That is not answering my question?" he retorted. "Either you need a doctor or your distress of mind calls for an adviser. Shall I hold your hand, and see if I can mesmerize you into telling me all your thoughts?" he continued half-laughing. Jewel drew back in alarm. She raised herself on her arm and looked away from him into the fire.

"You have no right to question me as you know."

"Why won't you give me the right?" he asked earnestly. "Look, Jewel, I love you and trust you so much, I am ready to take you on any terms. I should be glad and proud to marry you tomorrow, and wait for time to bring me love."

"Why will you tease me?" she asked desperately. "Be my friend without asking reward, but never hope to be anything else."

The girl was sitting now on the couch that had served her for a resting place. She bowed her head; the long silken lashes lay on her cheeks.

He still held her hand; and as he gazed down upon her face, so pale and sorrowing, his pulses throbbed with greater passion.

"Jewel you are an angel! Be one to me. You have many years to live; you could not, would not pass them alone. Be merciful then to one who worships the ground you tread! I know my heart. It is yours. None other can, shall ever share it. Accept my love and me, my darling!"

He was bending over her, his breath ruffled the soft rings of her hair. His feverish earnestness moved her. She felt a great pity for him. For the time she forgot her repugnance.

"He feels as I feel," she thought.

What would she not have done for him in her compassion! Anything but what his lips pleaded for; that was impossible.

"I am so sorry—so very sorry!" she said, and the light of her eyes, even the touch of her fingers confirmed her words. "But you see I have no love to give."

"Jewel," lightly he placed his arm about her, "I give you my love; I ask but, in return, you. Let me have the right of loving you through life. I will be content; for I shall live in hope that my affection shall one day win yours. If you must think your whole first love given, let me hold the second place in your heart."

"Is second love possible?" she asked.

"Most surely. Give me that; I will be satisfied." Her lips moved; assent seemed to quiver on them; when, looking up, she gazed directly into Cuthbert Sumner's eyes. He had been waited upon to the room by Sam, and had stood there looking at them without being noticed so absorbed had they been in their conversation.

With a cry Jewel staggered to her feet.

"Jewel, Jewel, hear me," cried Sumner in desperation, "I pray you, before you part us forever. Do not be rash; for God's sake, let me speak, hear me!" She waved him back as he stepped toward her.

General Benson was bewildered; his active mind comprehended instantly the peril of the moment—the frustration of his plans if he hesitated an instant—and his ready wit saved him. It was the time for decisive action. With a swift movement he placed himself at Jewel's side, took her hand in his, and thus faced Sumner.

"Mr. Sumner, this intrusion is unwarrantable. Miss Bowen is my promised wife."

Cuthbert bowed his head, and turning, rushed from the room and from the house.

(To be continued.)

"DID IT EVER OCCUR TO YOU, CUTHBERT SUMNER, THAT YOU ARE THE VICTIM OF A PLOT?" *Colored American Magazine* frontispiece (September 1901). Schomburg Center for Research in Black Culture.

CHAPTER XX.[1]

Cuthbert Sumner tendered his resignation to General Benson to take effect at the close of the official year, and it was accepted. "I have no feeling but friendship for you, Mr. Sumner," said the General after he had folded the document away. "I hope and trust that whatever happens we shall remember each other without enmity," he continued in his sweet voice so effective with most people. "Still, feeling that it must be unpleasant for you to serve under me, when we consider existing circumstances, without doubt what you propose is the best course."

It was ten o'clock the next day and Sumner sat at his desk looking out occasionally at the gathering storm that threatened to send March out with tumultuous blustering winds and heavy rain. The secretary and the stenographer occupied the same apartment with the chief. The ceiling of the apartment was lofty, there were elegant paintings on the walls, and the furniture was luxurious. There were rich hangings at the windows, carpets and rugs on the floor, lounges were grouped about the spacious room giving it more the appearance of a boudoir than a public office. The style of the wardrobes ranged about the walls would lead one to infer that all the conveniences for dining or lodging could be easily found within its four walls. Nor would one have been mistaken in inferring such to be the case; indeed, the chief's lunch was generally served in this room in sumptuous style by his valet. It was rumored, too, that here gay spreads and bachelor parties were not unknown; happenings at which grave questions of state were sometimes decided.[2]

A warm fire burned in the grate for there was chill in the air that furnace heat did not entirely remove, and the large pile of blazing coals shed a glowing radiance of cheerfulness on all around.

---

1 SYNOPSIS OF CHAPTERS XVII TO XIX. [The synopsis of Chapters I to XVI has not been repeated here. See Appendix A for the full text.] Jewel breaks her engagement with Sumner. Refuses to see him or read his letters. Accepts General Benson's attentions and at last their engagement is announced.

2 Lauren Dembowitz has shown in "Sources" that Hopkins derived much of this scene from Garry Moss's "The Mystery of the Hearth: A True History of Official Life in Washington" in *Frank Leslie's Popular Monthly* (1884).

General Benson, it was evident, though a servant of the people, was using their resources freely to gratify an extravagant taste. His was the life of a popular official floating at the ease of his own sweet will.

The only other occupant beside Cuthbert and Benson was Elise Bradford the stenographer. This woman was elegantly attired, and here again one noticed how utterly out of keeping her dress was with the work supposed to be performed by a simple government clerk. She was tall, fair and pale, with a countenance that impressed one with its resigned expression and sad dignity.

General Benson sat before his splendidly covered table where cut-glass bottles of eau de cologne gleamed, vases of fragrant flowers charmed the eye, and ornamental easels of costly style held pictures of fashionable ladies. He was looking over some papers which had just been submitted by Cuthbert. This morning he was abstracted and silent. Finally he called Sumner to him in a recess of a curtained window and said:

"Sumner, I have a favor to ask of you."

"I shall be happy to grant it if it is in my power, General."

"Thanks, I felt sure such would be your answer. I shall have to ask you and Miss Bradford to work overtime tomorrow and Sunday. This work must have our special attention. It is of such a nature that I can not confide it to an ordinary clerk. I cannot superintend the work myself because a party is to leave here on Saturday, myself among the number, for New York, on official business—two or three Senators and a Cabinet official to represent the President. We shall not return for ten days and I shall depend upon you to keep the office business in hand."

"I will do all that I can willingly," replied Sumner.

"And I think I'll go off now. The time is short until five to-morrow. I have some preparations to make. You may as well take charge at once."

Leaving Sumner he stepped to the side of Miss Bradford and engaged in a whispered conversation. Cuthbert was a discreet person and gave no heed to the couple. He was used to the manners of many high officials with their female clerks, and paid no attention to what did not concern him. He had observed that an apparent intimacy existed between his chief and Miss Bradford. If they knew that he had noticed them they gave no sign that his knowledge was an annoyance. His presence was treated with the utmost decorum.

The whispered talk kept on for some time. Finally, whatever subject had been under discussion seemed to have been satisfactorially arranged, and the chief arose from the seat he had occupied beside the lady and shook her hand warmly, with the words:

"At Easter then without fail."

"Poor Jewel," thought Cuthbert, "what will be her fate when she is the wife of this man who is but a reformed rake seeking to re-instate himself in society by a high political position and a rich marriage."

As the thought lingered in his mind, General Benson paused beside his desk. Sumner could not refrain from giving him an admiring glance nor could he wonder at the infatuation of most women for the handsome chief who stood there drawing on his gloves, his costly fur-lined coat unbuttoned and nearly sweeping the carpet giving an added charm to his handsome face, elegant figure and gracious manner.

"I have intrusted you with a delicate piece of business, Mr. Sumner." His voice was impressive. "The official relations between us have always been coordinate in character. I am confiding in you now as I would in a personal friend. You will find some additional papers to be collated in my desk," he continued drawing him behind the rich folds of the curtains back of the official desk. His gaze was fixed full in Sumner's face with such earnestness and anxiety that at once appealed to the secretary's sympathy. Sumner's face was like an open book in its candor and innocence of guile, as he replied quietly:

"You may trust me, General Benson, to respect your confidence. Personal matters have no entrance where they would interfere with obedience to my superiors."

"And, see here, Sumner, you may be detained later to-morrow night than tonight. Your work will probably keep you until sharp midnight, perhaps past. I have given the watchman notice of your being here by my orders. Here is my private entrance key and you can let yourself and Miss Bradford out without trouble. See that everything is safely closed up. You shall be handsomely compensated for your extra labor, although I know that you have no thought of the money," he added in answer to Sumner's deprecating wave of the hand. "Good-bye," and giving him his hand, the chief shook his warmly, and left the room.

They heard him descending the stairs, talking and laughing with messengers and others employed about the building, in the genial way for which he was noted among government employees.

CHAPTER XXI.

Time and tide wait for no man;[1] brains may throb, and hearts may ache or break, but the world rolls on just the same, for weal and woe,[2] whether the grim skeleton that comes an unbidden guest on so many a man's hearth is shrouded in elegance or bare in all its appalling hideousness.

It was not until two P.M. of Sunday that the secretary and stenographer had time to rest as they neared the close of their labors. Sumner felt a weariness of spirit and a dull aching of the heart that was not due to overwork. Worriment had removed the fresh heartful bloom from his face, but the paleness and thinness added to its refinement and intellectuality; while the restless feverish dilation of his dark eyes rendered them singularly striking and brilliant. More than once during this wretched time he had been possessed with a longing to be back with his father in their quiet New England home.

"Yes, this shall be my last year in politics. I'll go home and take up the business for which I was born; it will please my father."

As he turned to resume his work with a sigh, he became conscious that Miss Bradford was watching him. There had been a time when he had felt a passing admiration for the good-looking stenographer, and had paid her some attention, but after he met Jewel he had never pretended to give her a second thought.

She, on her side, had not resented his desertion but always seemed to retain a genuine regard for him which had shown itself in many neighborly acts of kindness which the close intimacy of office life often brings about between women and men. She had been rattling the keys of her typewriter at a furious rate of speed all day, and now, with a final pull of the carriage, finished her work. Then she rose with a sigh, crossed the room and flung

---

1 Proverb that appears in Geoffrey Chaucer's Prologue to the *Clerk's Tale* (line 119).

2 For good or bad.

herself down on one of the couches opposite Sumner's desk, evidently bent on conversation.

"Mr. Sumner, you look—oh, I don't know how you look, but I should say a rest would do you good."

"I shall have one when the vacation comes. I am going home and I shall not return to Washington."

"Are you going for good?" she asked in a surprised tone.

"Yes," he answered as he adjusted a pile of manuscript, and began folding up the papers scattered over his desk. "Washington holds no charm for me."

She was silent for a time and as she sat buried in deep thought she tapped the floor with one foot in restless fashion. At length she said:

"Don't think me intrusive, or that I seek to harrow your feelings, but isn't this sudden resolve the result of the misunderstanding between you and Miss Bowen?"

"I will answer you as frankly as you have asked, Miss Bradford; it is so."

There followed another pause, a silence so long that the young man thought that she had forgotten his presence. Suddenly she spoke again.

"Mr. Sumner, I like you; I trust you; why I know not, for my experience in life has not been of so pleasant a nature as to cause me to trust anyone; not a man, surely. But today I feel a desire to talk on forbidden subjects, to take someone into my confidence."

Sumner looked at her keenly as he said significantly:

"It is a safe rule, Miss Bradford, to keep one's own counsel."

"I feel impelled to tell you what I am about to disclose, by an unseen power. Do you not believe in unseen forces influencing our acts?" she asked wistfully.

"I cannot deny that I have sometimes felt the same influence of supernatural powers that you speak of, and I do firmly trust that the world of shadows and mystery to which we are all bound may be one of infinite love, infinite calm and rest."

"For those who have been upright here," while a look of pain crossed her face. "But what of those among us who have been guilty of many sins? That is the thought that haunts me to-night." She pushed her hair from her face with one hand as she looked up at him.

"Why trouble ourselves with such questions, Miss Bradford? Why not simply trust the judgment that sees not as man sees?"

She felt calmed as she looked into the true, earnest face opposite her. "Thank you," she said at last, simply. Then—

"May I tell you?"

"Whatever confidence you honor me by giving shall be sacredly respected."

"I know that. Did I not tell you that I trusted you? But you have my permission to tell Jewel Bowen as much as you think fit, for it is her due."

Sumner colored as he said:

"I am not on terms of intimacy with Miss Bowen."

"I know that, too," she replied impatiently, "but you probably will be after you hear what I have to tell you. I, too, am about to leave Washington. When I leave the office to-night I shall never return. Easter is two weeks off, and at Easter I am to be married to General Benson."

"Married—General Benson! Impossible! You jest!" exclaimed the startled man.

"To General Benson," she repeated emphatically.

"But—Miss Bowen—"

"Will have a welcome release," she broke in. "It is a long-delayed ceremony that should have been performed five years ago. I have a son four years old Mr. Sumner!"

Sumner could not answer her. He stared at the woman before him with unseeing eyes. He could not believe that he had heard aright.

"A son four years of age!" he repeated mechanically in shocked surprise. "This is most extraordinary! How can it be possible?"

"No wonder you are incredulous. Wait, wait!" she went on, "give me time. I will tell you all; it is your right to know. It has all been arranged so suddenly that my brain is in a whirl—I cannot think!"

She flung herself down against the cushions of the couch, and endeavored to grow calm. Sumner waited, disturbed, unhappy, heartsick, over this scene, fearing he knew not what. He watched her labored breathing, her clenched hands, and there was a long pause.

Sumner cast anxious glances over at the bowed head opposite him supported on its owner's hand. The fire blazed cheerily, and outside the wind rose, whirling the rain in great sheets against the window panes. It was a wild night.

Finally Elise Bradford sat up pushing her hair back restlessly from her temples, and faced him white and agitated.

"All this misery that you have endured for the past month," she began slowly,—"all the sorrow, you owe to one man. He has tortured you, fooled you, deceived you—Yes, it is true; but I—God help me—I love him."

"I do not comprehend your meaning, Miss Bradford, to whom do you refer?" he asked soothingly, for there was the glitter of fever in her eyes.

"Silence!" she interrupted sternly. "I must tell you certain things for your own welfare and the welfare of the girl you love. I dare not hide them. Perhaps—who knows—it may be put down to my credit in that great future life toward which we are all journeying. In the years that are coming, when you are both happy and forgetful of this present miserable time, remember me and my misery with pity."

Sumner could only wait in pained surprise for her to continue. She pressed her hands convulsively to her heart, as she sat there white as death, and trembling all over.

"Did it ever occur to you, Cuthbert Sumner, that you are the victim of a plot?"

"You will speak in riddles, Miss Bradford. I must confess that I do not understand you."

"And yet you are a man of remarkable intelligence, and not a child in the world's ways. I cannot swear to it, but I believe that you have fallen into the net of two adventurers and a daring adventuress. Have you noticed any intimacy between General Benson and the Madisons?"

"No; they seem to be merely chance acquaintances."

"And yet, they are partners in crime, and I believe that General Benson introduced the Bowens to the Madisons."

"Great heavens! No!" cried Sumner great light breaking in upon him at the bare possibility of such a thing being true. "Miss Bradford, are you sure?" he asked hurriedly.

"I am almost certain of the truth of what I say; you can easily ascertain if I am correct in my suspicions. I believe the intention was, your fortune for Aurelia Madison, Miss Bowen's for the General."

"But where do you get your information? Upon what are your suspicions based? Surely you have something to go upon," cried Sumner recovering from his first bewilderment.

"How can I tell you? Oh! The shame of it all will kill me," she said as she drew a long shuddering breath.

"Your distress pains me, Miss Bradford," said Cuthbert gently as he watched the wretched girl; he was moved more than he cared to show—indignant—furious over the conduct of this scoundrel in a high place. He went to one of the wardrobes and opened the door disclosing a compartment used as a wine closet. He quickly filled a glass from a costly cut-glass decanter, and carried it to the half-fainting woman urging her to drink it.

She took it eagerly from his hand and drained the glass.

"Yes, yes, I must go on. It is part of my punishment—my atonement! It is such misery, shame!" she sobbed brokenly. "I heard he was about to marry Miss Bowen. I accused him of treachery toward you in the matter. I threatened him with exposure. I told him that he must make atonement to me and the child at once. He must do it or I would speak; I would go to Miss Bowen with the whole miserable story."

"And he?" questioned Sumner gently, yet sternly, stifling his own feelings for the sake of the heart-broken woman before him, giving out strength and protection with womanly tenderness to soothe. "Tell me all, and be sure that I will speak of nothing that you desire kept secret."

"To have you understand the man known as General Benson, I must tell you a portion of my history."

"Excuse me," broke in Sumner, "you say 'known as General Benson,' is not that his true name?"

"No; it is not. And I cannot give you the true one. I have my own thoughts about it, however. When I was eighteen years of age, I came from Kentucky, where I was born, to Washington seeking employment.

"I was left an orphan while an infant, and brought up by my aunt who was too poor to support me after I entered womanhood. She did the best for me that she could, however, and I started out with high hopes, telling her that I should soon be able to repay her for her kindness and care. I had heard much of the large salaries paid to government clerks, and determined to seek employment here.

"Arriving in the city, I went to call upon the congressman from our district to whom I brought letters of introduction. He received me kindly, and said that he would do his best to have me appointed. After a week he sent me word to call at the

Treasury Building. There he introduced me to General Benson who wanted a clerk. The General immediately engaged me, and it is needless for me to say that I was overjoyed at my good fortune. I was able to send my aunt money, and for a time I was perfectly happy. It is useless to dwell on the details—I wish to hurry over this part of my life—suffice it that in six months' time I had become the chief's victim.

"I am abhorrent to you, no doubt. You who have been rich all your life may despise me; but I had tasted poverty, I appreciated its effect on my future welfare, and I sickened at the thought."

She paused a moment to take breath, for she had spoken rapidly, as if eager to have done with the shameful and painful details. "Official wealth, power and opportunity were my ruin. I was led to confide in the chief by his high position; and he, like others in such places, deceived me and betrayed that confidence. He was my first lover, for I was but eighteen, and I loved him as we always love the first man who teaches us what love is. I admired his genial ways, his distinguished air, and even this success in his vices was a source of pride to me. He took advantage of my youth to mold me to his fancy, and make me like himself. Oh, I can never make you realize the depravity of our elegant chief.

"For a long time he was content with my love. I was young enough and pretty enough to satisfy even him. But after a while he met Aurelia Madison, and then my agony began."

"What!" exclaimed Sumner, "do you know what you say? Aurelia Madison one of General Benson's mistresses?"

"That is not the worst thing about her," replied the woman with a bitter smile. "Will you believe me when I tell you that she is a quadroon?"[1]

"Impossible! you rave!" almost shouted the young man.

"I would it were not true. Yes, she is a quadroon, the child of Major Madison's slave, born about the time the war broke out. That is why the two men find in her a willing tool."

"My God!" exclaimed Sumner as he wiped the perspiration from his face, "a negress! this is too horrible." Repeated shocks had unnerved him, and he felt weak and bewildered.

"Do not blame her. Fate is against her. She is helpless. The education of generations of her foreparents has entered into her

---

1 A person who is one-quarter black.

blood. I should feel sorry for her if I could, but I feel only my own misery and degradation. I am selfish in my despair. Happy, prosperous people sympathize with the woes of others, but sometimes I feel like laughing at their mimic woes, my own are so much greater in comparison.

"Yet Aurelia in a measure deserves our pity. The loveliness of Negro women of mixed blood is very often marvellous, and their condition deplorable. Beautiful almost beyond description, many of them educated and refined, with the best white blood of the South in their veins, they refuse to mate themselves with the ignorant of their own race. Socially, they are not recognized by the whites; they are often without money enough to buy the barest necessities of life; honorably, they cannot procure sufficient means to gratify their luxurious tastes; their mothers were like themselves; their fathers they never knew; debauched white men are ever ready to take advantage of their destitution, and after living a short life of shame, they sink into early graves. Living, they were despised by whites and blacks alike; dead, they are mourned by none. You know yourself Mr. Sumner, that caste as found at the North is a terrible thing. It is killing the black man's hope there in every avenue; it is centered against his advancement. We in the South are flagrant in our abuse of the Negro but we do not descend to the pettiness that your section practises. We shut our eyes to many things in the South because of our near relationship to many of these despised people. But black blood is everywhere—in society and out, and in our families even; we cannot feel assured that it has not filtered into the most exclusive families. We try to stem the tide but I believe it is a hopeless task."

Sumner listened to her bound by the horrible fascination of her words. At last he said:

"But a white man may be betrayed into marrying her. I certainly came near to it myself."

"Very true; and if she had been a different woman, she would have succeeded, you would have been proud of your handsome wife because of your ignorance of her origin. As life, real life, has unfolded to my view, I have come to think that there is nothing in this prejudice but a relic of barbarism."

"Perhaps your reasoning is true; I will not attempt a denial. But I am thankful for my deliverance."

"Your feeling is natural; certainly, I do not blame you," she said, and after a slight pause resumed her narrative.

"One day the General came to me and told me that we must part. 'I owe you many obligations for your kindness. You have made the past few months very pleasant; of course you knew it was only for awhile, and that it must end some day. It is past now, and we will each go our way just as if we had never met. You must know that with men of the world these things are very natural and very pleasant. Here is some money'; and he thrust a well-filled purse in my hands.

"My heart was filled with terror and agony. 'But you said that you loved me.' I managed to falter in a dazed way. 'Well, perhaps, for the moment. But—can't you understand these things? I will spare you as much as I can; if I am harsh you press me to it.' He spoke lightly, carelessly, to me as I stood before him crushed for all eternity—to me, who had fallen, without a thought of resistance, under the charm of his manner and beauty, that have ruined more than one woman among those who are above me in wealth and position. It is left for men to change quickly. He seemed dumb, frozen, dead to all feeling. His heart and mind were filled with the dazzling beauty of his new love—the Negress Aurelia Madison. He had nothing left for me—not even pity. Then be continued,—

"'Elise, it is particularly necessary for my future plans that this affair of ours be kept secret. If you bury it in your heart, and seal your lips upon it, you shall be recompensed finally, I will never lose sight of you and the boy, but direct that a large sum shall be paid to you yearly. If not—people have died for a less offense than that.'

"While he was talking I was thinking deeply and rapidly. I felt that my only chance lay in matching his cunning with diplomacy. I made up my mind to compromise the matter. He was stronger than I; I could do nothing at present. Finally I told him that I would agree to all he asked if he would allow me to retain my position in the office with him, and would provide for the boy and educate him.

"This he agreed to do, and there has been a sort of armed neutrality between us ever since. I have learned much by being here. I know enough to ruin him. I planned for it and I have succeeded. He dares not go against me now, and so he has promised marriage, and I shall once more hold my head up among honest women."

Sumner felt a great wave of pity sweep over him at the thought of this delicate woman hoping to cope with the cunning deviltry of the man she had unmasked; but he could not find it in his heart to speak one discouraging word. His eyes filled with tears which were no shame to his manhood.

"Where is the child?" he asked when he could collect his scattered thoughts enough to speak.

"In Kentucky with my aunt," she replied naming a town.

"If what you tell me is true, and knowing what I do, I cannot doubt your story, General Benson is a consummate villain, a dangerous man," said Sumner as he paced the floor in excitement and wrath. "It is not possible that such things can be and go unpunished."

"You know now why I think it all a plot against you. Cannot you see for yourself?"

"Yes; I can never repay you for what you have done."

"Do not mention it. I shall be repaid if only you circumvent that woman, and all is made right between you and Miss Bowen."

It had grown very dark and Sumner lighted the gas.

"I will call a herdic[1] and see you home," he said, "if you will come now. It is long past the dinner hour. We have been here long enough. I feel it impossible to stop here longer, the place stifles me."

"I cannot go yet," she replied, "I have papers to sort and many articles to destroy as well as to gather up. I never wish to see the place again."

"I will stay then until you are ready to go."

"No; that is not necessary, thank you. Give me the key. I will lock up and leave it with the watchman."

"Well, then, if you are not afraid," he said reluctantly. He was dazed by all he had heard and wished to be alone. When he was ready to leave, he took her hand in his and shook it warmly.

"Good-bye, my friend; you have given me renewed hope."

In after years, Cuthbert remembered her face with its varying, changing tints—hope and despair—each struggling for the mastery.

"Yes," she said softly, "I am your friend, but friendships are short—made to be severed. Still, I am sure we shall meet again. How strange it is that lives are touching thus all the time— strangers yesterday, today helping each other—let us hope so

---

1 Two-wheeled carriage.

at least—touching—parting—but not forgotten—not utterly forgotten."

There was a new dignity in her manner that he had never noticed in the silent stenographer. But there was still a weary, listless tone in her voice.[1]

He pressed her white fingers with his strong eager hand, feeling his heart throb with suppressed excitement—the joy of living once more. He lifted her cold hand and touched it with his lips.

"Good-bye, then, once more; some one said once that meant 'God bless you'; I could say no more if I knew that our parting would be eternal which it is not. I want you to know Jewel."

She looked at him steadily a moment, then her face fell; a slight tremor passed over her face; she was unaccustomed to the chivalrous treatment that men give to women whom they respect. The hand he had kissed fell to her side. As he turned to close the door of the apartment, she was still standing where he had left her, with listless hands and bent head.

CHAPTER XXII.

Cuthbert's mind was in a tumult as he walked down the stairs and through the corridors of the great building. His strained nerves relaxed; he felt the intense relief of a man who throws a heavy load from his shoulders.

He accepted without question the story told him by Miss Bradford and her suggestion of a vile plot by these arch-conspirators to gain possession of a fortune. The story was feasible whichever way he viewed it. "Yes, it must be so." The more he thought of it, the more he wondered at his own blindness in not solving the problem before. His eyes flashed, and he clenched his hands in anger. His mood boded ill for his enemies. Already his mind was filled with plans to disconcert the plotters.

He hailed a passing herdic and was driven to his rooms. He felt sick, giddy, his hands trembled. This unexpected revelation, while it caused him intense happiness, nearly overcame

---

1 Lauren Dembowitz has shown in "Sources" that Hopkins derived much of the dialogue in this scene from a story entitled "Alixe," which was published anonymously in *Frank Leslie's Sunday Magazine* (1882).

him. He longed to be alone in his rooms where he could think over what he had heard. But in the midst of his joy and his plans to see Jewel and explain this great wrong and mystery to her, came thoughts—sorrowful thoughts of the woman who had befriended him. What would be her fate? he asked himself. Surely it was but a question of time before the chief, with his method of living, would disappear beneath the maelstrom[1] of his own unprincipled acts.

It was nine o'clock when he arrived at home thoroughly worn out. A splendid fire in the grate bade him a cordial welcome. John served him a good dinner. After making a pretense of eating, Sumner sat with his wine untasted on the table before him, smoking and staring into the fire. He sat there for hours smoking and thinking. Troubled thoughts disturbed him, shadows lingered on his face which the pleasant surroundings had not the power to dispel. He was deeply impressed by the insignificant trifles that had solved the secret of this wicked plot, in a skilful woman's hands, and more than thankful to know that through her he held the threads of the labyrinth in his own strong hands. He retired to rest worn out in mind and body. Physical and mental exhaustion brought some degree of calm, and he slept, but his slumber was fitful and broken, and he could still hear the moaning of the wind and the beating of the rain against the window panes. Mingled with these sounds were distorted dreams—bearing a shadowy relation to the scenes through which he had just passed.

In those uneasy slumbers he dreamed that he was in a deep, dark pit. Darkness blacker than the blackest night was all about him; but as he lay there, for he dreamed that he was reclining on the floor of the pit, suddenly beneath his body he felt a movement as of a monstrous body—a regular undulating movement. Then it seemed borne in upon his mind that the pit was a snake's den; the monsters—three in number—pythons of immense size to whom human victims were offered as sacrifices. He had been thrown to these sacred reptiles as their next victim. In his dream, horror and terror paralyzed both thought and action for a time. Then he realized that he must act quickly. As he looked into the dense darkness a tremulous ray of light pierced the gloom of the pit and for an instant Jewel's face smiled upon him,

---

1 Dangerous whirlpool.

then disappeared. In that instant of light he discerned a ladder leading to an opening at the top of the pit, through which he must have been thrown into the horrible dungeon. As he calculated his chances of escape, he heard the dragging and sweeping of a long ponderous body in motion moving toward him. With a determined wrench he broke the spell that bound him, sprang up the ladder and reached the blessed light of day.

He awoke bathed in perspiration, shivering with horror, his heart beating with fear. He lay there a while trying to shake off the effects of his dream, but for a time it seemed impossible; it would not slip away as dreams do; it was too vivid not to leave unpleasant thoughts behind.

Finally he sprang up. It was very early but he rang for John, and took time to make a careful and refreshing toilet. By half-past eight he was ready for the excellent breakfast brought by the delighted John who had not seen his master so cheerful for many weeks.

He wrote a note and despatched it by messenger to the department saying that he would be late, and to refer all matters to the assistant secretary until he came.

He wandered aimlessly about the rooms wondering how he could possibly content himself while he waited for a conventional hour to come for a call on Jewel. At length he resolved to go for a walk, and was just getting into his street garments when there was a loud ring at the outer door of the suite. John answered it. He heard a question in a man's voice:

"Is Mr. Sumner at home?"

Then as he turned from the window to answer John's call, he saw his servant's frightened face, and close behind him an officer. Sumner stood still in amazement.

"Mr. Cuthbert Sumner?" asked the officer.

"I am Mr. Sumner. What is your business with me?"

"Well, sir," said the man laboriously, "there's been a murder up at the Treasury Building there. Young woman found this morning. You're wanted to be at the inquest."

"But I know nothing of this affair. Who's the woman?"

The officer pulled a paper from his pocket and held it out awkwardly toward him:

"Sorry, sir, to disturb you. Miss Bradford is the victim; you are held on suspicion being the last gent, or person, seen in her company. Charge of murder!"

"Murder!" cried the horrified man.

The officer nodded as he replied:

"Ay, sir; and bad enough it is. Prussic acid was the means, sir, given in a glass of wine. Miss Elise Bradford, clerk at the Treasury Building. Body discovered by watchman early this morning."

"Great heavens!" said Sumner reeling back, "it can't be possible that the girl is dead—murdered!"

The officer's look said plainly enough,—"you know all about it." The police are quick to make victims.

"I know nothing about it. She was all right when I left her at eight yesterday after we had finished our work. I—"

"Stop, sir," said the man. "I am bound to warn you that whatever you say will be used as evidence against you."

"Let it be so," returned Sumner haughtily. "I have nothing to hide. I am absolutely guiltless of the crime as you will find."

"Maybe so, sir," replied the man civilly. "But meanwhile you must come with me."

Sumner was calm and self-possessed.

"You are free to examine my effects," he said. "I shall be ready to go with you in five minutes."

"I cannot lose sight of you, sir."

"Certainly not."

The faithful John stood by loudly protesting against the indignities put upon his master. Sumner gave him a few directions about the rooms. A herdic was called, and in five minutes the policeman and his prisoner were driven to the Police Court. The police evidence was given, and the prisoner having been remanded until after the inquest, was removed to the cells.

(To be continued.)

CHAPTER XXIII.[1]

Marthy Johnson knelt on the kitchen floor surrounded by heaps of fine white clothing sorting them into orderly piles. It was six o'clock on Monday morning. The gaudy little clock on the mantel, flanked by red vases elaborately gilded and filled with paper sunflowers, had just finished striking. The coffee pot was giving out jets of fragrant steam, and the pan of hot corn pone was smiling in an inviting manner from the back of the range. The square deal table between the windows held plates, mugs, knives and forks for three. The woman sang as she sorted:

> "Oh, the milk white hosses, milk white hosses,
> Milk white hosses over in Jerden,
> Milk white hosses, milk white hosses,
> I long to see that day.

> "Oh, hitch 'em to the chariot, hitch 'em to the chariot,
> Hitch 'em to the chariot over in Jerden,
> Hitch 'em to the chariot, hitch 'em to the chariot,
> I long to see that day."[2]

We last saw Marthy on the Enson plantation. Years have added to her weight, but other than that, hers is the same frank, fun-loving countenance, with its soft brown tint, its dazzling eyes and teeth.

---

1 SYNOPSIS OF CHAPTERS XX TO XXII. [The synopsis of Chapters I to XIX has not been repeated here. See Appendix A for the full text.] Cuthbert Sumner resigns his position under General Benson resolved to leave Washington. The latter goes on a trip with other government officials and leaves Sumner in charge of the office. He and Miss Bradford are obliged to work overtime on special work. She tells him of her former relations with General Benson, and says by threatening exposure she has induced him to promise her marriage at Easter. Sumner leaves her to finish her work at the office, stunned by what he has heard. She is murdered. The next morning he is arrested.

2 From "Gideon's Band," a plantation song. After the Civil War, both former abolitionists who established schools for newly freed blacks and certain members of the Ku Klux Klan referred to themselves as "Gideon's Band." For Gideon's role in the Bible, see Judges 6–8.

Her tidy calico gown was hidden by an immense blue-and-white-checked apron, and a snowy towel tied turban fashion hid her soft crinkly hair.

"Reckon I'd better fry that ham; it's gittin' on toward seven right smart," said Marthy with a glance at the clock. "My word, but where is mammy! I's clean worried out of my wits 'bout the ol' [lady.][1] Oliver—oh—Oliver!" she cried, opening a door which led from the kitchen to the regions above.

"What's wanting, mummy?" was wafted back in a male voice just turning into manhood.

"Your granny, Oliver; you must go hunt her child. I never knowed her to stay away all night but once befo'. You mus' git your breakfas' an' hunt her."

"Granny's all right, ma. I'm busy. Got a thesis for first recitation this morning. 'Deed I can't spare the time to go way over to the treasury from Meridian hill."[2]

"You, Oliver, you; move yourse'f now, hyar me? Your pa's never 'roun' when he's wanted, an' your sister's slavin' herse'f like a nigger to help ejekate yer. My Lord, how worthless men folks is! You've got a *teaseus*, have you?" she continued, waxing more wroth each moment. "An' your granny that's made of you like you was a baby may be daid up thar in the treasury or moulderin' in some alley an' you hollerin' down these stairs to me that you can't go an' holp her 'cause you's got a *teaseus*. I 'spec's we's all made a fool of you a-gettin' you into college. You's jes' like yer daddy; you's the born spit of him. My word, if you don't stir them long legs o' yourn out o' this lively, I'll take you down, sure's I'm yer mammy; I'll take yer down if you was as big as a house." The flood of angry words ended in a flood of tears. Her face was buried in the ample folds of her gingham apron when Oliver entered the kitchen.

He was a good-looking lad, tall and slender, a shade lighter brown than his mother, but with her pleasant, kindly face, laughing eyes and fun loving countenance. He had a gay and fearless bearing that was the pride of Marthy's heart. She often told her

---

1 This word is missing from the original installment in the *Colored American Magazine*. Marthy refers to Aunt Henny as "the ol' lady" later in this chapter.

2 Now part of Meridian Hill Park near the Adams Morgan section of Washington, DC.

mother in confidence, when Oliver was out of hearing:

"Mammy, yer gran'son's a born gin'ral; I never seen any man to 'pare with the swing dat's on him outside o' ol' Gin'ral Burnsis."[1]

And in this opinion Aunt Henny joined.

"Now, ma, don't cry," said the boy putting his arm about his mother's neck and kissing her cheek. "I'm going right off. I'm as fond of granny as can be. Don't now go and work yourself all up. I'm going this blessed moment." Marthy cried comfortably on the shoulder of her big son and allowed him to coax her into a better frame of mind. "You are a good boy, Ollie, and I didn't mean all them hard things I jes' said, honey. Don' you go an' lay 'em up agin me, son; your ol' mammy's jes' worried to death."

"Well, I ain't like dad, am I, ma?"

"No, bless yer heart, honey; yer ain't. You an' Venus is my comfits. Lawd, what a mis'able ol' 'ooman I'd be without you chilluns."

Marthy made Oliver sit down to his breakfast, waiting on him with a mother's fondness, piling his plate with the delicious fried ham and the smoking corn pone, and pouring his coffee with care.

"Do you know, ma," said Oliver between generous mouthfuls of bread and great gulps of coffee, as he ate with the hearty enjoyment of youth, "when I get through college, you shan't do a thing but wear a black silk dress every day and fold your hands and rock. I'm sick of seeing you in the washtub and Venus running to wait on the ladies fit to break her neck. I'm going to take care of you both."

"When you 'spec' that time goin' ter come, silly chile? Yer mammy 'spec' to wurk 'tell she draps inter the grave. Colored women wasn't made to take their comfit lak white ladies. They wasn't born fer nuthin' but ter wurk lak hosses or mules. Jes' seems lak we mus' wurk 'tell we draps into the grave."

"It won't be so always, ma. You'll see."

"Does you think money's jes' a-growin' on bushes ready to shuck into your hand when you gits through college? Pears lak to me, Oliver, you'd better make up yer min' to hussle aroun' fer awhile. I don' want ter feel that a chile o' min's too biggotty

---

1 Perhaps William Wallace Burns (1825–95), a brigadier general of the Union Army in the Civil War.

to do anything hones' fer a livin'. Don' you turn up yer nose at washin', an' yer may jes' thank God ef you gits a 'ooman when you git jined[1] that'll help you out in that business when college learnin' ain't payin'. An' don' spend yer extra money on silk dresses fer no 'ooman to lay roun' in. Caliker's done me all my life an' I ain't the worst 'ooman in the wurl' neither."

"Well, I'll wark fer you my own self, and I'll make money enough to keep you like a lady, college or no college."

"I wish it mote be so; but I jes' trimbles to have you talk that a-way, honey; jes' keep a still tongue and saw wood. Don't speak about your plans beforehan'. Never let anybody know what you reckon on doin' in the future 'cause the devil is always standin' 'roun' listenin' to you, an' that gen'man jes' nachally likes to put his cloven foot into a good basket of aigs an' smash 'em. 'Member what yer ma tells yer, honey."

"Now, ma, you don't believe all them old signs about hoo-dooing and such stuff. There isn't a thing in it, it's nothing but superstition."

"Don't talk to me 'bout yer suferstition; there is some things in this wurl that college edication won't 'splain, an' you can't argify an' condispute with 'em, neither. I've had my trials, Oliver, but tryin' to bring you an' yer sister to a realisin' sense of the sin in the wurl is hard on me, an' it lays on my mind. Now las' night I had a dream that a ghos' stood right up side 'o the bed lookin' at me. That's turrible bad luck; an' its bein' a female ghos' means that trouble is comin' to this family thro' a 'ooman. Now, this mornin' I gits up an' fin' yer granny ain't been here all night. It's borne in on me that sumthin' is wrong. Where 'bouts did you drap her, honey, when you picked the clos' up las' evenin'?"

"The last place we went, ma, was to Senator Bowen's. Granny went 'roun' to the kitchen to talk to Mis' Johnson while I went up to Venus. Granny said she was short off for breath and Mis' Johnson gave her a cup of coffee and a cutlet. Granny's fond of chicken cutlets."

"Um," replied his mother, "Mis' Johnson's a born lady cook or no cook. Chicken cutlets," she mused. "Some new Yankee fashion cookin' chicken, I reckon, bein' Mis' Johnson's from out Bos'n way. Wha's it taste like, Oliver, didn't they ask yer to have a bite with 'em?"

---

1 Joined, married.

"Chicken cutlets are common, ma," replied Oliver, with the indifference of familiarity. "Just slap your chicken in egg and bread crumbs, drop it into hot fat and there you are."

"Do you like 'em, son?" inquired his mother, while one could see in the watery look that lurked about the corners of her mouth a determination to try chicken cutlets at the first opportunity.

"I like 'em *fine* ma."

Marthy sighed, and then returned to the original subject. "What did granny say when you lef' her?"

"She said that she'd a right smart turn of washing up and dusting that she'd left over from Saturday afternoon because the clerks were working overtime in one of the departments. I left her at the foot of the steps on the north side."

"Well, honey, I don' kno'," and Marthy shook her head dubiously. "Run along to yer pa now, an' then up to the 'partment to fin' yer granny. 'Deed, God knows I hope the ol' lady's safe, but I mistrus' mighty much, I do."

"I think you're worrying for nothing, ma; I'm not a bit anxious. Sometimes has[1] to stop late, and she might have stayed all night because she was afraid to walk home alone."

Marthy shook her head solemnly. "Wha'd she be 'fraid of a po' black 'ooman with nuthin' to steal? 'Tain't a soul gwine tech her. She ain't young an' purty makin' a 'ticemen' fer people; men isn't chasin' 'roun' street corners in Wash'nt'n after ugly ol' 'oomen's. No Oliver; fifteen year ago this blessid winter when you and your sister was tweeny tots, jes' like this yer granny stayed away, an' sot all night on top o' ninety thousan' dollars wurth o' greenbacks.[2] The night befo' it happened I dreamt I was carried up to glory settin' on a cloud an' playin' on a golden harp, which means suddint honors an' el'vations; nex' thing I knowed the Presidunt 'pinted mammy prominen'ly to a firma-men'[3] persition in the 'partment at forty dollars a munf. Then I was able to sen' yer sister to school an' keep her nice in spite o' yer daddy's racketty ways. Yer granny's holped me powful. Yer pa's money don' 'mount to a hill o' beans in my pocket, but mammy's kep' him straigh, an' ennythin'd happen the ol' lady I'd be nachally obleeged to giv' up the ghos'."

---

1 I.e., sometimes she has.
2 Dollar bills.
3 Permanent.

"Ef you don' fin' your granny, stop at yer pa's an' bein' as the Gin'ral's away yer pester him to try an' hunt her up. An' don' fergit to stop inter Senator Bowen's an' see yer sister. Jes' ask her ef Miss Jewel's summer wrappers is to be clar-starched or biled-starched. 'Deed, my head's clean gone runnin' after mammy this mornin'. An' ef you see the madam or Miss Jewel, make yer manners. Them white ladies is a-payin' fer yer schoolin'. Git down ter bus'ness, now, hyar me, son? money talks."

As Oliver disappeared from view around the corner of the street, Marthy closed the outer door and re-entered the kitchen. Her naturally hopeful nature re-asserted itself and she took a brighter view of the situation. "I reckon I'll laugh if mammy comes in now all right. I wonder which way Ollie 'll go? Like as not he'll walk down G street an' mammy'll come on the keers.[1] Now, I'll jes' hussle roun' an' git them clo's out o' the tub agin' they git here."

Life had been checkered for Marthy since emancipation when she had joined her lot with St. Clair Enson's Isaac, in the "holy bonds of matrimony." "Like master like man," was a true prophecy in Isaac's case, and had caused the little brown woman a world of worry.

Isaac had obtained the billet of valet to General Benson, no one knew how, for up to that time he had been a ne'er-do-well, working when the notion pleased him or when actual starvation compelled him to exert himself, at other times swearing, drinking and fighting.

It was a time of rejoicing when, upon arriving home one night, after his daily lounge about the Bay or Buzzard's Nest,[2] looking for something to stimulate his weary system, he announced to his family that he had been "hired" by General Benson. Marthy rejoiced exceedingly although, as she told Aunt Henny,—

"What in the wurld the Gin'ral 'spects to git out o' Ike in the way o' wurk passes me."

Her mother shook her head ominously.

"De Gin'ral mus' be plum crazy. 'Twon'[3] las'."

After three months had rolled by, the poor little brown wife

---

1 Horse-drawn streetcars.
2 Peninsula formed at the meeting of the Potomac and Anacostia rivers in Washington, DC.
3 It won't.

began to take courage. Ike was working "stiddy"[1] although she had not yet seen the color of his money and she was still dependent upon the washing with which a number of families supplied her, and the substantial help given by her old mother's labor at the treasury.

"Pears lak, mammy, I can see some way to raise the mor'gage."

"Fu' w'y,[2] Marthy?"

"Ike's so stiddy."

Aunt Henny shook her head.

"Wha' you reckin de bill is, chile?" asked the old woman, removing her pipe from her mouth. Work was over and her chair and pipe in the warmest corner near the kitchen range, were comforting to the wornout frame. Aunt Henny was seventy, but save for rheumatism she had not changed since she left the Enson plantation. Sometimes she would bend her limbs, shake her head and sigh, "Dey neber be easy goin' 'gin, fuh sho', but I got a heap o' hope outen dem whilst dey ben limber, my soul; de bes' laigs I'll eber hab in dis wurl."

"We does owe on the mor'gage five hundred dollars," said Marthy in reply to her mother's question.

"My wurd, but de money grow slow; I got one hunder' dollars up stairs 'tween the feather bed an' de mattress. You make Ike fotch out de res'. Cayn't rightly feel de place is ourn till we's paid up. When I sees you an' de chillun under your own roof, I gwine ter gib up de ghos' in peace. An' Marthy, don't neber be a plum fool an let Ike wurrit you into raisin' money on de place, ef he gits inter scrapes let him git out as he gits in, widout any holp but de debbil. Ef you eber let dat mon take de bread outer yer mouf dat way, an I'm daid, I gwine ter riz up outer de grave an' hit yer; yas, I'll rawhide yer jes' as I user down on de plantation."

Marthy gasped but heaved a sigh of satisfaction over the thought of the hundred dollars.

"Well, I'se glad as glad 'bout the money, mammy. An' Ike's jes' got to pony up to the pint of that other fo' hundred dollars."

"Hump!" grunted Aunt Henny. "I don' trus' him. Dat niggah no leanin' pos' fer me. I'se gwine call on Gen'ral Benson myse'f, an' ef he de right kin' o' white gen'man, he gwine holp me in a 'spiracy ter make Ike raise dat money. Wha' you say to dat, Marthy?"

---

1 Steady.
2 Why.

"I likes it *fine*," Marthy cried, over joyed at what she considered a brilliant plan to subjugate the irresponsible Isaac.

Shortly after this conversation, Marthy applied to her husband for money.

"I ain't got no money fer ye, Marthy," he said in answer to her request.

"Ain't got no money, an' you been wurkin' stiddy fer munfs! What's gone come of it I'd like ter know." Isaac scratched his head in perplexity.

"I 'low to do better by yer, Marthy; you's ben a good gal to me, an' I 'low I ain't done the right thing by you in every way sence we was jined, but I'se turned over a new leaf; I ain't drawed a red cent o' my wages sence I went to wait on the Gin'ral. I jes' lef' it in his han's fer 'ves'men'. Major Madison an' Gin'ral's spec'latin' in mines. Dey owns de Arrow-head, an' all my wages an' all de money Gin'ral kin raise has ben put in dat gol' mine up in de Col'rady hills."

"The Lawd save us, Ike! Then we'll done lose this place," she cried. "The mor'gage money done come due in June, an' Mis' Jenkins been mighty kind, but he's boun' to fo'close 'cause I hear he want money pow'ful bad to meet his needcessities. O, Lawd! what is we gwine do?" she moaned rocking herself to and fro while the tears streamed down her cheeks.

"Don' you take on, Marthy," her husband said soothingly. "I'll git de money from de Gin'ral all right. I know I ain't been a 'sponsible man fer yer, but I'se got human feelin', ain't I? Ain't I proud o' my gal an' my boy what's in de college? Wha' you tink I'se turned over a new leaf fo' ef it warn't to see them chilluns holdin' up dar heads 'long wif de bes' ob de high-biggotty Wash'nt'n 'stockracy? Thar daddy's gwine ter make 'em rich an' when you an' me is moulderin' ter clay dem chillun's gwine ter be eatin' chickun an' a-settin' on thar own front do' steps jes' like de Presidun'."

"I don' trus' no white man. 'Member all the money went up in the Freedman's bank,[1] don' yer? I don' guess he'd be slow makin' a profit outen yer by keepin' yer wages. Plenty gentmen'd do it 'fore yer could bat yer eye."

"You tew ha'sh, Marthy. De Gen'ral an' de major been mighty fine ter your husban', gal. Don' you worry, dat money's safe."

---

1   A savings bank for formerly enslaved men and women established in 1865. It went bankrupt in 1874.

"I 'spicion him jes' the same," replied his wife sullenly.

"De major do be under some repetition as a bad character, but de Gin'ral's all right. Dar's heap o' his paw¹ in 'im," he continued in a musing voice. "Dar neber was a better man den ol' massa, an' I orter know. Lawse, de times me an young massa had t'gedder, bar hunts, an gamblin' 'bouts, an' shootin' and ridin'. He goin' so fas' I skacely cud keep up tuh him. We bin like brudders. All his clo's fits me *puffick!* Our size is jes' de same as ever. En jurin' de wah I jes' picked him twice outen de inimy's han's; my sakes dem was spurious² times."

"You, Isaac, wha' in the lan' you talkin' 'bout? Is you gone crazy? Them remarks o' yourn is suttinly cur'ous." Isaac started to his feet, and there was a guilty look on his face.

"What was I sayin', Marthy? 'Clar fo' it, my thoughts was miles 'way from hyar."

"Do hish! Ef I didn't kno' yer age, Isaac Johnson, I'd think you gone dotty. I 'clar fo' it, I hope you ain't goin' ter have sof'n o' the brain from drinkin' all Sam Smith's bad rum over to Buzzard's Nes'. I hern tell o' sech happenin's, but I pray the Lawd not to pile that trib'lation on top o' me."

After this occurrence, Aunt Henny sought General Benson's presence as the only hope of getting money out of Isaac. From this interview the old woman returned with a look of terror and consternation on her face. When questioned by Marthy as to the outcome of the interview she would say nothing of her success, only repeating the words: "I'se seed a ghos'! Lawd, my days is done."

Marthy went heavily about her work as spring approached. But for her children she would have given up the unequal struggle. Just at the darkest hour the Bowens had become interested in Venus and Oliver, and soon the little brown mother had felt a revival of hope in her breast, as she planned to make bold and go herself to Miss Jewel and ask the dear young lady to intercede with the Senator and get him to take up the hateful mortgage.

After Oliver left the house, his mother rubbed away industriously, and under her skilful fingers the delicate clothing was

---

1 Father.

2 Another example of the double meaning Hopkins achieves through dialect. Isaac means "glorious" here, but the author no doubt regarded supposed Confederate exploits as spurious (i.e., fraudulent).

soon floating like snow-capped billows in tubs and boilers. When noon was signalled from the observatory upon the hill, spotless garments waved in the keen air from every line in the large drying yard at the rear of the cottage.

"'Clar fo' it, Oliver's missed his school, an' mammy ain't come yet."

Half distracted with terror and fearing the worst, Marthy sat down in the midst of her disordered kitchen and sobbed aloud.

Suddenly she heard the click of the little gate. The next moment she saw Oliver's face at the door. It needed but a glance, to tell that something extraordinary had happened. He was breathless from running, his face ashen, his large eyes were distended to twice their usual size.

"O, ma, there's been a murder up to the treasury—"

"Don' tell me it's yer granny!" shrieked his mother.

"No'm; 'taint granny; it's a young lady; and Mr. Sumner that was Miss Jewel's beau is arrested, an' granny ain't been seen *nowhere* since she went into the building last night. Pa'll be home after he's been to the station to notify the police about granny, an' Venus can't leave Miss Jewel; she's taking on so."

"O, yer po' granny, Oliver! I jes' cayn't bar up under this. O, where's my mammy! Good Lawd, where's she at?"

CHAPTER XXIV.

"Terrible discovery this morning in Treasury building! Arrest, on suspicion, of Mr. Cuthbert Sumner!"

That was the startling head-line that met Jewel Bowen's eyes on that eventful Monday morning, and sent the blood back to her heart.

She had opened the paper lazily, glanced at the leaders, and with, "There's never anything interesting in the paper," turned to another sheet, and suddenly sat transfixed, her wide eyes seeing nothing but that one startling head-line that danced before her straining gaze, then stood still,—that at first appeared to be printed in great black type and then turned into blood-red letters!

In an instant the reserve and coldness of weeks was swept aside. He was again her lover. His deadly peril gripped her very heart-strings, and filled her whole being anew with all the strength and passion of woman's noblest love, that, at once, without a second's pause, throws aside all but honor itself for the being who is her world.

She had not read the account of the tragedy, but not for one instant did a thought of guilt associate itself in her mind with Cuthbert Sumner. *Guilty of a heinous crime!* She laughed aloud at the bare idea. In that moment she forgot the new duties lately assumed toward another. Promises had been forced upon her she had told herself often of late, with regret, and none could blame her if she swerved in the moment of trial from the exact path of duty. Now, she thanked God it was not yet a crime to think of the man she loved.

She calmed herself presently, and read the brief account given in the morning edition of the "Washington News." With the sheet closely clutched in her hand she sought her mother. Mrs. Bowen's maid was just serving her lady with breakfast as Jewel knocked and then entered the room. Mrs. Bowen was seated comfortably before the fire, opening her morning mail.

"Jewel, what on earth is the matter? What is wrong?" exclaimed her mother, startled at the strange look on her face.

"Cuthbert is arrested, charged with murder!"

Mrs. Bowen turned very white.

"Great heaven! Jewel! No, no, it is too horrible!"

"Read that," said the girl, laying the paper in her mother's lap.

The elder woman read the printed sheet and gazed up at her daughter with incredulous eyes.

"You do not believe him guilty?"

"*Guilty!*" the one word spoke volumes.

"What can we do to help him? It is unfortunate that your father is away."

"I have not thought yet." The determined woman spoke in the next sentence, "I shall visit him first of all."

"Jewel!" exclaimed her mother in a shocked tone. "What will the General think?"

"What he pleases," was the defiant answer.

Before Mrs. Bowen could protest, there was a hurried knock at the door, which, opening, admitted Venus. There were traces of tears on her face.

"Please, Miss, Mr. Sumner's man is in the hall asking if you will see him for a minute."

"Show him right up here, Venus."

John entered the presence of the two ladies with deep distress and alarm in his honest face. He looked years older than he did the day before. There was a strong affection between master and man. He came forward eagerly, his hands holding his cap and twitching nervously.

"Oh, Mrs. Bowen an' young Miss, I beg your pardon, but—but—I don't know what to do. I've telegraphed to the ol' gent'man—"

"Yes, John—when will he be here?" The ladies spoke together.

"The ol' gent'man's had shock, an' the doctor dassent to tell him, but the family lawyer will be here tomorrow to take charge; but I can't keep still, miss,—ma'am—I had to come an' see you. I've been in the Sumner family, boy an' man, for twenty years, an' they're used me white,[1] ma'am—miss, right straight through. 'Clare, I'd do anything on yearth for Mr. Cuthbert."

"How does your master bear it, John?"

"Like a lamb, miss—ma'am—I've been there now, jes' cam from there, been taking his orders an' things. All he says is 'John, there's a mistake; it'll be all right in a day or two.' But I don' b'lieve it. I feel oneasy. I thought maybe you all would tell what more I can do."

"That's right, John. We will help you all we can. These are evil days that have come to us lately." But in spite of her brave words, Mrs. Bowen looked about her in a helpless, bewildered way. Then she appealed to her daughter, "Jewel, what do you advise, dear?"

"The first thing to do is to see Cuthbert; I'm going to drive down to the jail and have a long talk with him."

"Jewel!"

"Well, mamma, if we intend to benefit him, there is but one way. Venus, order me a herdic; I won't wait for the carriage," she said, turning to her maid. "Why, what are you crying about, silly child; they can't hang Mr. Sumner without a trial."

"Yes'm; I know that. But it's my granny, too, miss. We can't find her," said the girl with a burst of tears. Again John spoke, trying to explain the matter to the bewildered ladies.

"It's ol' Mis' Sargean'—"

---

1 Honorably.

"What did you say?" interrupted Mrs. Bowen sharply, leaning forward in her chair.

"Sergeant, ma'am, Ol' Aunt Henny Sargeant, she's Venus's gran'mother. She's a cleaner up at the department, an' she's disappeared; ain't been seen sense last night, when she went into the building to clean up. Taking that an' putting it with the murder an' other funny things that's been happening about Mr. Sumner lately, it 'pears to me that something underhand is going on," he said with a deferential bow.

"Venus, come with me. John, be good enough to order the herdic. I will look into this matter and see what can be done," and Jewel turned to leave the room.

"Please, miss, do you mind if I take a seat on the box?"[1] asked John.

"Certainly not."

And the trio quitted the room leaving Mrs. Bowen alone.

CHAPTER XXV.

As the day grew older the excitement increased in the city over the murder of Elise Bradford. The circumstances surrounding the victim, as given out in the second editions of the press, the mysterious disappearance of the old scrub-woman and the high social and official position of the accused, gave rise to all sorts of sensational rumors.

"Very queer affair," said one man to another, nodding significantly. "A good deal behind it all, of course. Young men will be young men; you can't put an old head on young shoulders," he added, repeating the trite sayings as if they were original with himself.

"H'm, yes. Ugly facts, though, the wine-glasses especially. I take it the old Negress would be an important witness in the case."

"Yes. What about the wine-glasses? I haven't read the paper very carefully; just sketched it."

"Why, it seems they must have had wine together and he put prussic acid in her glass. But he denies it; says he gave her a glass of wine because she seemed faint, but he took none himself. In

---

1 A seat on the outside part of the carriage.

short, he cannot explain the presence of the *second* glass. The odd thing about it is his walking out and leaving the body there, if he did it, with no attempt at concealment."

"You don't say so! By Jove, what did he expect? And he claims to be innocent?"

"Yes; but of course he'd do that. I suppose his lawyers will claim that it was suicide. Fact is, he must have found himself in a mess and took this method of getting clear. These young bloods are as bad as the worst when you corner them."

"It must have been that way. And then, again, what he says may be true, somehow. From what one hears of him, he is incapable of a crime like this. He is called a man of spotless honor."

"Well, perhaps, except where there's a woman in the case. We are men ourselves, and we know."

The other nodded in acquiescence.

Will Badger and Carroll West met in the corridor of the jail, one just coming from a conference with the prisoner, the other seeking an interview.

Kind-hearted Badger was feeling very much cast down over his friend's predicament.

"Think he did it, Badger?" asked West after they had exchanged greetings.

"No more than you or I," was the decisive answer. "I would not believe the blackest evidence against his bare word. I know the man."

"I'm with you, but—well—confound the jade, I say, to get Sumner in this fix. Of course, there's another man. Who is he? Have you an idea?"

Badger shook his head and sighed. "The examination is tomorrow at ten. Try and be there, West."

"I will, sure. The Madisons are awfully cut up over this affair; she was almost in hysterics when I stopped in to talk it over. The Major isn't himself either."

"No wonder. Well, we shan't know anything positive until after the hearing. So long."

The friends separated.

Shortly after noon, Jewel arrived at the jail. The interview between her and Cuthbert was long and painful, but both were happier than they had been for many weeks. Sumner told Jewel the facts of his intimacy with Amelia,[1] blaming himself greatly for all the trouble that had followed his first deception. "I should have been frank with you, Jewel, and all would have been well."

Jewel's gentle heart was at last at rest; perfect confidence was established between the re-united lovers. As she rose to go, he said:

"It may go hard with me tomorrow at the examination; indeed, I know it will. There will be difficult work ahead for my attorneys. So many things have happened to separate us, Jewel, that I dread the future."

The tears stood in her eyes. She turned her head to hide them.

"Dare I express my selfish hopes—my wishes?"

For answer she threw herself into his arms again, and as he held her thus he whispered his request with an eager look upon his face.

She blushed violently, hesitated, then drawing herself up proudly said:

"I will do as you wish."

"Tomorrow morning then, at eight, I shall be waiting."

"I will not fail you," was her low reply, as snatching her hand hastily from his detaining clasp, she turned to accompany the officer from the cell.

As she passed through the office she asked the captain for the address of the chief of the secret service.

"You mean Mr. Henson, I take it, Miss?"

"If he is the celebrated detective, he is the very one."

"Well, Miss, it's No.— Pennsylvania Avenue; but he takes no outside cases. His government duties are all that he finds time for."

"Still, I will call on him."

The man bowed, and she passed on. Months ago she remembered hearing her father speak of the great powers of this detective. Why it had lingered in her mind she knew not, but now a hidden force impelled her to seek his aid.

She shrank from nothing that might benefit her lover. Shrink! was that like it, the proud flush on the soft cheek, the warm light in her eyes? Her heart throbbed fast in the excess of happiness it was to know that he was true, that all misunderstandings were buried spectres, and that she—she alone, held his heart. Let the

---

1 I.e., Aurelia Madison.

world do its worst, she could repay by showing every trust in him. After tomorrow she would have the right to stand beside him, though all the world should frown. Her thoughts did not go beyond the present. He would be proved innocent, she was sure. Money could do anything and there would be no sparing of any moment to clear him.

The herdic seemed to creep over the space between the station and the detective's chambers. Her very heart seemed on fire under intense, suppressed excitement and the emotion that surged beneath her calm, conventional exterior.

No.— Pennsylvania Avenue was a large brick building where lawyers congregated. Jewel alighted from the herdic, leaving Venus in it. Mr. Henson's office was on the second floor. She paused before a door upon the glass panels of which appeared the letters: "J. Henson, Detective." She opened the door and entered. There were a number of clerks in the room busily writing. One elderly man near the door was in charge.

"Yes, Mr. Henson was in and would no doubt see the lady if she could wait awhile," he said in reply to Jewel's inquiry. Placing a chair for her he took her card and disappeared behind a door marked "Private." Presently he returned saying that if she would come with him, Mr. Henson would receive her.

The great detective was seated at his desk writing. He did not look up as she entered, but said:

"Be seated, madam; I will give you my attention in one moment."

Jewel saw a well-preserved man of sixty odd years, middle height, and rather broad, but not fleshy. His thick iron gray hair covered his head fully and curled in masses over a broad forehead. He was well and carefully dressed. Presently he looked up from his work and glanced in her direction; then she saw that he had expressive dark eyes and a pleasant face which might have been handsome in youth, but for a long livid scar that crossed his face diagonally. A sabre might have made that deep, dangerous cut.

The light in the room was faint, and Jewel did not perceive the pallor that spread over the man's face as he gazed at her; the words he was about to utter died away unsaid, his chest heaved an instant in a convulsive movement which he controlled by a violent effort. There was silence as the man and girl gazed at each other, mutually attracted by a hidden affinity. It was but a second that the pause endured.

"You wish to speak with me, Miss?"

Then Jewel aroused herself from the spell which had held her since she encountered the piercing gaze of the quiet elderly man before her. The sound of his voice generated a feeling of relief in her breast, of trust and confidence. She could not analyze the sensation of complete rest that came to her with the few words just spoken.

"I wish to speak with you," she replied tremulously; then, recovering herself: "When I say that I am deeply interested in the murder that has just been committed, and that Mr. Sumner is my dearest friend, you will know what I want."

"I understand, Miss Bowen," he said, glancing at the card in his hand. "I seldom take cases outside of the government; still, I will hear what you have to tell me. I think this may be an exception to my rule."

He motioned her to the chair beside him and then placed a note-book on the desk before him.

"Mr. Summer is innocent," said the girl in a trembling voice. "He will have able counsel, I know; but I shall feel better if you will take charge. I have heard so much of your skill and wonderful powers of discernment that no one else could satisfy me."

The man looked at the beautiful girl before him with something akin to worship in his eyes. When he spoke again his voice had taken on an added softness, his words seemed to carry a caress hidden beneath their commonplace utterance.

"Thank you; I am greatly interested. Even the newspaper accounts bear evidence that this is a remarkable case, and there is generally a good deal hidden behind what they give out. Now tell me all you know of the matter."

Calmed by his gentle tones, Jewel gave a brief account of the affair as told her by Sumner. When she ceased speaking Mr. Henson, who had listened with down-cast eyes and unmoved countenance, said:

"It is a curious case, very. There seems no clue; but, if I mistake not, you have suspicions of someone." His eyes rested on her face in a peculiarly impressive manner.

"Why do you think so?"

"I trace it in the tones of your voice. Now tell me the name of the person you suspect and why."

The girl hesitated, then said in a low tone:

"General Benson!"

"Ah!" It was but a breath, but it spoke volumes. "And have you mentioned this to anyone?"

"Only to Mr. Sumner, but he will not entertain the thought. He thinks the idea absurd because the General is in New York, and can hardly know more than the bare outlines of the case as yet."

"Just so. But upon what do you base your thought?"

"Oh, Mr. Henson," and she clasped her hands and raised her wonderful, beseeching gray eyes to his face, "I cannot tell. There is a feeling of conviction that he knows all about the crime if he is not the assassin. There has been an adverse fate at work since General Benson crossed my path. There has been a train of unfortunate circumstances attending our whole acquaintance. It is absurd to suspect him I know, but I cannot help it." The detective looked at her again with the immovable expression peculiar to him.

"Your woman's intuition warns you; is that it?"

She bowed her head in acquiescence.

"And I have confidence in intuitive deductions," he muttered; then, aloud, "My dear child, gentlemen like General Benson sometimes do queer things under pressure of circumstances. You may be right. I will see Mr. Sumner; he will probably be more explicit with me than he could be with you. I will do my best for you. In fact, I shall put all my powers into my work, for it is an uncommon riddle you have set me to solve."

As she rose to go she asked his terms. He named a fair price. "But if you succeed in clearing him, and I know that you will, Mr. Henson, you shall receive a princely reward." Jewel laid her check for a goodly retainer, upon the desk before him. Henson looked and tapped the desk with his pencil, but did not notice the check. Then he rose, touched a bell, and accompanied his fair client to the door.

★ ★ ★ ★ ★ ★

Before nine o'clock on Tuesday morning, attended by her maid, with the jail officials for witnesses, Jewel Bowen became the wife of the suspected murderer, Cuthbert Sumner.

(To be continued.)

CHAPTER XXVI.[1]

The evening of the eventful day that made Jewel, Cuthbert Sumner's wife, closed in heavy and sombre. The hearing had the expected ending, and Sumner was held for trial in the following September, before the grand jury for wilful murder. The evidence was circumstantial, but damaging in the extreme. It showed exclusive opportunity for reasons unknown, but it was whispered about town that the girl had been an unwedded mother. Added to this was the knowledge of the broken engagement between the prisoner and Miss Bowen, and the fact that Miss Madison had at one time been affianced to him, and it was expected that she would be called by the prosecution to show the fickle nature of his relations with women.

At seven o'clock in the evening of that same day, robed in black velvet, Jewel paced restlessly up and down the floor of the library, sometimes pausing to listen to sounds from without, sometimes approaching the window and trying to pierce the gloom. The dinner bell rang; for no matter what our griefs, or how dark the tragedies which are enacted about us, meals are still served and eaten, just as if the hearts assembled about the board were never wrenched nor broken.[2]

The points brought out in the evidence were soon making their way about the city, and excitement and interest grew momentarily. Sumner smiled in bitterness of heart. He hardly knew himself in the picture drawn. Jewel sat in an obscure corner of the audience room of the court, heavily veiled, and listened to the testimony with a heart bursting with indignation. Each moment the load at her heart grew heavier. They both

---

1 SYNOPSIS OF CHAPTERS XXIII TO XXV. [The synopsis of Chapters I to XXII has not been repeated here. See Appendix A for the full text.] Aunt Henny Sargeant, scrub woman at Treasury Building, disappears on same night of the Bradford murder.

    Jewel Bowen visits Cuthbert Sumner in prison. Explanations are made, and they resolve to marry immediately. She visits J. Henson, chief of the secret service division, and places Sumner's case in his hands.

2 Lauren Dembowitz has shown in "Sources" that much of this paragraph derives from Joseph Fitzgerald Molloy's *Sweet Is Revenge* (1891).

realized at last that this was no child's play but a struggle to the death. Sumner clenched his hands and registered a vow to spend his fortune, if necessary, to clear his name, for the sake of the dear incentive, the thought of whom warmed his heart and made him bold to meet impending disaster.

The two ladies took their accustomed places at table, each secretly regretting the absence of the Senator. With him at home, dinner was wont to be a festive meal, where laughter and wit cheered the household or chance visitor. A dismal air hung over the room now; the servants moved to and fro with unaccustomed solemnity. The mother and daughter addressed each other seldom; each was buried in her own thoughts. Presently both rose from the table and passed into the library, where coffee was served.

After the servants had retired and they were safe from intrusion Mrs. Bowen broke the silence that brooded over them. She had watched Jewel closely all through the meal, studying her looks, thinking over her words and striving to arrive at satisfactory conclusions. At length she said quietly:

"Now, my dear, you have told me next to nothing, nor have I asked seeing how pale and tired you are, but I must talk with you about this marriage. I fear you have been very rash. My dear, I positively dread your father's return; dearly as he loves you, he will be very angry." After a pause she continued, clasping and unclasping her fingers nervously, "Oh, the talk there will be when this affair is known! Why didn't you consult me, child? I could have devised some way of helping the poor fellow without requiring you to sacrifice yourself. I am disappointed in Cuthbert Sumner."

"Do not use the word 'sacrifice,' mamma; I am glad to have the right to stand by Cuthbert in this dark hour. And why say anything to you of our intention? No one can blame you now. Beside, we have agreed to say nothing at present, about the marriage."

"But your whole life will be spoilt if he is found guilty."

"Mother," said the girl, sinking on her knees by Mrs. Bowen's side, "don't despair; it will all come right in a little while, I am sure it will. And you have always called yourself his friend, even when I was against him. You *cannot* believe him guilty; you are too just in your judgment, mamma."

Jewel was kneeling in the full light of the glowing fire, the ruddy glare fell on her white face, and the plaits of bright hair wound closely around her small head. Mrs. Bowen sighed, as she gazed in admiration at her daughter. The great gray eyes glowed like diamonds, but there was a world of passionate anguish in their depths. The flower-like mouth was compressed with the intensity of the pain which filled her breast.

Again Mrs. Bowen sighed and moved uneasily in her seat.

"Yes; but this is so different—a man accused of murder."

"How so, mamma? Is friendship in sunshine so different from friendship in shade?" There was sarcasm on the delicately chiselled features.

"What a champion you are, Jewel; once, perhaps, I should have acted and felt as you do."

"But now, mamma—?"

"Now, my child, I am of the world—worldly."

"Do you think papa will be very angry?" asked the girl with trembling lips after a short silence.

"We can expect nothing less. He is too fond of you to hold his anger long, however. I shall stand with you, Jewel, if it is any comfort for you to know it. I am glad, glad, glad, that you cannot marry General Benson." Jewel marvelled much at the strange look on her mother's face as she uttered these words.

"My dear mamma!" and the two women embraced each other. Then followed another silence broken by the elder woman.

"What impression did you receive from the evidence—I mean apart from the conclusions drawn by the jury?" A quiver went through the girl as she replied:

"I was confirmed in my belief in his innocence, although everything seemed to point the other way. Aurelia Madison's evidence was against him. She gave the impression that he came and went at her beck and call."

"She is false to the core—a dangerous woman."

"I agree with you, mamma. But her beauty blinds men. I dread her influence on the jury."

"There is no soul there—nothing but sensuality."

"Soul! there is no need for soul in a woman's beauty for it to dazzle most men," was the bitter answer.

"I marvel much over the matter. It seems to me there is something incomplete in the case—something to be explained. That poor girl! I can see no reason for murdering her. She may have been killed by mistake."

"That is scarcely likely."

"Cases of mistaken identity are common enough. It's a mysterious affair; I hope it may be cleared up without any delay."

"I hope so," added Jewel. "Murder will out;[1] there lies my hope for our success in tracing the murderer."

"What does Mr. Henson say?"

"Not much; we have had no time to talk. He has hardly got to work yet; but he told me to keep my courage up, and that he thought he should be able to throw some light on the dark points of the story. He has talked with Cuthbert."

Before Mrs. Bowen had time to reply the lace and satin portière[2] was pushed aside and Venus advanced toward them with a solemn and awe-stricken face.

"What, is it, Venus?" asked Mrs. Bowen, regarding her with surprise.

"Please, Mrs. Bowen," she said hesitatingly, "Senator Bowen—"

"Oh, papa is come," cried Jewel in delight.

"No, Miss—"

At this point General Benson's well-known figure appeared in the entrance.

"Mrs. Bowen—Jewel—" he exclaimed as he hurried toward them, "I am the bearer of evil tidings. Senator Bowen was taken ill in New York, and we have hastened to bring him home as soon as it was possible to move him. Have a room prepared instantly, the ambulance will arrive almost immediately."

Before another hour had elapsed, the great hush—which is the shadow of the grim visitant, whom no earthly power may shut out—had fallen on the Bowen mansion. The servants walked with noiseless tread and spoke in whispers.

Senator Bowen was ill unto death. He had been suddenly stricken down by a shock. The Washington delegation had been tendered a banquet at a famous New York club, and a hilarious time had been enjoyed. The New Yorkers had outdone themselves in catering for the amusement of their guests.

Senator Bowen had enjoyed himself hugely. Along in the early morning hours a servant passing the door of his room had caught

---

1   An old proverb that appears twice in Chaucer's *Canterbury Tales* and often thereafter.

2   Curtain hung over a doorway.

the sound of some one struggling for breath within. Entering, he beheld the Senator lying on the bed, one hand pressed to his heart, the other hanging inert. His eyes were wild, his pale countenance lined with purple marks.

The man went for help and soon medical aid had rendered all the relief possible. As soon as he could make himself understood the stricken man urged them to take him home.

After the first burst of grief, Mrs. Bowen and Jewel took up their places in the sick room along with the trained nurses. Each looked at the other in awe and consternation over the awful suddenness of this event. Surprising events had followed one another rapidly the past few days. They dared not think of the next cruel blow that Fate might deal them.

The doctors and nurses came and went softly. The hours drew out their long, anxious length. At the close of the third day the sick man fell into a heavy stupor, from which the doctors said he might rally—probably would—and he might linger two or three days longer; but the end was inevitable. Should he rally he must be kept quiet, and on no account excited; his heart was weak.

Mrs. Bowen undertook to see these instructions carried out. Jewel, pale and distressed, shared her mother's watch. She was in agony; her love for her father was strong, deep and tender. She was his idol, and he was hers, and until she met Cuthbert Sumner she had always felt that if he died she would not care to live another hour. She could never remember his having been cross to her in his whole life. In her eyes his very faults were virtues.

At midnight Mrs. Bowen persuaded her daughter to go and lie down.

"Keep your strength, my child, there is much to go through. If your father wakes I will surely call you."

When alone she drew her chair to the fire and sat there in shadow, watching the face of the silent figure on the bed that looked so ghastly in the light of the shaded light. It was very still; the tired nurses in the next room, dozed. Events long passed, returned in full force and pictured themselves vividly before her inner senses. How kind this man had been to her; how much she owed to his love and care. And now the hour had come for her to lose a protector who had never failed her. Wealth she might have, but it would not supply the tender deference and loving solicitude of wedded life that had been hers.

She shuddered at her thoughts. Why did the past haunt her so persistently? Presently she found herself weeping softly.

There are brave natures—women's perhaps, more often than men's—which bear up in a sea of adversity, and present a bold front to the buffeting winds of life's uncertainties. And sometimes these brave natures find a safe haven for their frail barks. Mrs. Bowen was one of these. She had never known trouble, save by name, since she met Zenas Bowen some twenty years before; and now behold, she is confronted by a very tempest of sorrow. In the midst of her reveries she was startled to hear her own name pronounced:

"Estelle."

It was Senator Bowen who spoke. In an instant his wife was at his side.

"Dear Zenas, you are better?" she said cheerfully.

"Yes, my brain is clear. I have been watching you, Estelle. Where is Jewel?"

"In her room; I made her lie down. Do you want her?"

"Poor child; let her sleep."

His eyes roved restlessly about the familiar room.

"It is good to be at home—so good."

"Yes—but you must not talk. Drink this and sleep." She held a soothing draught to his lips, lifting the powerless head in her arms with all a mother's tenderness. He drank it obediently and then lay back on his pillow and a satisfied look of peaceful rest overspread his pale features. He held his wife's hand in a nerveless grasp.

"We have been happy, Estelle. You have been a perfect wife. I have left you well provided for. Them rascals got some of it, but not the whole of it by a durned sight; Zenas ain't such a fool as he seems," a gleam of his old fun-loving spirit was on the pain-worn face.

"If Jewel marries the General—"

"No, Zenas," she interrupted; then she stopped remembering the doctor's caution. But the sick man did not grasp the significance of her words. His mind wandered.

"No you don't, General; my little girl shan't be forced. I, her father, say it. When, where and who she likes; that's my idee. I tell you, no!"

Then he looked at his wife with fast-glazing eyes, and said:

"The little hair trunk[1]—tell her—no difference—just the same."

Feebly he raised his arm. His wife knew his desire. She placed it about her neck. Then he drew her head nearer. A soft light radiated his features.

"My faithful wife!" he whispered. The cold lips touched her cheek.

"Zenas, Zenas!" exclaimed Estelle with a burst of emotion as she kissed the chill brow.

There was one long-drawn breath. The distracted wife sprang to the bell and rang a peal that brought the nurses hurrying in.

"Senator Bowen is worse!" she cried, wringing her hands helplessly.

The head nurse bent over the bed, then rising, said: "Senator Bowen is dead, madam."

Again Washington society was stirred by an unexpected calamity among its leading people. Interest was heightened because of the close association which existed between the Bowens and the chief actor in the Bradford tragedy. The ill-starred trip of the delegation that had started so gaily on its Canadian mission was the talk of the capital.

CHAPTER XXVII.

The funeral was over. Senator Bowen was at rest in the handsomest cemetery of the capital after many honors had been paid to the sterling worth of the rugged Westerner. Condolences flooded the widow and orphan. The contents of the will were not yet known, but it was supposed that both ladies were left fabulously rich.

One event had crowded so closely upon another that General Benson was given no opportunity for confidential conversation with the woman he desired to make his wife.

The loss of her father was a terrible shock to Jewel, and she kept to her rooms, weeping passionate tears and refusing to be comforted. A sense of horrible loneliness, of grief, apprehension, and the weight of some unknown calamity weighed her young heart down. Young, beautiful, well-born, and wealthy,

---

1 Trunk covered with a hairy hide.

surrounded by every luxury money could purchase or a cultivated taste long for, Jewel was supremely wretched. Her father
dead, her husband a prisoner, accused of the deadliest of crimes,
the girl was a prey to a thousand vague fears and haunting suspicions. She dreaded, too, the coming of the day set apart for reading the will, for General Benson could no longer be avoided. She
had written him a letter asking a release from promises made,
but as yet had received no reply.

Senator Bowen had been buried two weeks when, at an early
hour, the family lawyer appeared at the house and was ushered
into the breakfast room where, attired in deep mourning, Mrs.
Bowen sat in solitary state making a pretense of eating.

Mr. Cameron was a pale, small, dark-haired man, with sharp
eyes and thin lips; a hard, but honest face, and a short temper.

Somewhat alarmed by the troubled look on the solicitor's
face, Mrs. Bowen asked anxiously,—

"Is anything wrong, Mr. Cameron?"

"Well, madam, I hope not; but I thought I would ask you for
a cup of coffee, lay the case before you and talk it over. I heard
some surprising news last night," he continued, as he seated
himself and swallowed the steaming beverage that Mrs. Bowen
poured for him, the discreet servant having left the room at a
glance from his mistress. "Did you know that your husband
made a will while in New York?" he questioned abruptly, watching her with keen, bright eyes.

"A will in New York? No—surely not!"

"There is such a will in existence; it is held by General Benson, who came to me last night with the astonishing information. He will be here by eleven to have the instrument read. Of
course, this later document leaves the one in my possession null
and void."

Mrs. Bowen had grown very white as she listened to the lawyer, and a fixed look of intense thought was in her eyes.

"What are the terms of this new will? do you remember?"

"Not all of them; but Major Madison is left sole trustee, and
General Benson executor and guardian of Miss Bowen until she
is of age. Think of it!" cried the excitable man, "all the immense
business of the estate, ready money, etc., *absolutely* in the control
of these men!"

A wonderful change came over Mrs. Bowen at these words.
She was stung to the quick. She sprung from her chair as if

moved by a spring; her lips quivered, her eyes were dilated with what seemed like terror.

"General Benson and Major Madison!" she exclaimed in a hoarse voice, "surely you jest."

"Would it were a jest, my dear madam. Think of it! This magnificent estate and fortune to be left in the hands of two such villains as General Benson and his pal, Major Madison. Yes, villains, madam; and I will undertake to prove my position should they bring action against me for slander. What could my old friend, Bowen, have been thinking about! He must have lost his head completely," continued Mr. Cameron, looking with accusing eyes at the black-robed figure across his second cup of coffee. "Madison had done him out of a million in his bogus company already. A child could see that it was a cheat and a sham."

For one instant, at these words, Mrs. Bowen's face wore the look of a lioness bereft of her young; but her alarm seemed to subside as quickly as it arose. The lawyer was too excited himself to notice the expressions of consternation and alarm that flitted across the pale face of the silent woman before him. After a silence, she asked: "Have you examined this will, Mr. Cameron? Are you sure it is genuine?"

The old attorney put his cup down with emphasis and said with a bow: "Madam, it is a pleasure to talk with you. You have expressed my own thoughts in your question. The Bowen millions would be a great temptation to a set of sharpers. I have not examined the document, but I will; and you may trust me to find any flaw that exists."

"Let us be calm. If it is as we suspect, we shall gain nothing by allowing these men to see that we suspect them. Do not oppose them, but use every legal means to retain control of the estate until we prove our suspicions groundless."

The expression of her face was intense, even fierce; her mouth was tightly closed, her eyes strained as though striving to pierce the veil which hides from us the unseen.

Mr. Cameron looked his admiration of the fearless woman before him, and after a few more words they settled themselves to calmly wait developments.

At this same hour General Benson and his honored associate, Major Madison, sat in the former's room talking earnestly of the business in hand.

"Now, Madison, we have started on the last part of our

enterprise and it is full of peril; one flaw will destroy the whole structure which we have labored so hard to raise. We must preserve all our trumps. Aurelia has failed in her part; we must not fail."

"Pshaw!" said the Major, "we shall succeed. What is there to fear? the man is dead."

"There will be many questions asked, and, doubtless, that old fox of a lawyer is even now hunting for evidences of fraud. Don't underrate the danger, Madison. Our projects are dangerous, and the slightest mistake will prove fatal. But while there are one hundred chances against us, there are the same number in our favor. We know this, too, Madison,—necessity knows no law; we must go ahead!"

"There's the old woman; she'll kick on the will, and kick hard. What'll you do with her?"

There was a peculiar smile on the General's face as he said:

"She'll struggle a little; the scene today will be a story[1] one, so be prepared; but I hold a trump ahead of her."

"The deuce you do!"

"She can't escape from us any more than the girl can."

The Major whistled softly as he murmured "Amen," and then said: "I have faith in your judgment, Benson."

Benson took several turns up and down the long room and finally assumed his favorite attitude before the mantel.

"You do well to feel so, Major. I anticipate no difficulty in assuming full control of the Bowen millions, and how sorely we need them, you and I know, Major."

"But the girl—how will you manage her?"

Benson's face darkened, but he only waved his hand significantly. "Be calm. I wish the whole business was as easily disposed of as the girl."

"She's the only link in the chain that appears weak to my thinking, and she is the key of the old man's cash box. Who would ever have thought of her kicking over the traces so completely and marrying Sumner?" and the Major relighted his cigar, which had gone out while he was talking.

"Keep quiet about that, Madison; let them think us surprised by their news today. Pray observe my caution; I will explain later."

---

1 Possibly "stormy" or "sorry."

"I am glad it is all right. That old attorney worries me, too. Women are deceitful hussies; a man never knows what they are at." General Benson laughed softly at the Major's suggestion.

"What!" he said, "shall the foolishness of a mere girl stop us now, when we are so near the goal? By no means. If she attempts to thwart me, so much the worse for her. Wait for me, Major," and General Benson left the room to speak with Isaac.

Left alone, Major Madison went to the window and stood looking out at the passing throng.

"It is impossible not to admire Benson's nerve and his infernal penetration," he thought half-aloud. "He reasons out a position and plans from the most trivial circumstances. He always falls on his feet. How many close calls we have had since we joined forces; yet, thanks to his luck, we have come out first best every time. Yes, he has wonderful ability and his extraordinary audacity and nerve may be trusted to carry us safely through a difficult undertaking like the present one. What a profession we have adopted and practised for twenty years. Justice never sleeps, the old fogies tell us, but I'll be dog-goned if the old woman[1] ain't in a dead swoon when Benson's on the rampage."

Shortly after this the two friends stepped from their carriage before the Bowen mansion. The Major, in his black clothes, white cravat and spectacles, might readily have passed for an eminent divine about to administer consolation to the bereaved widow and orphan.

Jewel stood in the great library waiting for General Benson, who had requested an interview. The reading of the will had shown her how dependent she would be upon this man. The thought of him as a guardian made her sick at heart. What could her father have been thinking about? She was bewildered by the difficulties which had suddenly beset her path. She who had been petted and shielded all her life saw an existence of strife and danger opening dimly in the future.

"How will it all end," she asked herself drearily, "if Cuthbert should be condemned? He shall not be; he must not be," she told herself, shutting her teeth hard and drawing a long breath.

Presently General Benson entered the room closely followed by Mrs. Bowen, who crossed the room to Jewel's side and took

---

1 Justice is frequently depicted as a blindfolded woman with scales in one hand and a sword in the other.

her hand tenderly in hers. Together they faced General Benson, and this silent defiance filled the man with rage. He came to a halt immediately in front of the pale girl, who had risen to her feet on his entrance.

"I want to tell you, Jewel, in answer to your letter, that I shall not give you up," he began abruptly. "Nothing is changed since you gave me your promise and I shall hold you to it. Your father expected it, too, when he made me your guardian."

"Sir," said Jewel, in a voice almost unintelligible from agitation, "I know that my conduct is extraordinary, but so are the circumstances surrounding my acts; I do not propose to justify myself. It is a great favor that I ask at your hands, but I entreat you to relinquish a project so fraught with unhappiness for both of us. Your generosity will spare me many sad and sorrowful hours, and surely you could not desire an unwilling bride."

"All is fair in love,[1] Jewel," replied the General, who had listened apparently cold and unmoved, but inwardly a passion of rage and jealousy was gnawing at his heart. Then he continued with a malicious smile, "Why not yield gracefully to the inevitable?"

At these words the girl's every instinct arose in arms. She contrasted this scene with her father's fond indulgence and in hot anger longed to show this usurper how she despised his brief authority. There was a look of utter disgust on her face.

"I would have spared you, General Benson, but you need no leniency from me. There is no hope that I shall ever become your wife. I am already married to—Cuthbert Sumner!"

In a moment the man's manner changed.

"Ah!" he said, and the exclamation burst from his lips in a hiss; the elegant society man disappeared—hideous passion gave glimpses of depths of infamy—one beheld the countenance of a devil. "I have heard something of this before; but it does not concern me; it does not alter my plans. I should be foolish to allow a dead man to mar my future; and a dead man Sumner will be, for the law will remove him from my path. Nothing can save him." Jewel measured the man before her with flaming eyes; she turned from him toward the door with a gesture expressive of loathing; she halted on the threshold.

---

1 The statement "All is fair in love" first appears in John Lyly's 1578 prose work *Euphues: The Anatomy of Wit* and often thereafter.

"Hear me, General Benson, I will never become your wife; never, I swear it. Now do your worst."

As the door closed behind the angry girl the man turned to Mrs. Bowen, who stood watching the scene. "And you, madam, are you in league with the misguided girl who undertakes to defy my authority and rights?" The cool sarcasm of his tones was a combination of insolence and impudence.

"You are speaking to Senator Zenas Bowen's widow. You will kindly alter your words and tone when we are conversing, General Benson." Mrs. Bowen spoke in her usual calm, dignified tone. The General's face became purple, then pale; his white teeth gleamed savagely. His elaborate bow was full of mockery as he replied:

"I await your answer, madam, to my question."

"You shall have it," Mrs. Bowen exclaimed in exasperation. "I shall support Jewel in her desires. I am convinced that her father would never force her to act against her inclinations."

There ensued a moment of intense silence when she had finished speaking. General Benson was utterly transfigured. There was not the slightest vestige remaining of the elegant chief of a high official bureau; the sweet voice was changed—it was hard and rasping and had a ring in it that reminded one of the slums. He advanced toward Mrs. Bowen and seized her roughly by the arm.

"So you will assist that headstrong girl to defy me, will you? Well, do it at your peril! Do it, and I will tell your story to the world. I know you; I knew you instantly the first night I saw you in this house. This girl is not your child; why should you care. I have no desire to harm you. Just let things take their course and I will never disturb you in any way."

Uncontrollable terror had spread over Mrs. Bowen's features at these words. Her lips moved but gave forth no sound.

"You do not answer, madam!" exclaimed her tormentor. Then with a diabolical smile of evil triumph he added, "I am correct then in my surmise; you do not deny it?"

The white lips moved; this time her words were distinguishable,—"No! I do not understand what you mean." "I mean—," and he bent toward her and whispered in her ear. That whisper seemed to arouse her benumbed faculties. She moved toward him with disheveled hair, foaming lips, and one arm outstretched in menace. He sprang back from her with a smothered oath: "It is true; you cannot deny it."

"I admit nothing; I deny nothing. Prove it if you can," she muttered in a strained tone.

"Then it is war, is it? Very well, I give you until May to think it over. If you do not come to your senses by that time, I shall proceed to act. Think of it, madam; think well," and the General turned and abruptly left the room.

Mrs. Bowen stood there panting, crushed; her eyes alone gave signs of animation; they glared horribly. As the door closed behind her enemy she sighed; she sunk on the carpet. She had fainted.

CHAPTER XXVIII.

Time passed on, bringing in the early summer. It was the close of a beautiful June day and the sunset was still glowing and burning as it reluctantly bade the world good-night. Venus stood by an open window gazing anxiously into the twilight. Jewel had gone to the jail early in the day, leaving her maid at home. Mrs. Bowen had been in the room a number of times asking for her daughter. She was always uneasy now when Jewel was away from her, and her face wore a strained look of expectancy pitiful to see.

General Benson's anger seemed to have spent itself in the dire threats he had made on the day the will was read; he had left the women in peace, being scrupulously polite when they met to transact business.

Mrs. Bowen was anxious to leave the hot city, and it was agreed between her and Jewel to go to Arlington Heights, where the latter could still be in close proximity to the prisoner and continue her visits with ease. She had gone that day to tell him not to be depressed if the time between her calls was longer than usual.

The glow of sunset faded from the sky, and the summer twilight deepened into night, still Jewel did not appear. It was a warm night; the upper windows were all open; the diamond-studded sky was like a sea of glass. Another hour went by. Mrs. Bowen was pacing the floor restlessly. Venus came up from the servants' quarters with soup and wine for her mistress.

"Now do be persuaded to eat something, madam," said the maid. "You're just as white as death, and you've sat here waiting for Miss Jewel, without your dinner and you must be quite faint.

Here it's nine o'clock, and you always dine at half-past seven. I reckon my young lady's all right. She'll turn up presently as bright as a dollar, sure's your born."

So Mrs. Bowen smiled and allowed herself to be cheered by the devoted girl, and took some soup and a little of the wine; but she could not rest, and listened to every sound that came faintly to the great mansion from the outside.

Hour succeeded hour and it was eleven o'clock; nobody thought of going to bed.

As she sat listening there came a sharp quick ring at the outer bell. Venus herself, anxious for tidings from her loved mistress, rushed to the door ahead of the butler. It was a note which was handed her by a man well muffled up, who instantly disappeared in the thick shrubbery about the lawn. Venus hastened to Mrs. Bowen. With a smile she opened the envelope. The next moment she uttered a cry and gasped for breath.

"Whatever is the matter?" cried the frightened maid.

"This letter—this letter! Help me—help me! Your lady has been abducted!" Mrs. Bowen fell back unconscious in her chair.

The terror-stricken maid opened the letter with shaking hands and read the following lines:

"I always keep my word. If you value your reputation and your step-daughter's *welfare*, you will not seek to find her. In due time she will reappear."

★ ★ ★ ★ ★ ★

Meanwhile what had become of Jewel? She had elected to walk to the jail and back because of the beauty of the day. At the jail she found Mr. Henson, and they had stayed talking over the difficulties of the case until twilight was falling. But that did not disturb her for Mr. Henson would walk back with her, and the Washington streets, famous for their loneliness and seclusion, stretching like immense parks in all directions, would be robbed of their usual terrors for lone female pedestrians.

Mr. Henson accompanied her to the great entrance gates; there he left her, and she started up the carriage path at a rapid gait. Along the edges of the drive the underwood was so thick and the foliage of the trees arching overhead so full and dense that towards the centre of the drive it was in semi-twilight, and thick shades of darkness enveloped all things. In the half-light

Jewel thought she discerned a vehicle—a close carriage,[1] she fancied—standing at one side of the drive.

Surprised, but not startled, because of the close proximity of the house, the girl advanced. The next moment she was startled enough; a chill of fear went through her woman's heart and it stood still for one instant with a thrill of sickening terror, for suddenly out from the gloomy shade of the trees, into the drive, stepped two men, rough-looking ruffians wearing black half-masks.

The one who was evidently the leader said in a hoarse voice, probably disguised:

"Now, Jim."

Instantly both moved toward her.

Jewel was a Western girl. She did not scream. She had been brought up on a ranch; one of her early habits remained fixed, and even in Washington she, was never unarmed when without male escort. The jewelled toy she carried was a present from her father, and he had taught her to use it with deadly effect. Many a day they had hunted together, the young girl bringing down her game in true sportsmanlike style.

Instantly now her hand sought her pocket, in the very instinct of self-defense and desperation; she drew her revolver with intent to fire, but quick as a flash the leader flung himself upon her and wrenched the weapon from her hand. He then threw his arm about her slender form, drawing her towards the carriage.

The passion of terror and desperation lent the girl unnatural strength in her frantic struggle for freedom. The man was forced to place his other hand to stifle her screams.

"You come along quietly, missee, an' you'll be all right; but ef yer screams it won't be pleasant."

"You coward!" she gasped, as he bore her to the carriage. "You coward! Name your price, and let me go."

"Thar you are now slick as grease." She was in the carriage then. "Yer money won't help you with me, missee. You're a brave gal, but what's your strength to a man's? Drive on like h—, Jim."

The cold drops of agony stood on the girl's brow as the horror of her position grew upon her each moment.

"Where are you taking me?"

"I'm goin' ter take yer jes' a little journey outside o' Washington fer a few days. Don't you be feared; thar's nuthin' goin' hurt ye."

---

1 Closed (rather than open) carriage.

Who was this man holding her, refusing bribe, yet vowing to protect her from harm. She looked into the masked face in an agony of appeal and doubt and fear in the great gray eyes. The man was touched.

"Don't now, *don't*, missee, look that skeered. Nothin' ain't goin' hurt you, I tell you. Ise got a little gal o' my own."

The girl did not answer. Like a light it flashed across her who was the author of this outrage.

"I know your employer!" she said fiercely. "But he shall learn that I fear him not. I defy him still."

(To be continued.)

CHAPTER XXVIII (CONCLUDED).[1]

When Jewel came to herself she was lying on an old-fashioned canopied bed with a coverlet thrown over her. The room was evidently, originally designed for a studio, and was lighted by a skylight; even now a flood of sunlight streamed from above, making more dingy and faded by comparison the appearance of dusty canvases and once luxurious furniture scattered about the apartment. Evidences of decay were everywhere; a broken easel leant against the wall, and on a table odds and ends of tubes, brushes and other artistic paraphernalia were heaped in a disorderly mass. There were also a couch and easy chairs in faded brocade.

The girl looked about her with languid interest scarcely realizing what had happened to disturb the serenity of her daily life. Presently, however, the power of thought returned and with it a flood of memories concerning the outrage of the night before. She was a prisoner, but where?

What a terrible sensation it was to wake to the consciousness of being a prisoner! A prisoner! She, Jewel Bowen, who until recently had never known a care in her short existence of twenty years. Now all the waves and billows of life were passing over her threatening to engulf her. Could it be that all her bright hopes for the future were to end here in this lonely chamber?

With the thought she arose hastily from the bed and began walking despairingly about, examining the room. After a tour of the apartment she gave it up. Her prison was well-chosen. The doors were bolted, and no window gave a possibility of escape. There was no chance of attracting attention, by her cries, from passers-by, even if scores of persons traversed the streets about this house; no one would know that within its walls a desolate girl suffered the keenest of mental torture.

---

1 SYNOPSIS OF CHAPTERS XXVI TO XXVIII. [The synopsis of Chapters I to XXV has not been repeated here. See Appendix A for the full text.] Cuthbert Sumner and Jewel Bowen are married in the prison. At the hearing before the Grand Jury Sumner is held for trial in September. Senator Bowen, who is taken suddenly ill in New York, is brought home and dies the next day. After the funeral General Benson presents a will signed by Senator Bowen, that leaves the entire estate in his hands, together with Major Madison. Jewel Bowen is abducted at the very entrance to her home.

She paced the room frantically, and shook the doors of her prison violently until she was obliged to sink exhausted upon the couch. "They will hardly let me die of hunger," she told herself, resolving to save her strength for questioning whoever should bring her food.

Crouching upon the couch, she listened. Not a sound broke upon her ear. It seemed to her that desolation engulfed her. Presently, as she sat there, the sound of a footfall came to her strained ears, then a key grated in the lock, the door swung open, and a tall, pleasant-featured black man entered the room, bearing a tray. He carefully locked the door behind him, removing the key from the lock. He wheeled forward a small table and deftly arranged the contents of the tray upon it.

Jewel launched an avalanche of questions at him, but he returned no answer. He went and returned a number of times, bringing her clothing, books and luxuries of the toilet, all indicating that a long captivity was in prospect. At lunch time an aged Negress brought her food, but all efforts to engage her in conversation were unavailing; a more morose and repulsive specimen of the race Jewel had never met.

After this there was a monotonous interval of time passed in the agony of silence. Her meals were furnished regularly and all other needs lavishly supplied. One day was the record of another.

Four weeks must have passed since she was brought to this place, still she had no knowledge of her captors, nor where her prison was located. One change, however, was made—they gave her the freedom of an adjoining room as the summer heat increased, but the windows were barred and looked out upon extensive gardens filled with the ruins of what must once have been buildings and offices of a large plantation. The once well-kept walks were overgrown with weeds, and a heavy growth of trees obstructed the view in all directions.

One night she sat by the window gazing at the stars and eating her heart out in agony and tears. She could not sleep; insomnia had added its horrors to her other troubles. Suddenly the sky became overcast and the stars disappeared. A storm threatened. Low mutterings of thunder and gusts of rising wind foretold a summer shower. At intervals a lightning flash lit up the inky blackness of the scene. Finally the flashes became so vivid that the girl moved her seat from the window to a less exposed position with a scornful laugh at her own fear of death. "Truly," she thought bitterly, "self-preservation has been called the first law of nature. How we strive to preserve that which is of so little value."

Up and down the sides of the room her eyes wandered aimlessly; sometimes she felt that she was losing her mind. Presently a painting fixed into the wall arrested her attention. It was the portrait of an impossible wood nymph, but so faded that its beauty—if it had once possessed any—was entirely gone.

As she gazed at it indifferently the centre bulged outward, and a small strip of canvas swung to and fro as if from a draught of air.

Jewel sprang to her feet and ran to the picture. She trembled with sudden hope. Where did the draught come from? Carefully she raised the torn strip of canvas and inserted her hand beneath it, feeling along the wall back of the picture. There was a narrow recess behind it. Greatly excited by this discovery, she flew to the table where her dinner-service still remained, seized a knife and cut the canvas close to the frame for a good distance up. Then she tremblingly raised the cloth.

Oh! joy! It revealed a passage usually closed by a door which had become unfastened and now swung idly in the breeze made by the rising wind.

Thank heaven, it was an hour when she was free from interruption. No one would disturb her until morning. She took the lamp in her hand. Escape seemed very near. Scarcely waiting to widen the aperture, she crept through, and soon stood, covered with dust, trembling, shaken with emotion, in the dark passage which the canvas had hidden.

She paused and strained her ears to listen for sounds in the silent house. None came. Then she crept on very, very cautiously.

The passage was dark. It had evidently led to the servants' quarters at the back of the house when mirth and gaiety held high revel in the glorious old mansion. She went swiftly on, till she came to a black baize door. She pushed it open with little difficulty. Here she paused irresolute, for this door gave admission to the front of the house; there was a passage at right angles with the one just quitted, with stairs leading above and below. She glided toward the latter, seized hold of the banisters, descended into another passage with many doors opening into it. The doors were all closed.

What a rambling old place it was. In the excitement of the instant she had felt no terror, but now an icy chill seized her and her heart throbbed heavily.

She noticed now that one of the doors in the passage was ajar! Dare she pass it? To advance was appalling, but the case was a desperate one. With her heart throbbing wildly she stood motionless one instant, then she ventured past the unclosed door.

She shaded her lamp with one hand and with fascinated gaze took in, in one brief instant, the contents of the room. Her eyes wandered from the bare floor and walls to the table, the two chairs, and then to a bed in one corner. There her gaze lingered, for on the bed lay a woman of dark brown complexion and wrinkled visage; about her head was wound a many-hued bandanna handkerchief. The woman's eyes were open and fixed in terror and amazement upon the girl who had just entered the room. They gazed at each other for one moment, these two so strangely met, then the old woman threw her arms above her head, exclaiming:

"Bless Gawd! I'se ready! Praise de Lor'! He done sen' his Angel Gabriel to tote me home to glory."

The sound of her voice broke the spell that bound Jewel.

"Who are you, Auntie, and what makes you think me an angel?"

"Lor', honey, is you human sho' nuff? Why when I seen yo' face er-shinin' on me dar, an' hearn yer sof' step comin' en de lonely night, I made sho' it was de Lor' come to carry dis' po' sinner to er home in glory. I 'spec' I been shut up here so long I'se gittin' doaty. I'se a po' ol' black 'ooman, been dragged 'way from my home an' chillun an' locked up here by a limb o' de debbil 'cause he's 'fraid I tell his wicked actions. But 'deed chile, whar'd you come from? Does you live in dis place?"

Jewel shook her head sadly.

"I'm a prisoner, too, Auntie. I've been shut up here for four weeks now. I happened to find a way out of my room tonight, and I thought I might possibly escape. Can you tell me where I am?"

"Yes, honey, I can. You's down on de ol' Enson plantation in Ma'lan'. I was born on de nex' joinin' place myself. But who brung you here? What's your name, chile?"

"I haven't seen my captor yet, but I believe it to be General Benson. My name is Jewel Bowen."

"Mercy, King! My lovely Lor'd, but ain't dis curus?" exclaimed the old woman, greatly excited. "My gran'darter is yo' waiter, Venus Johnson!"

It was now Jewel's turn to become excited.

"Then you are?"

"Aunt Henny Sargent; dat's me."

CHAPTER XXIX.

Meanwhile there was mourning at the Bowen mansion, for the joy of the house had fled with Jewel. Mrs. Bowen sent for the family lawyer and then went to bed; trouble was wearing her out, and there was danger of her becoming a confirmed invalid.

Mr. Cameron put the machinery of the law in motion to find the missing girl, but there progress seemed to end.

Now the sorely tried mistress discovered what a treasure she had in the maid Venus. The girl was everywhere attending to the business of the house and waiting on the invalid mistress. She visited the jail with news for the restless unhappy man confined there, never seeming to weary in well-doing. Venus preserved a discreet silence concerning the letter received on the night of the abduction, but the brain of the little brown maid was busy. She had her own ideas about certain things, and was planning for the deliverance of her loved young mistress.

When Jewel had been absent about two weeks, Venus asked leave to pay her mother a visit one evening. Marthy had heard nothing from the police in relation to Aunt Henny, and she was overjoyed to see her daughter; it gave her an opportunity to pour her sorrows and griefs into sympathetic ears.

She bustled about the neat kitchen setting out the best that her home afforded for supper, and Oliver dropped his books in honor of his sister's visit, making it a festival.

When the meal was on the table, smoking hot,—corn pone, gumbo soup, chicken and rice and coffee of an amber hue,—the children ate with gusto. The mother's eyes shone with happiness as she watched their enjoyment, pressing upon them, at intervals, extra helps.

"Have some mo' this gumbo soup, my baby. I reckon you don' git nothin' like it up yonder with all the fixin's you has there."

"Well, my Lord, ma, I won't be able to walk to the cars if I keep on stuffing myself," replied Venus as her mother filled her plate again with the delicious soup.

"Say, Venus," broke in Oliver, with a grin on his mischievous face, "who's the good-looking buck that came to the end of the street with you the last time you were home?"

"What's that?" cried Marthy, sharply.

Oliver laughed and clapped his hands, "Ma's like a hen with chickens; she's afraid of the fellows, Vennie."

Venus laughed, too, a little shame-facedly. "Oh, now, Ollie, ain't you got no cover to your mouth? That was Mr. Sumner's man, John. I had to see him about a message from Mrs. Bowen to Mr. Sumner, and so he was polite enough to come with me to our street, it being pretty dark."

"That's all right," said Marthy in a relieved tone. "Mr. Williams is a perfec' gent'man. You're only a leetle gal, Venus, if you is out to work, an' there's time 'nuff for you to git into trubble. You don' wan' to fill yo' head up with 'viggotty[1] notions 'bout fellars yet. I got married young when I'd doughter been[2] playin' with baby rags; I don' want my gal to take on eny mo' trubble en her haid than she can kick off at her heels. You Venus, mark my wurds, an' 'member what I tell's you ef I'm moulderin' in the clay to dus' an' ashes tomorrer,—gittin' jined to a man's a turrible 'spons'bility, 'specially the man. You want to think well an' cal'ate the consequences of the prevus ac'.[3] Mymy, mymy!" she continued musingly, "how that carries me back to the las' time ol' Mis' Sargeant whopped me. She says to me, 'Marthy, did you take the money off my dresser table? tell me the troof,' and I dussan' lie, an' so I said 'Ys'm; Ike Johnson tol' me to do it an' he'd buy me a red ribbin fer my hair.' Ol' miss says 'Marthy, you's 'mitted the *prevus' ac'*, an' I'm gwine whop you,' an' the ol' lady laid it onto me right smart with her slipper. Ike Johnson's been gittin' me inter trubble ever sense that time.

"Oliver, when you was born an' I foun' you was a man chile I said to myself, 'Lord, how come you let me bring one of them mule[4] critters into the wurl to make trubble for some po' 'ooman?' An' ef ever you git jined, an' treat yo' wife as yo' pa's treated me, I hope you'll git yo' match, an' she'll wallop the yearth with you, 'deed I does."

---

1 Big-headed.
2 Ought to have been.
3 Hasty act.
4 Male.

"Daddy been home lately?" asked Venus carelessly after the meal was cleared away.

"No, chile, he ain't," replied her mother. "He was home— le' me see—jes' befo' the fus' of the munf. He brought me the mor'gage money."

"How much was it?"

"Four hundred dollars Venus, chile, you could have knocked me down with a feather, I was so outdone from 'stonishmen' when he throwed it into my lap and said 'dar's yo' mo'gage.'"

"Now, ma, where'd he get *all* that money I'd like to know? He never got it honest, that's my belief."

"Yes, I reckon he did, honey, this time. Gin'ral Benson give it to him. Yo' granny asked the Gin'ral about it 'way in the winter."

"Hump!" exclaimed Venus.

"He ain't been home sense. Gin'ral's bo't a plantation out o' Baltimo' a bit, an' yo' pa's holpin' to fix it up. I reckon he'll be thare 'bout all summer. He took a few clo's an' things with him when he was home." Venus looked at her mother intently, but remained silent.

"Dear, dear, Venus," Marthy continued beginning to cry, "ef I only knew where was yo' granny or what had come to her, I'd be a happy 'ooman this night. An' to think of Miss Jewel, too, that dear beautiful girl with a face like an angel out of glory. The ways of the Lord is pas' follerin', an' that's a fac'."

"What's dad say about granny?" asked Venus suddenly.

"*He* ain't worried none, bless yo' soul. He ain't studyin' 'bout the dear ol' so'l. He ain't got no mo' blood in him than a lizard. He's the onerist man! Says to me, 'quit frettin'; the ol' 'ooman 'll turn up safe quicker'n scat,' he says. 'She's tuf: nothin' ain't gwine kill the ol' hornet.' Them's yo' pa's words to me."

"What do you expect from dad, ma? you know him. You ought to if anybody does. Granny makes him toe the mark, that's why he dislikes her."

"That's so, sho' 'nuff, baby; an' what we know 'bout Ike Johnson's mean capers would fill a book. It's twenty years come nix Chris'mus sense we jumped the broomstick together.[1] We

---

1 Married. One of Hopkins's favorite sources, William Wells Brown, states in *My Southern Home*, "The mode of jumping the broomstick was the general custom in the rural districts of the South forty years ago; and, as there was no law whatever in regard to the marriage of

was the very las' couple jined befo' the s'render, an' ef it hadn't been for yo' granny, we'd all been in the po' house long ago an' fergit."

When it was time to start for home Oliver escorted his sister to the car. On the way she questioned him closely and learned many things concerning her father that her mother had failed to mention.

"It's as sure as preaching," she told herself late that night as she was preparing for bed, "it's as sure as preaching that some-body who knows something must take hold of Miss Jewel's case or that son of Sodom[1] will carry his point. The police are slower 'n death. Dad's up to his capers. He can fool ma, but he can't pull the wool over my eyes; I'm his daughter. Hump! well, we'll see about it. It's a burning shame for dad to go on this way after all Miss Jewel's kindness to us. But I'll balk him. I'll see him out on this case or my name ain't Venus Johnson."

"I'll see if this one little black girl can't get the best of as mean a set of villains as ever was born," was her last thought as her eyes closed in slumber.

Mr. Henson sat in his office the next morning thinking deeply. He had just returned from New York, where he had care-fully examined the ground, trying to find a flaw in the Bowen will, drawn and signed in that city, but not a particle of encour-agement had rewarded his efforts. He was much depressed over his failure to obtain a clue to what he was convinced was a clever forgery committed by two dangerous men. His vast experience did not aid him; he was forced to declare that the criminals had covered their tracks well.

Mr. Cameron had just left him after acknowledging *his* inabil-ity to fix a point that would legally stay the enforcement of the will.

All was dark; but the man felt that if he could obtain the slightest clue, he could unravel the whole plot without difficulty. But how to gain a clue was the question. He had determined to start the next day for Kentucky in the hope of finding Elise Bradford's aunt and the child of the dead woman, hoping that this might furnish the key to the mystery.

---

slaves, this custom had as binding force with the negroes, as if they had been joined by a clergyman" (46).

1 Wicked city destroyed by God in Genesis 19.

The morning sunshine streamed into the room. The intense heat was enervating. He drew his chair before the large open window on the side where the sun had not reached and directly in the wake of an electric fan. He leaned his head upon his hand and thought over the situation.

All his efforts had been to ascertain if there were any real grounds for the suspicions, which had been aroused in Miss Bowen's mind, and which his interviews with Sumner had confirmed. The news of her abduction had come as a distinct shock to him when it was given him upon his return from New York. The beautiful girl had aroused all the man's innate chivalry; springs of tenderness long dead to any influence had welled up in his soul, and he felt a mad desire, uncontrollable and irresistible, to rescue her, and take dire vengeance on her captors.

Her haunting influence was wrapped about him; he could see her, feel her presence and almost catch the tones of her low voice in the silent room. Ever and anon he glanced about him as if seeking the actual form of the fair spirit that had so suddenly absorbed his heart and soul.

He was satisfied in his own mind that General Benson was the criminal, but to this man who had become a legal machine, tangible evidence was the only convincing argument that he knew.

Presently a clerk entered the room and announced that a woman wished to speak with him.

"Show her in," he replied to the man's query.

A few seconds passed, and then the opening door admitted a young colored girl who had an extremely intelligent, wide-awake expression.

Venus was not at all embarrassed by the novelty of her surroundings, but advanced toward the chief with a business like air, after making sure that the retiring clerk had actually vanished.

"I'm Miss Jewel Bowen's maid," she declared abruptly. The detective whirled around in his chair at her words, and in an instant was all attention. His keen eyes ran over the neat little brown figure standing demurely before him, with a rapid mental calculation of her qualities.

"What is your name?"

"Venus Camilla Johnson."

"How long have you been in Miss Bowen's employ?"

"All the winter."

"Who sent you here?"

"Nobody. I keep my business to myself. Things are too curious around Wash'nton these days to be talking too much."

The shadow of a smile lurked about the corners of Mr. Henson's mouth.

"Well, what do you want? Time is precious with me."

"Yes, sir; I won't keep you long, but you see Miss Jewel's been my good angel and I jus' had to come here and unburden my mind to you or burst. You see, sir, it's this way,—the Bowen family is *white*[1] right through; mos' *too* good for this world. They've got piles of money, but mymy, mymy! since the Senator's gone, and Mr. Cuthbert's done got into trouble from being in tow with Miss Madison, they be the mos' miserablest two lone women you ever saw."

Venus forgot her education in her earnestness, and fell into the Negro vernacular, talking and crying at the same time.

Mr. Henson waited patiently. He knew that she would grow calmer if he did not notice her agitation.

"It's hard for me to go back on my own daddy," continued the girl, "but it's got to be done. I suspicion him more and more every minute I'm alive, I do. Miss Jewel's stolen away, and the old lady's taken down to her bed, an' my daddy is waltzing through the country looking after General Benson's business down on a plantation in Maryland. I'm no fool, Mr. Henson; he's my daddy, but Isaac Johnson's a bad pill. He's jus' like a bad white man, sir,—he'll do anything for money when he gets hard up."

Mr. Henson sat with pale face regarding the woman before him. His eyes gleamed and were fixed searchingly upon her. Finally he asked:

"Who are your parents? I take it they were once slaves. Where were they born?"

"Ma's Aunt Henny Sargeant's daughter Marthy, and daddy's Isaac Johnson. They lived on adjoining plantations in Maryland. Dad belonged to Mr. Enson, and Ma to Mrs. Sargeant. Ma says it was a terrible misfortune that she did live next door to the Ensons, leastwise Oliver and me'd never had Ike Johnson for our daddy."

"Any relation to the Aunt Henny who was employed by the government and who has disappeared?" the detective asked.

---

1 Upstanding.

"Yes, sir; that's her," replied the girl, nodding her head.

"Poor granny; I reckon she's dead all right. Ma takes it terrible hard. Does nothing but cry after granny all day while she's working. I tell her I *cain't* cry till I find Miss Jewel. Ma says I'm unfeeling; but, Lord, you cain't help being just as you're built. Say, Mr. Henson, I've made bold to bring you something. I took it away from the madam the night Miss Jewel was stolen."

Mr. Henson took the envelope that the girl extended to him, and read the note contained therein.

"Who do you think sent this, Venus?"

"No one but old Benson."

Again the chief smiled at the quaint answer. But he looked at her still more searchingly as he asked:

"Did anything of a particularly suspicious nature occur to make you hold that opinion?"

"Well, yes, sir; there did. Something I overheard General Benson say to the old lady."

"Oh, then, you were listening."

"I reckon I was, and a good job, too, or I wouldn't have this to tell you. It was the day the will was read. Mr. Cameron was gone, and the three of 'em—Mrs. Bowen, Miss Jewel and General Benson were in the library. Miss Jewel went out and left the other two together.

"He hollered at the madam like he was crazy, and I was standing there outside the door with the old Senator's boot-jack in my hand, expecting that I'd have to go in and hit the General over the head with it to protect the madam. He says to her, 'So, you will assist that head strong girl to defy me, will you? well, do it at your peril!' then he went close up to her—so close that their noses almost touched, and I thought it was about time for the boot-jack, sure,—but all he did was to whisper to her, and the old madam gave a screech and keeled over on the floor like she was dead.

"I 'clare to you, Mr. Henson, I was skeered enough to drop, but I didn't say a word, no sir; I just went in as soon as the General went out, and I picked the old lady up and got her to her room, and when she came to herself there was no body to ask her what was the matter because they didn't know what I could have told them. But Madam hasn't been herself since. I believe to my soul that he skeered the life out of her. When Miss Jewel didn't come home, and that note came instead, I just made up my mind it was Venus for General Benson, and that I'd got to cook his goose or he'd cook mine."

"You do not like General Benson, I see."

"Like him! who could, the sly old villain. He's mighty shrewd, and—" she paused.

"Well, what?"

"Foxy," she finished. "He tries to be mighty sweet to me, but I like a gentleman to stay where he belongs and not be loving servant girls on the sly. I owe Miss Jewel what money cain't pay, and I'm not ungrateful.

"*I* believe the old rapscallion has got her shut up somewhere down in Maryland, and dad's helping him. Oh, I didn't tell you, did I, that dad's his private waiter?"

"Ah!" exclaimed the chief, for the first time exhibiting a sign of excitement.

"Now we're getting down to business, my girl. I understand your drift now. You have done well to come to me."

Venus smiled in proud satisfaction at his words of praise. The man sat buried in deep thought for a time before he spoke again. Finally he said:

"I need help, Venus: are you brave enough to risk something for the sake of your mistress?"

"Try me and see," was her proud reply.

"It comes to just this: someone must go down to this planta-tion in Maryland, and hang around to find out if there is truth in our suspicions. Can you wear boys' clothing?" he asked abruptly.

Venus showed her dazzling teeth in a giggle. She ducked her head and writhed her shoulders in suppressed merriment as she replied:

"*Cain't* I? well, I reckon."

"Then you'll do. There's no time to be lost. Disguise your-self as a boy. Be as secret about it as possible. Tell no one what you are about to do, or where you are going, and meet me at the station tonight in time for the ten o'clock train for Baltimore. My agent will be waiting for you on the Avenue, just by the entrance, disguised as your grandfather Uncle Henry, a crippled old Negro, fond of drink. You are to be Billy, and both of you are going home to Baltimore. We will fix the rest of the business after you reach the village.

"God grant that this plan may hasten the discovery I have been seeking."

CHAPTER XXX.

Enson Hall reminded one of an ancient ruin. The main body of the stately dwelling was standing, but scarcely a vestige of the once beautiful outbuildings remained: the cabins in the slave quarters stood like skeletons beneath the nodding leaves and beckoning arms of the grand old beeches. War and desolation had done their best to reduce the stately pile to a wreck. It bore, too, an uncanny reputation. The Negroes declared that the beautiful woods and the lonely avenues were haunted after nightfall. It had grown into a tradition that the ghost of Ellis Enson "walked," accompanied by a lady who bore an infant in her arms.

The Hall was in charge of an old Negress, known all over the country as "Auntie Griffin." She was regarded with awe by both whites and blacks, being a reputed "witch woman" used to dealing and trafficking with evil spirits.

Tall and raw-boned, she was a nightmare of horror. Her body was bent and twisted by disease from its original height. Her protruding chin was sharp like a razor, and the sunken jaws told of toothless gums within.

Her ebony skin was seamed by wrinkles; her eyes, yellow with age, like Hamlet's description of old men's eyes, purged "thick amber and plum-tree gum."[1] The deformed hands were horny and toil-worn. Her dress was a garment which had the virtue of being clean, although its original texture had long since disappeared beneath a multitude of many-hued patches.

Auntie Griffin only visited the village for supplies; she was uncongenial and taciturn. She made no visits and received none. Lately, however, it was noticed that the old woman had a male companion at the Hall, an elderly, dudish[2] colored man whom she announced, on her weekly visit to the store, as her brother Ike, come to spend a short time with her.

It was well along in August when an old Negro calling himself Uncle William Henry Jackson, accompanied by his grandson Billy, a spritely lad, scarcely more than a boy, wandered into the village and took possession of one of the dilapidated antebellum huts, formerly the homes of slaves, many of which still adorned the outskirts of the little hamlet.

---

1 Shakespeare, *Hamlet* 2.2.197.
2 Dandyish.

Uncle William Henry claimed to be a former inhabitant who had belonged to a good old Southern family of wealth, made extinct by the civil strife. The oldest resident—a Negress of advanced age who was an authority on the genealogy of the settlement—claimed to remember him distinctly, whereupon he was adopted into their warm hearts as a son of the soil and received the most hospitable treatment; in two weeks he had settled down as a fixture of the place. The old man claimed to be a veteran of the late Civil War, and that he was in receipt of a small pension which provided food for himself and grandchild. Uncle William spent most of his time sitting on a half-barrel at the door of the general store, chewing tobacco, making fishing rods from branches which Billy brought him from the woods and telling stories, of which he had a wonderful stock. The rods he turned out were really pieces of artistic work when they left his hands, and the owner of the store agreed to find a market for the goods.

Thus the old man was happily established, to quote his own words, "fer de res' ob my days," sitting in the sun with a few old cronies of his own cut—white and black harmoniously blended—spinning yarns of life in camp, and, for the truth must be told, drinking bad moonshine rum.

He never tired of describing the battle scenes through which he had passed.

"Do I know anythin' 'bout Wagner?[1] I should say so, bein' I was in it," was his favorite prelude to a description of the famous charge.

"No, honey, I didn' lef' dat missin' leg dar. I lef' dat leg ober to For' Piller.[2] But fer all dat, Wagner was a corker,[3] yes, sah, a corker. From eleven o'clock Friday 'tel four o'clock Saturday we was gittin' on the transpo'ts, we war rained on, had no tents an' nothin' to eat. Thar was no time fo' we war to lead de charge. We came up at quick time an' when we got wifin 'bout one hunde'd

---

1 The Second Battle of Fort Wagner, the 18 July 1863 engagement on Morris Island outside of Charleston, South Carolina, in which many members of 54th Massachusetts, a black regiment, lost their lives.

2 Fort Pillow, the 12 April 1864 battle in Henning, Tennessee, in which Confederate soldiers massacred black troops and their white officers who were attempting to surrender.

3 Something special or memorable.

yards, de rebs[1] open a rakin' fire. Why, mon, they jes' vomited the shot inter us from de fo't, an' we a-walkin' up thar in dress parade order;[2] they mowed us down lak sheep. De fus' shot camed down rip-zip, an' ploughed a hole inter us big 'nuff to let in a squadron, an' all we did was ter close up, servin' our fire; but I tell you, gent'men, we looked at each other an' felt kin' o' lonesome fer a sight o' home an' fren's.

"Colonel Shaw[3] walked ahead as cool as ef he war up on Boston Common, singing out, 'steady, boys, steady!' Byme-by de order come in a clar ringin' voice, 'charge! Foreard, my brave boys!' We started on a double-quick, an' wif a cheer an' a shout we went pell-mell; wif a rush into an' over de ditch them devils had made an' fenced wif wire. But we kep' right on an' up de hill 'tel we war han' to han' wif de inimy. Colonel Shaw was fus' to scale de walls. He stood up thar straight an' tall lak de angel Gabrul, urgin' de boys to press on. I tell you, sah, 'twas a hot time.

"Fus' thing I 'member clearly after I got het up, was I seed a officer standin' wavin' his sword, an' I heard him holler, 'Now, give 'em h—, boys, give 'em h—!' an then thar come a shot; it hit him—zee-rip—an' off went his head; but, gent'men, ef you'll b'lieve me, dat head rolled by me, down de hill sayin' as it went, 'Give 'em h—, boys, give 'em h—!' until it landed in de ditch; an' all de time de mon's arms was a wavin' of his sword."

"Come off, Uncle," exclaimed one of the circle of listeners. "Who ever heard of a man's talkin' after his head was cut off?"

"Gent'men," replied Uncle William solemnly, "dat ar am a fac'; I see it wif my own two eyes, an' hyard it wif my own two ears. *It am a fac'.*"

"I've heard lies on lies," drawled another on-looker, "from all kinds of liars—white liars and niggers—but that is the mos' *infernal* one I ever listened to."

"I'll leave it to Colonel Morris thar[4] ef sech things ain't pos-

---

1 Rebels, Confederate soldiers.

2 Formal, closely packed marching formation.

3 Robert Gould Shaw (1837–63) was the commander of the first black regiment (the 54th Massachusetts). He was killed while leading his men during the Second Battle of Fort Wagner.

4 The detective Smith, disguised as Uncle Henry, is apparently referring to someone in the audience who also fought in the Civil War.

sibul. Ain't you seen cur'us capers cut when you was in battle, sah?"

"Don't bring me into it, Uncle William Henry, I'm listening to you," laughed the Colonel, who had just driven up and was about entering the store to make a purchase.

"It am a fac'; I 'clar it am a fac'," insisted the old man. "Thar was the officer talkin', and then the shot hit him so suddint dat he hadn't time to stop talkin'. Why de water in de ditch mus' have got in his mouf fer *I seen him when he spit it out!*" At this there was a roar of laughter from the crowd, and the first speaker slapped Uncle William Henry on the back with a resounding blow.

"That's a tough one for a professor, Uncle. I know you're dry. Come, have a drink."

When they had all returned to their places, the old man resumed his narrative.

"When I looked agin, Colonel Shaw was gone. The Johnnies[1] had pulled him over the parapet down onter de stockades, an' dat was de las' seen of as gallan' a gent'man as ever lived. I tell you, mon, when I seen dat, I fel' lak a she wil' cat, an' I jes' outfit[2] a blin' mule. I tore an' I bit lak a dog. I got clinched wif a reb, an' dog my cats, fus' thing I know'd I was chawin' him in de throat an' I never lef' go 'tel he give a groan an' I seed he was gone. Jes' then I seen three or fo' Johnnies running 'long de parapet toward me shoutin', 'S'render, you d— nigger.' I looked an' seen dat all 'bout me they was clubbin', stabbin' an' shootin' our boys to death, an' our men was fightin' lak devils themselves.

"Well, sah, when I seen them Mr. Whitemen makin' fer me, I jes' rolled down de hill to de ditch, an' plantin' my gun ba'net down in de water, I lepped acrost to de other side. I was flyin' fer sho, you may b'lieve, an' fus' thing I heard was, 'Halt! who goes thar?' It was de provy guard,[3] a black North Carolina regiment stationed thar to return stragglers to their posts. I sung out, clar an' loud, thinkin' I was suttinly all right then: 'Fifty-fourth Massachusetts!' But I felt de col' chills creep down my back when I heard de order: 'Git-a-back-a-dar, Fifty-fourth!' an' every mon's gun said 'click, clack.' You may b'lieve, gent'men, dat I got back.

---

1 Confederate soldiers.
2 Outfought.
3 Military police.

"I wandered aroun' fer a spell lak a los' kitten; finally, I stumbled into de lines, an' I crep' unner a gun-carriage[1] an' slep' thar 'tel mornin'."

Now it happened that Isaac Johnson was lonely in his enforced solitude, and being of a social disposition, soon made it a habit to wend his way to the corner store and listen to Uncle William Henry's stories. Having plenty of money, he treated freely and was soon counted a "good fellow" by all the frequenters of the place.

At first Isaac drank moderately, mindful of his responsibilities, but soon his old habits re-asserted themselves. Moreover, Uncle William liked the social glass also; and finally the two became so intimate that they would wend their way to the hut in the woods, where the latter had taken up his residence, and there enjoy to the full the contents of a gallon-jug which was concealed under a loose board in the floor. In short, Isaac got drunk, and losing all sense of caution, remained away from the Hall two days and nights, hidden in the hut from prying eyes. The first time this happened, old William Henry recovered control of himself as soon as Isaac was locked in drunken slumber upon Billy's bed, behind the curtains, which divided the one room into two sleeping apartments.

He went to the door then and waved a handkerchief three times, nailed it to the side of the hut and retired.

Ten minutes after this act the lad Billy entered the woods which led to Enson Hall.

The path, though often ill-defined, was never quite obliterated, and he came at last to where the trees grew thinner, and the Hall was visible. Then he emerged upon the broad stretch of meadow and crossing it was soon on the grounds. There he paused and looked cautiously about. Twilight was falling. The scene was wild and romantic. There was no sight nor sound of human beings.

He passed the rusty gates and sped swiftly across the lawn to the shelter of bushes near the wide piazzas. He sank down in their shadow and waited.

Nothing occurred to break the heavy silence. Not a human creature crossed the unkept grounds. The soft summer wind lazily stirred the grass growing in rank luxuriance. The scene

---

1 Cannon.

was desolate and depressing enough. So it continued for over an hour. Darkness finally succeeded the soft twilight. Then the lad re-appeared and skirted the sides and front of the building carefully.

Presently he espied a wild honeysuckle that had climbed to the third story of the house and blended its tendrils gracefully with the branches of a giant sycamore that stretched its arms so near to the house that they tapped gently against the irons that barred a window high above its head.

With the agility of a cat, the boy was quickly finding his way up, up, to the window of the room where Jewel was allowed to exercise and breathe the sweet summer air from the woods and fields. A subdued light gleamed in the window behind the iron bars.

Hush! what noise was that? It was the sound of voices in conversation. The lad ceased his climbing and rested, listening intently for a repetition of the sound. Again it came—first a sweet young voice that had a weary, despondent note; then, in answer the tones of an aged Negro voice in the endeavor to comfort and encourage.

The listener waited no longer, but rapidly mounted to the window just above his head, reached the lower end of the rusty iron bar which divided the broken casement into two, and drew himself up to the ledge, and peered in.

★ ★ ★ ★ ★ ★

Mr. Henson was aroused from slumber at midnight that night to receive an important telegram, which read: "All O.K. Just as we thought. Come on and bag the game."

(To be continued.)

CHAPTER XXXI.[1]

By the middle of September Washington awoke from the stagnation incident to the summer vacation, and was ready to begin the business of another working year. The departments were re-opened and hundreds of stragglers returned to work in the great government hives, all eager for the excitement of the great murder trial.

Sunday, the day before the opening of the trial, Cuthbert Sumner sat in his cell looking pale and careworn but still preserving his outward composure though racked by inward torture. Jewel's abduction had been a worse blow to him than his own arrest, and uncertainty as to her fate had nearly driven him wild; but today Hope had smiled her April smile from amid the clouds that threatened and he was at peace. His lawyer had just left him, bidding him to be of good cheer for all things pointed to a happy ending of his troubles.

Absorbed in thought he sat dreaming of the future and planning for a period of felicity that should atone for the suffering of the present time. Suddenly the key grated in the lock and the door swung open to admit a visitor. He recoiled as from a blow when he met the gaze of Aurelia Madison who stood staring at him with a glance in which curiosity, fear and love were mingled. She stood in the center of the gloomy cell like a statue, her dazzling beauty as marvellous as ever, the red-gold hair still shining in sunny radiance, the velvet eyes resting upon the man before

---

1 SYNOPSIS OF CHAPTERS XXVIII (CONCLUDED) TO XXX. [The synopsis of Chapters I to XXVIII has not been repeated here. See Appendix A for the full text.] Jewel comes out of a swoon to find herself imprisoned in a deserted mansion, waited on by an old Negress and a pleasant looking colored man who is Isaac Johnson. After a number of weeks she manages to get out of her room and in wandering over the house comes upon Aunt Henny, the missing witness in the Bradford murder case.

Meanwhile, Venus Johnson, from remarks made by her mother, infers that Gen. Benson has concealed Jewel at a place near Baltimore, where her father has gone to look after Gen. Benson's business for the summer. She goes to Chief Henson and tells him her thoughts.

Disguised as a boy, she discovers Jewel Bowen and her grandmother, Aunt Henny Sargeant, in the same house.

her with a hidden caress in their liquid depths. Sumner shuddered as he gazed and remembered the dead girl's story. When alone with this woman, she had always possessed an irresistible attraction for him, and in spite of the past the old sensation returned in full force at this unexpected encounter, mingled with fear and repulsion. She broke the spell which held them silent.

"Bert! my Bert!" She stretched out her hand to him, but he made no move to take it. The blood flushed her cheek.

"Why will you not take my hand?" She moved a step nearer to him; but he rose to his feet and drew back.

With a passionate cry she fell on her knees before him, seized his hand and covered it with kisses.

"Do not repulse me. See me at your feet. Bert! let me save you. Do not spurn me, I beseech you."

"Save me? Miss Madison, you jest," replied Sumner in a voice made quiet by a strong effort.

"I do not jest. I can and *will* save you." Her eyes were fixed upon his face in eager intensity. With a shock of surprise Sumner was convinced that she spoke the truth; but he stood there looking down upon her with all the coolness and sternness of a judge.

"You tell me news," he said at length.

"Great God! do not doubt me now. I can save you. All I ask in return is that you take me to your heart again as your affianced wife, and I shall be content."

"Ah! I thought so. There is a price attached to your generosity."

"Do not be so merciless. If you only knew—"

"I *do* know!" broke from Sumner's lips as he flung her off. She reeled back, gasping for breath. Still upon her knees, she gazed up into his immovable countenance. For a full minute there was dead silence. Then Sumner spoke.

"Do not let us have any more mistakes. If my acquittal depends upon the plan you have mentioned, Miss Madison, I shall never be free."

"Why do you speak thus?" she asked as she rose to her feet.

"For many reasons," he replied, significantly.

The woman looked utterly despondent. There was a pause— an exciting pause.

"Surely," she said at length, "you can have no hope that Jewel will return to you. Even if you were free, General Benson will hold her to her promise."

"Do not speak her name," cried Sumner, fiercely. "It is sacrilege for your perjured lips to name her whom you have so tricked, deceived and abused. A bad promise is better broken than kept, and *my wife*, formerly Miss Jewel Bowen, felt the truth of the old adage when she consented to *marry me in this very cell*." He could not repress the note of triumph in his voice as he uttered the words, but he was not prepared for what followed.

"No!" she cried out, with a passion terrible to see. "You have not dared—you could not dare—"

"Stop!" said Sumner sternly. "I warn you; do not try me too far. You will act wisely if you drop this whole matter and leave Washington and the society where you have queened it so long under false pretenses, for solitude and seclusion where you may escape the scorn of the world."

"What do you mean?" she demanded, her features pale to the very lips. She stood at bay, but in her face it could be seen that she measured his strength struggling with a new and horrible dread.

"God forbid that I should make you a social outcast!" he replied. "Need I speak plainer?"

Aurelia listened to him with the watchfulness of a tiger, who sees the hunter approaching, her strong, active brain was on the alert, but now her savage nature broke forth; she laughed aloud ferociously and then began a tirade of abuse that would have honored the slums.

Weary of the whole proceeding, disgusted with himself and the infatuation that had once enthralled him, he said at last, in desperation:

"Let us end this scene and all relations that have ever existed,—if you were as pure as snow, and I loved you as my other self, *I would never wed with one of colored blood, an octoroon!*"[1]

Wordless, with corpse-like face and gleaming eyes she faced him unflinchingly.

"If I had a knife in my hand, and could stab you to the heart, I would do it!"

"I know you would!"

"But such weapons as I possess I will use. I will not fly—I will brave you to the last! If the world is to condemn me as the descendant of a race that I abhor, it shall never condemn me as a coward!"

---

1 A person whose ancestry is one-eighth black.

Terrible though her sins might be—terrible her nature, she was but another type of the products of the accursed system of slavery—a victim of "man's inhumanity to man" that has made "countless millions mourn."[1] There was something, too, that compelled admiration in this resolute standing to her guns with the determination to face the worst that fate might have in store for her. Something of all this Sumner felt, but beyond a certain point his New England philanthropy could not reach.

He bowed his head at her words and said,—"As you will, I have warned you!"

She stood at the full of her splendid stature, her eyes gleaming, her ashen lips firmly set, then she turned from him and gave the signal that brought the warden to let her out. Silently, without a backward look, she passed from the cell, and the prisoner was once more left in solitude.

At nine o'clock that same night, Chief Henson stood near a gas-lamp on the platform of the Baltimore & Ohio railroad station, glancing through a few lines from his colored agent, placed in his hands by plucky little Venus Johnson that very morning. The latter had gone on to the Bowen mansion to prepare the mistress for an unexpected arrival.

Chief Henson was particularly pleased with the ability shown by his colored detectives. Smith, the male agent, was a civil war veteran who had left a leg at Honey Hill,[2] and on that account a grateful government had detailed him for duty on Chief Henson's staff of the secret service, and he had helped his chief out of many a difficult position, for which Mr. Henson was not slow nor meagre in his acknowledgments.

Five minutes after the train was in, Chief Henson saw Smith advancing toward him, accompanied by two females, closely veiled.

From out the swarming crowd the great detective stepped and motioned the man to follow with one of the females while

---

1 Robert Burns's "Man Was Made to Mourn: A Dirge" (1784) includes the lines "Man's inhumanity to Man / Makes countless thousands mourn" (lines 36–37).

2 A 30 November 1864 battle in Grahamville, South Carolina, in which Union forces, including the black 54th and 55th Massachusetts regiments, failed to cut the train line connecting Charleston and Savannah, Georgia.

he himself led the way with the other to the Bowen carriage outside the depot on the Avenue. Having placed the women in the carriage, and given the coachman his directions he and Smith entered a herdic and were driven rapidly to his office where they remained talking until the first hours of the morning.

Meanwhile Venus had resumed her duties as suddenly as she dropped them. The servants wondered among themselves, but not a comment was made. The news that the faithful girl brought seemed to restore Mrs. Bowen's lost vitality; she insisted on rising and being dressed, and received Jewel in her arms at the great entrance doors.

Supper was served in Mrs. Bowen's private parlor. Anyone who had entered the room would have been surprised at the kind solicitude and graciousness shown old Aunt Henny who was an honored guest. Mrs. Bowen's attention was evenly divided between her step-daughter and the old Negress. Venus waited on the company and for the time all thoughts of caste were forgotten while the representatives of two races met on the ground of mutual interest and regard.

Again and again Venus was called upon to repeat the story of her adventures.

"Yes, Mis' Bowen" she said for the twentieth time, "when I peeked in through that window and saw Miss Jewel an' gran sitting there talkin', I was plum crazy for a minute. Then I climb down as fas' as any squirrel an' I made tracks fer Mr. Smith, an' I told him what I'd seen. He says to me, says he, 'now, Venus, how in time 'm I goin' to get you into that house? We can't break the windows an' git in because they're ironed. 'Clar,' says he, 'I don't know where I'm at.' Well, you know Mis' Bowen, I ain't a bit slow, no'm, if I do say it, an' I jus' thought hard for a minute, an' then *it struck me!* Says I to him, 'git a move on dad there. You and me together mus' tote him to the house. When we git there you knock up the ol' woman an' make her let you put dad in; keep up all the fuss you can,' says I, 'an' in the kick-up why I'll sneak in and hide. You be waitin' by the front door, an' I'll have 'm out in a jiffy.' 'Good!' says he, 'two heads is better'n one if t'other is a sheep's head.' 'Much 'bliged for callin' me a fool,' says I. 'Welcome,' says he, 'but I take off my hat to you, young lady, I does, an' I'm goin' to give the chief a pointer to git you on the staff,' says he. 'Here's something to help the cause along,' an' he gave me a big bunch of keys an' a dark lantern.[1] 'Try the keys on the big front door,' he says.

"Well, everything worked pretically fine, Mis' Bowen. Dad was so drunk he couldn't stand, an' he didn't know whether he was afoot or ridin'. I slipped in all right, got my lady an' gran, an' got away as slick as grease.

"Dad ain't shown his head since; Mr. Henson's lookin' fer him, but I know he'll keep shy. I reckon he don't want to see ol' Ginral Benson fer one right smart spell. He's skeered all right—skeered to pieces."

Aunt Henny said nothing, but once in a while she would nod her turbaned head in seeming perplexity, as she furtively watched every movement made by Mrs. Bowen. For her part, Mrs. Bowen seemed uneasy under the old woman's persistent regard.

CHAPTER XXXII.

At last the eagerly looked for day of the Bradford murder trial came. Society had been on the qui vive[2] ever since Sumner's arrest, and in the twenty-four hours preceding the opening of the trial, public interest had gone up to almost unparalleled intensity of excitement, which the facts already known of the case increased as the time for the crisis approached. Among these facts was the one of the disappearance of the principal witness for the defense. Extraordinary disclosures were anticipated, and the wildest rumors were afloat, some of which contained a few grains of the truth.

The police told off for duty at the court had their work cut out for them, for crowds began to gather long before the opening hour, some to get in—some to see the notables in society, and the government swells arrive in quick succession. Before ten the room was crowded in every available place, and further admission was refused except to those engaged in the case.

Will Badger and Carroll West made their way slowly to their places among a nest of their set, including Mrs. Brewer and

---

1 A lantern with a movable door that can be used to direct or eliminate light.
2 French: on the look out for.

Mrs. Vanderpool and other friends of Sumner. Badger and West expected to be called by the defense.

The entrance of General Benson and Major Madison caused a flutter as they took their places in the space reserved for witnesses by the prosecution. Aurelia's tall, graceful form in a handsome dark gown followed the men. She received the various salutes which came to her from all parts of the crowded room with her usual polished elegance, but the fashionable world was puzzled; there was that in her appearance which suggested tragedy.

"Good heaven!" thought Carroll West, "I wonder if there can be any truth in the rumor I have just heard! How exquisite she looks, and pale—yes, and anxious too. I wonder if she cares for Sumner. I wonder what it all means anyhow. Heaven help her safely through this ordeal."

And she had need of all the sympathy that his kind heart could bestow, for the close of the trial would see her homeless, friendless, moneyless, under the ban of a terrible caste prejudice, doubly galling to one who, like herself, had no moral training with which to stem the current of adverse circumstances that had effectually wrecked her young life.

But all society missed its queen, Jewel Bowen, about whom the wildest reports were circulated, but no one knew the truth concerning her trip out of town. Jewel had an interview with her husband early in the morning, and it was decided that Mrs. Bowen and she would not enter the court room until the day when Aunt Henny was to give her testimony. Sure now of Cuthbert's acquittal the ladies were content to wait patiently the law's course.

General Benson was ignorant, as yet, of his prisoner's escape. Isaac had disappeared and Ma'am Griffin did not dare send him word. So in ignorance of the true state of affairs, he was his own imperious self.

Presently counsel were in their places. The Attorney General and a distinguished advocate for the government; and for the defense, ex-Governor Lowe, of Massachusetts, brilliant in criminal cases, had associated with him the Bowen family lawyer, Mr. Cameron, and—mightiest of all in interest of the accused, was the guidance and keen incisive intelligence of the sleuth hound E. Henson,[1] Chief of the Secret Service Division.[2]

---

1 Earlier the name was J. Henson.

2 Agency founded in 1865 following the death of Lincoln. Its purpose

Just after ten the buzz of talk suddenly ceased, hushed by the indescribable settling of a crowd long in expectancy, as the officials took their seats. The hush became breathless as the spectators waited the appearance of the one man for whom they had all gathered here that day—the prisoner. A buzz of admiration passed through the crowd as the accused passed to his seat. Erect, easy, dignified, Sumner took his place with the same grace that had marked his entrance into the crowded halls of pleasure. He met the steady stare of those thousand eyes cooly, steadily.

"How splendidly he bears himself!" whispered one to another. He had made a distinctly good impression.

Now came the necessary formalities. The jury to be called a mysterious algebraic proceeding to the uninitiated, where the value of the x is evolved to the amazement of the onlooker. The twelve men good and true were selected in this instance with very little trouble for a case so widely known and discussed. They were unchallenged and so, presently, were duly sworn; then the official question was put:

"How say you, prisoner at the bar—guilty or not guilty?"

The answer came in clear tones, low and steadily:

"Not guilty!"

The Attorney-General arose and began the trial with a recapitulation of the circumstances attending the murder of Elise Bradford, and the evidence adduced at the inquest. "And," said the learned counsel, "there can be little doubt that the secret of the crime lies in the victim's past. Clever detectives are of that opinion, and they argue logically enough that the fear of exposure of a guilty secret has been once more the motive of a terrible tragedy. The prisoner admits that he had been particularly attracted by the murdered girl at one time. It is known that they were alone together all that fatal Sunday afternoon in the deserted Treasury Building. He alone had exclusive opportunity to commit the crime. He admits that he gave her a glass of wine from the store kept for the chief's private use, but tells us that he left the victim in her usual health at eight that night, she refusing his escort home on a plea of wanting to pack up her belongings as she did not intend to return to work the next week having resigned her position.

---

was to protect the US president and root out currency counterfeiters.

All this story will be proved a tissue of falsehoods unless the prisoner has the power to prove who *did* administer poison to the dead woman—if he did not do it himself—after he left the office on that fatal night."

The learned counsel weighed strongly all these stubborn facts, in an eloquent speech, which told with[1] the audience. The case looked black for the accused. But the brilliant ex-governor smiled serenely as he glanced over the sea of faces. The trial dragged itself along with varying interest through two days. On the third day Aurelia Madison was called to prove the prisoner's gallantry and fickleness.

She did not glance at the prisoner as she passed to the witness box, impassive and lovely, but gave her evidence in a clear, concise manner that carried conviction with it. When she had finished, the tide of public opinion was strengthened against the prisoner. Like a whited sepulchre,[2] full of hatred, she attempted to swear away the life of an innocent man to gratify her wish for revenge. By her testimony society learned for the first time the secret of the broken engagement between the accused and Jewel Bowen. Her story caused a sensation.

"Heavens! It looks strange!" whispered Mrs. Vanderpool to her neighbor Mrs. Brewer. But the end was not yet. As the witness turned to leave the stand, Governor Lowe said blandly:

"One moment. Miss Madison; I wish to ask you a few questions."

The girl paused; a white shade passed over the classic features.

"You are Major Madison's daughter?"

"Yes."

"He is your father?"

"Yes; so I am told," this last haughtily.

"Describe your mother as you remember her."

"I do not remember my mother—I never saw her. I know nothing of her."

"Where were you born?"

"In Jackson, Mississippi, I am told."

"How much money were you to receive the day Mr. Sumner married you and General Benson married Miss Jewel Bowen?"

"I don't understand your meaning."

---

1 Had an effect on.
2 Hypocrite; see Matthew 23.27.

"Weren't you to have a million given you the day you married Mr. Sumner? Yes or no."

"My dowry was a million dollars, if that is what you mean."

"Call it what you like, young lady; that was your share of the boodle with the man thrown in. That is all."

A buzz of excitement went over the crowded room. The prosecution looked at each other in blank amazement. Major Madison moved about uneasily in his seat. He was the next one called.

He knew very little of the prisoner. He was abroad at the time the engagement was made between the accused and Miss Madison, and could add little to the testimony already given. Knew Mr. Sumner as a visitor at houses where they were mutually acquainted, and had invited him to card parties in his own home.

Again the brilliant advocate asked but few questions.

"Miss Aurelia Madison is your daughter?"

"Yes."

"Born in Mississippi?" The Major nodded.

"Who was her mother?"

"My wife."

"The servant—slave or what might you call her—that stood to you in that relation? Is it not so?" blandly insinuated the questioner.

"We object," interposed the Attorney-General hurriedly to the evident relief of the enraged witness.

"Your objection is sustained," returned the judge.

Not at all disconcerted, Governor Lowe bowed pleasantly to judge, jury, lawyers and witnesses, in token of submission.

"Well, Major, did you ever know a man by the name of Walker? Or, weren't you known by that name once yourself?"

"Yes, I took that name when I was in money difficulties and hiding from my creditors."

"The man I mean was a slave-trader, notorious all over the South, who was one of the band of conspirators that murdered President Lincoln. Did you ever meet him?"

"I never have," replied the witness visibly disturbed.

"Business good, Major? How are the Arrow-Head gold mine securities turning out?"

"As well as I can expect."

"But not so well as you could wish; meantime you run a faro[1]

---

1 Card game.

bank with your daughter as the snare and incidentally black mail and bunco[1] a rich family to repair your shattered fortunes. That is all, major."

The excitement increased momentarily among the spectators. It was easy to perceive that Governor Lowe was but reserving his forces. The last witness called by the prosecution was General Benson, and nothing was elicited from him but the fact that the murdered woman had worked in his department for five years, was competent and faithful. He had no knowledge of her family nor connections outside the office. He had noticed that Mr. Sumner was somewhat partial to the good-looking stenographer, but he attached no importance to that fact, he had been young once himself. The audience was captivated by his winning manners and genial smiles. Governor Lowe took all his rights in the cross-examination.

"You gave your name as Charles Benson, General? Ever known to the public by any other name?"

For a moment the General was nonplussed.

"Sir!" with freezing haughtiness, "I do not understand you."

"My question was a plain one; but I will put it in another form—Weren't you originally known as St. Clair Enson? Isn't that the only name you have a right to wear?"

Sensation in the court room.

"We object," from the Attorney-General.

"Your objection is sustained," from the judge.

Governor Lowe was in no wise disconcerted. Again he bowed to the judge, then faced the witness still bland and smiling.

"How old was Miss Bradford when she entered your employ?"

"Eighteen, I believe."

"Awhile back you said you thought nothing of Mr. Sumner's attentions to the good-looking stenographer because you were young once yourself. I hear you are still very partial to the ladies, age has not deadened your sensibilities to their infinite charms. Did you not also offer attention to your good-looking stenographer? Did not your attentions become so warm that for various *pressing* reasons you promised Miss Bradford marriage?"

"Your questions are an outrage, sir!"

"Plain yes or no, that is all I want."

"Most emphatically *No!*" thundered the witness, livid with

---

1 Swindle.

rage. Again Governor Lowe bowed.

"Just one question more. Where were you on the night of the murder, in New York or Washington?"

"I was in New York."

The silence in the room was intense. One sensational question had followed another so rapidly that the vast throng of people found no expression for their wonderment save in silence. What was this man showing?

"Thank you, General, that is all."

That closed the prosecution.

"By Jove! more lies under this than we can see," whispered West to Badger.

Still the testimony of the state was clear on all essential points strengthened by numberless details pointing toward the guilt of the prisoner. So the third day ended, and the public felt repaid for their interest; it bade fair[1] to go down in history as an extraordinary criminal incident.

CHAPTER XXXIII.

Thursday there was a settling down for a fresh start, an intense expectancy throughout the court. All felt that they were nearing a crisis. There were many new faces seen amid the throng and among them were the well-known features of Mrs. Bowen and Jewel, both closely shrouded in their sombre mourning robes.

Speculation was rife as to the line of the defense. What were they to hear now? What was, what could be the defense that could overpower the weight of evidence already given which seemed to make a fatal verdict a foregone conclusion? And yet, somehow, from the highest to the lowest of that hushed, excited throng, there was a curious, subtle feeling that some such resistless power lay in that reserved defense now about to be launched.

Perhaps the wish was "father to the thought."[2] The calm confidence and lack of anxiety on the part of the defense hinted of powerful resources.

One lawyer remarked to another, "It looks as if he had a reserve force that will absolutely reverse the battle."

---

1 Seemed likely.

2 Proverb that appears in Shakespeare's *Henry IV Part II*, 4.3.245.

The prisoner sat with folded arms, cool, motionless as a statue, outwardly, but within, the man's blood was on fire.

Now Governor Lowe, with courtly manner and in sonorous tones, took up his part in the drama, beginning with the prisoner's alleged reckless youth as brought out in Miss Madison's testimony, mainly. He admitted that his client had been wild but not to the point of profligacy. He spoke tenderly of the absent, aged father—a helpless invalid—and his indulgence of an only child—motherless, too, from birth—proud, passionate, high-spirited, indulged, uncontrolled personally and in the expenditure of money, and that at this most dangerous period of a lad's life, the young man had met Miss Madison and succumbed to her fascinations, whom he intended to show was but a beautiful adventuress.

"The court," he said, "has been prejudiced against my client more by this woman's evidence than by any other testimony introduced for the government, added to that the sympathy of the whole audience has been aroused by the spectacle of a helpless woman's trust betrayed. Bah! Let me briefly unfold to you, gentlemen of the jury, the truth of the garbled tale so skilfully woven by a designing woman."

Governor Lowe then related the story of the past winter and the broken engagement, as known to our readers, with added facts to show that his client had in no way wronged the woman, who knew perfectly well what she was about, having previously become a party in a conspiracy designed to force Cuthbert Sumner into marriage, and at the same time, give the control of the wealth of a well-known family into the hands of "the gang" through the daughter of the house, the betrothed of the accused.

Counsel then told of Aurelia's proposition of the day before the opening of the trial, and that the warden was a listener to the conversation between the prisoner and the witness; of her offer to give testimony at the trial which should free him, as she *knew the guilty party*; of the prisoner's scornful rejection of the offer, and his final retort when he told her that if she were as pure as snow, he would *never wed with one of colored blood*!

Here the astute counsel paused for his telling point to take effect. Nor was he disappointed in his calculations, for its action was as an electric shock upon the aristocratic gathering. "And now, your honor, and gentlemen of the jury," he resumed with solemn impressiveness, "I am going to prove that my client's version of his connection with this affair is absolutely true; that he was not the perpetrator of the deed, but by the irony of Fate he has been placed in a position where it was next to impossible for him to prove his innocence. After Mr. Sumner left Miss Bradford in the office on that fatal Sunday night, a person who shall be nameless still, for a time, a man high in official life, a leader in society, did enter said office and talk with the murdered woman whom he had promised to marry in a short time. While there they took wine together, he himself pouring it out and placing in her portion the arsenic, grains of which were found in the empty glass, and in the woman's stomach after death, as testified to before you by the coroner, et al."

Again he paused, for he could feel the horror that thrilled the crowd.

"This man, gentlemen of the jury, was aware of the relation formerly existing between Miss Madison and the accused, and scoundrel that he is, used the woman as a tool for the base purpose of blackmail which fortunately a higher power has frustrated; and for other reasons as well, planned to leave Mr. Sumner so surrounded and connected with Miss Bradford as to render it impossible for him to extricate himself from the charge of murder."

The counsel's manner was most effective as he made his charges; the whole scene so dramatic that only a sensational melo-drama could have rivalled its power. A subdued "whew-w!" went from mouth to mouth as a faint glimmer of the truth began to show something of the possibilities of the line taken by the defense.

"Finally, thanks to the astuteness, experience and daring of the very clever detective, who has really had active charge of the whole case, and to whom the highest praise is due, a *witness of the crime will be produced*!"

The audience was astounded; they had hoped for a sensation; their desire was more than realized.

Governor Lowe wound up his brilliant effort with a slight peroration—knowing well its good effect upon a jury—and amidst murmurs of applause, was ready to call his witness.

The first was John Williams, Sumner's valet, who testified to the regularity of his master's habits and his abstemious living. During the cross-examination, John got angry and told the Attorney-General that the Sumners were top-crust, sure; and never one of them had been known to show up as underdone dough nor half-and-half's,[1] if it wasn't so he'd eat his own head; he didn't object to meeting any man who disputed the "pint," in a slugging match, the hardest to "fend" off. The judge called him to order and the witness took his seat in a towering rage over the "imperdunce" of Southern white folks, anyhow.

Then West and Badger took the stand to refute the charge of inveterate gambling that had been made against the prisoner by Miss Madison. West was questioned only about Sumner and not of his own connection with the Madisons for which he was devoutly thankful. The fact was brought out that the Madison house was a gambling palace where men were fleeced of money for the sake of the smiles of the beautiful Aurelia, by the young fellow's tale of Sumner's warning to him against allowing himself to be ensnared by the Madison clique.

The watchmen and one or two cleaners were also placed upon the stand to prove that Mr. Sumner *did* leave the Treasury Building at the hour sworn to by him.

After that the motherless and worse than fatherless child—a beautiful fair-haired boy, was led forward and stood upon a chair in the witness-box, to give emphasis to the point made by counsel that the dead woman had a pressing claim upon some man who wished to rid himself of her as encumbrance. Some of the women spectators wept, and many men felt uncomfortable about the eyes. Then Gov. Lowe said: "I call Aunt Henny Sargeant." Two officers led the tottering old Negress from the ante-room to the witness chair. Aunt Henny had aged perceptibly since her imprisonment, but her faculties were as keen as ever. As she entered the crowded court-room, there was a cry, quickly suppressed, from the back seats of the room:

"Oliver, that's yer granny! My God, she's livin' yit!"

"Aunt Henny, I believe you have been in the employ of the government at the Treasury Building?"

"Yes, honey, I has."

"Tell the court how you came to be employed."

"Well, honey, I foun' a big pile o' greenbacks—mus' a bin 'bout a million dollars, I reckon,—one night when I was sweepin', an' I jes' froze to 'em all night. I neber turned 'em loose 'til de officers come in de mornin'; money's a mighty onsartin'

---

1 Anything less than consistently exemplary.

article, chillun. People won' steal if they don' get a chance, dat's my b'lief. Then de Presidun' an' lots of other gemman made a big furze over me, an' dey done gib me my job fer life."

"Now, Aunt Henny, do you remember where you were on Sunday evening, March 20, between six and ten o'clock?"

"Yas, honey, I does, fer I warn't in bed, nuther was I to home. I was at the Building doin' some dustin' in Gin'ral Benson's 'partmen', that I'd lef over from the afternoon befo'."

"Yes; well tell us what happened that evening at the Building."

"Well, honey, I wen' in pas' the watchman, who arst me wha' I was after, an' I tol' him. Den I wen' up to Gin'ral Benson's 'partmen', which was whar I'd lef' off. I has a skilton key dat let's me git in whar I wants to go. After I'd been in 'bout an hour, I hearn people talkin' in one ob de rooms—the private office—an' I goes 'cross de entry an' peeks roun' de corner ob de po'ter—"

"The what?" interrupted the judge.

"Po'ter, massa jedge; don' yer kno' what a po'ter am?"

"She means, portière, your honor," explained Gov. Lowe, with a smile. "Go on, aunty."

"I peeked 'roun' de corner ob de po'ter, an' I seed Miss Bradford an' de Gin'ral settin' talkin' as budge as two buzzards. He jes was makin' time sparkin' her like eny young fellar, an' fer a mon as ol' as I kno' *he* is, I tell you, gemmen, he was jes' makin' dat po' gal b'lieve de moon was made o' green cheese an' he'd got the fus' slice."

A suppressed laugh rippled through the room.

"What happened then?"

"Honey, my cur'osity was bilin' hot to see what was gwine on, an' I keep peekin' an' peekin'; byme-by I hearn de glasses clickin', an' I took another look, 'cause, tho' I'm a temprunce 'ooman, an' I b'long to de High Co't o' Gethsemne, an' de Daughters ob de Bridal Veil,[1] I neber' b'lieve dat good wine is gwine ter harm on' ol' rheumatiz 'ooman like me; no, sah; dar ain't none o' yer stiff-necked temp'runce 'bout yer Aunt Henny; I aint no better than quality. I know'd dat was good stuff dat de chief had in thar 'cause I'd done taste some ob it befo', an' I'd promis' myself to taste it agin dat very night soon as dat couple was gone. While I was thinkin' 'bout it, de Gin'ral turned his

---

1 Aunt Henny is presumably referring to temperance organizations here.

back to Miss Bradford as he poured de wine from de 'canter, an' dat brung him full facin' me whar I was a peekin' at him, an' bless my soul, gemman, I seed dat villyun drap somethin' white inter de glass an' then turn 'roun' an' han' it to Miss Bradford. I was dat skeered I thought I'd drap, an' while I was a makin' up my min' what to do, suddintly she throwed up both arms an' screeched out "*My God, Charles, you've pizened!*"

Great sensation in the court, and the crier restored order.

"What happened then, Aunty?"

"Bless my soul, honey, I don' know what did happen, somethin' dat neber come across me in all my life befo'. I tell you, gemmen, it takes somethin' to make a colored woman faint, but dat's jes' wha' I did, massa jedge; when I seed dat po gal fro up her arms an' hern her screech I los' all purchase[1] ob myself, an' I ain't got over it yet."

The old negress rocked herself to and fro in her chair. She made a weird picture, her large eyes peering out from behind the silver-bowed glasses, her turbaned head and large, gold-hoop earrings, and a spotless white handkerchief crossed on her breast over the neat gingham dress.

"And then, Aunty?" gently prompted Gov. Lowe.

"When I come to myself agin, I was in prison, an' my own son-in-law was a keepin' me locked up."

"Was that the reason you did not inform the authorities of what you had seen?" asked the judge.

"Yas, sah; yas, massa jedge."

"Now, Aunt Henny, I want you to tell the court when and where you knew General Benson before you saw him in the employ of the government," said Gov. Lowe.

"We object, your honor," promptly interrupted the Attorney-General.

"The objection is not well taken, Mr. Attorney-General. I think Gov. Lowe has a right to put the answer in evidence. We are not here to defeat the ends of justice. Proceed, Aunt Henny."

"He ain't Gin'ral Benson no more'n I'm a white 'ooman. His name's St. Clair Enson; he was born nex' do' to de Sargent place on the Enson plantation. Ise one ob de fus' ones what held him when he was born. Ise got a scar on me, jedge, where dat imp ob de debbil hit me wid a block ob wood when he warn't but seven

---

1 Control.

years ol'. Fus' time I seed him in dat 'partmen' I know'd him time I sot my eye on him, an' den I know'd thar'd be rucktions[1] kicked up, fer ef eber dar was a born lim' o' de debbil it's dat same St. Clair Enson."

"That will do, aunty. Perhaps my legal brother may wish to cross-examine."

The Attorney-General then took the witness in hand and conducted a skillful cross-examination without shaking the old woman's testimony. Finally he said:

"One last question and I am through: you spoke of your son-in-law—what has he to do with General Benson?"

"He!" snorted Aunt Henny indignantly, "thar ain't no kind ob devilmen' St. Clair Enson was ever mixed up in dat Ike Johnson warn't dar to help him. Ike's my gal's husban'; he's Gin'ral Benson's valley; he was gave to St. Clair Enson when dat debbil was a baby in de cradle."

During the testimony of this last witness, Gen. Benson and Maj. Madison were busily talking to each other, with an occasional word to the Attorney-General.

As Aunt Henny retired to her seat in the ante-room, Gov. Lowe arose, and in an impassioned speech moved the prisoner's release, and the taking into custody of the man really guilty—General Benson.

Scarcely waiting for him to finish, the Attorney-General sprang to his feet and attacked the defense fiercely. Then ensued a scene unparalleled in the history of courts of justice.

"On what would you base such an unheard of precedent? on the evidence of a Negress? Would you impugn the honor of a brilliant soldier, a brave gentleman—courteous, genial, standing flawless before the eyes of the entire country? Such a man as General Benson cannot be condemned and suspicioned by the idiotic ramblings of an ignorant *nigger* brought here by the defense to divert attention from the real criminal, who attempts to shield himself under the influence of the Bowen millions. In the same spirit that has actuated my legal brother, while deprecating violence of any kind as beneath the dignity of our calling, I would feel myself justified in sounding the slogan of the South—lynch-law![2] if I thought this honorable body could be

---

1 Trouble.

2 The practice by which a mob presumes to take justice (*continued*)

influenced to so unjust a course as is suggested by Gov. Lowe."

Instantly a chorus of voices took up the refrain—"That's the talk! No nigger's word against a white man! This is a white man's country yet!"

For a brief space, judge, jury and advocates were nonplussed; women shrieked and men flinched, not knowing what the end might be. But above the uproar, which was answered by the crowd outside, rang the voice of the police-sargeant as he formed his men in line at the door ready to charge the would-be violators of the peace. Before the determined front of the police, the crowd quieted down and order was restored.

Then Gov. Lowe arose once more:

"May it please your honor, and gentlemen of the jury, I have still another witness to present, and the last one, I call the chief of the Secret Service Division."

Once again there was silence in the room. Curiosity was on tiptoe. Many men in high places knew the chief well by reputation but had never met him. He had successfully coped with many important cases and had saved the government millions of dollars. He entered the witness-box calmly as if oblivious of the curiosity of the crowd.

"Mr. Henson, I believe that for many years you have been in the secret service."

"Yes, for fifteen years I have served the government in the capacity of a detective. Previous to that time I was a soldier and served three years, on the Federal side, at the front."

"Now, Mr. Henson, we will ask you to tell the court what you know of this case, in your own way."

At the first sound of his voice, Mrs. Bowen, who up till this time had been sitting with lowered veil, suddenly swept it one side and stared at the man in the witness-box with a strained, startled gaze. His eyes, wandering over the audience, rested on her white face. For one instant he wavered and seemed to hesitate, then by an effort he regained his composure and began his story.

"I was first called into this case by Miss Jewel Bowen. I took hold of it because of the interest she aroused in my mind, and out of pity for her distress. After I met and conversed with Mr.

---

into its own hands without legal authority, which often resulted in the torture, mutilation, and burning of African Americans.

Sumner, I was satisfied in my own mind of his innocence, and that he was the victim of a conspiracy."

In a brief, incisive way, which carried weight to many doubting minds, he detailed the substance of the information he had obtained.

"Being brought into the issues growing out of the intimacy between General Benson and the Bowen family because of his engagement to Miss Bowen, I, very naturally, was placed in charge of the business of accumulating the facts in regard to Senator Bowen's death in New York. I have found out that he made no will while there, and that the one offered here for probate by Gen. Benson *is a forgery*.

"After Senator Bowen's death his daughter was abducted, and in the search which I caused to be made for her, we found, concealed in the same house, the old Negress, Aunt Henny. So, step by step, we have been able to fix the murder of Miss Bradford, the forged will of Senator Bowen, the abduction of Miss Bowen and of Aunt Henny—the most important witness in this case—upon a band of conspirators numbering three people, all well known in society and having the entrée to the best houses."

"Do we quite understand you, Mr. Henson," asked the judge, "that in your opinion the prisoner at the bar has been the victim?"

"Yes, your honor, but only because he stood in the way of their obtaining the Bowen millions. That was the intention in the start—to obtain that immense fortune. Other than the strong attachment existing between Miss Bowen and Mr. Sumner, he would never have been molested.

"It now becomes my duty to make a statement in regard to the testimony of the last witness."

His face was set and stern. It was evident that he struggled to maintain his composure.

"What she has said concerning Gen. Benson is absolutely true. It is a long story, gentlemen, but I will be as brief as possible."

Then in graphic words that held the vast crowd spellbound, he told the story of Ellis and St. Clair Enson, as our readers already know it up to the discovery of Hagar's African descent. The judge forgot his dignity, a shock waved over the court-room. People seemed not to breathe, the interest was so intense, as they listened to the burning words of the speaker.

"When Ellis Enson returned home after completing his arrangements for taking his wife abroad, he was set upon in Enson woods by his brother and the unprincipled slave driver, Walker, and beaten into unconsciousness. When he came to himself he was in South Carolina enrolled as a member of the Confederate army. Here he remained until a good opportunity offered, when he deserted and returned home to find that his wife, child and slaves (of whom Aunt Henny was a valued house servant), had been driven to the Washington market, where his wife in desperation had thrown herself and infant into the Potomac river.

"Stripped of his fortune, home and family, cursing God and man, he entered the army on the Federal side, seeking death, but determined to carry destruction first to those who had so cruelly wronged him. But death comes not for the asking, and the ways of God are inscrutable."

He paused and passed his hand over his beaded forehead. Gen. Benson sat like a marble statue, and his nails reddened where he gripped the arms of his chair. The sound of voices came in from the street through the open window. Inside there was silence like the grave.

"Ellis Enson always supposed that his brother St. Clair stayed abroad where he had hidden after he was found guilty as one of the conspirators against the life of President Lincoln, but when I was called into this case, I found that he was in this country, serving the government he had basely betrayed, and still steeped in crime, along with his pal, Walker. Gentlemen, General Benson is St. Clair Enson, and his friend, Major Madison, is the notorious trader, Walker.

"As for me, I no longer need to conceal my identity. Gentlemen—" he gasped and faltered, and put his hand to his throat as though the words choked him.

"*General Benson is my brother—I am Ellis Enson!*"

As he finished speaking Mrs. Bowen sprang to her feet with a scream; she made a step towards him—then stopped—while these words thrilled the hearts of the listeners:

"*Ellis! Ellis! I am Hagar!*"

(To be concluded.)

CHAPTER XXXIV.[1]

At Mrs. Bowen's impassioned cry, Chief Henson turned an appealing look upon the judge, who bowed his head as if understanding the mute question; he reached the fainting woman's side with one stride, and lifted her tenderly in his strong arms, then he bore her from the crowded room, followed by the maid and weeping step-daughter. The spectators fell back respectfully before the stern man over whose white face great tears, that did not shame his manhood, coursed unheeded.

When the excitement incident to Chief Henson's story (or Ellis Enson, as we must now call him) had somewhat subsided, the trial was resumed.

Governor Lowe called no other witnesses, but at once rose to address the jury for the prisoner, and never, perhaps, had the great politician and leader been more eloquently brilliant than on that occasion. He ranged up the whole mass of evidence with a bold and masterly grasp that could not be outrivalled.

In burning words he laid bare the details of the plot for millions, explaining that when General Benson found himself defeated in all directions, and threatened with exposure by the woman he had ruined, if he persisted in marrying Miss Bowen, he had conceived the idea of a diabolical deed—to murder Miss Bradford and allow the guilt to rest upon Cuthbert Sumner, thus ridding himself of two obstacles at one stroke.

He painted vividly the stealthy return of General Benson from New York to Washington, his arrival at the Treasury Building, his concealment in the great wardrobes, with which his

---

1 Synopsis of Chapters XXXI to XXXIII. [The synopsis of Chapters I to XXX has not been repeated here. See Appendix A for the full text.] Aurelia Madison visits Sumner in prison and offers to prove his innocence, if he will marry her. He refuses to do this, announces his marriage with Jewel, accuses her of bearing colored blood, and she leaves him vowing vengeance. At the trial Aunt Henny is produced as an eye-witness of the murder. Lynching is threatened by the crowd when Gov. Lowe moves to arrest Gen. Benson on her evidence. To prove the truth of the old negress' story, Chief Henson declares himself to be Ellis Enson, supposed to have been murdered twenty years before. Mrs. Bowen recognizes her former husband and claims that she is the unfortunate Hagar.

department was supplied, his long wait for the departure of Mr. Sumner, during which he heard the dead woman's confession to the secretary; his meeting with Miss Bradford, down to the last awful move in the tragedy witnessed by the old Negress, Aunt Henny, who fainted with horror at the tragedy of the night. "He returned to New York as secretly as he left the city," continued the Governor, "because his flight had occurred on the Sabbath, when all the members of the committee were bent on individual pleasure, and as he was in his place on Monday morning no one noticed his absence. Then, in his devotion to his employer's interests, the faithful servant and ex-slave, Isaac Johnson, knowing no law save the will of his former owner, faithful to the traditions of slavery still, concealed the only witness of the crime, failing only in one point—that he did not murder the old woman (his mother-in-law) as commanded by General Benson, but kept her in confinement. In attempting to force Miss Bowen to marry him by abducting her and concealing her in an old country house, detectives searching for her found the missing witness, whom we have heard here to-day.

"The romance of the situation is enhanced by the fact that in just retribution the brother so inhumanly betrayed and abandoned, even as was Joseph[1] of old, by his brethren, was the Nemesis[2] placed upon the criminal's track to put him in the power of outraged justice."

With a splendid peroration, and a tender reference to the unexpected meeting of the cruelly-separated husband and wife, the Governor sat down and the Attorney-General followed him in a speech of great ability; but he knew the verdict was a foregone one, that his own remarks were but a form, that the weight of evidence in "this most extraordinary case" left him but one course. He felt, too, a savage bitterness towards Benson or Enson, that made him pant for the trial which he knew must come. In fact, officers were already stationed near the precious trio ready to take them in charge the moment all preliminary proceedings were over.

The Attorney-General concluded his speech with the words, "Justice is all that we are seeking, gentlemen of the jury, and in

---

1 In Genesis 37, Joseph's jealous brothers tear off his coat, throw him in a well, and sell him into slavery in Egypt for 20 pieces of silver.
2 The Greek goddess of retribution; a bitter enemy or antagonist.

your hands I leave the prisoner's interests, knowing that you will return a verdict in accordance with the evidence given, that will give us all the right to welcome Mr. Sumner among us again fully reinstated in the confidence and esteem of the whole country."

The judge's charge followed, with a finely-balanced summing up which displayed all the power and glory of English jurisprudence; even the prisoner followed him with admiring forgetfulness of self. Finally the case was given to the jury; they consulted together a few minutes for the sake of appearances, without leaving their seats, then the foreman rose and announced: "We find the prisoner not guilty."

"Is this your verdict, Mr. Foreman?" asked the clerk.

"It is," he answered.

"So say you all, gentlemen of the jury?"

"We do," in chorus from the box.

If there had been much doubt which way public opinion and sympathy had set during the trial, there was absolutely none when the verdict "not guilty" was given, for the long-repressed excitement found vent in an outburst of applause that for a time defied official control. Like wildfire the news spread to the people outside, and cheer after cheer rent the air, the crowd swaying and pushing in a vain attempt to get a glimpse of the late prisoner; but as soon as he could, Sumner left in a carriage with Badger and West, faithful John Williams on the box, for his apartments, and later the Bowen mansion.

Sumner could never have told very precisely what passed after the verdict had been given, save that as in a dizzy dream he heard applause within and cheers without; then he saw the fetters on the wrists of General Benson and saw him hurried from the room between two officers, followed by Major Madison and Aurelia. The two villains had sat nonplussed and dumbfounded during the stirring events just chronicled, making no effort to escape. Governor Lowe rushed the business of their arrest, and in this was ably seconded by the judge and the Attorney-General.

Presently Sumner found himself in a mass of humanity in a room with Governor Lowe and Mr. Cameron, receiving congratulations and invitations. He thanked all in his pleasant way and declined; he could not bear society just yet.

That verdict gave back life to Jewel and to him, but he was unhappy and anxious over her situation with her stepmother; the wonderful revelation of Mrs. Bowen's identity with the slave

Hagar was a shock to him. It was a delicate situation, but, of course, he told himself, "Mrs. Bowen could see that with all sympathy for her and her sad story, it was impossible for Jewel to be longer associated with her in so close a relationship as that of mother and daughter." He comforted himself with the thought that the unfortunate woman was the second wife of Senator Bowen, and that was a fortunate fact. He would do all that he could for Mrs. Bowen, but the social position of Mrs. Sumner demanded a prompt separation.

Cuthbert Sumner was born with a noble nature; his faults were those caused by environment and tradition. Chivalrous, generous-hearted—a manly man in the fullest meaning of the term—yet born and bred in an atmosphere which approved of freedom and qualified equality for the Negro, he had never considered for one moment the remote contingency of actual social contact with this unfortunate people.

He had heard the Negro question discussed in all its phases during his student life at "Fair Harvard," and had even contributed a paper to a local weekly in which he had warmly championed their cause; but so had he championed the cause of the dumb and helpless creatures in the animal world about him. He gave large sums to Negro colleges and on the same principal gave liberally to the Society for the Prevention of Cruelty to Animals, and endowed a refuge for homeless cats. Horses, dogs, cats, and Negroes were classed together in his mind as of the brute creation whose sufferings it was his duty to help alleviate.

And Jewel? She, too, felt that straining of the heart's chords as she waited in her private sitting room for her lover-husband. She was alone. Ellis Enson was with her step-mother. After Mrs. Bowen returned to consciousness, Jewel had stolen away unnoticed by the strangely reunited pair, leaving them in sacred seclusion.

She held the evening paper in her hand. It contained a column headed, "Sensational Ending of the Famous Bradford Tragedy."

After detailing the day's events, the editor gave the story of the white slave Hagar (Mrs. Bowen), and her extraordinary recognition of her former husband and master in the person of Chief Henson of the Secret Service Division. The editor went on to say:

"No trace of woman or child was found after her leap over the bridge into the river. She was supposed to have been drowned. The woman, however, was picked up by a Negro oyster-digger and concealed in his hut for days. At the breaking out of the war she drifted to California and in a few years married the wealthy miner, Zenas Bowen. This story, showing, as it does, the ease with which beautiful half-breeds may enter our best society without detection, is a source of anxiety to the white citizens of our country. At this rate the effects of slavery can never be eradicated, and our most distinguished families are not immune from contact with this mongrel race. Mrs. Bowen has our sympathy, but we cannot, even for such a leader as she has been, unlock the gates of caste and bid her enter. Posterity forbids it. We wait the action of Mr. Ellis Enson (Chief Henson) with impatience, praying that sentiment may not overcome the dictates of duty."

Jewel's tender heart was full of pity and love for her stepmother. Now she knew for the first time whence came the fountain of love so freely lavished upon her by this heart-broken mother.

"How she must have suffered," murmured the girl to herself. Then, as she mentally counted up the years that had passed since the events chronicled by the paper, she said aloud in some surprise, "Why, I must be about the age of the poor baby girl. How wonderful!" She was glad to be alone after all these weeks of tempest and to-day's climax, with its reaction. Mingled with her own joy at Cuthbert's release was a silent, wordless awe of Chief Henson's declaration in the court room and her stepmother's avowal. But, strange to say, the girl felt none of the repugnance that the announcement of Mrs. Bowen's origin had brought to Sumner. Her own happiness was so great that all worldly selfishness was swept away.

Hush! She suddenly rose from the couch where she was sitting, with wide eyes and quivering form, hearing the soft musical voice outside, so yearned for all these dreadful weeks, now fast disappearing like a horrible nightmare before the rosy glow of Hope's enchanting rays. She saw the door open and shut— saw Cuthbert's tall form enter—she sank upon the couch, putting out her hands to him in a trustful, childlike way.

Without a word he flung himself beside her and folded her in his arms with a passion and strength that were resistless.

"Mine at last! My darling! My one love—my wife!" For a second there was a blank—life itself seemed to stand still, and time and space were obliterated.

"Husband!" she said at length with smothered passion.

He stooped and kissed her in a strange, awed way—silently, solemnly, as a man might who had been so near the grave—heart to heart, soul to soul, conscious only in that supreme moment paradise was touched! So for some minutes they sat in soul communion. Sumner broke the silence after a time.

"Heaven only can reward Chief Henson and Venus Johnson for their rescue of you, my treasure. May heaven forget me if I ever forget their devotion to my dear wife. I tell you, Jewel, I was maddened when the news was brought to me of your abduction. I would have been a murderer in truth could I have been free for one moment to meet Benson!"

The wife's lips touched his softly, lovingly—true woman to the core—as a "ministering angel."[1]

"But, dearest, God protected me."

There was another eloquent pause. Then Sumner said abruptly:

"To-morrow our marriage must he properly advertised. It is Thursday now; on Monday you must come with me to my father. After you have seen him, you shall plan our future."

Jewel laid her head against him. "Your wishes are mine, Cuthbert."

Then they talked a while of the strange revelations made at the trial, of the discovery of Negro blood in Aurelia Madison and Mrs. Bowen.

"With the knowledge that we now possess of her origin, we can no longer wonder at her wicked duplicity," said Sumner.

"That is true in her case," replied Jewel, "but a truer, sweeter, more perfect woman than mamma does not live on the earth; how do you account for it?"

"Depend upon it, those characteristics are but an accident of environment, not the true nature of her parent stock. I have always heard that the Negro race excelled in low cunning."[2]

"True," replied Jewel, dreamily, "but then there are Venus and Aunt Henny."

"Yes, and my faithful John. I suppose these exceptions prove the rule. Still I am thankful that Mrs. Bowen is only your step-mother."

---

1 An echo of Hebrews 1.14.

2 A belief widely held by white people in the nineteenth and early twentieth centuries.

Then they drifted back into their lovers' talk once more.

"Look thro' mine eyes with thine, true wife,
Round my true heart thine arms entwine;
My other dearer life in life,
Look thro' my very soul with thine!"[1]

It was midnight when the wedded lovers separated. In the hall, they met Ellis Enson, as we shall hereafter call him.

The man's face wore a look of solemn joy. He shook Jewel's hand silently. He urged Sumner to go to his room with him and spend the night, for he had much to say to him in regard to the late trial. Sumner felt obliged to accept the invitation, and the two men went away together.

The early morning hours found them still talking over the trial, but their greatest interest was in the story of the elder man—the strange trials in two lives.

"How do you intend to fix it?" questioned Sumner.

"Of course Mrs. Bowen is very much shaken, but we shall be quietly remarried on Sunday, and then I shall take my wife away. When we return I hope to have possession of Enson Hall, where we shall take up our permanent abode. I hand in my resignation to-day, to take immediate effect."

"I honor you for your resolution, Enson, but indeed I have not your strength of character. I could never solve the social problem in that high-handed manner. Have you no fear of public opinion?"

"My dear boy, I know just where you are. I went all through the old arguments from your point of view twenty years ago. I wavered and wavered, but nature was stronger than prejudice. I have suffered the torments of hell since I lost my wife and child."

He rose from his seat and strode once down the room, then back again, pausing before the young man.

"Sumner," he said, with impressive solemnity, "race prejudice is all right in theory, but when a man tries to practice it against the laws which govern human life and action, there's a weary journey ahead of him, and he's not got to die to realize the tortures of the damned. This idea of race separation is carried

---

1 Alfred, Lord Tennyson, "The Miller's Daughter" (1842), lines 221–24.

to an extreme point and will, in time, kill itself. Amalgamation[1] has taken place; it will continue, and no finite power can stop it."

"But, my dear Enson, you do not countenance such a—such a—well—terrible action as a wholesale union between whites and blacks? Think of it, my dear man! Think of our refinement and intelligence linked to such black bestiality as we find in the slums of this or any other great city where Negroes predominate!"

Enson smiled at the other's vehemence.

"Certainly not, Sumner; but, on the other hand, take the case of Aurelia Madison. Did you ever behold a more gorgeously beautiful woman, or one more fastidiously refined? Had her moral development been equal to her other attainments, and you had loved her, how could you endure to have a narrow, beastly prejudice alone separate you from the woman pre-destined for your life-companion? It is in such cases that the law of caste is most cruel in its results."

"I think that the knowledge of her origin would kill all desire in me," replied Sumner. "The mere thought of the grinning, toothless black hag that was her foreparent would forever rise between us. I am willing to allow the Negroes education, to see them acquire business, money, and social status within a certain environment. I am not averse even to their attaining political power. Farther than this, I am not prepared to go."

"And this is the sum total of what Puritan New England philanthropy will allow—every privilege but the vital one of deciding a question of the commonest personal liberty which is the fundamental principle of the holy family tie."

"When one considers the ignorance, poverty and recent degradation of this people, I feel that my position is well taken," persisted Sumner. "Ought we not, as Anglo-Saxons,[2] keep the fountain head of our racial stream as unpolluted as possible?"

Enson smiled sadly; a holy light for one instant illumined the scarred face of the veteran:

"'A boy's will is the wind's will,
And the thoughts of youth are long, long thoughts,'"[3]

---

1 Miscegenation, race mixture.
2 White people, particularly of English stock.
3 Henry Wadsworth Longfellow, "My Lost Youth" (1855). These two

he quoted softly. "You will learn one day that there is a higher law than that enacted by any earthly tribunal, and I believe that you will then find your nature nobler than you know."

"You make me feel uncanny, Enson, with your visionary ideas. Thank God, I have my wife; there I am safely anchored."

"Amen!" supplemented Enson softly, as they clasped hands in warm goodnight.

CHAPTER XXXV.

On Friday the court room was again crowded to the doors by spectators eager to view the closing scenes in the celebrated case.

The soi-disant[1] General Benson was arraigned on a charge of wilfully murdering Elise Bradford, and was committed for trial in October. Major Madison, or Walker, the ex-slave driver, and his daughter Aurelia were also in court, Madison for forgery in connection with Senator Bowen's will.

Nothing criminal was charged against Aurelia; in fact, no one desired to inflict more punishment on the unfortunate woman, and when she left the court room that day she vanished forever from public view.

Deadly pale, but proudly self-possessed, Ellis Enson gave his testimony at the hearing, fixing a steadfast, unflinching gaze on the livid, haggard face that glared back with sullen hate and fear in every line. So for a moment of dead silence, of untold pain to one, those two men, sons of one father, but with a bridgeless gulf between them, stood face to face after many years.

The story had to be told again, however deeply it racked one soul to be forced to give deadly testimony against the murderer, who, outcast by his own evil deeds, was still his father's son. The ghastly facts stood out too clearly for hesitation, and St. Clair Enson, alias Gen. Charles Benson, was remanded for trial.

Owing to the unsavory character of the prisoner extra precautions were taken by the warden to prevent a rescue or an escape.

At one o'clock Saturday morning the guard upon the outer wall that surrounded the jail saw a shadow that seemed to move. At first he thought it a stray cat or dog, then as he watched he

---

lines appear at the end of each of the ten stanzas in the poem.

1 French: so-called, self-styled.

saw that it stole along the wall suspiciously; obedient to orders, he fired; the shadow fell to earth.

The men who came running at the sound of the shots bore the wounded man back to the jail, where they found that their burden was the body of St. Clair Enson, and that he was dead. The guard's bullet had taken a fatal effect.

In the prisoner's bed crouched Isaac Johnson in a vain endeavor to cover up his former owner's flight. A gaping hole at one side of the cell told where an entrance had been effected. How Isaac had managed to cut his way through the solid masonry always remained a mystery to the authorities.

Thus ended St. Clair Enson's career of vice and crime. Walker, alias Major Madison, died in the state prison.

CHAPTER XXXVI.

Late Saturday afternoon, Hagar, so long known to us as Mrs. Bowen, reclined in semi-invalid fashion on the couch in her boudoir. She had exchanged her deep mourning for a house dress of white cashmere, profusely touched with costly lace. Her dark hair, showing scarcely a touch of silver, was closely coiled at the back of her shapely head. In spite of a shade of sadness her countenance was serene.

She was happy—happier than she had ever hoped to be in this life. True, no callers begged admittance into the grand mansion, no cards overflowed the receivers in the spacious entrance hall, since the sensational items disclosing her identity had appeared in the columns of the daily press; that fact did not disconcert her in the least. One thing alone troubled her,—Sumner's determination to separate her from Jewel.

The tender-hearted woman who had been his champion and friend throughout dark days of suspicion and despair, could not understand his antipathy to her. The two ladies did not worry themselves unduly, however, trusting that time and their united persuasions would win him to a better frame of mind.

The ceremony of the morrow would see her united to the husband of her youth. She thought only of that.

Ellis wished to settle the whole of Senator Bowen's immense fortune upon Jewel, but the latter would not hear of so unjust a proceeding. So the mansion was to be left in the care of Marthy

Johnson, Aunt Henny and Oliver, while Mr. and Mrs. Enson were abroad. Venus was to go to Massachusetts with her young mistress, and the plan was that she and John Williams should be married about Christmas. The travellers were to start on their journeys early Monday morning. Suddenly Senator Bowen's last words, "The little hair trunk!" flashed across the lady's mind. It had been his in his first wife's time. He had clung to it through poverty and prosperity. It was in the late Senator's dressing-room which opened into the room where she was lying. Secretly blaming herself for neglecting the shabby object of his love and care, Hagar rose hastily and passed into the adjoining room.

Everything was as he had left it. How lonely it seemed without the jovial, genial presence of the man who had saved her from despair. Tears came to her eyes as she stood gazing upon familiar objects, each bearing the personality of the man who had gathered them about him. Over in a corner stood the little hair trunk. She moved slowly toward it, and presently was on her knees before it with the lid thrown back.

She sat there, prone upon the floor, for a time, gazing in mute sadness upon the contents—shabby, peculiarly made garments of the fashion in vogue before the war, mementoes of that other wife of his young manhood, and, strange mixture, a number of clay pipes, burned black by use, and fishing tackle, all mingled in a motley heap.

She took up the first wife's picture, opened the case and gazed into the eyes of the blowzy[1] girlish face in its hideous cape bonnet, the long spiral curls falling outside the ruche[2] that faced the head covering. Not a pretty face; no, but honesty and kindliness of heart were written there, silently claiming their tribute, turning the contemptuous smile to gentle reverence.

Hagar closed the case softly and placed it beside her on the floor with the other articles which her sense of neatness and order had caused her to fold carefully in regular piles, ready to replace in the shabby receptacle.

She had often wondered who Jewel resembled and where she had obtained the dainty, high-bred elegance of face and figure; surely not from father nor from mother. To-day her curiosity was

---

1 Coarse, unkempt, fleshy, red-faced.
2 Decorative frill or pleat for trimming a dress or hat.

again aroused; the desire to know pursued her so persistently that she was amazed.

The small velvet case containing Senator Bowen's daguerreotype,[1] taken in early youth, had a peculiar fascination for her. His face smiled up at her, round, jolly, rubicund, a dimple in his chin and a laugh in his eyes, which the straight hair, combed flatly to the sides of his head, could not render sedate. Hagar felt a film gather to her eyes. What a god he had been to her! How devoted! How gentle! And he was a man of strong intellect and staunch integrity. She had no cause to be ashamed of him. He had saved her from despair. Next to her God she placed this man, whom she knew instinctively would never have forsaken her, never for one instant would he have wavered from his constancy to her, no matter what the cause, were she but true to him.

Ellis had come back to her; yes, but although love forgave, love worshipped at his shrine, love could not blot out the bitter memory of the time when he had failed her.

She closed the case with a nervous click, and went on with her sorting and folding. The very last thing that she found was a brown paper parcel, tied with coarse string. She undid the knot with the feeling of pride which attends the operation of succeeding in untying a string without cutting it. She smoothed out the kinks and curls and laid it carefully at her side ready for use again; then she removed the paper, expecting to see a man's wearing apparel; to her surprise a roll of white cashmere, yellow with age, met her eyes; it was wrapped about other articles. The kneeling woman felt the room spinning round her as she held the packet in her hand. There was something vaguely familiar in that ordinary piece of yellow cashmere; one side being visible showed a deep embroidered design tracing the edge of the deep hem. She could not move. Every muscle was paralyzed, and a flood of memories rushed in turmoil through her brain.

Trembling, breathless with excitement, she began to unroll the bundle. The last fold, as it fell apart, revealed the outer covering to be an infant's cloak of richest material and beautifully embroidered. With quivering fingers the agitated woman continued to shake out the garments that the cloak enfolded—a tiny dress, dainty skirts, a lace cap—in short, all the articles necessary to make up the attire of a child of love and wealth.

---

1 An early type of photograph.

"Oh, merciful heaven! How came these here?" she whispered with white lips, as she pressed each tiny garment to her lips, and rained tremulous kisses on the exquisite lace cap. "My baby, my baby!"

She threw herself upon the floor and lay there weeping scalding tears. Before her lay the garments that her own hands had fashioned twenty years before, for the little daughter who had come to bless the union of Ellis Enson and herself. Half in terror she gazed upon them as upon the ghost of one long since departed. She made a movement and a metallic sound drew her attention to an object that slipped from among the clothing to the floor. It was a gold chain, from which depended a locket.

"My mother's locket!" she gasped. "Ah! Until this hour I had forgotten it; it was about my darling's neck when last I dressed her. My God! How comes it here? Why do I find it in Zenas Bowen's trunk?"

She touched a spring and the outer lid sprang back, showing a piece of paper pressed in the space usually devoted to pictures. The paper fell upon the floor unheeded. The writing was in Senator Bowen's hand, but she did not notice it; she was pressing her fingers along the margin of filagree work which decorated the edge of the locket; presently the back fell apart; then she pressed again and a third compartment opened and from it the face of Ellis Enson in his first youth smiled up into her own.

How well she remembered all the minute details of the history of the locket in the shadowy past, brought so vividly to her memory by the dramatic events of the last few days. Her mother had given her the locket at the time of her father's death, and had told her that it was a valued heirloom, and had explained to her the intricate working of the triple case. Probably no one had ever discovered the secret spring, and the case was supposed to be empty. After Mrs. Sargeant's death, she had in turn explained to Ellis, she had placed his pictured face there, and when, tortured and tormented by persecution, she was driven from her home to the slave market, she had placed the locket about the baby's neck; why, she knew not.

Gazing at it now with sick and whirling brain, there came a step outside in her sitting room. She dragged her leaden limbs to the door and beheld Ellis. The bright smile on his face at sight of her seemed to chase away the years and renew his lost youth.

"My darling," he began, "you see I have managed to return

earlier than I expected. I could not support the purgatory of absence from you longer. But what is the matter?"

Hagar could not answer him. Leaning against the door-frame, she looked him in the eyes, then extended her hand, the open locket lying on her palm.

"Ellis," she said, in a husky whisper, "I have just found this—here—in this room—in Senator Bowen's old trunk of relics. What can it mean? For God's sake, try and explain it to me. I cannot grasp the meaning of it at all."

Ellis's face was as white as her own, but he spoke soothingly to the distracted woman. Then his trained eye travelled beyond her to where the folded paper lay forgotten.

Taking her in his arms, he placed her upon the couch in the sitting-room, and then picked up the paper, first tenderly straightening each tiny garment and placing them all together in a pile upon a chair. Closing the door carefully behind him, he drew a chair to the side of the couch where Hagar lay weeping.

"Now, Hagar, my dear," he said, coaxingly, "you will try and be good and command yourself. God grant by these tokens that we may trace our darling's last resting place—a message from Heaven!"

"Oh, how selfish I am, Ellis! You need comfort as much as I do," she cried, her love on fire at sight of the tears in his eyes, which he tried in vain to suppress. And then for a little while the childless parents held each other's hands and wept. Presently Ellis opened the paper from the locket. It seemed but a leaf from a memorandum book, but what a change it wrought in the lives of four people!

March, 1862.—Went up the Potomac on the "Zenas Bowen" for oysters. Brought off[1] 100 guns, 300 pounds of ammunition, Charleston, S.C. Picked up log floating outside the bay with a girl baby less than one year old attached to it by clothing. Must have floated many hours, but the sleeping child was unhurt. Clothing rich; no clue to parents or relatives.

November, 1862.—Have adopted child and shall call her "Jewel." Have placed this mem. inside locket found on child for future reference.

Zenas Bowen.

Mary Jane Bowen.

---

1 Seized or recovered from a shipwreck.

There was a sound of weeping in the quiet room. "The Divine Father hears all prayers, sees all suffering. In His own good time the All-Merciful has had mercy."[1] The solemn words broke from Ellis.

"And I have said in my anguish, there is no God. He does not heed my woes. Blasphemer that I am!" cried Hagar.

"And she is here in this very house! My God, I thank Thee! Ellis, do not fear, I am strong go, I beseech you, lose not a moment, bring her to me—bring my Jewel, my daughter, to my arms. Ah, did not my heart yearn over her from the first, when, as a tender baby girl, I held her to my aching heart, and soothed my deep despair? Go, go—at once—Ellis! This suspense is more trying than all that has gone before. You do not know a mother's feelings. Shall I live till your return?"

Ellis, alarmed at her state, choked down his own feelings, and left the room in search of Jewel.

★ ★ ★ ★ ★ ★

Who can paint the most sacred of human emotions? Clasped in her mother's arms, and shown the proofs preserved by her adopted father of her rescue from the death designed by her distracted mother, Jewel doubted not that she was Hagar's daughter.

CHAPTER XXXVII.

All night the new-found daughter and husband watched beside Hagar's couch. They feared for her reason. But joy never kills, and at length she slept, and Jewel stole away to take her needed rest.

When alone again in her room, after the startling revelation that had come to her, she sat a long time, trying to realize the complete change in her future which this discovery would bring. She did not deceive herself; the cup of happiness was about to be snatched from her lips. Cuthbert, who was the one object of her passionate hero worship, would turn from her with loathing. There were dark circles about her eyes and her cheeks were ghastly. She loved her mother, she was proud of her father but

---

1 Rosa Nouchette Carey, *Not Like Other Girls: A Novel* (1884).

feelings engendered for twenty years were not to be overcome instantly. It was horrible—a living nightmare, that she, the petted darling of society, should be banned because of her origin. She shrank as from a blow as she pictured to herself the astonishment, disgust and contempt of her former associates when they learned her story. The present was terrible, the future more awful still. Overcome by her thoughts, moans burst from her overcharged heart; she stretched out her arms in an abandonment of grief and dropped senseless in the middle of her room, and so Venus found her in the early morning hours. Heaven help her, for it must also be written for her as for her ill-fated mother:

"Better the heart strings had never known
The chord that sounded its doom."[1]

Venus knew the whole story. Mr. Enson had called Marthy, Aunt Henny and Venus into the room and told them very solemnly the facts in the case. There was much weeping and rejoicing.

"My soul," cried Venus to her mother when they were alone, "what about Mr. Sumner? If he goes back on Miss Jewel it'll kill her; it will break her heart."

"It's my 'pinion dat it's already broke, honey; a gal brung up like her has been's gwine break her heart to fin' herself nuthin' but common nigger trash. I jes' hope de debbil's give St. Clair Enson a good hot place down thar to pay him for his devilmen' here on yearth, 'deed I does," said Aunt Henny.

Jewel sent for her father and they talked the matter over. Mr. Enson could give her little hope. He was forced to acknowledge that Sumner was strongly prejudiced. He promised to see him, however, and tell him the story and hear his reply to Jewel, who sent also a pathetic note bidding him farewell:

"I know your prejudice against amalgamation; I have believed with you. My sin, for it is a sin to hold one set of God's creatures so much inferior to the rest of creation simply because of the color of the skin, has found me out. Like Miriam[2] of old, I have scorned the Ethiopian and the curse has fallen upon me, and

---

1 Maria I. Forster, "Sunshine and Shade" (1859), lines 45–46.

2 In Numbers 12, Miriam is rebuked by God and stricken with leprosy for criticizing her brother Moses's Cushite/Ethiopian wife.

I must dwell outside the tents of happiness forever. I know you pity my poor mother; she has been so unhappy. I am proud of my father; he is a noble man. I will write again to-morrow and perhaps see you; but, oh, pray not to-day!"

Twenty-four hours passed and left Sumner as they found him, in mental torture. Then his good angel triumphed. He swore he would not give her up, and then he learned the power of prayer. He was ready to overlook and forgive all if only Jewel were left him. As his entreaties went up to a compassionate God the words rose ever before him.

"Many waters cannot quench love, neither can the floods drown it."[1] "All Thy waves and Thy billows have gone over me, but the heart is not easily closed. Love is strong as death."[2]

Evening found him hastening toward the Bowen mansion. The house looked desolate. He rang the bell at the great entrance doors. Marthy Johnson answered the imperative summons.

"Lor', Mr. Sumner, Lor', sir!"

"Where are they all, Marthy?" he asked abruptly.

"Gone to de continen', Mr. Sumner. Massa Ellis say, you young folks'll git better lef' by your lonesomes; dat's what he tol' me tell you, sir."

Sumner left her in deep despair. He went home to his father for a brief time and then started for the Continent himself.

At the end of a year, mindful of poor John's devotion, for he vowed not to marry Venus till his master settled down, Sumner returned to America and again sought the Bowen mansion. Again Marthy answered his summons, and told him that the family were at Enson Hall. He did not notice the pity on the woman's face.

He never paused until he reached the pretty little rustic town in Maryland that held his heart, his dove of peace. And then a great fear fell upon him, undefined and foreboding. He sent John on with his luggage to the Hall, and wandered up the country road with beating heart and feverish pulses. In a few minutes he would see her, she would be beside him, loving, forgiving. The tears came into his eyes, and he whispered a prayer. He drew his hat over his face and wandered off across a daisied field until he had overcome his emotion. A little graveyard nestled

---

1 Song of Solomon 8.7.
2 Psalms 42.7.

close beside the road. He was on the broad Enson acres, and in that enclosure dead and gone Ensons had slumbered for centuries. It was cool and shady and restful, and unconsciously he stepped into it.

Suddenly with a great cry he stood still before a fair, slender shaft of polished cream-white marble.

Jewel, aged 21.
"Not my will, but Thine be done!"[1]

He fell down with his face upon her grave. She had died abroad of Roman fever.[2]

★ ★ ★ ★ ★ ★

Cuthbert Sumner questioned wherein he had sinned and why he was so severely punished.

Then it was borne in upon him: the sin is the nation's. It must be washed out.[3] The plans of the Father are not changed in the nineteenth century; they are shown us in different forms. The idolatry of the Moloch of Slavery[4] must be purged from the land and his actual sinlessness was but a meet offering to appease the wrath of a righteous God.

Across the lawn of Enson Hall a child—a boy—ran screaming and laughing, chasing a gorgeous butterfly. It was the child of St. Clair Enson and Elise Bradford, the last representative of the Enson family.

Cuthbert watched him with knitted brows. In him was embodied, in a different form, a lesson of the degradation of slavery. Cursed be the practices which pollute the soul, and deaden all our moral senses to the reception of the true doctrines of Divinity.

The holy institution of marriage ignored in the life of the

---

1 The words of Christ to his Father while on the cross. See Luke 22.42.
2 Malaria.
3 An implicit reference to Adam's (original) sin.
4 Cf. John Greenleaf Whittier's "Moloch in State Street" (1851), about the return of the fugitive slave Thomas Sims to his master in the wake of the Compromise of 1850. See Appendix C2.

slave, breed[1] indifference in the masters to the enormity of illicit connections, with the result that the sacred family relation is weakened and finally ignored in many cases. In the light of his recent experiences Cuthbert Sumner views life and eternity with different eyes and thoughts from what he did before he knew that he had wedded Hagar's daughter. Truly had Ellis Enson spoken when he judged him nobler than he knew.

"A boy's will is the wind's will,
And the thoughts of youth are long, long thoughts."

THE END.

---

1 Bred.

Appendix A: Hagar's Daughter Synopsis in the Colored American Magazine (1902)

[In the June 1901 issue of the *Colored American Magazine*, the fourth installment of *Hagar's Daughter* began with a synopsis that summarized the plot of the previous installments. The text of the combined synopses, from the June 1901 to the March 1902 issues, is reproduced below.]

DURING December, 1860, the rebellious political spirit of the country leaped all barriers and culminated in treason.

Closely associated with the Confederate leaders was St. Clair Enson, son of an aristocratic Maryland family, who hoped, by rendering valuable aid to the founders of the new government, to re-establish himself socially and financially. While in Charleston, S.C., attending the convention preliminary to the formation of the new government, he received a letter announcing the birth of his brother's heiress. This enraged Enson who saw in it the loss of his patrimony. He fell in with a notorious slave-trader named Walker, who accompanied him on his homeward trip on the steamer "Planter." Walker offers to show him a way out of his difficulties for ten thousand dollars.

St. Clair Enson's brother Ellis had married Miss Hagar Sargeant a beauty and an heiress. A daughter was born. Soon after this St. Clair arrives at Enson Hall accompanied by Walker. He claims that Enson has a slave of his on the plantation. Enson denies the charge.

Walker explains that, being childless, Mr. and Mrs. Sargeant, while living at St. Louis, took an octoroon[1] slave from him to bring up. He declares that Hagar is that child, and produces papers to prove his claim. Hagar recognizes the man, and faints at the sight of him.

Ellis buys Hagar and the child of Walker. Unable to bear the disgrace of having married a Negress, he decided to leave

---

1 See p. 230, n. 1.

home, but loving his wife very dearly, concludes to go abroad, and live where they are unknown. St. Clair overhears the plan and informs Walker. Enson leaves home to make arrangements for the journey. At end of three weeks his dead body is found in some woods on the estate.

Hagar accuses St. Clair and Walker of murdering Ellis. Then St. Clair gives Walker permission to sell Hagar and the child in the Washington slave market. Hagar, with the child, leaps into the Potomac River.

The story next opens in the winter of 1882, in the city of Washington, D.C.

The event of the season is a grand ball about to be given at the home of Senator Zenas Bowen who has a charming wife and a beautiful young daughter, Jewel, engaged to Cuthbert Sumner, a rich New Englander, private secretary for General Benson, chief of a department.

At the theatre one night, society is stirred by the advent of a new beauty, Miss Aurelia Madison, to whom Sumner was at one time engaged, a fact that he has concealed from Jewel.

General Benson has fallen in love with Jewel and determines to win her and her fortune of ten million. To this end, he plots with Major Madison and Aurelia to separate the lovers.

Aurelia Madison becomes fast friends with Jewel on the strength of an old school acquaintance at the Canadian convent. She secures an invitation to the ball and appears there, creating a sensation.

On the night of the ball, and near its close, by a series of pre-concerted arrangements, Jewel, who had gone to the conservatory with General Benson, sees Aurelia in Sumner's arms; she believes him in love with her beautiful friend.

Jewel breaks her engagement with Sumner. Refuses to see him or read his letters. Accepts General Benson's attentions and at last their engagement is announced.

Cuthbert Sumner resigns his position under General Benson resolved to leave Washington. The latter goes on a trip with other government officials and leaves Sumner in charge of the office. He and Miss Bradford are obliged to work overtime on special work. She tells him of her former relations with General Benson, and says by threatening exposure she has induced him to promise her marriage at Easter. Sumner leaves her to finish her work at the office, stunned by what he has heard. She is murdered. The next morning he is arrested.

Aunt Henny Sargeant, scrub woman at Treasury Building, disappears on same night of the Bradford murder.

Jewel Bowen visits Cuthbert Sumner in prison. Explanations are made, and they resolve to marry immediately. She visits J. Henson, chief of the secret service division, and places Sumner's case in his hands.

Cuthbert Sumner and Jewel Bowen are married in the prison. At the hearing before the Grand Jury Sumner is held for trial in September. Senator Bowen, who is taken suddenly ill in New York, is brought home and dies the next day. After the funeral General Benson presents a will signed by Senator Bowen, that leaves the entire estate in his hands, together with Major Madison. Jewel Bowen is abducted at the very entrance to her home.

Jewel comes out of a swoon to find herself imprisoned in a deserted mansion, waited on by an old Negress and a pleasant looking colored man who is Isaac Johnson. After a number of weeks she manages to get out of her room and in wandering over the house comes upon Aunt Henny, the missing witness in the Bradford murder case.

Meanwhile, Venus Johnson, from remarks made by her mother, infers that Gen. Benson has concealed Jewel at a place near Baltimore, where her father has gone to look after Gen. Benson's business for the summer. She goes to Chief Henson and tells him her thoughts.

Disguised as a boy, she discovers Jewel Bowen and her grandmother, Aunt Henny Sargeant, in the same house.

Aurelia Madison visits Sumner in prison and offers to prove his innocence, if he will marry her. He refuses to do this, announces his marriage with Jewel, accuses her of bearing colored blood, and she leaves him vowing vengeance. At the trial Aunt Henny is produced as an eye-witness of the murder. Lynching is threatened by the crowd when Gov. Lowe moves to arrest Gen. Benson on her evidence. To prove the truth of the old negress' story, Chief Henson declares himself to be Ellis Enson, supposed to have been murdered twenty years before. Mrs. Bowen recognizes her former husband and claims that she is the unfortunate Hagar.

Appendix B: Promoting Hagar's Daughter

[By the time *Hagar's Daughter* first appeared in the *Colored American Magazine*, Pauline Hopkins had already published several articles in the periodical, as well as a novel, *Contending Forces*, as a bound book. Although Hopkins used her mother's maiden name, Sarah A. Allen, as a pseudonym, the editors decided to reveal that she was *Hagar's Daughter*'s true author when the final installment was published in March 1902. By connecting this serial to *Contending Forces*, the editors hoped to expand the magazine's readership by capitalizing on the notoriety Hopkins was gaining with her first novel.]

1. Cover of the *Colored American Magazine*, vol. 2,
   no. 5 (March 1901)

Reproduced from *The Digital Colored American Magazine*,
coloredamerican.org. Original held at the Beinecke Rare Book
and Manuscript Library, Yale University.

2. **Advertisement for *Contending Forces,
Colored American Magazine,* vol. 4, no. 4
(March 1902)**

[The first indication that Sarah A. Allen was one of Hopkins's
pseudonyms appears in this advertisement placed in the front of
the March 1902 issue of the *Colored American Magazine*.]

Reproduced from *The Digital Colored American Magazine*,
coloredamerican.org. Original held at the Beinecke Rare Book
and Manuscript Library, Yale University.

3. Subscription Advertisement for the *Colored American Magazine*, vol. 4, no. 4 (March 1902)

[The *Colored American Magazine* editorial staff hoped to attract more readers—and subscribers—by offering a free copy of Hopkins's novel, *Contending Forces*, with each paid subscription to the magazine. *Hagar's Daughter* is identified as a work by the same author.]

Reproduced from *The Digital Colored American Magazine*, coloredamerican.org. Original held at the Beinecke Rare Book and Manuscript Library, Yale University.

4. From "Editorial and Publishers' Announcements," *Colored American Magazine*, vol. 4, no. 4 (March 1902), p. 335

[At the close of the magazine's March 1902 issue, Hopkins is explicitly identified as the author of *Hagar's Daughter.*]

With this issue of the magazine, the popular serial story "Hagar's Daughter" reaches its close. It has proved a wonderful success, and the great interest manifested in it from all sections of the country is most encouraging to both author and publishers. In this connection we must let our readers into a little secret. While the story "Hagar's Daughter" has been announced as being written by Sarah A. Allen, it has in reality been written by our own Miss Pauline E. Hopkins, who chose her mother's name, under which to write this powerful story. We make this statement at this time in justice to Miss Hopkins, as well as in response to the general inquiry regarding the personality of the author of "Hagar's Daughter."

In this special connection we would call attention to that other powerful race book from Miss Hopkins' pen entitled "Contending Forces." It is a most interesting study of race conditions told in story form, and it has received very favorable comment from the press of the country.

In order that our readers may have an opportunity to secure a copy of "Contending Forces" FREE, we have made a most remarkable offer, which appears in the front part of this magazine. In order to be sure of securing a copy of this book you should take advantage of this remarkable offer at once, as it may not appear again.

Appendix C: Race/History

[In the Preface to her 1900 novel *Contending Forces*, Pauline Hopkins encourages African Americans to *"faithfully portray the inmost thoughts and feelings of the Negro with all the fire and romance which lie dormant in our history"* (14). According to C.K. Doreski, Hopkins "acknowledged her obligation not simply to cultivate but to create an audience for her revisionist race history. She assumed the authority of race historian and mediated between the issues of race and gender to incite a readership to pride and action" (72). In her fiction and nonfiction, Hopkins places a great deal of emphasis on history. In *Hagar's Daughter*, she demonstrates her extensive knowledge about the events and the literature of the 1850s and 1860s in particular. This knowledge can be seen in the novel's reference to the fate of self-emancipated people in Boston following the passage of the Compromise of 1850, its allusion to white abolitionist John Greenleaf Whittier's 1851 poem "Moloch in State Street" about one of these fugitives, and its highlighting of Robert Smalls's heroics in Charleston harbor in 1862. Like *Hagar's Daughter*, Hopkins's 1902 essay "Munroe Rogers" reflects her neo-abolitionist agenda at the *Colored American Magazine*, emphasizing a clear post-Reconstruction-era connection with—rather than a break from—antebellum conditions.]

1. From Pauline E. Hopkins, "Hon. Frederick Douglass," *Colored American Magazine*, vol. 2, no. 2 (December 1900), pp. 121–32

[In *Hagar's Daughter*, Hopkins refers to events that she discusses in her December 1900 Famous Men of the Negro Race installment devoted to Frederick Douglass (1818–95), such as mob violence against abolitionists (including the killing of Rev. Elijah Lovejoy [1802–37]), the enacting of a national Fugitive Slave Law, the return to the South of the fugitives Thomas Sims (1834–1902) and Anthony Burns (1834–62), and the US Supreme Court's 1857 *Dred Scott* decision.]

What were the times and conditions which tended to produce this inspired enthusiast and to place the slave-holder's chattel before the world on the same platform with Phillips, engaged in the same mission, the confidante of Wm. Lloyd Garrison, Parker Pillsbury and others?[1]

The introduction of the cotton-gin into the South enhanced the value of slave-property and there seemed no immediate prospect of the gradual emancipation of the slaves, which question had begun to be agitated in several states. Then came the formation of the Anti-slavery society in 1832, one year after the publication of "The Liberator," in Boston. The agitation of the question in Congress, the mobbing of Wm. Lloyd Garrison who was driven from the Anti-slavery platform in Boston by the cultured, rich Puritan patriots of the great commonwealth. They laid hands on Garrison with cries of violence, put a rope about his waist, and dragged him to imprisonment! Mobs quickly followed this act of Massachusetts, in Utica, New York, and in New York City. The experience of Rev. Elijah P. Lovejoy, a native of Maine, who in St. Louis edited the "St. Louis Times" and advocated through its columns justice to the enslaved Negro, recalls the story of Ida Wells Barnet, colored journalist and lecturer, in these more recent years. Lovejoy was murdered; Mrs. Barnet lost all her property but escaped with her life. In New York colored people were hunted like wild beasts, their churches and homes burned, with no attempt at protection.

It was suggested to the Legislature of one of the Southern States, that a large reward be offered for the head of a citizen of Massachusetts who was the pioneer in the Anti-slavery movement. A similar reward was offered for the head of a citizen of New York. This insult was not received in either State. The position of the American churches on the question of slavery did great damage to the cause of Christianity. Christmas[2] defended slavery out of the Bible.

The enactment by Congress of the Fugitive Slave Law caused the friends of freedom to feel that the General Government was fast becoming the bulwark of slavery. The rendition of Thomas Sims, and later that of Anthony Burns, was humiliating to the friends of the Blacks.

---

1 Along with editor William Lloyd Garrison (1805–79), lawyer Wendell Phillips (1811–84) and minister Parker Pillsbury (1809–98) were high-profile abolitionists.

2 It is likely that Hopkins intended to write Christians here.

The "Dred Scott Decision" added to the smouldering fire. By this decision in the highest court of American law, it was affirmed that no free Negro could claim to be a citizen of the United States, but was only under the jurisdiction of the separate State in which he resided; that the prohibition of slavery in any Territory of the Union was unconstitutional; and that the slave-owner might go where he pleased with his property, throughout the United States, and retain his right. This decision created much discussion, both in America and in Europe, and injured the good name of the country abroad.

The Constitution thus interpreted by Judge Taney,[1] became the winding sheet of liberty, and gave boldness to the Southerners. The slave-holders in the cotton, sugar and rice growing states began to urge the re-opening of the slave-trade, and the driving out of all free colored people from the Southern States. In the Southern Rights' Convention, Baltimore, June 8, 1860, a resolution was adopted calling on the Legislature to pass a law to that effect. Every speaker took the ground that such a law was necessary to preserve the obedience of the slaves. Judge Catron of the Supreme Court of the United States, opposed the law.[2] He said the free colored people were among the best mechanics, artisans, and most industrious laborers in the States, and that to drive them out would be an injury to the State itself. (The governments of the Southern States in 1900, will please take notice.)

2. John Greenleaf Whittier, "Moloch in State Street" (1851), *Anti-Slavery Poems: Songs of Labor and Reform* (Houghton, Mifflin and Co., 1888), pp. 165–68

[Near the end of *Hagar's Daughter*, Hopkins alludes to John Greenleaf Whittier's "Moloch in State Street." She was likely drawn to the headnote to the poem, which blames wealthy, politically connected, white citizens of Boston for the return to the South of a fugitive from slavery, Thomas Sims.]

---

1 US Supreme Court Chief Justice Roger Taney (1777–1864) wrote the majority opinion in the *Dred Scott* case.
2 Associate US Supreme Court Justice John Catron (1786–1865) sided with the majority in the *Dred Scott* decision.

In a foot-note of the Report of the Senate of Massachusetts on the case of the arrest and return to bondage of the fugitive slave Thomas Sims it is stated that—

"It would have been impossible for the U.S. marshal thus successfully to have resisted the law of the State, without the assistance of the municipal authorities of Boston, and the countenance and support of a numerous, wealthy, and powerful body of citizens. It was in evidence that 1500 of the most wealthy and respectable citizens—merchants, bankers, and others—volunteered their services to aid the marshal on this occasion.... No watch was kept upon the doings of the marshal, and while the State officers slept, after the moon had gone down, in the darkest hour before daybreak, the accused was taken out of our jurisdiction by the armed police of the city of Boston."

> The moon has set: while yet the dawn
>   Breaks cold and gray,
> Between the midnight and the morn
>   Bear off your prey!
>
> On, swift and still! the conscious street   5
>   Is panged and stirred;
> Tread light! that fall of serried feet
>   The dead have heard!
>
> The first drawn blood of Freedom's veins
>   Gushed where ye tread;   10
> Lo! through the dusk the martyr-stains
>   Blush darkly red!
>
> Beneath the slowly waning stars
>   And whitening day,
> What stern and awful presence bars   15
>   That sacred way?
>
> What faces frown upon ye, dark
>   With shame and pain?
> Come these from Plymouth's Pilgrim bark?
>   Is that young Vane?   20

Who, dimly beckoning, speed ye on
    With mocking cheer?
Lo! spectral Andros, Hutchinson,
    And Gage are here![1]

For ready mart or favoring blast   25
    Through Moloch's[2] fire,
Flesh of his flesh, unsparing, passed
    The Tyrian[3] sire.

Ye make that ancient sacrifice
    Of Man to Gain,   30
Your traffic thrives, where Freedom dies,
    Beneath the chain.

Ye sow to-day; your harvest, scorn
    And hate, is near;
How think ye freemen, mountain-born,   35
    The tale will hear?

Thank God! our mother State can yet
    Her fame retrieve;
To you and to your children let
    The scandal cleave.   40

Chain Hall and Pulpit, Court and Press,
    Make gods of gold;
Let honor, truth, and manliness
    Like wares be sold.

Your hoards are great, your walls are strong,   45
    But God is just;
The gilded chambers built by wrong
    Invite the rust.

---

1 Henry Vane the Younger (1613–62), Thomas Hutchinson (1711–
    80), Edmund Andros (1637–1714), and Thomas Gage (1718/19–87)
    were all British governors of Massachusetts.
2 Moloch was a Canaanite god associated with fiery human sacrifice,
    especially of children.
3 Tyrian refers to the Mediterranean port city of Tyre as well as to a
    royal purple dye for clothing.

What! know ye not the gains of Crime
    Are dust and dross;   50
Its ventures on the waves of time
    Foredoomed to loss!

And still the Pilgrim State remains
    What she hath been;
Her inland hills, her seaward plains,   55
    Still nurture men!

Nor wholly lost the fallen mart;
    Her olden blood
Through many a free and generous heart
    Still pours its flood.   60

That brave old blood, quick-flowing yet,
    Shall know no check,
Till a free people's foot is set
    On Slavery's neck.

Even now, the peal of bell and gun,   65
    And hills aflame,
Tell of the first great triumph won
    In Freedom's name.[1]

The long night dies: the welcome gray
    Of dawn we see;   70
Speed up the heavens thy perfect day,
    God of the free!

3. From "Gen. Robert Smalls," *National Republican* (6 March 1886), p. 3

[In *Hagar's Daughter*, Hopkins places St. Clair Enson, Isaac Johnson, and Walker on board the *Planter* so that she can draw attention to Robert Smalls's (1839–1915) daring commandeering of the vessel during the Civil War. The following article in

---

1 [Whittier's note:] The election of Charles Sumner to the United States Senate "followed hard upon" the rendition of the fugitive Sims by the United States officials and the armed police of Boston.

the *National Republican*, which Hopkins may have consulted, describes this exploit in detail.]

He was born at Beaufort, S.C., on the 5th of April, 1839, and now lives on the very place where he was born. He lived in Beaufort, leading the monotonous life of his race, until the year of 1851, when he went to Charleston and worked at the rigger's trade, and also led a seafaring life in sailing along and about the coast of South Carolina and Florida. It was here that he acquired that knowledge of the bars and harbors of the seacoast which he afterward used to such signal advantage to the Union cause. For two years he was a stevedore in Charleston, and in July, 1861, went on board the steamer Planter, then a confederate transport plying between the city and Fort Sumter and other points in Charleston harbor. This craft was also the special dispatch boat of Gen. Ripley.[1] After being on this vessel about two months he was made wheelsman. (At that time it was not in accordance with coastwise, nautical etiquette to call a colored man a pilot.) In this situation he continued until the 13th of May, 1862.

The captain, chief engineer, and mate of the Planter all had gone ashore up into the city the previous night, where they slept, leaving on board a crew of eight men, all colored, among whom was Gen. Smalls.

A consultation was held and it was resolved by these eight men, Gen. Smalls at their head, to seize the boat and carry it out to the United States fleet outside the harbor. The design was hazardous in the extreme. The little boat would have to pass beneath the guns of the batteries. Failure and detection would have been certain death. Fearful was the venture, but it was made. The daring resolution had been formed, and under command of Robert Smalls, the wheelsman, steam was put on, and with her valuable cargo of guns and ammunition, intended for Fort Ripley, a new fortification just constructed in the harbor, about 2 o'clock in the morning, the Planter silently moved off from her dock, steamed up to North Atlantic wharf, where the wife and two children of Robert Smalls, and the wife and children of another of the crew were waiting to embark. Noiselessly the vessel approached the wharf, and in silence and in haste

---

1 Brigadier General Roswell S. Ripley (1823–87), the Confederate commander at Charleston.

received the waiting women and children on board, and then started down the river out to sea. The regular signal was given as Fort Johnson was passed and was answered, and so at Fort Sumter. As soon then as the boat was out of range of the guns of these grim guardians of the city, the flag of truce was raised and out for the ocean she steamed.

In the misty morning a frigate was described off the bar. The Planter approached her. In the mist the white flag was not seen, and, to the terror and surprise of the Planter's crew, the strange ship hove round and presented her broadside and opened her ports. The command had already been given, "Ready," and the captain was about to speak the "Fire," when one of the officers on the quarter deck discerned the flag of truce. The vessels were now within hailing distance, and the captain of the Union ship asked, "What boat that was, and what was wanted." The reply was given and the Planter's errand explained. The captain ordered her to come alongside, but his order was not heard by Smalls and his men, who proceeded to go around the stern of the ship, when they were brought to a stand-still by the captain's thundering tones as he called out, "Stop, or I will blow you out of the water." The Planter then came alongside, the movement of her was explained, and an officer named Watson and four men were put on board. The strange ship proved to be the sailing frigate Onward and the officer Capt. Nichols. Smalls was transferred to the gunboat Augusta, the flag ship off the bar, under the command of Capt. Parrot, whence he afterward proceeded to Port Royal to Commodore Dupont, then in command of the southern squadron, where the Planter was received, and Robert Smalls was entered upon the navy list as a pilot. The Planter was put under command of an officer from the ship Wabash, named Phœnix.

4. From Pauline E. Hopkins, "Munroe Rogers," *Colored American Magazine*, vol. 6, no. 1 (November 1902), pp. 20–26

[Hopkins's article about Munroe Rogers, whom the Attorney General of Massachusetts turned over to North Carolina to face a bogus charge of arson, serves as a kind of coda to her Famous Men of the Negro Race and Famous Women of the Negro Race biographical series. She begins by raising the subject of betrayal through her references to Thomas Sims and Anthony Burns, indicating that she regards Rogers as a latter-day fugitive from slavery. The thrust of *Hagar's Daughter* is that the United States is reverting to the conditions that existed before the Civil War. In keeping with the novel, "Munroe Rogers" argues that the South requires "a new moral code" because the Republican Party has shirked "a responsibility of its own making"; moreover, it contends, "[t]he question of disenfranchisement has speedily resolved itself into one of serfdom; that means a gradual resumption of all the relations of slavery." Consequently, Hopkins sees a revolution of some kind on the horizon and calls for a great race leader to provide direction at this critical period.]

It has been truly said that there is nothing new under the sun.

Who among the rejoicing millions could have been persuaded that in less than forty years from the day they celebrated— Emancipation day—this American people would have turned their backs upon the lessons of humanity learned in the hard school of sanguinary war, and repeated in their entirety the terrible acts exemplified by the surrender of Sims and Burns by a conservative North at the brutal demand of a domineering South!

Alas, that today we must record this fact!

[...]

A short sojourn in any Southern village or city would supply abundant practical argument against the status quo which no newspaper will supply. Arson, murder and rape are crimes not punished when committed by white men. There is a town in South Carolina where a white man has not been hanged for twenty-five years, and not because he has not committed crimes. The white people of the South are pitiless as is proven by nearly every issue of the daily press. A people who can look with apathy upon horrible scenes of lynching must be pitiless, and without justice, and with no sympathy for fair play. They are not in the Southern blood. In the Negro's case, they do not pity, because they despise; they give him no cardinal help, because they disdain.

There is always a word to be said in extenuation for inherited morals. For the Southern attitude toward the Negro we must blame the grandfathers. These outrages are conducted on a mistaken standard of self-preservation. The South needs nothing less than a new moral code. That does not come in one generation. Yet we cannot wait for time to be their Solon.[1] There are crises in human history which pause not for the manufacture of new laws. The human emergency pits itself against tradition.

The question of disfranchisement has speedily resolved itself into one of serfdom; that means a gradual resumption of all the relations of slavery, with, perhaps, the exception of the auction block, which in the end will also return for short periods, for the punishment of minor offenses.

There are 8,000,000 of the children of Ham[2] who above all things want manhood—free and expansive—and they mean to have it. They do not want to lord it over white neighbors, though in some states they hold the balance of power; they simply want a fair interpretation of all laws and a share in decent citizenship, and this they are bound to get. They have been patient, more patient than any other nominally free people in the world, but the end is approaching. There is no fierceness, no impulse, but only a steady resolve that is significant. We have our leaders, we are banding together, our clubs are on the increase, our young men's forums are rapidly forming all over the country. These things mean something.

It is a startling fact that, if our prosperity increases in the present ratio, the Negro in 50 years from now will own the greater part of the private landed property in several Southern states. Herein lies the prime cause for Southern antipathy. All the Negro asks is a chance to prove to the world that he is an orderly, capable citizen, and the aristocratic Southerner can pursue his political way in peace. But this they will not do.

If affairs remain as they are now in this unnatural and strained condition, where the manhood of both races is debased, the one by the consciousness of a wrong committed, the other of a wrong endured, there must come a revolution. The air breathes a spirit of restlessness which precedes self-defense. If some Toussaint L. Overture[3] should arise!

---

1   The lawmaker, politician, and poet Solon proposed reforms that eventually led to the development of democracy in ancient Athens.

2   I.e., people of African descent (derived from the fate of Noah's son Ham and his offspring in Genesis).

3   Toussaint L'Ouverture (1743–1803), a formerly enslaved Haitian

[...]

Black slavery has been abolished, and upon this virtue Republicanism rests, while the great masses are being enslaved by the power of gold, and crushed in the great folds of gigantic monopolies.

The labor question, the question of suffrage, rested in the hands of immigrants, the Negro question—all are slowly being merged into one great question involving the herd of common people of whom the Negro is a recognized factor. The solution of one of these living issues must eventually solve the other two, and no finite power can stay the event. Herein lies our only hope.

The fight is on; neither by the eloquence of the South nor by the wealth of Republicanism can the government hope to escape the iron hand of Destiny, whose fingers relentlessly manipulate the mill machinery of a just God.

Not agitate![1]

Republics exist only on the tenure of being constantly agitated. We cannot live without the voice crying in the wilderness—troubling the waters that there may be health in the flow.

---

general who led that nation's revolution against France. Hopkins's variant spelling was not uncommon in the early 1900s.

1 It is possible that *"Not agitate!"* is a typographical error and Hopkins instead intended *"Not agitate?"* It is also possible that "Not agitate!" is a reference to the poem "Song of the Agitators," by an anonymous author, originally published in the *Ohio Star* and reprinted in the *Liberator* (19 November 1852 and 3 October 1862) and the *Anti-Slavery Bugle* (9 October 1862), which repeatedly asserts that agitation will stop only when all the horrors of slavery have ended, e.g., "'Cease to agitate' we will, / When the slave's whip's sound is still" (1–2).

Appendix D: The Figure of Hagar

[Significant to the Jewish, Christian, and Islamic religions, the biblical Hagar speaks with an angel on two occasions, calls on God directly, and bears the first child of and is later banished by Abraham. She figured prominently in black and, paradoxically, white American literature and culture during the nineteenth and early twentieth centuries. The February 1901 issue of the *Colored American Magazine* includes "Fascinating Bible Stories IV: Hagar and Ishmael" by Charles Winslow Hall, and there is a reprint of a painting of the mother and son on page 288 of that issue. Moreover, in an installment of her Famous Women of the Negro Race series, Hopkins compares black clubwomen to Hagar and their white counterparts to Sarah in recounting the recent actions of the latter to draw the color line against the former. On the one hand, African Americans closely identified with this enslaved Egyptian who became the mother of Ishmael, an outcast among humankind with a long line of descendants, such that the phrase "Aunt Hagar's children" became synonymous with US blacks. On the other hand, as Janet Gabler-Hover has shown, Hagar became the focus of narratives and poems by white women writers who celebrated her defiance of male authority yet stripped her of an African heritage in texts that in some cases offered apologies for slavery.]

1. Genesis 16 and 21 (King James Version)

[In Genesis 16, the elderly Sarah gives her aged husband, Abraham, the young handmaiden Hagar, who conceives and gives birth to a male child named Ishmael. In Chapter 21, Abraham complies with the demand of Sarah, who has recently given birth to her own son, Isaac, that Hagar and Ishmael be sent away. With only a loaf of bread and a pitcher of water, the mother and son set off into the desert, where Hagar despairs until comforted by an angel.]

Chapter 16

Now Sarai Abram's wife bare him no children: and she had an handmaid, an Egyptian, whose name was Hagar.

²And Sarai said unto Abram, Behold now, the Lord hath restrained me from bearing: I pray thee, go in unto my maid; it may be that I may obtain children by her. And Abram hearkened to the voice of Sarai.

³And Sarai Abram's wife took Hagar her maid the Egyptian, after Abram had dwelt ten years in the land of Canaan, and gave her to her husband Abram to be his wife.

⁴And he went in unto Hagar, and she conceived: and when she saw that she had conceived, her mistress was despised in her eyes.

⁵And Sarai said unto Abram, My wrong be upon thee: I have given my maid into thy bosom; and when she saw that she had conceived, I was despised in her eyes: the Lord judge between me and thee.

⁶But Abram said unto Sarai, Behold, thy maid is in thine hand; do to her as it pleaseth thee. And when Sarai dealt hardly with her, she fled from her face.

⁷And the angel of the Lord found her by a fountain of water in the wilderness, by the fountain in the way to Shur.

⁸And he said, Hagar, Sarai's maid, whence camest thou? and whither wilt thou go? And she said, I flee from the face of my mistress Sarai.

⁹And the angel of the Lord said unto her, Return to thy mistress, and submit thyself under her hands.

¹⁰And the angel of the Lord said unto her, I will multiply thy seed exceedingly, that it shall not be numbered for multitude.

¹¹And the angel of the Lord said unto her, Behold, thou art with child, and shalt bear a son, and shalt call his name Ishmael; because the Lord hath heard thy affliction.

¹²And he will be a wild man; his hand will be against every man, and every man's hand against him; and he shall dwell in the presence of all his brethren.

¹³And she called the name of the Lord that spake unto her, Thou God seest me: for she said, Have I also here looked after him that seeth me?

¹⁴Wherefore the well was called Beerlahairoi; behold, it is between Kadesh and Bered.

¹⁵And Hagar bare Abram a son: and Abram called his son's name, which Hagar bare, Ishmael.

¹⁶And Abram was fourscore and six years old, when Hagar bare Ishmael to Abram.

Chapter 21

And the Lord visited Sarah as he had said, and the Lord did unto Sarah as he had spoken.

²For Sarah conceived, and bare Abraham a son in his old age, at the set time of which God had spoken to him.

³And Abraham called the name of his son that was born unto him, whom Sarah bare to him, Isaac.

⁴And Abraham circumcised his son Isaac being eight days old, as God had commanded him.

⁵And Abraham was an hundred years old, when his son Isaac was born unto him.

⁶And Sarah said, God hath made me to laugh, so that all that hear will laugh with me.

⁷And she said, Who would have said unto Abraham, that Sarah should have given children suck? for I have born him a son in his old age.

⁸And the child grew, and was weaned: and Abraham made a great feast the same day that Isaac was weaned.

⁹And Sarah saw the son of Hagar the Egyptian, which she had born unto Abraham, mocking.

¹⁰Wherefore she said unto Abraham, Cast out this bond-woman and her son: for the son of this bondwoman shall not be heir with my son, even with Isaac.

¹¹And the thing was very grievous in Abraham's sight because of his son.

¹²And God said unto Abraham, Let it not be grievous in thy sight because of the lad, and because of thy bondwoman; in all that Sarah hath said unto thee, hearken unto her voice; for in Isaac shall thy seed be called.

¹³And also of the son of the bondwoman will I make a nation, because he is thy seed.

¹⁴And Abraham rose up early in the morning, and took bread, and a bottle of water, and gave it unto Hagar, putting it on her shoulder, and the child, and sent her away: and she departed, and wandered in the wilderness of Beersheba.

¹⁵And the water was spent in the bottle, and she cast the child under one of the shrubs.

¹⁶And she went, and sat her down over against him a good way off, as it were a bowshot: for she said, Let me not see the

death of the child. And she sat over against him, and lift up her voice, and wept.

[17]And God heard the voice of the lad; and the angel of God called to Hagar out of heaven, and said unto her, What aileth thee, Hagar? fear not; for God hath heard the voice of the lad where he is.

[18]Arise, lift up the lad, and hold him in thine hand; for I will make him a great nation.

[19]And God opened her eyes, and she saw a well of water; and she went, and filled the bottle with water, and gave the lad drink.

[20]And God was with the lad; and he grew, and dwelt in the wilderness, and became an archer.

[21]And he dwelt in the wilderness of Paran: and his mother took him a wife out of the land of Egypt.

2. From Pauline E. Hopkins, "Artists," Famous Women of the Negro Race, X, *Colored American Magazine*, vol. 5, no. 5 (September 1902), pp. 362–67

[In the installment of her Famous Women of the Negro Race series devoted to artists, Hopkins provides a biographical sketch of the sculptor Edmonia Lewis (1844–1907) and refers to her statue of *Hagar*, presumably completed in the late 1860s and now in the possession of the Smithsonian Museum of Art. A photograph of the statue appears on the cover of this Broadview edition.]

The annals of statuary record few artists of the fair sex, but it is pleasant to learn that a taste for this art is developing among women; and numbered among the few there is one who has made famous not only her race, but the American people, over the entire globe:

Miss Edmonia Lewis, the colored American artist, was born near Albany, New York, July 4, 1845. She is of mingled African and Indian descent, her father being a full-blooded African, and her mother a Chippewa Indian. Both parents died young, leaving the orphan girl at the age of three, and her brother, to be brought up by the Indians. Her opportunities for an education were very meagre, but she was sent to school by her brother, finally entering Oberlin College[1] contemporary with Mrs. Fanny Jackson Coppin.[2]

Miss Lewis is below the medium height; her complexion and features betray her African origin; but her hair is more of the Indian type, being black, straight and abundant. Her head is well-balanced, exhibiting a large, well-developed brain. Her manners are unassuming, and most winning and pleasing; her character displays all the proud spirit of her Indian ancestors.

On her first visit to Boston she saw a statue of Benjamin Franklin. She was filled with amazement and delight. The "stone image" was magical in her sight, and new powers stirred within her. "I, too, can make a stone man," she told herself, and she went at once to visit William Lloyd Garrison, and told him her desires, and asked him how she could best set about accomplishing her wishes.

Infused by her enthusiasm, Mr. Garrison gave her a note of introduction to Mr. Brackett,[3] the Boston sculptor, and after talking with her, he gave her a piece of clay and the mould of a human foot as a study. "Go home and make that," said he; "if there is anything in you, it will come out."

The young girl went home and toiled at the piece of clay with all the stoical determination of her Indian ancestors not to be defeated in her purpose, and when it was finished, she carried it to the sculptor. He looked at her model, broke it up, and said, "Try again." She tried again, modelling this time feet and hands, and finally attempted a medallion of the head of John Brown,[4] which was pronounced excellent.

Her next essay was the bust of Colonel Robert G. Shaw. The family of the young hero heard of the bust which Miss Lewis was making as a work of love, and went to see it, and were delighted with the portrait which she had taken from a few poor

---

1 Oberlin College, founded in 1833, became one of the first colleges in the United States to admit African American students, in 1835.

2 African American educator and missionary to South Africa (1837–1913) who enrolled at Oberlin College in 1860.

3 Edward Augustus Brackett (1818–1908), sculptor and artist whose works include a bust of John Brown.

4 John Brown (1800–59), abolitionist who led and was executed as a consequence of an ill-fated raid on the federal arsenal at Harpers Ferry, Virginia, in 1859.

photographs. Of this bust she sold one hundred copies, and with the money she set out for Europe, full of hope and courage, in 1865.

Arrived at Rome, Miss Lewis took a studio, and devoted herself to hard study and hard work, and there she made her first statue—a figure of Hagar in her despair in the wilderness. It is a work full of feeling, for, as she says, "I have a strong sympathy for all women who have struggled and suffered. For this reason the Virgin Mary is very dear to me." And we may believe this, for Miss Lewis had suffered, almost to the last extremity, from the baleful influence of slavery and caste prejudice.

The first copy of Hagar was purchased by a gentleman from Chicago. A fine group of the Madonna with the infant Christ in her arms, and two adoring angels at her feet, was purchased by the young Marquis of Bute, Lord Beaconsfield's (Disraeli) Lothair,[1] for an altarpiece.

In 1867, she gave the world "The Freedwoman." "The Death of Cleopatra," a vividly realistic work, was sent to the Centennial Exhibition of 1876; she has also given us "The Old Arrow-Maker and His Daughter," "Rebecca at the Well," and portrait busts of Henry W. Longfellow,[2] Charles Sumner and Abraham Lincoln. The last mentioned work is in the San José library, California.

Among Miss Lewis' other work are two small groups, illustrating Longfellow's poem of Hiawatha. Her first, "Hiawatha's Wooing," represents Minnehaha seated, making a pair of moccasins, and Hiawatha by her side with a world of love-longing in his eyes. In the "Marriage," they stand side by side with clasped hands. In both, the Indian type of features is carefully preserved, and every detail of dress, etc., is true to nature. The sentiment is equal to the execution. They are charming hits, poetic, simple, natural; and no happier illustrations of Longfellow's poem were ever made than those by Miss Lewis. A fine marble bust of Longfellow was ordered from Miss Lewis by Harvard College.

---

1 John Crichton-Stuart (1847–1900), the Third Marquess of Bute, reputed to be the richest man in the world, was the inspiration for the 1870 novel *Lothair* by Benjamin Disraeli (1804–81), the Earl of Beaconsfield.

2 Henry Wadsworth Longfellow (1807–82), poet known for his lyrical verses.

At Rome this talented woman is visited by strangers from all nations, who visit the "Eternal City," and everyone admires her great genius. Her works show great ideality, a pure heart and an awakened mind. She has, of course, found her chief patronage abroad, where her ability has removed all barriers to association with the most aristocratic leaders, and communion with the greatest minds of the age.

Portrait of Edmonia Lewis taken by Henry Rocher (c. 1870). National Portrait Gallery. Smithsonian Institution.

3. Eliza Poitevent Nicholson, "Hagar," *The Cosmopolitan; a Monthly Illustrated Magazine*, vol. 16, no. 1 (November 1893), pp. 10–13

[In Chapter VI of *Hagar's Daughter*, Hopkins reproduces the last stanza of the 165-line blank verse dramatic monologue "Hagar," which originally appeared in *Cosmopolitan* magazine in November 1893, by the Southern white writer and editor Eliza Poitevent Nicholson (1843–96). Speaking directly to Abraham, Hagar describes his heartlessness at length, accuses him of being cowardly, and tempts him to choose her and "Egypt's mighty gods" over his wife and his "cruel god of Israel."]

Go back! How dare you follow me beyond
The door of my poor tent? Are you afraid
That I have stolen something? See! my hands
Are empty, like my heart. I am no thief!
The bracelets and the golden finger rings   5
And silver anklets that you gave to me,
I cast upon the mat before my door,
And trod upon them. I would scorn to take
One trinket with me in my banishment
That would recall a look or tone of yours.   10
My lord, my generous lord, who sends me forth,
A loving woman, with a loaf of bread
And jug of water on my shoulder laid,
To thirst and hunger in the wilderness!
    Go back!   15
Go back to Sara! See! she stands
Watching us there, behind the flowering date,
With jealous eyes, lest my poor hands should steal
One farewell touch from yours. Go back to her,
And say that Hagar has a heart as proud,   20
If not so cold, as hers; and, though it breaks,
It breaks without the sound of sobs, without
The balm of tears to ease its pain. It breaks—
It breaks, my lord, like iron: hard, but clean;
And, breaking, asks no pity. If my lips   25
Should let one plea for mercy slip between
These words that lash you with a woman's scorn,
My teeth should bite them off, and I would spit

Them at you, laughing, though all red and warm with blood.
"Cease!" do you say? No, by the gods   30
Of Egypt, I do swear that if my eyes
Should let one tear melt through their burning lids,
My hands should pluck them out; and if these hands,
Groping outstretched in blindness, should by chance
Touch yours, and cling to them against my will,   35
My Ishmael should cut them off, and, blind
And maimed, my little son should lead me forth
Into the wilderness to die. Go back!

Does Sara love you as I did, my lord?
Does Sara clasp and kiss your feet, and bend   40
Her haughty head in worship at your knee?
Ah! Abraham, you were a god to me.
If you but touched my hand my foolish heart
Ran down into the palm, and throbbed, and thrilled,
Grew hot and cold, and trembled there; and when   45
You spoke, though not to me, my heart ran out
To listen through my eager ears and catch
The music of your voice and prison it
In memory's murmuring shell. I saw no fault
Nor blemish in you, and your flesh to me   50
Was dearer than my own. There is no vein
That branches from your heart, whose azure course
I have not followed with my kissing lips.
I would have bared my bosom like a shield
To any lance of pain that sought your breast.   55
And once, when you lay ill within your tent,
No taste of water, or of bread, or wine
Passed through my lips: and all night long I lay
Upon the mat before your door to catch
The sound of your dear voice, and scarcely dared   60
To breathe, lest she, my mistress, should come forth
And drive me angrily away; and when
The stars looked down with eyes that only stared
And hurt me with their lack of sympathy,
Weeping, I threw my longing arms around   65
Benammi's¹ neck. Your good horse understood

---

1   In Genesis, Ben-ammi is Lot's son by his own daughter. However, in

And gently rubbed his face against my head,
To comfort me. But if you had one kind,
One loving thought of me in all that time,
That long, heart-breaking time, you kept it shut   70
Close in your bosom as a tender bud
And did not let it blossom into words.
Your tenderness was all for Sara. Through
The door, kept shut against my love, there came
No message to poor Hagar, almost crazed   75
With grief lest you should die. Ah! you have been
So cruel and so cold to me, my lord;
And now you send me forth with Ishmael,
Not on a journey through a pleasant land
Upon a camel, as my mistress rides,   80
With kisses, and sweet words, and dates and wine,
But cast me off, and sternly send me forth
Into the wilderness with these poor gifts—
A jug of water and—a loaf of bread—
That sound was not a sob; I only lost   85
My breath and caught it hard again. Go back!
Why do you follow me? I am a poor
Bondswoman, but a woman still, and these
Sad memories, so bitter and so sweet,
Weigh heavily upon my breaking heart   90
And make it hard, my lord—for me to go.
"Your god commands it?" Then my gods, the gods
Of Egypt, are more merciful than yours.
Isis and good Osiris never gave
Command like this, that breaks a woman's heart,   95
To any prince in Egypt. Come with me
And let us go and worship them, dear lord.

Leave all your wealth to Sara. Sara loves
The touch of costly linen and the scent
Of precious Chaldean[1] spices, and to bind   100
Her brow with golden fillets, and perfume
Her hair with ointment. Sara loves the sound
Of many cattle lowing on the hills;

this poem Hagar puts her arms around the neck of Abraham's horse.
1 I.e., Babylonian.

And Sara loves the slow and stealthy tread
Of many camels moving on the plains.   105
Hagar loves you. Oh! come with me, dear lord.
Take but your staff and come with me; your mouth
Shall drink my share of water from this jug
And eat my share of bread with Ishmael;
And from your lips I will refresh myself   110
With love's sweet wine from tender kisses pressed.
Ah! come dear lord. Oh! come, my Abraham.
Nay, do not bend your cold, stern brows on me
So frowningly; it was not Hagar's voice
That spoke those pleading words.   115
                    Go back! Go back.
And tell your god I hate him, and I hate
The cruel, craven heart that worships him
And dares not disobey. Ha! I believe
'Tis not your far-off, bloodless god you fear   120
But Sara. Coward! Cease to follow me!
Go back to Sara. See! she beckons now,
Hagar loves not a coward; you do well
To send me forth into the wilderness,
Where hatred hath no weapon keen enough   125
That held within a woman's slender hand
Could stab a coward to the heart.
                    I go!
I go, my lord; proud that I take with me
Of all your countless herds by Hebron's brook,   130
Of all your Canaan riches, naught but this—
A jug of water and a loaf of bread.
And now, by all of Egypt's gods, I swear
If it were not for Ishmael's dear sake
My feet would tread upon this bitter bread,   135
My hands would pour this water on the sands;
And leave this jug as empty as my heart
Is empty now of all the reverence
And overflowing love it held for you.
                    I go!   140
But I will teach my little Ishmael
To hate his father for his mother's sake.
His bow shall be the truest bow that flies
Its arrows through the desert air. His feet,

The fleetest on the desert's burning sands;   145
Aye! Hagar's son a desert prince shall be,
Whose hand shall be against all other men;
And he shall rule a fierce and mighty tribe,
Whose fiery hearts and supple limbs will scorn
The chafing curb of bondage, like the fleet   150
Wild horses of Arabia.
                I go!
But like this loaf that you have given me,
So shall your bread taste bitter with my hate;
And like the water in this jug, my lord,   155
So shall the sweetest water that you draw
From Canaan's wells, taste salty with my tears.

Farewell! I go, but Egypt's mighty gods
Will go with me, and my avengers be.
And in whatever distant land your god,   160
Your cruel god of Israel, is known.
There, too, the wrongs that you have done this day
To Hagar and your first-born, Ishmael,
Shall waken and uncoil themselves, and hiss
Like adders at the name of Abraham.   165

Appendix E: Popular Genres and Literary Experimentation

[Critics have long noted Hopkins's mixing and subversion of popular genres and literary tropes, especially in her *Colored American Magazine* serial novels. This hallmark of her writing can be traced back to her first work to appear on stage. According to Jessica Metzler, Hopkins's "genre-blending" 1879 play *Peculiar Sam* "featured an all-black cast and a cohesive narrative structure that turned minstrel stereotypes against themselves," thereby serving "as an important link between blackface minstrel shows and turn-of-the-century black musical theater" (110, 116, 118). In addition to reworking melodrama, the Gothic, the Western, and the African adventure tale in her fiction, Hopkins draws on and responds with a black difference to the conventions of detective fiction in *Hagar's Daughter* and "Talma Gordon" (1900), widely recognized as the first detective and mystery story by an African American author. Furthermore, Hopkins's 1901 short story "A Dash for Liberty" boldly and strategically recasts and updates black and white accounts (by Frederick Douglass, Lydia Maria Child [1802–80], and William Wells Brown [c. 1814–84]) of the successful 1841 mutiny on the slave ship *Creole*.]

1. From Pauline E. Hopkins, *Peculiar Sam* (1879), Fisk University, John Hope and Aurelia E. Franklin Library, Special Collections, Pauline E. Hopkins Collection, box 1, folder 5

[Hopkins's Papers at Fisk University contain both the four-act *Peculiar Sam*, which was performed in various cities in the Midwest from March through June of 1879, and the three-act *Slaves' Escape; or, The Underground Railroad*, which was staged in Boston in December 1879, July 1880, and September 1881. Anticipating *Hagar's Daughter* to a degree, *Peculiar Sam* portrays some African American characters whose language remains the same before and after slavery and others whose manner of speaking has changed along with their circumstances. Having led his mother (Mammy), sister (Juno), love interest (Virginia), and close friends northward from Mississippi via the Underground Railroad, Sam rapturously describes the freedom they are on the brink of attaining in Act Three. Jim, the mixed-race overseer whom the young white master has allowed to marry Virginia against her will, arrives too late to stop them.]

Act III

Time, night. Banks of a river. River at back, entrances l. & r.[1] Trees and shrubbery along banks.

{Enter party led by Sam.}

Sam— {Looks around.} See hyar Mammy, I hope nuthin' aint happened to Jinny, kase when I was on de top ob dat las' hill we crossed, pears like I seed a lot ob white folks comin'.

Mammy— It's only through de blessin' ob de Lor', we haint been tooken long 'go. I don't neber see wha's got inter Marser's dogs.

Sam— Mammy dar aint a dog widin' ten mile roun' Marser's place, dat aint so sick he kan't hol' his head up. 'Deed mammy a chile could play wif 'em.

Mammy— {Holds up her hands in astonishment.} Wha! Wha' you been doin' to Marser's dogs? Why boy he'll kill us.

Sam— He will sho nuff Mammy ef he ketches us. Marse he hab plenty ob money an' I thought I'd done nuff to 'sarve[2] some ob it, an' I jes helped mysel' to a pocket full. An' wif som' ob it I bought de stuff wha' fixed dem dogs; deed I did, kase dis chile am no fool.

Mammy— {More surprised.} Been stealin' too. {Groans.} I neber 'spected dat ob you Sam.

Sam— No use Mammy, we mus' hab money, de 'litioners am

---

1 Abbreviations for stage left and stage right.
2 Deserve.

good frien's to us, but money's ebery man's frien', an'll neber 'tray eben a po' forsook coon.

Juno— {Has been looking anxiously up the road.} Dey's comin Mammy! Here's Jinny Sam!

{All rush <u>r. l.</u>,[1] to look up road. V[IRGINIA] sings solo, all join in chorus ["Old Kentucky Home"].[2] At close enter CAESAR, V[IRGINIA], & PETE, throw down bundles, embrace.}

Caesar— Well my chillern, we's almos' free de dark valley, le's sing one mo' hymn 'fo we bids good-bye to de sunny Souf. {Chorus.}

Sam— {As they close.} (Picks up bundle.) Come on Mammy, come on Jinny, le's git on board de raf'. I tell you chillern I feels so happy I doesn't kno' mysel'. Jes feel dis air, it smells like freedom; jes see does trees, dey look like freedom, {Points across river.} an' look ober younder chillern, look dar good, dat ar am ol' freedom himsel'. {Gets happy, begins to sing.} "Dar's only one mo' riber to cross."[3]

{All join in song, shake hands, laugh and shout, exit <u>l. h.</u> singing grows fainter, but louder as raft shoots into sight from <u>l. h.</u> with all on board. Dark stage. Moon rises. From <u>r. h.</u>[4] JIM rushes panting on the stage, peers after raft. Tableau, music growing fainter.}

Curtain.

---

1 I.e., cross stage right to stage left.
2 The state song of Kentucky (1853) by Stephen Collins Foster (1826–64). It is considered an abolitionist song despite its frequent use of the racial slur "darkies."
3 From the spiritual "One More River."
4 L.h. and r.h. are Hopkins's stage directions for house left and house right, from the audience's perspective.

2. Pauline E. Hopkins, "Talma Gordon," *Colored American Magazine*, vol. 1, no. 5 (October 1900), pp. 271–90

[Employing plots within plots—a murder mystery, a racial mystery, a pirate mystery, and a marital mystery—"Talma Gordon" is at once a tragic mulatta tale with a happy ending, a detective story that signifies on Edgar Allan Poe's "The Murders in the Rue Morgue" (1841) and "The Gold-Bug" (1843), and a powerful anti-imperialistic polemic.]

THE Canterbury Club of Boston was holding its regular monthly meeting at the palatial Beacon-street residence of Dr. William Thornton, expert medical practitioner and specialist. All the members were present, because some rare opinions were to be aired by men of profound thought on a question of vital importance to the life of the Republic, and because the club celebrated its anniversary in a home usually closed to society. The Doctor's winters, since his marriage, were passed at his summer home near his celebrated sanatorium. This winter found him in town with his wife and two boys. We had heard much of the beauty of the former, who was entirely unknown to social life, and about whose life and marriage we felt sure a romantic interest attached. The Doctor himself was too bright a luminary of the professional world to remain long hidden without creating comment. We had accepted the invitation to dine with alacrity, knowing that we should be welcomed to a banquet that would feast both eye and palate; but we had not been favored by even a glimpse of the hostess. The subject for discussion was: "Expansion; Its Effect upon the Future Development of the Anglo-Saxon throughout the World."

Dinner was over, but we still sat about the social board discussing the question of the hour. The Hon. Herbert Clapp, eminent jurist and politician, had painted in glowing colors the advantages to be gained by the increase of wealth and the exalted position which expansion would give the United States in the councils of the great governments of the world. In smoothly flowing sentences marshalled in rhetorical order, with compact ideas, and incisive argument, he drew an effective picture with all the persuasive eloquence of the trained orator.

Joseph Whitman, the theologian of world-wide fame,

accepted the arguments of Mr. Clapp, but subordinated all to the great opportunity which expansion would give to the religious enthusiast. None could doubt the sincerity of this man, who looked once into the idealized face on which heaven had set the seal of consecration.

Various opinions were advanced by the twenty-five men present, but the host said nothing; he glanced from one to another with a look of amusement in his shrewd gray-blue eyes. "Wonderful eyes," said his patients who came under their magic spell. "A wonderful man and a wonderful mind," agreed his contemporaries, as they heard in amazement of some great cure of chronic or malignant disease which approached the supernatural.

"What do you think of this question, Doctor?" finally asked the president, turning to the silent host.

"Your arguments are good; they would convince almost anyone."

"But not Doctor Thornton," laughed the theologian.

"I acquiesce which ever way the result turns. Still, I like to view both sides of a question. We have considered but one tonight. Did you ever think that in spite of our prejudices against amalgamation,[1] some of our descendants, indeed many of them, will inevitably intermarry among those far-off tribes of dark-skinned peoples, if they become a part of this great Union?"

"Among the lower classes that may occur, but not to any great extent," remarked a college president.

"My experience teaches me that it will occur among all classes, and to an appalling extent," replied the Doctor.

"You don't believe in intermarriage with other races?"

"Yes, most emphatically, when they possess decent moral development and physical perfection, for then we develop a superior being in the progeny born of the intermarriage. But if we are not ready to receive and assimilate the new material which will be brought to mingle with our pure Anglo-Saxon stream, we should call a halt in our expansion policy."

"I must confess, Doctor, that in the idea of amalgamation you present a new thought to my mind. Will you not favor us with a few of your main points?" asked the president of the club, breaking the silence which followed the Doctor's remarks.

---

1 See p. 256, n. 1.

"Yes, Doctor, give us your theories on the subject. We may not agree with you, but we are all open to conviction."

The Doctor removed the half-consumed cigar from his lips, drank what remained in his glass of the choice Burgundy, and leaning back in his chair contemplated the earnest faces before him.[1]

We may make laws, but laws are but straws in the hands of Omnipotence.

"There's a divinity that shapes our ends,
Rough-hew them how we will."[2]

And no man may combat fate. Given a man, propinquity, opportunity, fascinating femininity, and there you are. Black, white, green, yellow—nothing will prevent intermarriage. Position, wealth, family, friends—all sink into insignificance before the God-implanted instinct that made Adam, awakening from a deep sleep and finding the woman beside him, accept Eve as bone of his bone; he cared not nor questioned whence she came. So it is with the sons of Adam ever since, through the law of heredity which makes us all one common family. And so it will be with us in our re-formation of this old Republic. Perhaps I can make my meaning clearer by illustration, and with your permission I will tell you a story which came under my observation as a practitioner.

Doubtless all of you heard of the terrible tragedy which occurred at Gordonville, Mass., some years ago, when Capt. Jonathan Gordon, his wife and little son were murdered. I suppose that I am the only man on this side the Atlantic, outside of the police, who can tell you the true story of that crime.

I knew Captain Gordon well; it was through his persuasions that I bought a place in Gordonville and settled down to spending my summers in that charming rural neighborhood. I had rendered the Captain what he was pleased to call valuable medical help, and I became his family physician. Captain Gordon was a retired sea captain, formerly engaged in the East India trade. All his ancestors had been such; but when the bottom fell out of that business he established the Gordonville Mills

---

1 The framing narrative pauses here. Dr. Thornton's tale begins with the next paragraph.

2 Shakespeare, *Hamlet* 5.2.10–11.

with his first wife's money, and settled down as a moneymaking manufacturer of cotton cloth. The Gordons were old New England Puritans who had come over in the "Mayflower"; they had owned Gordon Hall for more than a hundred years. It was a baronial-like pile of granite with towers, standing on a hill which commanded a superb view of Massachusetts Bay and the surrounding country. I imagine the Gordon star was under a cloud about the time Captain Jonathan married his first wife, Miss Isabel Franklin of Boston, who brought to him the money which mended the broken fortunes of the Gordon house, and restored this old Puritan stock to its rightful position. In the person of Captain Gordon the austerity of manner and indomitable willpower that he had inherited were combined with a temper that brooked no contradiction.

The first wife died at the birth of her third child, leaving him two daughters, Jeannette and Talma. Very soon after her death the Captain married again. I have heard it rumored that the Gordon girls did not get on very well with their stepmother. She was a woman with no fortune of her own, and envied the large portion left by the first Mrs. Gordon to her daughters.

Jeannette was tall, dark, and stern like her father; Talma was like her dead mother, and possessed of great talent, so great that her father sent her to the American Academy at Rome, to develop the gift. It was the hottest of July days when her friends were bidden to an afternoon party on the lawn and a dance in the evening, to welcome Talma Gordon among them again. I watched her as she moved about among her guests, a fairy like blonde in floating white draperies, her face a study in delicate changing tints, like the heart of a flower, sparkling in smiles about the mouth to end in merry laughter in the clear blue eyes. There were all the subtle allurements of birth, wealth and culture about the exquisite creature:

"Smiling, frowning evermore,
Thou art perfect in love-lore,
Ever varying Madeline,"[1]

quoted a celebrated writer as he stood apart with me, gazing upon the scene before us. He sighed as he looked at the girl.

---

1 Alfred, Lord Tennyson, "Madeline" (1830), lines 25–27.

"Doctor, there is genius and passion in her face. Sometime our little friend will do wonderful things. But is it desirable to be singled out for special blessings by the gods? Genius always carries with it intense capacity for suffering: 'Whom the gods love die young.'"[1]

"Ah," I replied, "do not name death and Talma Gordon together. Cease your dismal croakings; such talk is rank heresy."

The dazzling daylight dropped slowly into summer twilight. The merriment continued; more guests arrived; the great dancing pagoda built for the occasion was lighted by myriads of Japanese lanterns. The strains from the band grew sweeter and sweeter, and "all went merry as a marriage bell."[2] It was a rare treat to have this party at Gordon Hall, for Captain Jonathan was not given to hospitality. We broke up shortly before midnight, with expressions of delight from all the guests.

I was a bachelor then, without ties. Captain Gordon insisted upon my having a bed at the Hall. I did not fall asleep readily; there seemed to be something in the air that forbade it. I was still awake when a distant clock struck the second hour of the morning. Suddenly the heavens were lighted by a sheet of ghastly light; a terrific midsummer thunderstorm was breaking over the sleeping town. A lurid flash lit up all the landscape, painting the trees in grotesque shapes against the murky sky, and defining clearly the sullen blackness of the waters of the bay breaking in grandeur against the rocky coast. I had arisen and put back the draperies from the windows, to have an unobstructed view of the grand scene. A low muttering coming nearer and nearer, a terrific roar, and then a tremendous downpour. The storm had burst.

Now the uncanny howling of a dog mingled with the rattling volleys of thunder. I heard the opening and closing of doors; the servants were about looking after things. It was impossible to sleep. The lightning was more vivid. There was a blinding flash of a greenish-white tinge mingled with the crash of falling timbers. Then before my startled gaze arose columns of red flames reflected against the sky. "Heaven help us!" I cried; "it is the left tower; it has been struck and is on fire!"

I hurried on my clothes and stepped into the corridor; the

---

1 Attributed to the Greek dramatist Menander (342–291 BCE).
2 Lord Byron, *Childe Harold* (1812), Canto III, Section XXI, line 8.

girls were there before me. Jeannette came up to me instantly with anxious face. "Oh, Doctor Thornton, what shall we do? Papa and mamma and little Johnny are in the old left tower. It is on fire. I have knocked and knocked, but get no answer."

"Don't be alarmed," said I soothingly. "Jenkins, ring the alarm bell," I continued, turning to the butler who was standing near; "the rest follow me. We will force the entrance to the Captain's room."

Instantly, it seemed to me, the bell boomed out upon the now silent air, for the storm had died down as quickly as it arose; and as our little procession paused before the entrance to the old left tower, we could distinguish the sound of the fire engines already on their way from the village.

The door resisted all our efforts; there seemed to be a barrier against it which nothing could move. The flames were gaining headway. Still the same deathly silence within the rooms.

"Oh, will they never get here?" cried Talma, wringing her hands in terror. Jeannette said nothing, but her face was ashen. The servants were huddled together in a panic-stricken group. I can never tell you what a relief it was when we heard the first sound of the firemen's voices, saw their quick movements, and heard the ringing of the axes with which they cut away every obstacle to our entrance to the rooms. The neighbors who had just enjoyed the hospitality of the house were now gathered around offering all the assistance in their power. In less than fifteen minutes the fire was out, and the men began to bear the unconscious inmates from the ruins. They carried them to the pagoda so lately the scene of mirth and pleasure, and I took up my station there, ready to assume my professional duties. The Captain was nearest me; and as I stooped to make the necessary examination I reeled away from the ghastly sight which confronted me—*gentlemen, across the Captain's throat was a deep gash that severed the jugular vein!*

The Doctor paused, and the hand with which he refilled his glass trembled violently.

"What is it, Doctor?" cried the men, gathering about me.

"Take the women away; this is murder!"

"Murder!" cried Jeannette, as she fell against the side of the pagoda.

"Murder!" screamed Talma, staring at me as if unable to grasp my meaning.

I continued my examination of the bodies, and found that the same thing had happened to Mrs. Gordon and to little Johnny.

The police were notified; and when the sun rose over the dripping town he found them in charge of Gordon Hall, the servants standing in excited knots talking over the crime, the friends of the family confounded, and the two girls trying to comfort each other and realize the terrible misfortune that had overtaken them.

Nothing in the rooms of the left tower seemed to have been disturbed. The door of communication between the rooms of the husband and wife was open, as they had arranged it for the night. Little Johnny's crib was placed beside his mother's bed. In it he was found as though never awakened by the storm. It was quite evident that the assassin was no common ruffian. The chief gave strict orders for a watch to be kept on all strangers or suspicious characters who were seen in the neighborhood. He made inquiries among the servants, seeing each one separately, but there was nothing gained from them. No one had heard anything suspicious; all had been awakened by the storm. The chief was puzzled. Here was a triple crime for which no motive could be assigned.

"What do you think of it?" I asked him, as we stood together on the lawn.

"It is my opinion that the deed was committed by one of the higher classes, which makes the mystery more difficult to solve. I tell you, Doctor, there are mysteries that never come to light, and this, I think, is one of them."

While we were talking Jenkins, the butler, an old and trusted servant, came up to the chief and saluted respectfully. "Want to speak with me, Jenkins?" he asked. The man nodded, and they walked away together.

The story of the inquest was short, but appalling. It was shown that Talma had been allowed to go abroad to study because she and Mrs. Gordon did not get on well together. From the testimony of Jenkins it seemed that Talma and her father had quarrelled bitterly about her lover, a young artist whom she had met at Rome, who was unknown to fame, and very poor. There had been terrible things said by each, and threats even had passed, all of which now rose up in judgment against the unhappy girl. The examination of the family solicitor revealed the fact that Captain Gordon intended to leave his daughters only a small annuity, the bulk of the fortune going to his son Jonathan, junior.

This was a monstrous injustice, as everyone felt. In vain Talma protested her innocence. Someone must have done it. No one would be benefited so much by these deaths as she and her sister. Moreover, the will, together with other papers, was nowhere to be found. Not the slightest clue bearing upon the disturbing elements in this family, if any there were, was to be found. As the only surviving relatives, Jeannette and Talma became joint heirs to an immense fortune, which only for the bloody tragedy just enacted would, in all probability, have passed them by. Here was the motive. The case was very black against Talma. The foreman stood up. The silence was intense: We "find that Capt. Jonathan Gordon, Mary E. Gordon and Jonathan Gordon, junior, all deceased, came to their deaths by means of a knife or other sharp instrument in the hands of Talma Gordon." The girl was like one stricken with death. The flower-like mouth was drawn and pinched; the great sapphire-blue eyes were black with passionate anguish, terror and despair. She was placed in jail to await her trial at the fall session of the criminal court. The excitement in the hitherto quiet town rose to fever heat. Many points in the evidence seemed incomplete to thinking men. The weapon could not be found, nor could it be divined what had become of it. No reason could be given for the murder except the quarrel between Talma and her father and the ill will which existed between the girl and her stepmother.

When the trial was called Jeannette sat beside Talma in the prisoner's dock; both were arrayed in deepest mourning. Talma was pale and careworn, but seemed uplifted, spiritualized, as it were. Upon Jeannette the full realization of her sister's peril seemed to weigh heavily. She had changed much too: hollow cheeks, tottering steps, eyes blazing with fever, all suggestive of rapid and premature decay. From far-off Italy Edward Turner, growing famous in the art world, came to stand beside his girl-love in this hour of anguish.

The trial was a memorable one. No additional evidence had been collected to strengthen the prosecution; when the attorney-general rose to open the case against Talma he knew, as everyone else did, that he could not convict solely on the evidence adduced. What was given did not always bear upon the case, and brought out strange stories of Captain Jonathan's methods. Tales were told of sailors who had sworn to take his life, in revenge for injuries inflicted upon them by his hand.

One or two clues were followed, but without avail. The judge summed up the evidence impartially, giving the prisoner the benefit of the doubt. The points in hand furnished valuable collateral evidence, but were not direct proof. Although the moral presumption was against the prisoner, legal evidence was lacking to actually convict. The jury found the prisoner "Not Guilty," owing to the fact that the evidence was entirely circumstantial. The verdict was received in painful silence; then a murmur of discontent ran through the great crowd.

"She must have done it," said one; "who else has been benefited by the horrible deed?"

"A poor woman would not have fared so well at the hands of the jury, nor a homely one either, for that matter," said another.

The great Gordon trial was ended; innocent or guilty, Talma Gordon could not be tried again. She was free; but her liberty, with blasted prospects and fair fame gone forever, was valueless to her. She seemed to have but one object in her mind: to find the murderer or murderers of her parents and half-brother. By her direction the shrewdest of detectives were employed and money flowed like water, but to no purpose; the Gordon tragedy remained a mystery. I had consented to act as one of the trustees of the immense Gordon estates and business interests, and by my advice the Misses Gordon went abroad. A year later I received a letter from Edward Turner, saying that Jeannette Gordon had died suddenly at Rome, and that Talma, after refusing all his entreaties for an early marriage, had disappeared, leaving no clue as to her whereabouts. I could give the poor fellow no comfort, although I had been duly notified of the death of Jeannette by Talma, in a letter telling me where to forward her remittances, and at the same time requesting me to keep her present residence secret, especially from Edward.

I had established a sanitarium for the cure of chronic diseases at Gordonville, and absorbed in the cares of my profession I gave little thought to the Gordons. I seemed fated to be involved in mysteries.

A man claiming to be an Englishman, and fresh from the California gold fields, engaged board and professional service at my retreat. I found him suffering in the grasp of the tubercle-fiend[1]—the last stages. He called himself Simon Cameron.[2] Sel-

---

1 Tuberculosis, a disease of the lungs.

2 This character shares a name with Simon Cameron *(continued)*

dom have I seen so fascinating and wicked a face. The lines of
the mouth were cruel, the eyes cold and sharp, the smile mocking and evil. He had money in plenty but seemed to have no
friends, for he had received no letters and had had no visitors in
the time he had been with us. He was an enigma to me; and his
nationality puzzled me, for of course I did not believe his story
of being English. The peaceful influence of the house seemed
to sooth him in a measure, and make his last steps to the mysterious valley as easy as possible. For a time he improved, and
would sit or walk about the grounds and sing sweet songs for the
pleasure of the other inmates. Strange to say, his malady only
affected his voice at times. He sang quaint songs in a silvery
tenor of great purity and sweetness that was delicious to the listening ear:

> "A wet sheet and a flowing sea,
> A wind that follows fast,
> And fills the white and rustling sail
> And bends the gallant mast;
> And bends the gallant mast, my boys;
> While like the eagle free,
> Away the good ship flies, and leaves
> Old England on the [lee]."[1]

There are few singers on the lyric stage who could surpass
Simon Cameron.

One night, a few weeks after Cameron's arrival, I sat in my
office making up my accounts when the door opened and closed;
I glanced up, expecting to see a servant. A lady advanced toward
me. She threw back her veil, and then I saw that Talma Gordon,
or her ghost, stood before me. After the first excitement of our
meeting was over, she told me she had come direct from Paris,
to place herself in my care. I had studied her attentively during
the first moments of our meeting, and I felt that she was right;
unless something unforeseen happened to arouse her from the
stupor into which she seemed to have fallen, the last Gordon was

---

(1799–1889), who was Abraham Lincoln's first—and allegedly cor-
rupt—secretary of war.

1   From Scottish poet Allan Cunningham's "A Wet Sheet and a Flowing Sea" (1825), lines 1–8.

doomed to an early death. The next day I told her I had cabled Edward Turner to come to her.

"It will do no good; I cannot marry him," was her only comment.

"Have you no feeling of pity for that faithful fellow?" I asked her sternly, provoked by her seeming indifference. I shall never forget the varied emotions depicted on her speaking face. Fully revealed to my gaze was the sight of a human soul tortured beyond the point of endurance; suffering all things, enduring all things, in the silent agony of despair.

In a few days Edward arrived, and Talma consented to see him and explain her refusal to keep her promise to him. "You must be present, Doctor; it is due your long, tried friendship to know that I have not been fickle, but have acted from the best and strongest motives."

I shall never forget that day. It was directly after lunch that we met in the library. I was greatly excited, expecting I knew not what. Edward was agitated, too. Talma was the only calm one. She handed me what seemed to be a letter, with the request that I would read it. Even now I think I can repeat every word of the document, so indelibly are the words engraved upon my mind:

MY DARLING SISTER TALMA: When you read these lines I shall be no more, for I shall not live to see your life blasted by the same knowledge that has blighted mine.

One evening, about a year before your expected return from Rome, I climbed into a hammock in one corner of the veranda outside the breakfast-room windows, intending to spend the twilight hours in lazy comfort, for it was very hot, enervating August weather. I fell asleep. I was awakened by voices. Because of the heat the rooms had been left in semi-darkness. As I lay there, lazily enjoying the beauty of the perfect summer night, my wandering thoughts were arrested by words spoken by our father to Mrs. Gordon, for they were the occupants of the breakfast-room.

"Never fear, Mary; Johnny shall have it all—money, houses, land and business."

"But if you do go first, Jonathan, what will happen if the girls contest the will? People will think that they ought to have the money as it appears to be theirs by law. I never could survive the terrible disgrace of the story."

"Don't borrow trouble; all you would need to do would be to show them papers I have drawn up, and they would be glad to take their annuity and say nothing. After all, I do not think it is so bad. Jeannette can teach; Talma can paint; six hundred dollars a year is quite enough for them."

I had been somewhat mystified by the conversation until now. This last remark solved the riddle. What could he mean? teach, paint, six hundred a year! With my usual impetuosity I sprang from my resting-place, and in a moment stood in the room confronting my father, and asking what he meant. I could see plainly that both were disconcerted by my unexpected appearance.

"Ah, wretched girl! you have been listening. But what could I expect of your mother's daughter?"

At these words I felt the indignant blood rush to my head in a torrent. So it had been all my life. Before you could remember, Talma, I had felt my little heart swell with anger at the disparaging hints and slurs concerning our mother. Now was my time. I determined that tonight I would know why she was looked upon as an outcast, and her children subjected to every humiliation. So I replied to my father in bitter anger:

"I was not listening; I fell asleep in the hammock. What do you mean by a paltry six hundred a year each to Talma and to me? 'My mother's daughter' demands an explanation from you, sir, of the meaning of the monstrous injustice that you have always practised toward my sister and me."

"Speak more respectfully to your father, Jeannette," broke in Mrs. Gordon.

"How is it, madam, that you look for respect from one whom you have delighted to torment ever since you came into this most unhappy family?"

"Hush, both of you," said Captain Gordon, who seemed to have recovered from the dismay into which my sudden appearance and passionate words had plunged him. "I think I may as well tell you as to wait. Since you know so much, you may as well know the whole miserable story." He motioned me to a seat. I could see that he was deeply agitated. I seated myself in a chair he pointed out, in wonder and expectation,—expectation of I knew not what. I trembled. This was a supreme moment in my life; I felt it. The air was heavy with the intense stillness that had settled over us as the common sounds of day gave place to the early quiet of the rural evening. I could see Mrs. Gordon's face as she sat within the radius of the lighted hallway. There was a smile of triumph upon it. I clinched my hands and bit my lips until the blood came, in the effort to keep from screaming. What was I about to hear? At last he spoke:

"I was disappointed at your birth, and also at the birth of Talma. I wanted a male heir. When I knew that I should again be a father I was torn by hope and fear, but I comforted myself with the thought that luck would be with me in the birth of the third child. When the doctor brought me word that a son was born to the house of Gordon, I was wild with delight, and did not notice his disturbed countenance. In the midst of my joy he said to me:

"'Captain Gordon, there is something strange about this birth. I want you to see this child.'

"Quelling my exultation I followed him to the nursery, and there, lying in the cradle, I saw a child dark as a mulatto, with the characteristic features of the Negro! I was stunned. Gradually it dawned upon me that there was something radically wrong. I turned to the doctor for an explanation.

"'There is but one explanation, Captain Gordon; there is Negro blood in this child.'

"'There is no Negro blood in my veins,' I said proudly. Then I paused—*the mother!*—I glanced at the doctor. He was watching me intently. The same thought was in his mind. I must have lived a thousand years in that cursed five seconds that I stood there confronting the physician and trying to think. 'Come,' said I to him, 'let us end this suspense.' Without thinking of consequences, I hurried away to your mother and accused her of infidelity to her marriage vows. I raved like a madman. Your mother fell into convulsions; her life was despaired of. I sent for Mr. and Mrs. Franklin, and then I learned the truth. They were childless. One year while on a Southern tour, they befriended an octoroon girl who had been abandoned by her white lover. Her child was a beautiful girl baby. They, being Northern born, thought little of caste distinction because the child showed no trace of Negro blood. They determined to adopt it. They went abroad, secretly sending back word to their friends at a proper time, of the birth of a little daughter. No one doubted the truth of the statement. They made Isabel their heiress, and all went well until the birth of your brother. Your mother and the unfortunate babe died. This is the story which, if known, would bring dire disgrace upon the Gordon family.

"To appease my righteous wrath, Mr. Franklin left a codicil to his will by which all the property is left at my disposal save a small annuity to you and your sister."

I sat there after he had finished his story, stunned by what I had heard. I understood, now, Mrs. Gordon's half contemptuous toleration and lack of consideration for us both. As I rose from my seat to leave the room I said to Captain Gordon:

"Still, in spite of all, sir, I am a Gordon, legally born. I will not tamely give up my birthright."

I left that room a broken-hearted girl, filled with a desire for revenge upon this man, my father, who by his manner disowned us without a regret. Not once in that remarkable interview did he speak of our mother as his wife; he quietly repudiated her and us with all the cold cruelty of relentless caste prejudice. I heard the treatment of your lover's proposal; I knew why Captain Gordon's consent to your marriage was withheld.

The night of the reception and dance was the chance for which I had waited, planned and watched. I crept from my window into the ivy-vines, and so down, down, until I stood upon the window-sill of Captain Gordon's room in the old left tower. How did I do it, you ask? I do not know. The house was silent after the revel; the darkness of the gathering storm favored me, too. The lawyer was there that day. The will was signed and put safely away among my father's papers. I was determined to have the will and the other documents bearing upon the case, and I would have revenge, too, for the cruelties we had suffered. With the old East Indian dagger firmly grasped I entered the room and found—that my revenge had been forestalled! The horror of the discovery I made that night restored me to reason and a realization of the crime I meditated. Scarce knowing what I did, I sought and found the papers, and crept back to my room as I had come. Do you wonder that my disease is past medical aid?

I looked at Edward as I finished. He sat, his face covered with his hands. Finally he looked up with a glance of haggard despair: "God! Doctor, but this is too much. I could stand the stigma of murder, but add to that the pollution of Negro blood! No man is brave enough to face such a situation."

"It is as I thought it would be," said Talma sadly, while the tears poured over her white face. "I do not blame you, Edward."

He rose from his chair, rung my hand in a convulsive clasp, turned to Talma and bowed profoundly, with his eyes fixed upon the floor, hesitated, turned, paused, bowed again and abruptly left the room. So those two who had been lovers, parted. I turned to Talma, expecting her to give way. She smiled a pitiful smile, and said: "You see, Doctor, I knew best."

From that on she failed rapidly. I was restless. If only I could rouse her to an interest in life, she might live to old age. So rich, so young, so beautiful, so talented, so pure; I grew savage thinking of the injustice of the world. I had not reckoned on the power that never sleeps. Something was about to happen.

On visiting Cameron next morning I found him approaching the end. He had been sinking for a week very rapidly. As I sat by the bedside holding his emaciated hand, he fixed his bright, wicked eyes on me, and asked: "How long have I got to live?"

"Candidly, but a few hours."

"Thank you; well, I want death; I am not afraid to die. Doctor, Cameron is not my name."

"I never supposed it was."

"No? You are sharper than I thought. I heard all your talk yesterday with Talma Gordon. Curse the whole race!"

He clasped his bony fingers around my arm and gasped: "*I murdered the Gordons!*"

Had I the pen of a Dumas[1] I could not paint Cameron as he told his story. It is a question with me whether this wheeling planet, home of the suffering, doubting, dying, may not hold

---

1 Alexandre Dumas *père* (1802–70), a nineteenth-century French writer of African descent.

worse agonies on its smiling surface than those of the conventional hell. I sent for Talma and a lawyer. We gave him stimulants, and then with broken intervals of coughing and prostration we got the story of the Gordon murder. I give it to you in a few words:

"I am an East Indian, but my name does not matter, Cameron is as good as any. There is many a soul crying in heaven and hell for vengeance on Jonathan Gordon. Gold was his idol; and many a good man walked the plank, and many a gallant ship was stripped of her treasure, to satisfy his lust for gold. His blackest crime was the murder of my father, who was his friend, and had sailed with him for many a year as mate. One night these two went ashore together to bury their treasure. My father never returned from that expedition. His body was afterward found with a bullet through the heart on the shore where the vessel stopped that night. It was the custom then among pirates for the captain to kill the men who helped bury their treasure. Captain Gordon was no better than a pirate. An East Indian never forgets, and I swore by my mother's deathbed to hunt Captain Gordon down until I had avenged my father's murder. I had the plans of the Gordon estate, and fixed on the night of the reception in honor of Talma as the time for my vengeance. There is a secret entrance from the shore to the chambers where Captain Gordon slept; no one knew of it save the Captain and trusted members of his crew. My mother gave me the plans, and entrance and escape were easy."

So the great mystery was solved. In a few hours Cameron was no more. We placed the confession in the hands of the police, and there the matter ended.[1]

"But what became of Talma Gordon?" questioned the president. "Did she die?"

"Gentlemen," said the Doctor, rising to his feet and sweeping the faces of the company with his eagle gaze, "gentlemen, if you will follow me to the drawing-room, I shall have much pleasure in introducing you to my wife—*nee* Talma Gordon."

---

1 Dr. Thornton's tale ends here.

3. Pauline E. Hopkins, "A Dash for Liberty," *Colored American Magazine*, vol. 3, no. 4 (August 1901), pp. 243–47

[Apart from some speculative details in a handful of newspaper articles, little was known about the life of Madison Washington before and after he led a successful revolt aboard a slaver traveling between Virginia and New Orleans in 1841. To fill the gaps, Frederick Douglass moved beyond biography in "The Heroic Slave" (1853), producing what is widely regarded as the first African American fictional text. William Wells Brown and the white abolitionist Lydia Maria Child likewise published accounts of the *Creole* rebellion. In her version, Hopkins takes calculated liberties with her source materials: she changes the protagonist's name from Washington to Monroe, identifies the revolt leader's wife Susan as the descendant of a founding father (similar to the title character of William Wells Brown's *Clotel*), and emphasizes the ongoing need for unified action to respond to the oppression of African Americans in general and the exploitation of black women in particular. Despite the note at the start stating that Hopkins's story is based on a June 1861 *Atlantic Monthly* article, the piece in that issue by Thomas Wentworth Higginson (1823–1911), who commanded black troops during the Civil War, makes no specific mention of Madison Washington or the revolt on the *Creole*, although it does refer to other slave rebellions (Gruesser, "Taking Liberties").]

Founded on an article written by Col. T.W. Higginson, for the Atlantic Monthly, June, 1861.

"So, Madison, you are bound to try it?"

"Yes, sir," was the respectful reply.

There was silence between the two men for a space, and Mr. Dickson drove his horse to the end of the furrow he was making and returned slowly to the starting point, and the sombre figure awaiting him.

"Do I not pay you enough, and treat you well?" asked the farmer as he halted.

"Yes, sir."

"Then why not stay here and let well enough alone?"

"Liberty is worth nothing to me while my wife is a slave."

"We will manage to get her to you in a year or two."

The man smiled and sadly shook his head. "A year or two would mean forever, situated as we are, Mr. Dickson. It is hard for you to understand; you white men are all alike where you are called upon to judge a Negro's heart," he continued bitterly. "Imagine yourself in my place; how would you feel? The relentless heel of oppression in the States will have ground my rights as a husband into the dust, and have driven Susan to despair in that time. A white man may take up arms to defend a bit of property; but a black man has no right to his wife, his liberty or his life against his master! This makes me low-spirited, Mr. Dickson, and I have determined to return to Virginia for my wife. My feelings are centred in the idea of liberty," and as he spoke he stretched his arms toward the deep blue of the Canadian sky in a magnificent gesture. Then with a deep-drawn breath that inflated his mighty chest, he repeated the word: "Liberty! I think of it by day and dream of it by night; and I shall only taste it in all its sweetness when Susan shares it with me."

Madison was an unmixed African, of grand physique, and one of the handsomest of his race. His dignified, calm and unaffected bearing marked him as a leader among his fellows. His features bore the stamp of genius. His firm step and piercing eye attracted the attention of all who met him. He had arrived in Canada along with many other fugitives during the year 1840, and being a strong, able-bodied man, and a willing worker, had sought and obtained employment on Mr. Dickson's farm.

After Madison's words, Mr. Dickson stood for some time in meditative silence.

"Madison," he said at length, "there's desperate blood in your veins, and if you get back there and are captured, you'll do desperate deeds."

"Well, put yourself in my place: I shall be there single-handed. I have a wife whom I love, and whom I will protect. I hate slavery, I hate the laws that make my country a nursery for it. Must I be denied the right of aggressive defense against those who would overpower and crush me by superior force?"

"I understand you fully, Madison; it is not your defense but your rashness that I fear. Promise me that you will be discreet, and not begin an attack." Madison hesitated. Such a promise seemed to him like surrendering a part of those individual rights for which he panted. Mr. Dickson waited. Presently the Negro said significantly: "I promise not to be indiscreet."

There were tears in the eyes of the kind-hearted farmer as he pressed Madison's hand.

"God speed and keep you and the wife you love; may she prove worthy."

In a few days Madison received the wages due him, and armed with tiny saws and files to cut a way to liberty, if captured, turned his face toward the South.

★ ★ ★ ★ ★

It was late in the fall of 1840 when Madison found himself again at home in the fair Virginia State. The land was blossoming into ripe maturity, and the smiling fields lay waiting for the harvester.

The fugitive, unable to travel in the open day, had hidden himself for three weeks in the shadow of the friendly forest near his old home, filled with hope and fear, unable to obtain any information about the wife he hoped to rescue from slavery. After weary days and nights, he had reached the most perilous part of his mission. Tonight there would be no moon and the clouds threatened a storm; to his listening ears the rising wind bore the sound of laughter and singing. He drew back into the deepest shadow. The words came distinctly to his ears as the singers neared his hiding place.

"All dem purty gals will be dar,
    Shuck dat corn before you eat.
Dey will fix it fer us rare,
    Shuck dat corn before you eat.
I know dat supper will be big,
    Shuck dat corn before you eat.
I think I smell a fine roast pig,
    Shuck dat corn before you eat.
Stuff dat coon an' bake him down,
I spec some niggers dar from town,
    Shuck dat corn before you eat.
Please cook dat turkey nice' an' brown,
By de side of dat turkey I'll be foun',

Shuck dat corn before you eat."[1]

"Don't talk about dat turkey; he'll be gone before we git dar."
"He's talkin', ain't he?"
"Las' time I shucked corn, turkey was de toughes' meat I eat fer many a day; you's got to have teef sharp lak a saw to eat it."
"S'pose you ain't got no teef, den what you gwine ter do?"
"Why ef you ain't got no teef you muss gum it!"
"Ha, ha, ha!"

Madison glided in and out among the trees, listening until he was sure that it was a gang going to a corn-shucking, and he resolved to join it, and get, if possible some news of Susan. He came out upon the highway, and as the company reached his hiding place, he fell into the ranks and joined in the singing. The darkness hid his identity from the company while he learned from their conversation the important events of the day.

On they marched by the light of weird, flaring pine knots, singing their merry cadences, in which the noble minor strains habitual to Negro music, sounded the depths of sadness, glancing off in majestic harmony, that touched the very gates of paradise in suppliant prayer.

It was close to midnight; the stars had disappeared and a steady rain was falling when, by a circuitous route, Madison reached the mansion where he had learned that his wife was still living. There were lights in the windows. Mirth at the great house kept company with mirth at the quarters.

The fugitive stole noiselessly under the fragrant magnolia trees and paused, asking himself what he should do next. As he stood there, he heard the hoof-beats of the mounted patrol, far in the distance, die into silence. Cautiously he drew near the house and crept around to the rear of the building directly beneath the window of his wife's sleeping closet. He swung himself up and tried it; it yielded to his touch. Softly he raised the sash, and softly he crept into the room. His foot struck against an object and swept it to the floor. It fell with a loud crash. In an instant the door opened. There was a rush of feet, and Madison stood at bay. The house was aroused; lights were brought.

"I knowed 'twas him!" cried the overseer in triumph. "I heern

---

1　This slave work song appears in William Wells Brown's *My Southern Home* (1880).

him a-gettin' in the window, but I kept dark till he knocked my gun down; then I grabbed him! I knowed this room'd trap him ef we was patient about it."

Madison shook his captor off and backed against the wall. His grasp tightened on the club in his hand; his nerves were like steel, his eyes flashed fire.

"Don't kill him," shouted Judge Johnson, as the overseer's pistol gleamed in the light, "Five hundred dollars for him alive!"

With a crash, Madison's club descended on the head of the nearest man; again, and yet again, he whirled it around, doing frightful execution each time it fell. Three of the men who had responded to the overseer's cry for help were on the ground, and he himself was sore from many wounds before, weakened by loss of blood, Madison finally succumbed.

★ ★ ★ ★ ★

The brig[1] "Creole" lay at the Richmond dock taking on her cargo of tobacco, hemp, flax and slaves. The sky was cloudless, and the blue waters rippled but slightly under the faint breeze. There was on board the confusion incident to departure. In the hold and on deck men were hurrying to and fro, busy and excited, making the final preparations for the voyage. The slaves came abroad in two gangs: first the men, chained like cattle, were marched to their quarters in the hold; then came the women to whom more freedom was allowed.

In spite of the blue sky and the bright sunlight that silvered the water the scene was indescribably depressing and sad. The procession of gloomy-faced men and weeping women seemed to be descending into a living grave.

The captain and the first mate were standing together at the head of the gangway as the women stepped aboard. Most were very plain and bore the marks of servitude, a few were neat and attractive in appearances; but one was a woman whose great beauty immediately attracted attention; she was an octoroon. It was a tradition that her grandfather had served in the Revolutionary War, as well as in both Houses of Congress. That was nothing, however, at a time when the blood of the proudest

---

1 A two-masted sailing vessel.

F.F.V.'s[1] was freely mingled with that of the African slaves on their plantations. Who wonders that Virginia has produced great men of color from among the ex-bondmen, or, that illustrious black men proudly point to Virginia as a birthplace? Posterity rises to the plane that their ancestors bequeath, and the most refined, the wealthiest and the most intellectual whites of that proud State have not hesitated to amalgamate with the Negro.

"What a beauty!" exclaimed the captain as the line of women paused a moment opposite him.

"Yes," said the overseer in charge of the gang. "She's as fine a piece of flesh as I have had in trade for many a day."

"What's the price?" demanded the captain.

"Oh, way up. Two or three thousand. She's a lady's maid, well-educated, and can sing and dance. We'll get it in New Orleans. Like to buy?"

"You don't suit my pile," was the reply, as his eyes followed the retreating form of the handsome octoroon. "Give her a cabin to herself; she ought not to herd with the rest," he continued, turning to the mate.

He turned with a meaning laugh to execute the order.

The "Creole" proceeded slowly on her way towards New Orleans. In the men's cabin, Madison Monroe lay chained to the floor and heavily ironed. But from the first moment on board ship he had been busily engaged in selecting men who could be trusted in the dash for liberty that he was determined to make. The miniature files and saws which he still wore concealed in his clothing were faithfully used in the darkness of night. The man was at peace, although he had caught no glimpse of the dearly loved Susan. When the body suffers greatly, the strain upon the heart becomes less tense, and a welcome calmness had stolen over the prisoner's soul.

On the ninth day out the brig encountered a rough sea, and most of the slaves were sick, and therefore not watched with very great vigilance. This was the time for action, and it was planned that they should rise that night. Night came on; the first watch was summoned; the wind was blowing high. Along the narrow passageway that separated the men's quarters from the women's, a man was creeping.

---

1 First Families of Virginia; i.e., prominent early settlers of the Virginia colony.

The octoroon lay upon the floor of her cabin, apparently sleeping, when a shadow darkened the door, and the captain stepped into the room, casting bold glances at the reclining figure. Profound silence reigned. One might have fancied one's self on a deserted vessel, but for the sound of an occasional footstep on the deck above, and the murmur of voices in the opposite hold.

She lay stretched at full length with her head resting upon her arm, a position that displayed to the best advantage the perfect symmetry of her superb figure; the dim light of a lantern played upon the long black ringlets, finely-chiselled mouth and well-rounded chin, upon the marbled skin veined by her master's blood,—representative of two races, to which did she belong?

For a moment the man gazed at her in silence; then casting a glance around him, he dropped upon one knee and kissed the sleeping woman full upon the mouth.

With a shriek the startled sleeper sprang to her feet. The woman's heart stood still with horror; she recognized the intruder as she dashed his face aside with both hands.

"None of that, my beauty," growled the man, as he reeled back with an oath, and then flung himself forward and threw his arm about her slender waist. "Why did you think you had a private cabin, and all the delicacies of the season? Not to behave like a young catamount, I warrant you."

The passion of terror and desperation lent the girl such strength that the man was forced to relax his hold slightly. Quick as a flash, she struck him a stinging blow across the eyes, and as he staggered back, she sprang out of the door way, making for the deck with the evident intention of going overboard.

"God have mercy!" broke from her lips as she passed the men's cabin, closely followed by the captain.

"Hold on, girl; we'll protect you!" shouted Madison, and he stooped, seized the heavy padlock which fastened the iron ring that encircled his ankle to the iron bar, and stiffening the muscles, wrenched the fastening apart, and hurled it with all his force straight at the captain's head.

His aim was correct. The padlock hit the captain not far from the left temple. The blow stunned him. In a moment Madison was upon him and had seized his weapons, another moment served to handcuff the unconscious man.

"If the fire of Heaven were in my hands, I would throw it

at these cowardly whites. Follow me; it is liberty or death!"[1] he shouted as he rushed for the quarter-deck. Eighteen others followed him, all of whom seized whatever they could wield as weapons.

The crew were all on deck; the three passengers were seated on the companion smoking. The appearance of the slaves all at once, completely surprised the whites.

So swift were Madison's movements that at first the officers made no attempt to use their weapons; but this was only for an instant. One of the passengers drew his pistol, fired, and killed one of the blacks. The next moment he lay dead upon the deck from a blow with a piece of a capstan bar in Madison's hand. The fight then became general, passengers and crew taking part.

The first and second mates were stretched out upon the deck with a single blow each. The sailors ran up the rigging for safety, and in short time Madison was master of the "Creole."

After his accomplices had covered the slaver's deck, the intrepid leader forbade the shedding of more blood. The sailors came down to the deck, and their wounds were dressed. All the prisoners were heavily ironed and well guarded except the mate, who was to navigate the vessel: with a musket doubly charged pointed at his breast, he was made to swear to take the brig into a British port.

By one splendid and heroic stroke, the daring Madison had not only gained his own liberty, but that of one hundred and thirty-four others.

The next morning all the slaves who were still fettered, were released, and the cook was ordered to prepare the best breakfast that the stores would permit; this was to be a fête[2] in honor of the success of the revolt and as a surprise to the females, whom the men had not yet seen.

As the women filed into the captain's cabin, where the meal was served, weeping, singing and shouting over their deliverance, the beautiful octoroon with one wild, half-frantic cry of joy sprang towards the gallant leader.

"Madison!"

---

1   Through Monroe's rallying cry, Hopkins evokes Patrick Henry's famous statement made in St. John's Church in Richmond in 1775 during the Second Virginia Convention.

2   A celebration or festival.

"My God! Susan! My wife!"

She was locked to his breast; she clung to him convulsively. Unnerved at last by the revulsion to more than relief and ecstasy, she broke into wild sobs, while the astonished company closed around them with loud hurrahs.

Madison's cup of joy was filled to the brim. He clasped her to him in silence, and humbly thanked Heaven for its blessing and mercy.

★ ★ ★ ★ ★

The next morning the "Creole" landed at Nassau, New Providence, where the slaves were offered protection and hospitality.

Every act of oppression is a weapon for the oppressed. Right is a dangerous instrument: woe to us if our enemy wields it.

Appendix F: Gender

[Women of color assume prominent roles in Hopkins's writings, as indicated by the impressive and accomplished heroines of her novels and her biographical sketches, and she takes great pains to champion their virtuousness in the face of white beliefs to the contrary. All of this is amply demonstrated in the opening entry of her Famous Women of the Negro Race series, devoted to "Phenomenal Vocalists." Because several of her fictional characters are mixed raced, early critics assumed that Hopkins advocated miscegenation and valued light-skinned heroines over darker ones. On the contrary, she frequently uses lighter-skinned female characters to castigate the widespread sexual exploitation of black women by white slaveholders that produced an African American population with a range of skin hues, from "ebony to alabaster." In one of these texts, "Furnace Blasts. II. Black or White—Which Should Be the Young Afro-American's Choice in Marriage," Hopkins explicitly advises US black men not to forsake black women. In addition to attesting to the animosity that her writings elicited in the former slave states, her lengthy 1905 letter to William Monroe Trotter, who shared her opposition to Booker T. Washington's public policies and behind-the-scenes machinations, painstakingly documents the harassment she encountered because of her gender. As the de facto chief editor of the *Colored American Magazine*, Hopkins had to endure male resentment, hostility, and unrelenting efforts to undermine her authority.]

1. **From Pauline E. Hopkins, "Phenomenal Vocalists," Famous Women of the Negro Race, I, *Colored American Magazine*, vol. 4, no. 1 (November 1901), pp. 45–53**

[Although it does include profiles of Sojourner Truth (c. 1797–1883) and Harriet Tubman (c. 1820–1913), Famous Women of the Negro Race otherwise provides composite portraits—of literary workers, educators, club women, artists, and college students. Appropriately enough, it begins with an installment about five singers, including the Hyers Sisters with whom Hopkins worked when she herself was a "Phenomenal Vocalist." In this installment, she celebrates the nobility and altruism of black women who have tirelessly supported their male counterparts in the face of extreme conditions.]

In giving the life-stories of five great artists it is pleasant to worship before these half-deserted shrines and drink in the beauty and inexhaustible charm of these singers, two of whom are of a past generation. It is profitable, too, for us to appreciate the fact that the women of the race have always kept pace with every advance made, often leading the upward flight. The work accomplished by these artists was more sacred than the exquisite subtleness of their art, for to them it was given to help create a manhood for their despised race.

In writing of the attainments of a people it is important that the position of its women be carefully defined—whether endowed with traits of character fit for cultivation, bright intellects and broad humanitarianism, virtuous in all things, tender, loving and of deep religious convictions. Given these attributes in its women and a race has already conquered the world and its best gifts.

Maligned and misunderstood, the Afro-American woman is falsely judged by other races. Nowhere on God's green earth are there nobler women, more self-sacrificing tender mothers, more gifted women in their chosen fields of work than among the millions of Negroes in the United States. The opening of the same scenes, the same pursuits and interests, with the same opportunity for education as is enjoyed by more favored people, have brought out the noblest and best in the women of our race. But an assertion is of no value unless proven. To this end we give the achievements of Negro women who were beacon lights along the shore in the days of our darkest history.

2. From J. Shirley Shadrach, "Furnace Blasts. II. Black or White—Which Should Be the Young Afro-American's Choice in Marriage," *Colored American Magazine*, vol. 6, no. 5 (March 1903), pp. 348–52

[In order to reduce the number of times her own name appeared in the *Colored American Magazine* and the *New Era Magazine*, Hopkins used two pseudonyms: her mother's maiden name,

Sarah A. Allen (the byline for *Hagar's Daughter*), and J. Shirley Shadrach, which she likely intended as an homage to Shadrach Minkins (c. 1814–75), the fugitive who was liberated from a Boston jail and later escaped to Canada. In the second of two pieces entitled "Furnace Blasts," both attributed to Shadrach, Hopkins addresses prejudice against black women and takes a firm stand against intermarriage. Ira Dworkin notes that the "unambiguously issue-oriented nonfiction model" Hopkins uses in the short-lived "Furnace Blasts" series "differs from her biographical approach in Famous Men and Famous Women" (199).]

The purpose of every race lover should be to familiarize the public mind with the fact that the Negro is a *human being*, amenable to every law, human and divine, that can affect any other race upon the footstool. The greatest objection to Negro enfranchisement is found in the menace of social equality which it is contended will inevitably lead to amalgamation.

The Anglo-Saxon argues that no fouler blight can fall upon his race than the curse of intermarriage with former slaves, forgetting that the "shaded Afghan"[1] which represents the present conglomeration, once pure African, was contributed by the blood of the Southern whites.

In the fear of social equality, no allowance is made for the chance that the Negro may not care for the joys (?) of such association; it is taken for granted that he will jump at the opportunity of pushing himself into a circle where he is not wanted. The truth is, the intelligent, self-respecting Afro-American finds every intellectual and social want more than filled among his associates of his own class. Among them he finds all the refinements of life which enhance the beauty of home and woman, with that freedom of association in which is a certain cordial exhilaration only found in social equality. There vulgarity, ignorance, coarseness, do not exist, but pleasant jets of affection, delicious fountains of association metamorphose the earth, and in this happy social affinity he forgets that there is a world where prejudice bars the door of pleasure for Negroes.

But the question of marriage is one of three about which no man can speak with certainty; it defies all laws and bows only to the will of Infinity.

---

1 I.e., race mixture.

We are born; we marry; we die; and no power on earth can change the circumstances under which these vital happenings occur; had we such power, then would Infinity cease to be Infinity.

Shall the Anglo-Saxon and the Afro-American mix?
They have mixed.
Shall they continue to mix?
This is the question which underlies all personal and public prejudice and legislation against the Negro.

[...]

"From ebony to alabaster!"

It was the privilege of the writer to listen to the eloquent and scholarly Prof. Price,[1] in Tremont Temple, Boston, shortly before his death.

In speaking of the wide range of choice spread out before our youth he said that there was no call for a man or woman of color to marry outside racial lines, for there was every color necessary for choice ranging from ebony to alabaster. But in spite of the variety, many Negroes are availing themselves of the privileges granted by our Northern States, to unite themselves with the Caucasian race; and this is more prevalent among men than among women.

We find no fault in this if the Negro unites himself to one who is in all things his equal—morally and intellectually. But we are sorry to say, the reverse often happens, and so men entail upon themselves and their children the deadly association of a nature vile, miasmatic and filthy, dealing death to all hope of moral cleanliness.

There is still another point to consider.

The Negro woman is not tolerated by the Anglo-Saxon; he can stand the black man but not the black woman save in the menial position of a servant or the degraded one of a concubine. Positions calling for refined service are barred to the female

---

1 Joseph Charles Price (1854–93), the founder of Livingstone College.

Afro-American, generally speaking, and the hatred of the white sister is so implacable as to become revolting.

If, then, the male of our race contracts alliance with the dominant race, by preference, what becomes of his sisters and the other female members of his family when the time comes for them to select life-partners? The sequence is inevitable under certain circumstances: an alliance of shame or the lonely celibacy from which nature revolts.

[...]

To the young Afro-American who hesitates between black or white in his choice of a life partner, I say "Don't!" The time for amalgamation is not yet. In the company of the beautiful, virtuous and intellectual of your own race, lie health, happiness and prosperity.

3. **From Pauline E. Hopkins to W[illiam] M[onroe] Trotter (16 April 1905), Fisk University, John Hope and Aurelia E. Franklin Library, Special Collections, Pauline E. Hopkins Collection**

[Seeking to document Booker T. Washington's takeover of periodicals that were critical of him and his policies, W.E.B. Du Bois wrote to fellow Harvard alumnus William Monroe Trotter (1872–1934), the editor of the black newspaper the *Boston Guardian*, seeking information about the *Colored American Magazine*. Hopkins prepared a ten-page letter with twenty enclosures in response to Trotter's inquiry. In these documents she elaborates on the internal politics at the journal and reveals personal information about herself that is not available elsewhere. She details the intense pressure she faced from John C. Freund (1848–1924), a white ally of Washington, to alter her editorial policies. She also describes being fired by Washington's associate Fred Moore, the nominal purchaser of the periodical, who moved it from Boston to New York in 1904. The letter also refers to the strong opposition to Hopkins's fiction in the South.]

My dear Mr. Trotter:

Herewith I send you a detailed account of my experiences with the Colored American Magazine as its editor and, incidentally, with Mr. Booker T. Washington in the taking over of the magazine to New York by his agents. It is necessarily long and perhaps tedious at the outset, but I trust that you will peruse it to the end. I have held these facts for a year, but as my rights are ignored in my own property, and I am persistently hedged about by the revengeful tactics of Mr. Washington's men, I feel that I must ask the advice of some one who will give me a respectful hearing, and judgment as to the best way to deal with this complicated case. I hope that you will do what you can for me.

[...]

Early in February, 1904, Mr. Freund sent me a bouquet of Russian violets by his Boston representative, Mr. Adelbert Loomis; the book "Self-Help" by Smiles,[1] an expensive set of furs, a $25-check and a book "Eternalism."[2] I had seemed to be a favorite with our benefactor and these special attentions made my position in the office very uncomfortable. As I am not a woman who attracts the attention of the opposite sex in any way, Mr. Freund's philanthropy with regard to myself puzzled me, but knowing that he was aware of my burdens at home, I thought that he was trying to help me in his way. I was so dense that I did not for a moment suspect that I was being politely bribed to give up my race work and principles and adopt the plans of the South for the domination of the Blacks.

[...]

Mr. Dupree[3] received a letter dated April 6,[4] which threw a firebrand into the office and made my position unbearable. See letter marked "17." In this letter we note the following:

"There is, however, one rock right squarely ahead of us. That is the persistence with which matter is put into the

---

1 Samuel Smiles, *Self-Help; With Illustrations of Character, Conduct, and Perseverance* (1859).
2 Orlando J. Smith, *Eternalism: A Theory of Infinite Justice* (1902).
3 Virginia native William Dupree (1839–1934) was, at the time, the president of the Colored Co-operative Publishing Company.
4 Hopkins is referring to a letter from Freund.

magazine, which has no live interest, and furthermore, is likely to alienate the very few friends who might help us. Now, I have spoken on the subject already more than I care to. Either Miss Hopkins will follow our suggestion in this matter and put live matter into the magazine, eliminating anything which may create offense; stop talking about wrongs and a proscribed race, or you must count me out absolutely from this day forth."

[...]

"Proscribed race," was a hit at my book "Contending Forces" and my serial story "Hagar's Daughter" both of which had aroused the ire of the white South, male and female, against me many of whom had paid me their compliments in newspaper squibs and insulting personal letters sent to the old management of the magazine.

[...]

Messrs. Dupree, West and Watkins[1] were influenced by Mr. Freund's threat of withdrawal, and matters grew unbearable for me at the office; I was absent for a number of days. During this absence I wrote to Mr. Freund outlining to him some of the difficulties I was encountering not knowing that they were caused by him. See letter marked "18."

In letter "19" he virtually gives up the enterprise and tells me of the unflattering comments made upon my work (the work so recently eulogized by himself) by Boston people. See letters marked "19" and "20."

My Boston critics were all men working for and under Mr. Washington. $150 promised us by Mr. Freund was given right after the reception in March, to Mr. Charles Alexander, Editor of "The Boston Colored Citizen" a paper publicly believed to have been born at Mr. Washington's suggestion for the express

---

1 William O. West (b. 1859) was the manager of the *Colored American Magazine* and secretary of the Colored Co-operative Publishing Company. Virginia native Jesse W. Watkins (b. 1872) was the treasurer and one of the four founders of the Colored Co-operative Publishing Company.

purpose of putting "The Boston Guardian" out of business.

About the last of April or the first of May, 1904, negotiations were opened with Mr. Dupree by Mr. Fred R. Moore, National Organizer of the Business League, looking to the purchase of the Colored American Magazine. It was planned to remove this plant to New York and have T. Thomas Fortune[1] as the Editor and Pauline E. Hopkins as Associate Editor. It was understood by the force that Mr. Moore represented and covered Mr. B.T. Washington. I was offered $12 per week which I decided to accept having determined that I would accept the situation as I found it, succumb to the powers that were, and do all I could to keep the magazine alive unless they asked me to publicly renounce the rights of my people. They held, also, the plates of my book "Contending Forces" and 500 bound and unbound copies of the same. The book had been sold to the former management on the monthly instalment plan, and when the company failed they still owed me $175. So, being a creditor and a shareholder and a member of the Board of Directors, I had a deep interest in the business of the corporation.

After I settled in New York, Mr. Freund wrote me a letter congratulating me on my earnest and faithful work for the purchases [sic] of the magazine. Many promises were made me, but I soon found that I was being "frozen out" for Mr. Roscoe Conkling SIMMONS[2] a _nephew_ of MRS. B.T. WASHINGTON who now holds the position which I was forced to resign last September.

---

1 Timothy Thomas Fortune (1856–1928) was the long-time editor of the _New York Age_ and an advisor to Booker T. Washington.

2 Roscoe Conkling Simmons (1881–1951) was an African American journalist who became a columnist for the _Chicago Tribune_.

Appendix G: Borrowings/Plagiarism/ Signifying

[Although scholars have long known that Hopkins incorporated material by others into her writings without acknowledgment, widespread digitization of books and periodicals has begun to make it possible to calculate just how extensive this was. Responding to recent critical discoveries along these lines, Richard Yarborough states that, given "the vast array of source texts from which Hopkins took material," one must be "impressed with the absolutely extraordinary range of her reading": "What boggles the mind is the extent to which Hopkins's approach depended, in part, upon her ability not simply to remember specific details of the texts from which she borrowed but to weave these plot turns, snippets of description, and passages of dialogue into coherent narratives informed by her racially progressive goals. Judge her intertextual appropriations as you will, it hardly resulted from any reluctance to expend the creative labor necessary to produce fiction" (Introduction). Hopkins derives a significant portion of *Hagar's Daughter* from other sources. She does so in at least three distinct ways. First, in a more or less conventional manner, she reprints, with or without quotation marks and without attribution, short passages from canonical authors, such as Shakespeare and Tennyson, as well as writers of popular fiction. Second, she borrows extended plotlines, entire scenes, character structures (to use JoAnn Pavletich's term), and key themes from (often well-known) literary texts, including her evocation of Satan and his minions from John Milton's *Paradise Lost* in her depiction of the Southern secessionist conference, her casting of Hagar Sargeant as a racialized "madwoman in the attic" through her echoes of Charlotte Brontë's *Jane Eyre*, and her explicit nod at the end of Part I to "Death Is Freedom," the climactic twenty-fifth chapter of William Wells Brown's *Clotel*, when Hagar suicidally leaps with her infant into the Potomac river to avoid a life of slavery. Third, she frequently lifts—often verbatim—dialogue, narration, and background description from popular magazine fiction, as Lauren Dembowitz has established. In some instances, she combines the second and third of these approaches, appropriating not only a plotline, episode, and/or motif, but also (sometimes copious) phrasing from the same text, as she does, for example, with the gambling scene early in Brown's *Clotel* and, as Dembowitz discusses at length, Fanny Driscoll's 1884 story "Two Women," approximately 80 per cent of which has been sewn into the fabric of Hopkins's novel (Dembowitz, "Appropriating"). Adam Sonstegard contends that J. Alexandre Skeete's rendering of Hagar leaping off of Long Bridge with her infant daughter was influenced by and served as a response to a late 1852 illustration of Eliza Harris escaping across the ice floes in the Ohio River with her child in Harriet Beecher Stowe's *Uncle Tom's Cabin*. Another image that Hopkins and Skeete very likely had in mind was the 1853 frontispiece illustration of the title character hurling herself into the Potomac in William Wells Brown's *Clotel*. Dembowitz notes, moreover, the resemblance between Skeete's drawing of Jewel Bowen seeing Aurelia Madison in the arms of her fiancé Cuthbert Sumner and the illustration that accompanied Fanny Driscoll's *Frank Leslie's Popular Monthly* story "Two Women," in which Mignon Trevor beholds June Langdon with her arms clasped around Don Eastern's neck ("Sources").]

1. Illustration from Harriet Beecher Stowe, *Uncle Tom's Cabin* (J. Cassell, 1852), p. 50B

[Hammatt Billings (1818–74) did seven illustrations for the original two-volume edition of *Uncle Tom's Cabin* in 1852. At the end of that year, Jewett & Company of Boston brought out a one volume "Christmas" edition of the novel featuring 117 additional engravings by Billings, including the headpiece for Chapter Seven, which depicts Eliza Harris fleeing across the ice in the Ohio River with her child.]

From Harriet Beecher Stowe's *Uncle Tom's Cabin* (1852). University of Virginia.

2. From William Wells Brown, *Clotel; or, The President's Daughter* (London, Partridge & Oakey, 1853), pp. 69–70, 216–18

[An image of the protagonist pitching herself into the Potomac River served as the frontispiece for the first edition of William Wells Brown's *Clotel*. The gambling scene early in the novel, in which a slave is wagered and lost in a poker game, clearly inspired the one on board the *Planter* in *Hagar's Daughter*, which includes language taken directly from Brown. In Chapter VIII of *Hagar's Daughter*, Hopkins again pays homage to Brown: she positions Hagar in the same location (she flees across a bridge linking Washington, DC, and Virginia), places her in the same situation (she is pursued by slave catchers from both directions), and portrays her performing the same desperate act (she leaps into the Potomac River) as the title character in Chapter 25 of *Clotel*. As Holly Jackson has established, Brown himself borrowed this scene from an account published 11 years earlier, and other writers, including Frederick Douglass and Frances Harper (1825–1911), reproduced it as well.]

THE DEATH OF CLOTEL.   *Page* 218.

From William Wells Brown's *Clotel* (1853). Charles L. Blockson Afro-American Collection. Temple University.

From Chapter 2: "Going to the South"

It was now twelve o'clock at night, and instead of the passengers
being asleep the majority were gambling in the saloons. Thousands of dollars change hands during a passage from Louisville
or St. Louis to New Orleans on a Mississippi steamer, and many
men, and even ladies, are completely ruined. "Go call my boy,
steward," said Mr. Smith, as he took his cards one by one from
the table. In a few moments a fine-looking, bright-eyed mulatto
boy, apparently about fifteen years of age, was standing by his
master's side at the table. "I will see you, and five hundred dollars better," said Smith, as his servant Jerry approached the
table. "What price do you set on that boy?" asked Johnson, as
he took a roll of bills from his pocket. "He will bring a thousand
dollars, any day, in the New Orleans market," replied Smith.
"Then you bet the whole of the boy, do you?" "Yes." "I call you,
then," said Johnson, at the same time spreading his cards out
upon the table. "You have beat me," said Smith, as soon as he
saw the cards. Jerry, who was standing on top of the table, with
the banknotes and silver dollars round his feet, was now ordered
to descend from the table. "You will not forget that you belong
to me," said Johnson, as the young slave was stepping from the
table to a chair. "No, sir," replied the chattel. "Now go back to
your bed, and be up in time to-morrow morning to brush my
clothes and clean my boots, do you hear?" "Yes, sir," responded
Jerry, as he wiped the tears from his eyes.

Smith took from his pocket the bill of sale and handed it to
Johnson; at the same time saying, "I claim the right of redeem-
ing that boy, Mr. Johnson. My father gave him to me when I
came of age, and I promised not to part with him." "Most certainly, sir, the boy shall be yours whenever you hand me over a
cool thousand," replied Johnson. The next morning, as the passengers were assembling in the breakfast saloons, and upon the
guards of the vessel, and the servants were seen running about
waiting upon or looking for their masters, poor Jerry was entering his new master's state-room with his boots.

From Chapter 25: "Death Is Freedom"

At the dusk of the evening previous to the day when she was to
be sent off, as the old prison was being closed for the night, she

suddenly darted past her keeper, and ran for her life. It is not a great distance from the prison to the Long Bridge, which passes from the lower part of the city across the Potomac, to the extensive forests and woodlands of the celebrated Arlington Place, occupied by that distinguished relative and descendant of the immortal Washington, Mr. George W. Curtis.[1] Thither the poor fugitive directed her flight. So unexpected was her escape, that she had quite a number of rods[2] the start before the keeper had secured the other prisoners, and rallied his assistants in pursuit. It was at an hour when, and in a part of the city where, horses could not be readily obtained for the chase; no bloodhounds were at hand to run down the flying woman; and for once it seemed as though there was to be a fair trial of speed and endurance between the slave and the slave-catchers. The keeper and his forces raised the hue and cry on her pathway close behind; but so rapid was the flight along the wide avenue, that the astonished citizens, as they poured forth from their dwellings to learn the cause of alarm, were only able to comprehend the nature of the case in time to fall in with the motley mass in pursuit, (as many a one did that night,) to raise an anxious prayer to heaven, as they refused to join in the pursuit, that the panting fugitive might escape, and the merciless soul dealer for once be disappointed of his prey. And now with the speed of an arrow—having passed the avenue—with the distance between her and her pursuers constantly increasing, this poor hunted female gained the "*Long Bridge*," as it is called, where interruption seemed improbable, and already did her heart begin to beat high with the hope of success. She had only to pass three-fourths of a mile across the bridge, and she could bury herself in a vast forest, just at the time when the curtain of night would close around her, and protect her from the pursuit of her enemies.

But God by his Providence had otherwise determined. He had determined that an appalling tragedy should be enacted that night, within plain sight of the President's house and the capital of the Union, which should be an evidence wherever it should be known, of the unconquerable love of liberty the heart may inherit;

---

1 This is George Washington Parke Custis (1781–1857), the Arlington (Virginia) plantation owner and Washington biographer, not "Curtis" as Brown has it.

2 A rod is equal to five and one-half yards.

as well as a fresh admonition to the slave dealer, of the cruelty and enormity of his crimes. Just as the pursuers crossed the high draw for the passage of sloops, soon after entering upon the bridge, they beheld three men slowly approaching from the Virginia side. They immediately called to them to arrest the fugitive, whom they proclaimed a runaway slave. True to their Virginian instincts as she came near, they formed in line across the narrow bridge, and prepared to seize her. Seeing escape impossible in that quarter, she stopped suddenly, and turned upon her pursuers. On came the profane and ribald crew, faster than ever, already exulting in her capture, and threatening punishment for her flight. For a moment she looked wildly and anxiously around to see if there was no hope of escape. On either hand, far down below, rolled the deep foamy waters of the Potomac, and before and behind the rapidly approaching step and noisy voices of pursuers, showing how vain would be any further effort for freedom. Her resolution was taken. She clasped her *hands* convulsively, and raised *them*, as she at the same time raised her *eyes* towards heaven, and begged for that mercy and compassion *there*, which had been denied her on earth; and then, with a single bound, she vaulted over the railings of the bridge, and sunk for ever beneath the waves of the river!

Thus died Clotel, the daughter of Thomas Jefferson, a president of the United States; a man distinguished as the author of the Declaration of American Independence, and one of the first statesmen of that country.

3. **Fanny Driscoll, "Two Women,"** *Frank Leslie's Popular Monthly,* **vol. 17, no. 5 (May 1884), pp. 561–67**

[In Fanny Driscoll's 1884 short fiction "Two Women," a man who has broken off an engagement to a beautiful, exotic, assertive woman falls in love with a pretty, meek, conventional one, only to have the former resort to subterfuge to get him back. Similarly, in *Hagar's Daughter,* Cuthbert Sumner's impending marriage to Jewel Bowen is called off because of the conniving actions of Aurelia Madison, to whom he was once betrothed. However, whereas the unscrupulous woman wins her man in Driscoll's narrative, Aurelia's stratagem does not succeed in Hopkins's novel. More significantly, although in Driscoll's story the "Two Women" are white, in Hopkins's novel both Jewel and

Aurelia possess some African blood, which profoundly affects their circumstances and largely determines their fates. The illustration for "Two Women" depicts the key scene in which Mignon Trevor finds June Langdon embracing Don Eastern.]

TWO WOMEN.—"MRS. LANGDON'S ARMS WERE ABOUT HIS THROAT. A DEEP SIGH STARTLED HIM. STANDING IN THE ARCH BETWEEN THE BOUDOIR AND THE LIBRARY, PALLID AS A GHOST, STOOD MIGNON."—SEE NEXT PAGE.

Vol XVII No 5.—26

Illustration from Fanny Driscoll's "Two Women." *Frank Leslie's Popular Monthly*, May 1884, 561.

"Come to me. I am dying.   JUNE."

Don Eastern's brow was knit, and he muttered a very impatient imprecation under his breath, as he stood studying the telegram which had just been put in his hand.

"I thought that was all over and done with. Must we go through with it again, I wonder?"

And then he took up a time-table and studied it attentively for a moment.

"Of course, a thousand miles in this beastly cold is a mere nothing for a busy man! That's understood. A woman's caprice must be gratified at all hazards. My arch-enchantress isn't dying any more than I am, but I suppose I must go."

Glancing hurriedly through the mail on his desk, he then picked up, from the midst of commonplace, practical, business-like looking letters, a slim, satiny envelope of palest pink, with a faint perfume clinging to it. His whole face softened and his hand shook for a moment as he eagerly opened, and read the few lines.

"My little Mignon!" he said, gently.

But his little Mignon did not keep him from taking a journey of a thousand miles to see June Heatherton, to whom he had been betrothed a year ago; with whom he had quarreled fiercely over some palpable flirtation on her part; from whom he had parted in bitterness and pain, and yet with a half-relieved feeling in a corner of his heart.

Six months he had been reckless, as a man sometimes will when a woman has been false and untrue in any particular; and then she had written him, proudly, tenderly, saying that, as she had sinned, so must she be supplicant—in her anger she had said she did not love him, but now she knew better; she would never love any one else—would he not come back to her?

But this he had declined, politely and firmly. Now that it was all over, he knew he had never loved her, and that it was a most fortunate thing that he had found it out in time.

Her grace, her beauty, her wonderful fascination had thrilled his blood with a rapture that he thought then was Love, but it was only her false twin-sister. Love had come to him, indeed, but it was a later guest, and then a sweet face leaned to him through the shadows, and its purity and tenderness blotted out the warm Summer beauty of June Heatherton from before his vision.

Yet, a week later he was in her presence.

"She evidently still lives!" he murmured, sardonically, as he entered the magnificent hall of Heatherton, *pater*,[1] in which no signs of mourning fluttered.

A moment later June entered the drawing-room, where he waited, feeling very much like an accomplished chess player after a close long game, with "checkmate" still in doubt.

Ah, yes, she could stir even his unbelieving, cold heart.

In some soft, white woolen *négligé* that clothed her from foot to throat like snow, with her golden hair caught in a careless, crinkling mass low down on her neck, with her lips scarlet and dewy, and a deep light in her dusky eyes, she came swiftly to him—the white arms were about his throat, the sweet, warm lips against his.

"My love! my love!" she murmured, softly.

And certainly Don Eastern was not the kind of man to let the memory of a little Mignon prevent him from holding a beautiful, yielding form closely in his arms, and returning clinging kisses with interest, when such a rare opportunity offered.

I question if there are many men that would.

But for all this propitious beginning, Don Eastern went back to his own home, a week later, as free as when he left it. He alone knew the full power of June Heatherton's siren charms, for he was the only man she had ever loved. He alone knew of the tears she had shed; he alone knew that she had thrown herself at his feet in all her exquisite, gleaming beauty, and begged him to take her back to his heart, with all the despairing passion that a woman like her can feel when she sees the man that was once her abject slave beyond her reach.

What was her pride compared to the desolation that swept over her when she realized that the heart she had trifled with was hers no longer, when she had learned to prize it most?

And so he went back to his little Mignon, whose calm, pure face was continually before him through all his journey in the bitter Winter cold.

A dainty little missive would be awaiting him—the last week or two would drop away from him then. But to his intense disappointment, no letter was here; he only waited to grasp this fact fully, and to freshen up after his tiresome trip, when once more he started out.

---

1 Father.

It was a very different woman from June Heatherton that greeted him at the end of this journey. Not tall, nor voluptuous, nor passionate; but flower-sweet and fragile, with dreaming eyes and a sweet mouth, and a radiant smile.

A faint flush stole into her cheeks as she came quietly to him and laid her hands in his outstretched ones for a brief moment. She did not even see the love and longing in his eyes, and then he took her in his arms.

"Mignon, I can wait no longer," he said, earnestly. "Say you love me."

She looked up into his face a little startled, and trembled like a bud the wind has shaken too roughly; but she did not strive to leave her prison, and, after a pause which was breathless and terrible to Don Eastern, she said, gravely and sweetly:

"I love you."

"My angel!" he said, passionately. "I am not worthy of you— not worthy to touch your hand; but I love you so, little Mignon, I shall make you happy."

And she laid her cheek against his, perfectly happy and trusting and content, deeming him

> —— "the goodliest man
> That ever among the ladies ate in Hall,
> And noblest."[1]

Strangely enough, he told her all about June Heatherton. He hid nothing—not even his long journey last week—and Mignon's face was shadowed for a moment.

"Did you ever love her?"

"No, my darling; I thought I did, but I know better now."

"She is very beautiful?"

"Yes."

"And she loves you?"

He bent down and kissed her, but did not answer.

"Are you sure—*quite* sure—that you love *me*?"

"My blossom," he murmured, with infinite tenderness, "if you are not the other half of my soul, I pray God I may go to my grave bereft."

---

1 From lines 253–55 of the "Lancelot and Elaine" section of Alfred, Lord Tennyson's *The Idylls of the King*, first published in 1859.

"But you would have married *her*," she said, after a little.

"I don't think Fate would have been so cruel, knowing my little unknown Mignon was my rightful portion. Remember, dear, I did not know *you* then."

And she was silenced.

★ ★ ★ ★ ★ ★

Three months later Don brought her June's wedding cards.

"You see, dear," he said, "that she did not love me."

But in a day or two came a mad letter to him, written by June on her wedding-day. And Don Eastern was sorry, indeed; for June Heatherton, despite her coquetry, was a girl with a really fine nature. She was good and noble in most things, but this unreasoning love seemed to have overwhelmed her, and swept her off her feet.

He said nothing to Mignon. He destroyed the letter, and did not answer it.

He was beginning to hope she had found a new love to fill her heart, when another letter came.

She had tried to love her husband; she had imagined, if she were married to some good man, she could forget her wild love for *him*. But it was in vain, and she was the most miserable woman on the face of the earth.

He said nothing to Mignon. It would only grieve her, and she was too white and innocent to know anything of such stormy passions.

A third letter came, and a fourth, and he began to be seriously annoyed, when one day a little note came from June—Mrs. Langdon—saying she was in town visiting her sister; would he not call?

In his perplexity (men are such stupids) he went to Mignon.

He told her Mrs. Langdon was in town; and that she had written him to call. Should he do so?

And then, to her questions: No, she was not happy, and she had not yet learned to love her husband, whom she had married in one of her freaks, but in time, perhaps—

And poor little Mignon, with a very sore heart and a calm face, told him to go if he wished. It would be only courtesy.

She had seen June's picture, and the beautiful sorceress face was something to remember—the sweet smiling lips, the languid, dark eyes, the pearl softness and fairness. Often, when she was nestled in her lover's arms, the thought would steal to her that that beautiful head had lain where hers was now; that his kisses had been pressed upon other, redder lips, and she felt a little pang, as a loving jealous heart will, for there is little love in this world that does not walk hand-in-hand with jealousy. It is all very well to talk about a perfect trust, a noble confidence, but this is the nineteenth century, and one must be vain, and arrogant, and self-sufficient, indeed, when no doubt ever creeps in of one's own power and fascination when pitted against another's.

June Langdon had wealth, beauty and passion. Mignon had twice her intellect, and tenderness, and capacity for pain and self-sacrifice and love. June was a magnificent cactus-blossom, scarlet and gold, and subtle; Mignon was a fair day-lily, pallid and fragrant and pensive.

And men have such an unfortunate weakness for tropical flowers, they cannot pass them by carelessly or unconsciously, even though they have already plucked the lily and laid the frail petals above their hearts. The white flower brought out all the beauty of Don Eastern's soul, its chivalry and tenderness, its belief in the good and true, its higher impulses and aspirations; but he could not ignore the scarlet brilliant cactus-bud; it caused his blood to flow faster, it gave a new zest to living—for an hour.

Mignon was his saint, his nun, his good angel, and he loved her truly, with all the high love a man of the world can ever know. He reverenced her for her womanly goodness and truth; he trusted her as he never supposed he could trust any one. She rested him and soothed him unspeakably.

And little Mignon loved him with a strange power and intensity that was the very breath of her life to her.

But he went to see Mrs. Langdon just the same.

She came to him more royally beautiful than ever, with eyes more lustrous and filled with a starrier dusk, with redder lips and a deeper flush on her delicate cheeks; her garments clung about her lissome form, a faint, mystic perfume rose from her laces—*Circe*, indeed.

He stood up silently and gravely, but she laid her head on his shoulder and drew his lips down to hers. She had once been delicately reserved, and high and proud, but a mad, unthinking love had changed her strangely. And, married though she was, this man, Don Eastern, held all her soul in his keeping, and with a tropical nature like hers love is everything.

She would have preferred heaven and the "lilies and the languors of virtue"; debarred from that, she would take hell and the "raptures and roses" of a love to which she had no shadow of right. By-and-by, she said, "Don, you love some one?"

He bowed, with a deep look in her face.

"Not me—you do not love *me*!" she said, impatiently. "It is some one else, some one I do not know—tell me about her!"

"My dear June, could a man ever find room for two women in his heart, when one of them was you?"

"Tell me about *her*," she said, steadily. "I have not loved you all these years, Don Eastern, without learning every phase of your mood. Does she live here?"

"No, but she is visiting here at present."

"Is she beautiful?"

"No."

"Brilliant?"

"No."

"Wealthy?"

"No."

"What *is* she, then?"

"An angel, whose garments it is a profanation to touch."

She looked at him wonderingly and sighed heavily.

"Can I see her?"

"I am sure I do not know. You may possibly meet her at some party or something."

"Are you going to hear Modjeska to-morrow night?"

"Yes."

"With *her*?"

"I believe so."

"Then I shall see her—Oh, my God!"

She caught her breath sharply, and fell down at his feet in all her exquisite beauty.

"Can you never, *never* love me again, Don? My life, my soul, it is all yours! Can you not give me a little love in return?"

He lifted her up gently.

"It is too late to ask that now, June. Try and forget you ever loved any one but your husband. Believe me, you will be happier. No one can more bitterly regret than I the misery of our past. Let us begin anew."

But she thrust him away from her wildly, and bade him to go, if he did not wish her to fall dead at his feet.

So he went away sadly.

★ ★ ★ ★ ★ ★

Mignon was visiting a schoolfriend, Mrs. Barrymore, and the next night they all sat listening to the heart breaking story of "Camille"—Mrs. Barrymore, piquant and gypsy-like; Mr. Barrymore, blonde and languid, but very devoted to his pretty, dashing wife; Mignon, and Don Eastern. She was listening earnestly to Modjeska, who interpreted so well a passionate, loving, erring, noble woman's heart. The high-bred grace, the dainty foreign accent, the naturalness of this actress, held her in thrall, and she never took her eyes from the stage; but as the curtain went down on the second act, she lifted her glass and slowly scanned the house. Suddenly she paused with a heart that throbbed strangely. Directly across from her sat a woman, whom surely she had seen somewhere—a woman with great dusky eyes and golden hair and a brilliant scarlet on her lips, and a fitful flush on her cheeks—a woman in gold satin that fell away from snowy neck and arm on which opals gleamed ominously, with a knot of crimson roses in her hand.

"Don," she said, tremulously, "is not that an old friend of yours in the box opposite?"

He lifted his glass.

"You recognize her from her picture, I see. She is looking remarkably well, is she not?" nonchalantly.

"She is glorious!" but the tender heart contracted.

The dusk eyes across were looking in her direction with a restless, smoldering fire in their depths that pained her to see.

June Langdon had glanced over her with a hungry intensity that seemed to search her. She passed over Mrs. Barrymore's bright, dark beauty, and settled directly on Mignon's face, studying it intently. The dark eyes, the wistful mouth, the dreaming, calm sweet face.

"Not beautiful? No; but a face that any man would shrine in his heart and love more recklessly than any mere beauty of form and coloring," she murmured. "Yet she dresses like an actress. There is not another woman in the house like her. She is odd and picturesque. She is like a strain of Mozart, a spray of lilies, a cool pool in the heart of a desert. My God! how he looks at her—he never looked at me like that! He respects her, he worships her—"

She sank back, breathless with misery, and yet, again and again she found herself gazing intently at Mignon.

In a long, black velvet gown, cut after the fashion of an old picture, with rare lace at throat and elbow, with long black gloves and a black fan, and a large bouquet of creamy, odorous jasmine in her hand, she was a contrast, indeed, to most women there.

Mrs. Barrymore was more of a gypsy than ever in pale amber and dark ruby; all about her were color and glow and shimmer, but from the rich darkness her clear pallor, like the leaf of one of her jasmine-buds, the sweet red lips, the dreaming eyes, shone out, and attracted a thousand eyes. She was like a picture of repose. She was the twilight, tender and pensive, after the hot, tumultuous day.

And Don Eastern, looking across at the beautiful enchantress, in her gold-satin draperies, without a thrill, knew that for one touch of the small gloved hand at his side he would brave death.

As *Camille* was parting with *Armand* after her interview with his father, looking so sadly changed from the lighthearted, joyous girl, in her pretty pink dress and garden hat, of an hour before, laughing and sobbing in a breath, kissing him in despairing, parting love, smiling in a grand self-renunciation, weeping over her dead and broken hopes all together, June Langdon, glancing over, saw that the sorrowful blossom-face had grown strangely white, and that Don Eastern was fanning her anxiously, and that he had drawn a mass of black, Spanish drapery about the slim form.

She saw Mignon look up with unspoken thanks, lifting her eyes with such devotion and love and faith in them; she saw him look down eagerly, with truest, tenderest love and anxiety; and then she waited no longer, but rose impatiently, with rage and hatred in her heart.

She paused for one last look.

Mrs. Barrymore had leaned forward to speak to Mignon, and as June's eyes fell on her face she started.

"Why, it is Blythe Hart! I knew she had married, but did not know what had become of her. Ah, everything is easy now."

The next day Mrs. Langdon's carriage dashed up to the Barrymore mansion, and a moment afterward Mrs. Langdon was announced.

Mrs. Barrymore and Mignon were seated together in the drawing-room, Mignon nestled in a great chair before the grate, Mrs. Barrymore lying luxuriously on a low Turkish divan.

Mrs. Barrymore stood up, with a very faint surprise in her face, that changed to delight as she recognized an almost forgotten friend.

"Why, June, are *you* Mrs. Langdon? Three years in Europe have set me quite outside the pale of all my old friends. This is my dear friend, Mignon Trevor. Little Mignon, you have often heard me speak of June Heatherton?"

And Mignon, with a faint color in her cheeks, bowed quietly, but did not speak, and relapsed into her reverie, gazing with dark, dreaming eyes into the flames.

How did it happen? Circe alone knew. But after that these two were often together.

"Such a lovely morning, little Mignon! You must come for a drive with me." Or, "I shall be alone to-day; you must come and make the hours bright for me."

And, although Mignon felt a vague dread and dislike, it was so intangible, and the beautiful voice and face and manner so enchanting, that she could not resist, and felt ashamed of her distrust and fears.

The days had flown swiftly, and they had been days of rapture for Mignon; the gayety and life and bustle were quite new to her. Every day Don was with her, morning and evening; he watched over her with a jealous care and loving devotion that were a marvel to himself. He took her for drives, and accompanied her to the opera; he sent her rare flowers from his own greenhouses; he brought her his favorite books and music, and late in the evenings he lingered beside her, parting from her reluctantly, and thinking of her every moment he was away from her. He realized that this pure, gentle, loving girl was the one supreme love of his life—her white hand could lead him unscathed over every sin and temptation; her sweet, dark eyes draw him to the uttermost ends of the earth. He was proud of her intellect and culture, he worshiped her for her innocence and trust, and for the first time in his life the restless cynical man of the world was happy.

June Langdon was less than nothing to him. He had never been near her since that day. He never even thought of her.

But to-day he held an ivory sheet of paper in his hand, with a monogram emblazoned in violet and gold upon it. And a line in the elegant running hand he knew so well:

"I am going away. Come just once more, for the sake of the old days, when no other woman was dearer than I. I am going to Paris to live, and may never see you again.   JUNE."

And he went. Reluctantly and distastefully—but he went.

He was ushered into a dainty little boudoir, scented and flower-filled.

Mrs. Langdon came forward from the library to meet him, in a creamy, clinging robe, with a scarlet poppy on her bosom, that gleamed out white and satiny from the yellow, enshrouding laces.

She did not give him unasked kisses this time; she did not offer him even her hand, but threw herself down in a great chair, with a sad languor that would have touched any heart but his. They talked a little while, indifferently, of a thousand things, and then he arose to go.

"Good-by, Mrs. Langdon. I hope you will enjoy Paris, and not quite forget all your old friends."

But with a low and exceedingly bitter cry she stood up.

"*Must* we part like this? Oh, my God! I cannot bear it! Have you no mercy, no pity?"

The tears streamed down her cheeks, and she held out her hand imploringly.

With deepest pity and sympathy, he took her hands in his.

"June, you will forget. Believe me, dear, you will forget all this in a very little while. What good would my love do you now? It could bring you nothing but sorrow. We must never meet again. I hope—I *know* you will be very happy yet. Good-by. God be with you, dear."

He bent down and touched the trembling hands with his lips, feeling wretchedly sorry for this beautiful, undisciplined woman in her misery.

But she flung her arms about his throat, and clung to him in a very abandonment of grief and parting, sobbing hysterically, with low, sharp moans that cut him to the heart.

"June, dear child, do not weep so. You will be ill. It is torture to hear you."

She faltered and shivered, and he put his arms about her, and kissed her on her fair brow once, twice.

Her arms were about his throat, the beautiful, quivering, wet face pressed close against his cheek.

A deep sigh startled him. He lifted his head.

Standing in the arch between the boudoir and the library, with the *portière* dropping behind her, pallid as a ghost, with frightened woful eyes and despair in every feature, stood Mignon.

With a loud exclamation, with rage and impatience and disgust, he shook the exquisite form from his bosom and strode across the room.

But the *portière* had fallen back into its place, and Mignon had vanished.

He called a servant and gave him a message for Miss Trevor, but the man returned with word that she had just gone out. He left the house without another look at the woman who had brought that despairing look into his sweet love's face, and rushed to Mrs. Barrymore's. But the servant, with no expression at all in his well-trained and very expansive face, informed him that the ladies were not at home.

Perforce, he was obliged to wait until night, and then he found himself once more at the Barrymore mansion.

Mrs. Barrymore received him coldly. Mignon had gone home; she would write to him from there, probably.

He waited two days, then the little rosy missive reached him. He kissed it passionately before he opened it.

"I never wish to see you again. My one prayer now is that I may forget you utterly. Good-by for all time. MIGNON."

With a mad and bitter wrath, he cursed June Langdon— cursed her fiercely and cruelly—and then he started for Mignon's home, only to find it closed and deserted. And then despair overtook him, too.

Everything, every one, was repulsive to him.

He went to California, and from one end of the Pacific coast to the other. He speculated wildly. He was insanely reckless.

One day, six months after he had first gone through the Golden Gate, he saw a notice in a paper that made June Langdon a widow. He tore the paper in two, and trampled upon it.

★ ★ ★ ★ ★ ★

A year went by, and then he grew calm. He would go home and seek Mignon. He would make her believe in him; life was not worth the living without her. For one touch of her cool hand, one glance of the calm, dark eyes, one smile of the sweet, wistful lips, he would barter wealth and fame, and all the world had to offer—ay, life itself!

He never paused after he had started, nor night nor day, until he had reached the pretty rustic town that held his pearl of price, his snow-white lily, his dove of peace.

And then a great fear fell upon him, undefined and foreboding. He wandered up the wide, irregular street with beating heart and feverish pulses. In a few minutes she would be beside him, gentle, loving, forgiving.

The tears came into his eyes, and he muttered a wordless prayer, sneering, cold man of the world that he was.

He drew his hat over his eyes, and wandered off across a wide, daisied field that opened from the street, until he had shaken off his unwonted emotion.

The little graveyard nestled close beside the field; it looked cool, and shady and restful, and unconsciously he stepped into it.

Suddenly, with a great cry, he stood still before a fair, slender, marble shaft.

Mignon: Aged 19.
"Blessed are the pure in heart."

There was only one Mignon in the world. He fell down with his face upon her grave. She had died in Rome of the fever.

Two years later June Langdon was Mrs. Don Eastern.

Appendix H: Contemporary Responses to Hagar's Daughter

[Hopkins's 1905 letter to William Monroe Trotter (see Appendix F3) refers to the negative responses of Southerners to her *Colored American Magazine* serial stories. A March 1901 article in the *Weekly Economist*, a white North Carolina newspaper, contains the only known review of *Hagar's Daughter*, which dismissively connects Hopkins's politics with those of Harriet Beecher Stowe (1811–96) and faults the narrative for its reliance on black dialect. During Hopkins's tenure with the periodical (and even for a few months after she had been fired from it), she received many letters from readers, several of which were published in the magazine. In March 1903, the *Colored American Magazine* published one about its serial fiction that has the distinction of being the only letter that Hopkins responded to in print. The white, Northern writer does not fault the publication's novels for their language but rather for their portrayal of mixed-race relationships. Hopkins's memorable response, which applies equally well to the *Weekly Economist* review, declares that white people "don't understand *what pleases Negroes.*"]

1. "The Colored Magazine," *Weekly Economist* [Elizabeth City, NC] (15 March 1901), p. 3

[In response to a request from the *Colored American Magazine*'s local agent, the Elizabeth City, North Carolina, *Weekly Economist* published a review of the journal's March 1901 issue, including the initial installment of *Hagar's Daughter*. The newspaper praises the look and much of the content of the magazine but disparages the "copious use of negro folklore" in and the "fanaticism" and "uncharitableness" of the plot of Hopkins's novel. The article also offers opinions on the intellectual capacity and temperament of US blacks. On the one hand, it claims to differ from those who believe "the negro race is deficient in ... intellect" and prone to "imbecility or barbarism" without white guidance, and commends the culture, shrewdness, and common sense of three local African Americans. On the other hand, it asserts that "the negro is an imitative, kindly, credulous, unsuspecting, sympathetic and gullible race."]

We were handed, a few days ago, the March number of the "Colored American Magazine," of Boston, Mass., of which Walter W. Wallace is editor, with an associate staff, all of whom are colored, with a request from the agent, A.W. White, of Elizabeth City, to give our opinion of the work.

It is handsomely illustrated and the original contributions are quite creditable. The agent informs us that many of its conductors and contributors are Southern negroes and that it aims to express all its opinions with fairness and impartiality, without taint of race or class prejudice and with the best ability that the colored race can furnish. A carefully written or printed book or magazine article gives the measure of a man. This is the only monthly magazine, under the conduct of negroes, published in the United States, and it challenges the world to an examination of their claim to culture and intellectuality.

There is a large class of people of culture and observation who have no unfriendly feeling for the race, who think that the negro race is deficient in the higher capabilities of intellect; that the most distinctive feature of its intellectual conformation lies in its power of imitation, and that when left alone without the object lesson of a superior race, it rapidly falls back into imbecility or barbarism. We are not of that class. We believe that generally the negro is an imitative, kindly, credulous, unsuspecting, sympathetic and gullible race.

We have read with critical carefulness "Hagar's Daughter," to which attention is called editorially, and which we suppose is the prize story of the magazine, and it displays the imitative character of the author, Sarah A. Allen. The writer has evidently read a book by the late Harriet Beecher Stowe, called Uncle Tom's Cabin. It is a close imitation of that "devil fish"[1] of our literature, which drew upon its imagination for its facts, and upon its fanaticism and uncharitableness for its fancy sketches.

We think the author of Hagar's Daughter had better discard Uncle Tom as a hero, Mrs. Stowe as a model in fiction, and abbreviate her copious display of negro folk lore. One touch of

---

1 A marine animal perceived to have a sinister appearance, like a devil ray, stonefish, or octopus.

kindness in the life of the "Old Mammy" of the slavery days, will reach the heart and do justice to the negro race, more than a thousand pages of slang and pigeon English that the friends and foes of the negro race are doing what they can to make as distinct a part of the intellectual characteristics of the race, as the wide mouth and wall eyes are of their physical characteristics.

We believe that the negro race is capable of the highest culture, and that they are improved by hybridizing. We have the proof of it in this town. Prof. P.W. Moore,[1] an Afro-American, is the equal of Booker Washington in culture, and perhaps, his superior in some other respects. Isaac Leigh, another Afro-American, is as shrewd a business man as you can find anywhere, and Charles McDonald,[2] another Afro-American, cannot be beaten anywhere in strong, hard, horse sense.

2. From "Editorial and Publishers' Announcements," *Colored American Magazine*, vol. 6, no. 5 (March 1903), pp. 398–400

[According to the biographical note attached to her papers held at the Burke Library of Union Theological Seminary at Columbia University, Cornelia A. Condict (1835–1926) worked as a Sabbath-school missionary and superintended the primary department of the Central Presbyterian Church in Newark, New Jersey; was married to the Rev. Walter C. Condict, who held pastorates during the nineteenth century in New Jersey, Minnesota, and New York; and traveled extensively in Asia in connection with her missionary work. Condict objects to the prevalence of "tragic mixed loves" in the *Colored American Magazine*'s serial stories, contending that they "will not commend themselves to your white readers and will not elevate the colored readers." Hopkins's blistering response rejects the double standards and hypocrisy of white people who claim to be religious and defends her depiction of the injustices committed against black people.]

---

1 Peter Weddick Moore (1859–1934), the first principal of Elizabeth City State Colored Normal School, now Elizabeth City State University.

2 Isaac Leigh (1855–1945), a local barber; Charles McDonald (d. 1935), a community leader.

We are constantly in receipt of letters from our readers in all sections of the country, in fact of the world, and it gives us a great deal of pleasure to note how warm a reception is given our publication among all classes and races. Some friends offer kindly suggestions as to how we can improve and make more helpful "The Colored American Magazine," while others tell of the grand work already accomplished by our periodical. The following letter, recently received from one of our *white* readers, is of more than passing interest to us all:

Dear Sirs:—

With Miss Floto I have been taking and reading with interest the COLORED AMERICAN MAGAZINE.

If I found it more helpful to Christian work among your people I would continue to take it.

May I make a comment on the stories, especially those that have been serial. Without exception they have been of love between the colored and whites. Does that mean that your novelists can imagine no love beautiful and sublime within the range of the colored race, for each other? I have seen beautiful home life and love in families altogether of Negro blood.

The stories of these tragic mixed loves will not commend themselves to your white readers and will not elevate the colored readers. I believe your novelists could do with a consecrated imagination and pen, more for the elevation of home life and love, than perhaps any other one class of writers.

What Dickens did for the neglected working class of England, some writer could do for the neglected colored people of America.

For several years I worked (superintended a Sunday school) among a greatly mixed people, Indian, Negro, Spanish and Anglo-Saxon.

My sympathies are with the earnest and spiritual work that is being done for your people, by yourselves or others.

We have kindred who are cultured Christian ladies, who for years have borne the ostracism of the white women of the South for the sake of the colored girls and women of the great South land.

Very respectfully,

CORNELIA A. CONDICT.

Following is Miss Hopkins' reply, which we feel will be of general interest:—

With regard to your enclosure (letter from Mrs. Condict) will say, it is the same old story. One religion for the whites and another for the blacks. The story of Jesus for us, that carries with it submission to the abuses of our people and blindness to the degrading of our youth. I think Mrs. Condict has a great work to do—greater than she can accomplish, I fear—to carry religion to the Southern whites.

My stories are definitely planned to show the obstacles persistently placed in our paths by a dominant race to subjugate us spiritually. Marriage is made illegal between the races and yet the mulattoes increase. Thus the shadow of corruption falls on the blacks and on the whites, without whose aid the mulattoes would not exist. And then the hue and cry goes abroad of the immorality of the Negro and the disgrace that the mulattoes are to this nation. Amalgamation is an institution designed by God for some wise purpose, and mixed bloods have always exercised a great influence on the progress of human affairs. I sing of the wrongs of a race that ignorance of their pitiful condition may be changed to intelligence and must awaken compassion in the hearts of the just.

The home life of Negroes is beautiful in many instances; warm affection is there between husband and wife, and filial and paternal tenderness in them is not surpassed by any other race of the human family. But Dickens wrote not of the joys and beauties of English society; I believe he was the author of "Bleak House" and "David Copperfield." If he had been an American, and with his trenchant pen had exposed the abuses practiced by the Southern whites upon the blacks—had told the true story of how wealth, intelligence and femininity has stooped to choose for a partner in sin, the degraded (?) Negro whom they affect to despise, Dickens would have been advised to shut up or get out. I believe Jesus Christ when on earth rebuked the Pharisees in this wise: "Ye hypocrites, ye expect to be heard for your much speaking"; "O wicked and adulterous (?) nation, how can ye escape the damnation of hell?"[1] He didn't go about patting

---

1 Hopkins seems to combine Matthew 6.7, 16.4, and 23.33 when she talks of Christ rebuking the Pharisees.

those old sinners on the back and saying, "All right, boys, fix me up and the Jews will get there all right. Money talks. Divy on the money you take in the exchange business of the synagogue, and it'll be all right with God." Jesus told the thing as it was and the Jews crucified him! I am glad to receive this criticism for it shows more clearly than ever that white people don't understand *what pleases Negroes*. You are between Scylla and Charybdis:[1] If you please the author of this letter and your white clientele, you will lose your Negro patronage. If you cater to the *demands* of the Negro trade, away goes Mrs.——. I have sold to many whites and have received great praise for the work I am doing in exposing the social life of the Southerners and the wickedness of their caste prejudice.

Let the good work go on. Opposition is the life of an enterprise; criticism tells you that you are doing something.

Respect.,

Pauline E. Hopkins

---

1 I.e., between a rock and a hard place. In Book Ten of the *Odyssey*, Odysseus must decide whether to sail by one of these female monsters or the other.

Works Cited and Select Bibliography

"A Few of the Good Things to Be Found in the *Colored American Magazine* during the Year 1901." *Colored American Magazine,* vol. 1, no. 5, October 1900.

Allen, Sarah A. [Pauline E. Hopkins]. *Hagar's Daughter: A Story of Southern Caste Prejudice. Colored American Magazine,* vol. 2, no. 5, March 1901, pp. 337–52.

Ammons, Elizabeth, editor. *Short Fiction by Black Women, 1900–1920.* Oxford UP, 1991.

"Anti-Roosevelt-Taft Meeting of Colored Voters to Raise Money to Send Delegates." *Boston Herald,* 31 May 1908, p. 7.

Bergman, Jill. *The Motherless Child in the Novels of Pauline Hopkins.* Louisiana State UP, 2012.

Brooks, Kristina. "Mammies, Bucks, and Wenches: Minstrelsy, Racial Pornography, and Racial Politics in Pauline Hopkins's *Hagar's Daughter." The Unruly Voice: Rediscovering Pauline Elizabeth Hopkins,* edited by John Cullen Gruesser, U of Illinois P, 1996, pp. 119–57.

Brown, Lois. *Pauline Elizabeth Hopkins: Black Daughter of the Revolution.* U of North Carolina P, 2008.

Carby, Hazel V., editor. *The Magazine Novels of Pauline Hopkins.* Oxford UP, 1988.

—. *Reconstructing Womanhood: The Emergence of the Afro-American Woman Novelist.* Oxford UP, 1987.

"Central Square Business Man Rescues Woman Afire." *Cambridge Sentinel,* 16 August 1930, p. 8.

"Charles-Street Church." *Boston Daily Advertiser,* 19 September 1881, p. 8.

"Colored Folks Thanksgiving." *Boston Globe,* 26 November 1897, p. 17.

"The Colored Magazine." *Weekly Economist* [Elizabeth City, NC], 15 March 1901, p. 3.

"Colored Women Protest. They Denounce the Leasing System in the South." *Boston Herald,* 27 December 1897, p. 6.

Crawford, Shawn. "No Time to Be Idle: The Serial Novel and Popular Imagination." *World & I,* vol. 13, no. 11, November 1998, pp. 323–31.

Dahn, Eurie, and Brian Sweeney. *The Digital Colored American Magazine,* 31 May 2019, www.coloredamerican.org.

DeLamotte, Eugenia. "Collusions of Mystery: Ideology and the Gothic in *Hagar's Daughter*." *Gothic Studies*, vol. 6, no. 1, May 2004, pp. 69–79.

Dembowitz, Lauren. "Appropriating Tropes of Womanhood and Literary Passing in Pauline Hopkins's *Hagar's Daughter*." Yarborough et al., pp. e21–e27.

—. "Sources for *Hagar's Daughter: A Story of Southern Caste Prejudice*." Pavletich, *Inspired Borrowings*.

Doreski, C.K. "Inherited Rhetoric and Authentic History: Pauline Hopkins at the *Colored American Magazine*." Gruesser, *The Unruly Voice*, pp. 71–97.

Dworkin, Ira, editor. *Daughter of the Revolution: The Major Nonfiction Works of Pauline E. Hopkins*. Rutgers UP, 2007.

"Editorial and Publishers' Announcements." *Colored American Magazine*, vol. 6, no. 5, March 1903, pp. 398–400.

Elliott, R.S. "The Story of Our Magazine." *Colored American Magazine*, vol. 3, no. 1, May 1901, pp. 43–77.

Fanning, Patricia J. *Through an Uncommon Lens: The Life and Photography of F. Holland Day*. U of Massachusetts P, 2008.

Gabler-Hover, Janet. *Dreaming Black/Writing White: The Hagar Myth in American Cultural History*. UP of Kentucky, 1999.

Gruesser, John Cullen. *Edgar Allan Poe and His Nineteenth-Century American Counterparts*. Bloomsbury, 2019.

—. *The Empire Abroad and the Empire at Home: African American Literature and the Era of Overseas Expansion*. U of Georgia P, 2012.

—. *Race, Gender and Empire in American Detective Fiction*. McFarland, 2013.

—. "Taking Liberties: Pauline Hopkins's Recasting of the *Creole* Rebellion." Gruesser, *The Unruly Voice*, pp. 98–118.

—, editor. *The Unruly Voice: Rediscovering Pauline Elizabeth Hopkins*. U of Illinois P, 1996.

Hopkins, Pauline E. *Contending Forces*. Edited by Richard Yarborough, Oxford UP, 1988.

—. Famous Men of the Negro Race. VI. Lewis Hayden. *Colored American Magazine*, vol. 2, no. 6, April 1901, pp. 473–77.

—. Famous Men of the Negro Race. IV. Robert Browne Elliott. *Colored American Magazine*, vol. 2, no. 4, February 1901, pp. 294–301.

—. *The Magazine Novels of Pauline Hopkins*. Edited by Hazel V. Carby, Oxford UP, 1988.

Ihara, Rachel. "'The Stimulus of Books and Tales': Pauline Hopkins's Serial Novels for the *Colored American Magazine*." *Transnationalism and American Serial Fiction*, edited by Patricia Okker, Routledge, 2012, pp. 127–47.

"In the West End." *Boston Globe*, 24 December 1894, p. 5.

Jackson, Holly. "Another Long Bridge: Reproduction and Reversion in *Hagar's Daughter*." *Early African American Print Culture*, edited by Lara Langer Cohen and Jordan Alexander Stein, U of Pennsylvania P, 2012, pp. 192–202.

Knight, Alisha R. *Pauline Hopkins and the American Dream: An African American Writer's (Re)Visionary Gospel of Success.* U of Tennessee P, 2012.

Laski, Greg. *Untimely Democracy: The Politics of Progress after Slavery.* Oxford UP, 2018.

McKay, Nellie Y. Introduction. Gruesser, *The Unruly Voice*, pp. 1–20.

Metzler, Jessica. "'Course I Knows Dem Feet!': Minstrelsy and Subversion in Pauline E. Hopkins's *Slaves' Escape; or, The Underground Railroad*." *Loopholes and Retreats: African American Writers and the Nineteenth Century*, edited by John Cullen Gruesser and Hanna Wallinger, Lit Verlag, 2009, pp. 101–23.

"Miss Lee Entertained." *Boston Herald*, 5 February 1907, p. 7.

Nickerson, Catherine Ross. *The Web of Iniquity: Early Detective Fiction by American Women.* Duke UP, 1999.

"Pauline E. Hopkins." *Colored American Magazine*, vol. 2, no. 3, January 1901, pp. 218–19.

Pavletich, JoAnn, editor. "Inspired Borrowings: Pauline Hopkins's Literary Appropriations." *Pauline Elizabeth Hopkins Society*, www.paulinehopkinssociety.org/inspired-borrowings/.

—. "The Practice of Plagiarism in a Changing Context." Yarborough et al., pp. e9–e13.

—. "'... we are going to take that right': Power and Plagiarism in Pauline Hopkins's *Winona*." *CLA Journal*, vol. 59, no. 2, December 2015, pp. 115–30.

Porter, Dorothy B. "Hopkins, Pauline Elizabeth." *Dictionary of American Negro Biography*, edited by Rayford W. Logan and Michael R. Winston, W.W. Norton, 1982, pp. 325–26.

"Protest at Faneuil Hall. Public Mass Meeting Condemns the Killing of Negro Men and Women." *Boston Globe*, 29 September 1906, p. 4.

"Read a Paper on Lynching." *Boston Globe*, 29 November 1899, p. 6.

"The Rise of the Black Republic: Miss Pauline E. Hopkins Lectures at Tremont Temple." *Boston Post*, 18 October 1889, p. 8.

Robinson, M. Michelle. *Dreams for Dead Bodies: Blackness, Labor, and the Corpus of American Detective Fiction*. U of Michigan P, 2014.

"Sam Lucas' Theatrical Career Written by Himself in 1909." *New York Age*, 13 January 1916, p. 6.

Sanborn, Geoffrey. *Plagiarama! William Wells Brown and the Aesthetic of Attraction*. Columbia UP, 2016.

—. "The Winds of Words: Plagiarism and Intertextuality in *Of One Blood*." *J19: The Journal of Nineteenth-Century Americanists*, vol. 3, no. 1, Spring 2015, pp. 67–87.

Shand-Tucci, Douglass. "American Aristocracy: Gods of Copley Square; Magic II." *Open Letters Monthly: An Arts and Literature Review*, 1 June 2013, www.openlettersmonthly.com/issue/american-aristocracy-gods-of-copley-square-magic-ii/.

Shockley, Ann Allen. "Pauline E. Hopkins: A Biographical Excursion into Obscurity." *Phylon*, vol. 33, Spring 1972, pp. 22–26.

Short Fiction by Black Women, 1900–1920. Collected by Elizabeth Ammons, Oxford UP, 1991.

Soitos, Stephen F. *The Blues Detective: A Study of African American Detective Fiction*. U of Massachusetts P, 1996.

Sonstegard, Adam. *Artistic Liberties: American Literary Realism and Graphic Illustration, 1880–1905*. U of Alabama P, 2014.

Southern, Eileen. Introduction [to *Peculiar Sam*]. *African American Theater Volume 9: Out of Bondage (1876) and Peculiar Sam; or, The Underground Railroad (1879)*. Garland, 1994, pp. xxiii–xxix.

Sweeney, Brian. "Throwing Stones across the Potomac: The *Colored American Magazine*, the *Atlantic Monthly*, and the Cultural Politics of National Reunion." *American Periodicals*, vol. 29, no. 2, September 2019, pp. 135–62.

Tate, Claudia. "Pauline Hopkins: Our Literary Foremother." *Conjuring: Black Women, Fiction, and the Literary Tradition*, edited by Marjorie Pryse and Hortense J. Spillers, Indiana UP, 1985, pp. 53–66.

Thomas, Brook. *The Literature of Reconstruction: Not in Plain Black and White*. Johns Hopkins UP, 2017.

"To Protest Lynching. Mass Meeting to Be Held Tomorrow Night." *Boston Globe*, 20 August 1911, p. 11.

Tuhkanen, Mikko. "'Out of Joint': Passing, Haunting, and the Time of Slavery in *Hagar's Daughter*." *American Literature*, vol. 79, no. 2, May 2007, pp. 335–61.

Wallinger, Hanna. *Pauline E. Hopkins: A Literary Biography*. U of Georgia P, 2005.

"West End News." *Boston Post*, 6 December 1894, p. 3.

"Woman's World." *Freeman* [Indianapolis], 12 November 1892, p. 2.

Yarborough, Richard, editor. *Contending Forces*. Oxford UP, 1988.

—. Introduction. Yarborough et al., pp. e4–e8.

Yarborough, Richard, et al. "Rethinking Pauline Hopkins: Plagiarism, Appropriation, and African American Cultural Production." *American Literary History*, vol. 30, no. 4, Winter 2018, pp. e3–e30, doi.org/10.1093/alh/ajy014.

From the Publisher

A name never says it all, but the word "Broadview" expresses a good deal of the philosophy behind our company. We are open to a broad range of academic approaches and political viewpoints. We pay attention to the broad impact book publishing and book printing has in the wider world; for some years now we have used 100% recycled paper for most titles. Our publishing program is internationally oriented and broad-ranging. Our individual titles often appeal to a broad readership too; many are of interest as much to general readers as to academics and students.

Founded in 1985, Broadview remains a fully independent company owned by its shareholders—not an imprint or subsidiary of a larger multinational.

For the most accurate information on our books (including information on pricing, editions, and formats) please visit our website at www.broadviewpress.com. Our print books and ebooks are also available for sale on our site.

broadview press
www.broadviewpress.com